D0356338

# THE
# VESUVIUS
# ISOTOPE

P.O. Box 178963
San Diego, CA 92177
www.murderlab.com

This book is a work of fiction. Names, characters, places, incidents, and, especially, any references to the pharmaceutical industry are strictly products of the author's imagination or are used fictitiously. Any resemblance to actual events or locales or persons or companies, living or dead, is entirely coincidental.

ISBN: 978-0-9893819-0-1 (print book)
ISBN: 978-0-9893819-1-8 (ebook)

Ordering Information: Quantity sales. Special discounts are available on quantity purchases by corporations, associations, and others. For details, contact the publisher at the address above.

Manufactured in the United States of America

# ACKNOWLEDGEMENTS

I thank two brilliant ladies who dedicated countless hours to making this work possible: My editor, Cyndie Duncan, for her encyclopedic knowledge of em dashes and ellipses, and for stopping me from creating a world in which the dead have mood swings and pianos are portable; and my alpha, beta, epsilon, kappa, gamma, mu and zeta reader, Sara McBride, for reading every single chapter just *one more time*, and never being afraid to tell me when I have "pulled a total wanker."

I thank my mom, Glenna Fraser, for not letting me watch *The Dukes of Hazzard* because they used bad grammar, for instead teaching me Scrabble and Teakettle, and for convincing me that I could do anything I wanted with this life (sorry to have taken that advice *so* literally...) And for putting the manuscript back on the right track when it wandered off into Never-Never Land.

I thank the pharmaceutical company that laid me off so that I could finally *finish* the manuscript.

I thank good friends and family who have encouraged this endeavor and convinced me it would be worth the effort—the Lissner/Swann/Boddie family, my brothers, Lindsay, Amy and Bryan, Jenn, Ashley, Gray, Laurie...

I thank Damonza's Awesome Book Covers for the awesome book cover.

I thank my chicho, Senior Antonio; my beautiful step-daughters, Nataly and Christina; and my little love, Harmoni, for their friendship and keeping it real; and my kids, Rambo, Haley, and Pilgrim, for always listening to Mommy reading aloud.

Most importantly, I thank my wonderfully loving and encouraging husband, Sonny, for working twice as hard as the rest of us put together, for date nights and family days, for sending me off to Egypt well-prepared, for being a marketing genius, and for thinking it was a great idea for me to publish a book instead of pursuing another "real" job. You are my Jeffrey Wilson, except that you don't die in the first paragraph.

# THE
# VESUVIUS
# ISOTOPE

KRISTEN ELISE, PH.D.

Murder Lab Press

San Diego, CA

ASHES WERE ALREADY FALLING, NOT AS YET VERY THICKLY. I LOOKED ROUND: A DENSE BLACK CLOUD WAS COMING UP BEHIND US, SPREADING OVER THE EARTH LIKE A FLOOD. "LET US LEAVE THE ROAD WHILE WE CAN STILL SEE," I SAID, "OR WE SHALL BE KNOCKED DOWN AND TRAMPLED UNDERFOOT IN THE DARK BY THE CROWD BEHIND." WE HAD SCARCELY SAT DOWN TO REST WHEN DARKNESS FELL, NOT THE DARK OF A MOONLESS OR CLOUDY NIGHT, BUT AS IF THE LAMP HAD BEEN PUT OUT IN A CLOSED ROOM.

-LETTERS OF PLINY THE YOUNGER (CA. 61—112 CE)

# PROLOGUE

Thousands perished in the ashes the day the darkness fell as if the lamp had been put out in a closed room. So, too, was buried a medical breakthrough that today, nearly two millennia later, could save thousands. Six weeks ago, it emerged.

The person who rediscovered the ancient isotope did not at first realize the magnitude of the find. Except for the curious property of restoring life, it is inert. It is harmless to humans— indeed, to all living things. It survives for only moments. Yet, despite its transient nature, it appears to bring death as well as life; a trail of cadavers has followed the isotope through the centuries.

Is it magic, as believed by the ancients? As a scientist in 2023, I have a more logical hypothesis. But when it comes to murder of the strictly mortal variety, I must admit, empirically I know for certain of only one. My husband, Jeff.

When I find it, or recreate it in a lab as the case may be, I will name the isotope Vesuvium. I think Jeff would appreciate that. Like the erupting volcano, in fact, like Jeff himself, it is as majestic as its lifespan is fleeting.

He was my world. I loved him more than anything. I hope he would forgive me for all that I have done.

YOU COULD HEAR THE SHRIEKS OF WOMEN, THE WAILING OF INFANTS, AND THE SHOUTING OF MEN; SOME WERE CALLING THEIR PARENTS, OTHERS THEIR CHILDREN OR THEIR WIVES, TRYING TO RECOGNIZE THEM BY THEIR VOICES. PEOPLE BEWAILED THEIR OWN FATE OR THAT OF THEIR RELATIVES, AND THERE WERE SOME WHO PRAYED FOR DEATH IN THEIR TERROR OF DYING. MANY BESOUGHT THE AID OF THE GODS, BUT STILL MORE IMAGINED THERE WERE NO GODS LEFT, AND THAT THE UNIVERSE WAS PLUNGED INTO ETERNAL DARKNESS FOR EVERMORE.

-LETTERS OF PLINY THE YOUNGER (CA. 61—112 CE)

# CHAPTER ONE

T*here is a crash. I feel wetness, and pain. I see a thousand memories.*

*My husband was naked the first time we met. The image of him at that moment has not faded from my mind in our five short years together. Now, as I feel myself slipping beneath the surface, there is another image as well—of the last time I saw my husband. He was lying dead from two gunshot wounds. Again, he was naked.*

The first time I saw Jeff, I was sprinting along Black's Beach in La Jolla, California. The secluded strip of coastline is world-renowned as a runner's paradise, with its intense four-mile loop of steep mountain switchbacks and deep sand. Black's has long been my favorite place to jog, despite the fact that it is a clothing-optional beach.

That morning, as I rounded the corner into a nook beside a jutting shoreline cliff, I almost crashed into him before managing to change course. My first impression was beach bum, not nudist as I later liked to teasingly call him. At five o'clock in the morning, the beach appeared totally abandoned. I assume he thought he was alone and, therefore, felt comfortable stripping out of his wetsuit to dress after his morning surf session. Black's was, after all, a nude beach.

He was no more than five feet away from me, so nothing escaped my attention. Seawater was running down his lean surfer's body as he tossed a dripping wetsuit onto a boulder beside him and then reached for a towel lying next to a pile of clothing.

He glanced up. As he did, a lock of sandy hair fell over his forehead. His eyes met mine, and then he flashed a mischievous grin of straight white teeth.

"Whoops, *that's* embarrassing!" The handsome nude man with the smoky blue eyes chuckled while belatedly bringing the towel up to shield himself.

"Morning," I said casually, continuing past him with a smirk.

Less than a month later, it was my turn to be caught off guard. I was at the International Conference on Emerging Infectious Diseases delivering a lecture about biological terrorism. The conference was held in Paris that year, and attendance was at an all-time high. I was at the podium in the main lecture hall speaking to an audience of approximately five thousand. In the midst of my speech, I glanced up from the microphone, and one audience member sitting front row center of the auditorium caught my eye.

My voice faltered when I saw him. The handsome, well-dressed man with the smoky blue eyes looked familiar, but I couldn't place him. Then he flashed that mischievous grin, and our brief moment on Black's Beach returned to me.

I completely lost my train of thought.

My presentation trailed off mid-sentence. A few people in the audience cleared their throats. I felt my face flush. I took a few well-rehearsed steps to recover my composure—three deep breaths, a sip of water from my glass on the podium, another deep breath.

"Whoops, *that's* embarrassing!" I said into the microphone. I could feel myself smiling.

Later, as I sat sipping coffee and reviewing my notes between sessions, he approached me. This time, with the advantage of seeing him coming toward me, I was prepared.

"Dr. Stone," he said with a professional nod.

"Naked surfer," I said and nodded back.

A pair of women at an adjacent table glanced toward us. He acknowledged them with a smile before returning his attention to me.

"I'm surprised you recognized me," he said.

"I *was* looking at your face, for the most part."

It was then that I noticed his conference-issued name badge. Jeffrey Wilson had been granted the Nobel Prize in Chemistry a few years prior for the creation of a new chemical element, one of the very few so-called superheavy elements in existence at the time. He had received the Nobel both for creating the new element and for the ground-breaking method by which it was created.

I remembered the media circus that surrounded his winning the Nobel. The majority of press attention was concentrated at The Scripps Research Institute where Jeff was a principal investigator. That facility is less than a mile from Black's Beach.

Jeff must have known immediately that he would die.

The shot to his back passed all the way through his body. The bullet had to have come from within our bedroom.

He was still standing. The waist-high wrought iron railing enclosing our bedroom terrace stopped him from falling forward. As he stood naked, leaning against the railing, with a bullet hole through his middle, a steady red river gushed from the exit wound. The blood gathered along the edge of the railing and then trickled down, tracing the intricate ironwork like lava flowing through a vertical maze. A small crimson pool formed on the edge of the terrace's natural stone floor, but the majority spilled over. Down it poured, past the second and first floor windows of our house and onto the forward deck of my yacht.

Jeff's right hand went first to the exit wound in his bare stomach and then to the terrace railing, where it left a bloody handprint. It must have been at that moment that he turned to look at the shooter behind him.

The second bullet hit him in the upper chest, sending my husband—the most handsome, brilliant, kind, charming, Nobel laureate chemist in the history of the prize—plunging backward over the terrace railing to his death.

The yacht was a gift from Jeff for our first wedding anniversary, but I always teased him that *Teresa* was as much his gift as mine. While the small yacht was easily maneuvered by one person, Jeff and I almost always took her out together.

I was standing on our bedroom terrace enjoying the panoramic view of the Pacific Ocean when I first saw her. I was wearing a backless evening gown of shimmering royal blue, a color Jeff loved on me for the way it accentuated my blue eyes and long auburn waves. The dress was floor length and fitted to my slender, petite frame. A single alluring slit in the gown exposed my left leg to the thigh.

Jeff stepped out of our bedroom and joined me on the terrace. His standard attire of jeans, T-shirt, and tennis shoes had been transformed, and Jeff was dashing in a black jacket and tie. The thick sandy brown hair that almost always fell over his forehead was now smoothly slicked back. In each of Jeff's hands was a glass of champagne. He handed one to me and appreciatively ran his eyes over my dress before pulling me close for a kiss.

"Happy anniversary," he said. "You look gorgeous."

I set my champagne down on the terrace railing to embrace my husband with both arms. "Where are we going for dinner?" I whispered between kisses.

Instead of answering, Jeff stepped away from me and leaned casually against the railing. He glanced down at the water below, and his face lit up with the same mischievous grin I had first seen three years earlier on Black's Beach.

"You know what has always bugged me?" he said.

"What's that, love?"

"That we had a boat dock but no boat."

Instead of thinking to look down, I looked at Jeff. He dipped his eyes downward once more. This time mine followed, and I saw her for the first time.

The yacht was directly beneath us, moored unassumingly in the formerly empty space as if she had always been there. On *Teresa*'s forward deck was an elegantly set table for two. Standing next to the table was a man in a chef's hat who announced, as if on cue, that dinner was served.

It was upon that very same spot on *Teresa*'s deck that Jeff's body landed after falling from our bedroom terrace three years later.

The front door was unlocked, so I was certain my husband would be there. "Jeff," I called as I entered the house, "I'm home." I was not surprised there was no answer. If he was still in the shower, he would not have heard me. Or maybe he was out on our private terrace lost in his own thoughts. Or perhaps he had simply ignored me.

I dropped my purse and my laptop on the living room sofa and began climbing the stairs.

It had been a chilly three days between us. We had barely spoken since the biggest fight of our marriage, and I now wondered if our relationship could ever return to the way it had been. A part of me wanted so badly to just forget the events of three days prior and to surprise him on the terrace in the nude, as I had done so many times before.

I opened the bedroom door, and I was stopped in my tracks. On the floor near my nightstand was a small metal object. The back of my neck came alive with chills.

I recognized the gun immediately. It was mine.

I stepped timidly toward it as a light breeze ruffled the curtains framing the French doors to our terrace. A sudden gust of wind brought the curtains billowing into the bedroom. One of them kissed the pistol lying on the floor before shrinking back again.

I glanced up. The glass doors were standing wide open, as if beckoning me out between them. Slowly I moved toward the terrace.

There I saw it. The blood on the metal railing, framed theatrically by the ruffling curtains. It had already begun to congeal. The pools along the top of the railing and upon the stone floor beneath it were a brighter red than the thinner traces down the vertical metal. The handprint smeared along the top rail was a sickening blotchy swirl of multiple hues. It appeared to be the exact size of my husband's hand.

My mind was not my own as I stepped forward and crossed the terrace.

Naked and vulnerable, Jeff's body was displayed in the center of *Teresa*'s forward deck. All four of his limbs were jutting out unnaturally from his torso. Also radiating out from the center of his body were two overlapping ovals of varying shades of red, one from his chest and the other from his abdomen.

The expression on Jeff's face was one of horror, and there was something else there as well. I think it was sorrow.

I could make no sound. I could only stare. I have no idea how long I stood there.

A flash of light roused me. Another gust of wind had just blown past, and the boat was now rocking gently. A single ray from the setting sun danced mockingly into my eyes, drawing them to the small object from which the light was ricocheting. Until that moment, I had not noticed the pistol silencer lying beside Jeff's body. It was nearly concealed within the pool of blood that had flowed from my husband's heart.

The message to me was clear: Be quiet.

It was perversely fortunate that Jeff's body had landed on the yacht. Our dock was built on a private, narrow canal that led directly out into the Pacific Ocean. It would be surprisingly easy, albeit very expensive, to hide his body. And I knew I had to hide his body.

So I bribed a mortician.

I pulled Larry Shuman's information from a hasty Internet search on one lone criterion: his business was still open that late in the evening.

Shuman greeted me with a professional handshake, but his eyes were sympathetic as he offered condolences for my loss. He then ran a pudgy hand through the sparse hair on his head and motioned for me to sit across from him as he sat behind his desk. He looked at me questioningly, as if wondering what I had not said on the phone.

The easiest way to explain what I wanted from Shuman was to show him. I opened my purse and pulled out my iPhone, where I had stored a collection of photos. Shuman examined them academically for quite some time before speaking. "Why, may I ask," he said finally, "did you call my funeral home instead of the police?"

I took a deep breath before answering. "Because I need this to remain unreported for a short period of time. You can still do the necessary post-mortem work-up, but I'm asking, please, do not report this. Not yet."

Shuman stood up from his desk so abruptly that his chair tipped over backward behind him. He pulled the receiver of his desk phone off its cradle and began to dial.

"I have heard quite enough, Dr. Stone."

I lunged forward.

Shuman jerked back in an effort to escape my clutching hand, but I was quicker than he was. My hand closed around his, and we began to struggle for the telephone receiver. As we did, the unclasped purse dangling from my arm banged across Shuman's desk with sufficient force to spill its contents. Several thick wads of rubber banded cash fell out onto the desk.

My strength was no match for his, but Shuman replaced the receiver of the phone, his eyes dropping once or twice to the cash on the desk and then returning to meet my own. Finally, he reached backward and righted his chair to sit down again.

"Dr. Stone, I know who you are. I have read about you and your husband several times over the past few years. Your biotechnology company, founded on the very science that earned Dr. Wilson the Nobel Prize, is among the most successful in the history of the industry—"

"And today," I interrupted, "I became its sole surviving founder, and one of the wealthiest individuals in California.

"Mr. Shuman, the murder weapon is my own gun. The only prints on it are certain to be mine. The murderer walked into our home through an unlocked front door. And if the police are called, they will quickly discover the same thing that I myself have recently discovered..."

My voice cracked, and I paused and looked down at my lap for a moment before continuing. "I have reason to believe that Jeff might have been having an affair.

"I don't know with whom, but I believe that if I can find that person I might be able to identify Jeff's killer. I'm not asking you to cover this up indefinitely, only to allow me a brief sliver of time to come to terms with the loss of my husband. And to find some answers."

"Absolutely not," Shuman said, reaching again for the telephone on his desk. "At best, I would be interfering with a criminal investigation. At worst, I would be aiding and abetting a murderer." He began dialing.

"One million!" I shouted. Shuman hesitated and looked up. I reiterated, this time calmly, "One million dollars. With proper preservation of the body and no cause for suspicion after your examination, that sliver of time will make no difference to you whatsoever. Except, of course, that you'll be a million dollars richer."

Shuman replaced the receiver once again. He glanced around the dingy office as if regarding it for the first time. He looked back down at the money lying on his desk, and then he met my gaze again.

"And what if I personally doubt your innocence, especially given that you are now attempting to bribe an undertaker?"

"You say you know who I am. If you should doubt me for even a moment, then, by all means, turn me in."

Shuman shook his head. He looked weary and sad. "Dr. Stone, I don't believe you are behaving rationally, which is completely understandable under the circumstances. I may know who you are, but you don't know anything about me. You have no idea what I might do. Why would you deliberately put yourself at this kind of risk? Your reputation? Your career? Your very freedom?" He rubbed his face with his hands and sighed. "Please, just follow the rules. Report your husband's murder."

"Mr. Shuman, if you know my history as you claim to, then you should already understand why that is something I cannot do."

I next saw Larry Shuman at two o'clock in the morning. We met that very night on Fiesta Island, a small stretch of barren coastline within San Diego's Mission Bay. I pulled *Teresa* as close to the shore as I could, and Shuman collected my husband's body.

I had covered Jeff with a blanket, and I was grateful that

I did not have to view him again in that condition. I turned away as the chubby middle-aged man grunted while hoisting Jeff's body onto a gurney. He then heaved the gurney through knee-high waves and onto the shore.

"You have two weeks," he said, and, not waiting for my response, he returned to his hearse.

Without looking back, I turned *Teresa* and sailed out beyond the edge of the bay, where I cast the silencer overboard.

*I will not remain quiet.*

It was seven days ago that I placed my trust and my husband's corpse, only weakly insured by a million dollar bribe, in the hands of a total stranger. Now, as I feel myself slipping beneath the surface, my two weeks have been cut short. I am out of time to find Jeff's killer because the authorities have just found his body.

CAESAR MARRIED CALPURNIA, THE DAUGHTER OF PISO, AND GOT PISO MADE CONSUL FOR THE YEAR FOLLOWING.

-*LIVES OF THE NOBLE GRECIANS AND ROMANS*
PLUTARCH (CA. 46–120 CE)

HE HAD SEEN HIM FAVOURED BY THE WOMAN WHOM HE IMAGINED HE LOVED, AND WHOSE POSSESSION HE HAD BEEN PROMISED BY THE SECRET SCIENCE OF THE EGYPTIANS, WHOSE POWER TO UNVEIL THE MYSTERIES OF THE FUTURE HE FIRMLY BELIEVED.

-*CLEOPATRA*
GEORG EBERS (1837–1898)

## CHAPTER TWO

*T*here are hundreds of them, thousands. Agonized, nameless faces and ransacked bodies writhing in desperation on white mattresses. An IV drips into one arm of each.

*The beds are clean, the facilities immaculate. The glaring lights upon the brilliant white beds only accent the appalling conditions of the patients. They are crammed together, side by side and end to end. Thousands of adjacent hospital beds.*

*A phone is ringing. I ignore it and walk like a zombie down the rows of beds; my eyes cast from one face to the next. Beside me, a feeble plea comes forth from a teenaged voice.*

*"Please..."*

I jerked awake. The familiar dream began to fade. I could feel a rocking motion beneath me, and I rolled over onto my back. Directly above me was the underside of our bedroom terrace. I slowly became aware that I was on my own yacht, lying in the center of the pool of dried blood that was now all that remained of Jeff. I could not remember how I got there.

My left hand hurt, and I realized my fist was tightly clenched. As I opened it, four tiny trickles of blood seeped from indentations in my palm as my husband's wedding ring fell from my hand. The boat rocked again, and a subtle rattling broke the early morning silence as the small gold circle rolled across the smooth wood of the yacht's deck.

I sobbed endlessly as I scrubbed Jeff's blood from our terrace floor and the wrought iron railing. While sopping up the blood on *Teresa*'s deck, twice I had to pause to vomit into the bucket I was using to clean. When I had finished erasing the evidence of my husband's death, I began clawing through our home in search of clues to his life.

I rifled through the pockets of Jeff's work attire in our walk-in closet. I yanked his weekend clothes from our dresser drawers and shoved the upper mattress from our bed to examine the space beneath it.

I began ransacking the entire house, pulling out every drawer, climbing shelves in every closet to access the highest nooks, shoving items haphazardly to the ground. I bored through dusty boxes in our garage and clambered over old furniture in our attic, using a flashlight to peer into every dark corner.

I scoured Jeff's side of the ocean view office we shared. I had never looked anywhere in Jeff's desk except the front center drawer where he kept a checkbook and some house money. This time, I frantically tore through his desk, his file cabinets, and his bookshelves. Nothing.

I began looking through the files on his computer desktop, and then I realized that his iPhone had been sitting on the desk the entire time. How stupid! Here was the true record of his most recent, most personal activities. My hands were shaking as I picked up the phone.

I had never previously suspected that Jeff was cheating. His behavior had never been that of a cheater. In recent weeks, he seemed distracted, but that was not unusual for a man so dedicated to his work that he retained his academic position even while leading a successful biotechnology company.

But even in those recent weeks, Jeff did not exhibit the sudden, complete detachment of someone who is straying, the obvious physical revulsion in the presence of a woman he used to love. I never would have considered my husband capable of infidelity. Until three days before his murder.

Three days before his murder, I was clearing our dinner dishes from the table when the phone rang. Jeff had just retired to the living room with a stack of paperwork, and I could hear the sounds of a football game coming from our large-screen TV. I put the plates I was holding into the sink and reached across the kitchen island for the telephone receiver.

"Well, hello, my lady," said a familiar voice. "And how are *you* doing this evening?"

"Hi, John. I'm great!" I said to my husband's best friend. "You?"

"I'm fine... except... well... I have a lot of patients these days asking about the latest advancements in superheavy-isotope-based therapeutics. Especially the people that—you know—have, uh, failed other therapies and don't have many options left. So I was really looking forward to Jeff's presentation at the conference in Seattle last week.

"When Jeff didn't speak, and then when I couldn't find him anywhere, I went to the conference organizers to ask if his time slot had changed. They said he had not checked in..."

The cheers coming from the living room TV grew to a roar as a touchdown was scored. Two commentators began shouting over each other.

I, too, wanted to scream. The familiar background noises of our home, normally so comforting, had just become unrelenting cacophony.

I slid off the barstool at the kitchen island where I had sat down in a daze while listening to John. I felt sick to my stomach. I took a few deep breaths, but they did little to quiet my nerves.

I stepped out of the kitchen.

Jeff was in sweatpants, a T-shirt, and socks, reclining beneath a blanket on the living room sofa. In his lap was a stack of papers. His eyes moved up and down between his work and the football game on the TV mounted on the wall.

I took another deep breath. "That was John," I said.

Jeff's face paled, and he looked up from his papers. "What did he need?"

"He was calling about the conference in Seattle. He was wondering why you missed your lecture."

Jeff's eyes dropped back down to the pages in his lap, and he continued to shuffle through them. His complexion was now changing quickly from white to red. "I'll be sure to call him back."

I stood motionless.

"GO!" Jeff shouted suddenly at the TV, and the audience in the football stands began to cheer wildly. The redness on Jeff's face deepened.

"So why *did* you miss your lecture?" I pressed, and he

paused before answering.

"I decided my presentation wasn't ready for prime time yet."

"Since when are you unprepared to deliver a lecture, especially one scheduled months in advance to be given to several thousand people?"

Jeff tossed the papers onto the coffee table and sat up. "What is this, Katrina, the third degree?"

"Of course not. But why didn't you tell me? I thought you were really looking forward to presenting. You love presenting! And it's not like you to flake out without even extending the courtesy of canceling."

"I've had a lot on my mind," Jeff said with a shrug. "I guess I just forgot."

"You just forgot?"

"Yes."

"You just forgot that you skipped the entire conference?"

Jeff's eyes flashed. "What the... this is unbelievable! You checked up on me?"

"I didn't check up on you," I found myself explaining. "John blurted it out. He said he started looking around for you when you didn't speak and ultimately found out that you had never checked in at the registration desk. He obviously didn't think you would have lied to me about your whereabouts. He was just worried about you. And now, so am I. Frankly, I'm also worried about the future of our relationship! What were you doing in Seattle all that time? Did you even go to Seattle? Did you even *intend* to go to Seattle?"

Jeff stood up from the sofa and switched off the TV. "Of course I intended to go to Seattle!"

It was the first time I had ever heard my husband shout in anger.

"I registered for the conference, Katrina. Do you want to

21

see my receipt? Is that how it's going to be now? I had every intention of going... it's just that I... I..."

"Are you cheating on me?"

"No!" he shouted. "Absolutely not! Of course not!" His voice softened. "Honey, listen. Don't you remember those nights? Don't you remember talking to me every night like we always do when one of us is away? Sometimes we talked late, late into the night. Long conversations. Remember?"

I did. I also remembered that he had looked tired.

Jeff and I used video calls to keep in touch when one of us was away on business. At that moment, I distinctly remembered that when Jeff was allegedly in Seattle he looked exceptionally tired.

I remembered lying in bed one night, my bare breasts covered with our comforter, and watching him through my phone's video screen. I remembered Jeff leaning his own iPhone against something so that he could speak to me while also rubbing his eyes, his shoulders, his temples. And behind him, I remembered that I could see the nightstand of his hotel room with a Marriott welcome package upon it.

I remembered him smiling, shaking his upper body as if shaking off a rough day, and asking me what was beneath the blanket...

"Come on, Katrina!" Jeff began shouting at me again in our living room. "Use logic. Ask yourself if I am behaving like a cheater."

"You mean like disappearing for four days solid?"

Jeff swallowed and looked down. Then he approached me and put both hands on my shoulders. He looked into my eyes, and in his I thought I saw desperation for the first time since meeting him.

"I meant that a cheating man is not interested in the conversations we had while I was away," he said quietly. "A cheating man is eager to get off the phone with his wife."

"Sure," I scoffed, "unless his lover knows he's married! Maybe she's also married and has something to lose. Maybe she would sit there and wait for you to talk to me. Maybe she was off somewhere talking to her own husband at the same time. You're not stupid, Jeff! You would know exactly how not to get caught. God, I can't believe we are actually having this conversation!"

But in my heart, I also could not believe Jeff would want that, any of that. It was not Jeff. Either I was wrong now, or I had been wrong about my husband all along.

"Where were you for four days, Jeff?"

He let out a sigh and sank back down onto the living room sofa. There were tears in his eyes.

"Sweetheart, listen," he said quietly. "I can't tell you. I am sorry for that, I really am. I have never lied to you before. I have never kept anything from you. I am sorry for lying to you about the conference. I hate myself for that. But I can't tell you now, either. Please, you just have to trust me..."

Four days later, the silence of the empty house was maddening. Apart from my own ragged breathing and the steady, persistent ticking of our grandfather clock—a nagging reminder of the transience of time—there was only a void where a couple in love had lived.

I sat down heavily on the carpeted floor next to Jeff's desk in our office. My eyes were burning from a morning of almost constant crying. My fingers were swollen and sore from scrubbing Jeff's blood from our terrace and the yacht, and they trembled as I scrolled through the screens on Jeff's cell phone.

In Jeff's recent call history was an international phone number. I did not recognize the country code, and I might not have noticed the number at all—except for the fact that it appeared fifty-six times over five weeks.

The record began with an incoming call to Jeff. After that, both incoming and outgoing calls between Jeff's cell phone and the international number occurred daily, sometimes several times per day, with the exception of a single four-day time span.

I recognized the dates immediately. They were the same four days as the conference in Seattle. This was the number of the person Jeff was with over those four days.

For a few long moments, I only stared at Jeff's phone as if the number itself would suddenly speak, explaining to me the inexplicable. Finally, I dialed the number.

"Dr. Wilson!" a woman answered with an excessive enthusiasm that made me prickle. Her voice held a barely perceptible accent.

"Actually, this is Dr. Stone," I said coolly. "Jeff Wilson's wife. With whom am I speaking?"

There was a long pause, and when the woman spoke again the enthusiasm was gone. "I'm sorry, Dr. Stone," she said. "This is Alyssa Iacovani. I am an old classmate of your husband's from UCLA."

Jeff had done his undergraduate work at UCLA, and we kept in touch with several of his college buddies. None of them had ever mentioned an Alyssa Iacovani.

"I am the director of the Piso Project," the woman went on. "This is an antiquities research project with *Il Museo*

*Archeologico Nazionale,* the National Archeological Museum in Naples, Italy. I apologize for my sense of urgency, Dr. Stone, but I was expecting a call from your husband several hours ago, and he has not called. I was just about to phone him instead. I must see Jeff immediately."

For a moment, I struggled to comprehend her audacity as well as her statements. *Antiquities research? Italy? What could she possibly need to speak to Jeff about?*

"I'm sorry," I said finally. "My husband has been called away on family business and will be unavailable for at least the next couple of weeks." Another lengthy pause ensued, and I began to wonder if she was still on the line.

"In that case," the woman said at last, "Dr. Stone, I apologize again, but I must see *you* immediately."

In one of these buildings there has been found an entire library, compos'd of volumes of the Egyptian Papyrus, of which there have been taken out about 250; and the place is not yet clear'd or emptied... Of these there are many in my custody.

-Director of the Museum Herculanese

Camillo Paderni (1720–1770)

# CHAPTER THREE

I caught the next flight to Naples, Italy.

When it landed, I stepped off the airplane, found my driver, and instructed him to take me directly to the National Archeological Museum.

Once in the limousine, I laid my head back and closed my eyes. Well accustomed to the frequent travel mandated by my career, I usually sleep as soundly on an overnight flight as in my own bed at home. This time, my restless, shallow sleep was a theater for recurrent loops of horrifying dreams.

Act One starred my husband, a river of blood flowing from his abdomen, steadying himself with our terrace railing, turning to look at the shooter in our bedroom whose face I could never see. In Act Two, Jeff would lie dying on the deck of my otherwise gleaming anniversary gift, a circle of blood expanding around him, a red death slowly enveloping his life. In Act Three, a black blanket would enfold his naked corpse, and then a black hearse would enfold the blanket, and then a black night would enfold the hearse.

I was the star of the finale, desperately sopping blood from my home, where it continued pouring in faster than I could clean, like a macabre variant on Mickey Mouse's unruly swirling basin in *The Sorcerer's Apprentice.*

Three times, this grisly Shakespearean tragedy was interrupted by flight turbulence, which brought on highly uncharacteristic airsickness. By the time the plane landed at ten o'clock in the morning Italian time, I was exhausted, hungry, dizzy, and cross.

"Ma'am, we have arrived," the limousine driver said, waking me. I shook my head to clear the fuzziness.

I stepped out of the car and entered the museum.

I passed through a ground floor lobby adorned with marble sculpture to arrive at the museum's coat check desk, where I checked my hastily over-packed luggage. Following the directions given at the desk, I went back across the lobby to the stairwell, my pace and my heart rate increasing with every step. By the time I reached the lower floor, I was practically running.

I rounded a corner and skidded to an abrupt halt as I almost collided with a six-foot-long crocodile. Mummified and encased in glass, the large reptile appeared a bit thin, but otherwise it looked almost normal and as if it were sleeping. An accompanying description, written in both Italian and English, explained that crocodiles were thought by the ancient Egyptians to have special powers.

I glanced around the room and realized I was in the section of the museum I had been looking for. Several mummified human forms surrounded me, along with a second crocodile, this one just a baby. It was bright green, no more than a foot in length, and could have been confused with someone's pet lizard. It, too, was impeccably mummified.

"Dr. Stone?" a voice behind me inquired.

I turned and sized her up for a moment before answering. I had been expecting Alyssa Iacovani to be a brunette, given the Italian last name and slight accent. Instead, straight pale blonde hair flowed like spun gold to her shoulders, which were tan beneath a lightweight sleeveless top. Her green eyes were both intelligent and inquisitive.

I briefly remembered the first time Jeff passed a hand through my waist-length auburn hair. "I love that you're a redhead," he had said. "I've always thought redheads were the sexiest."

"We have the most fun, too," I teased. "My sister always told me that was supposed to be blondes, but, then again, she's a dumb blonde."

"I have never been into blondes, dumb or otherwise," Jeff had responded with a smile.

"Dr. Iacovani," I said, stepping forward to shake the hand of the lovely blonde woman who might have been my husband's classmate.

"Please, call me Alyssa," she said.

"Katrina," I said in kind.

"Nice to meet you, Katrina, and thank you for coming so quickly. I'm sure you have gathered that time is of the essence, so I apologize for dispensing with any small talk. I'll get straight to the point. How well do you know your husband's research?"

I raised an eyebrow. "I am the co-founder of *our* company," I said.

"Of course"—Alyssa appeared unfazed by the jab—"but you are the head of the biology division. Jeff is head of chemistry. What I was asking is this: How well do you understand the chemistry? Do the biologists and chemists fully understand each other's work, or are the two areas too different from one another?"

"We have a loose understanding of each other's work," I said. "He and the other chemists design and chemically synthesize the molecules, but once I see the synthesis scheme I can follow it. My function is to design and implement the biological assays, but Jeff and the other chemists can follow what we biologists are doing once we explain it to them. Why do you ask?"

"Ugh, where do I begin?" Alyssa looked around and made a sweeping gesture with both hands, calling my attention to the artifacts in the museum exhibit. "I noticed you surveying the Egyptian rooms when you arrived. I put these rooms together.

"I did my doctoral work at the Yale Egyptological Institute in Egypt, mostly doing field research at the Fayoum Oasis outside of Cairo. After graduate school, I came here.

"*Il Museo Archeologico Nazionale* is the direct descendent of the Royal Bourbon Museum, one of the largest and oldest museums in all of Europe. It contains one of the world's most valuable collections of Roman and Greek antiquities.

"I believed that my expertise in Egyptian antiquities could be a valuable asset here. As I'm sure you are aware, it is impossible to fully appreciate any one of these ancient cultures without an in-depth knowledge of the others. I came to Naples to strengthen my understanding of the Greek and Roman cultures while bringing my extensive background in Egyptian culture to the museum. I have been here ever since." She smiled. "People tell me I have even picked up the accent a little."

"Indeed," I said.

"As I mentioned to you on the phone, I was an undergraduate at UCLA with Jeff—"

"Excuse my rudeness," I said, "but I don't remember Jeff ever mentioning you in the past. I only heard your name for the first time a few weeks ago." It was a lie. I had first heard her name the previous day—from her—on the phone.

"He probably didn't remember me," she said, shrugging. "We were not friends in college; in fact, I doubt he even knew who I was." She smiled sheepishly. "In my required freshman chemistry sequence—which I *loathed*, by the way—I knew him by name and by sight as the guy who was in the habit of throwing off the curve. I even knew people who tried to sabotage his efforts. They didn't succeed, as Jeff published his first paper in *Nature* one year later, as a college sophomore. Aside from that, Jeff was gorgeous, charming, brilliant, and an outstanding surfer. He was hard to miss, and everyone knew he would one day do something extraordinary. After graduation, I read about Jeff from time to time when he would receive yet another prestigious award, so I was always vaguely aware of his career path.

"Recently, I stumbled upon a puzzle in my own research. I believed that this puzzle had a strong and unique chemical component. Knowing that Jeff would be the absolute best person on Earth to riddle it out, I decided to give it a shot. I looked him up and I called him. I don't think he had any idea who I was.

"The thing that surprised me, to be honest, was his eagerness to help. Jeff became practically obsessed with the document. He started calling me daily, sometimes several times a day. I think he forgot about the time difference between Naples and San Diego because a few times he even woke me up in the middle of the night." She laughed heartily.

I felt a sudden, intense wave of nausea and struggled to process the information I had just been hit with. *Ancient Egypt? Unique chemical component? What document?* Panic welled up inside me when I realized I was supposed to already know.

Jeff should have told me.

"Of course," I bluffed. "As you said, he is certainly very excited about... the document. But I must admit, I have been so busy lately that I haven't followed the development of the situation as closely as I should have. Perhaps it's best for you to bring me up to speed from the beginning."

Alyssa gave me a strange look.

"Would you like a cup of coffee?" she asked then.

"No, thank you, I'm fine." It was another lie. I felt dizzy and nauseous. I looked again at the mummified humans and animals surrounding me and wished for a moment of fresh air.

"Katrina, how well do you know ancient Egypt?"

"Not very well," I said, gazing longingly out the open door of the room.

"Of course not. That's what I was afraid of. History is not your area any more than biology is mine.

"Obviously, I cannot make you an expert on the subject in one conversation, but there are certain concepts that you *must* grasp. Please feel free to stop me if I am either speaking over your head or insulting your intelligence."

Alyssa motioned toward the mummified crocodile. "One thing you need to understand about the ancient Egyptians is that they were a culture of superstition. Natural phenomena were explained as acts of the gods. The Greeks were similar, and the Romans borrowed heavily from both cultures.

"During the time of the first Caesars, just before the birth of Christ, all three cultures were heavily intermingled. And it was during that time that a powerful change in thinking began to evolve.

"The ancients became increasingly motivated by empirical data, things they observed. They began to build hospitals instead of temples to cure their sick. They conducted autopsies to explain causes of death. They developed sophisticated sur-gical instruments, some of them similar to instruments still used to this day. They developed scientific methods and drew conclusions based on hard, experimental evidence—"

I snapped to attention. "Sorry, what?"

"In short," she said, "during this era, these three cultures began a shift in thinking, from superstition to true science."

"And this is the era you study?" I asked.

"It is."

"What caused the change? What led these cultures toward science and away from superstition?"

Alyssa smiled. "That is the central question around which my research has been focused for nearly twenty years," she said. "I believe it was the work of one woman."

Alyssa guided me to an elevator. We stepped inside, and she pushed the button for the top floor of the museum. When we stepped out, in sharp contrast to the mummified crocodiles, ordinary objects now surrounded us.

Curio cabinets lining the walls contained a large assort-ment of metal and ceramic dishes and vases. Centered in the room was a large case containing a single blue vase, clear-ly a treasure from a lost era. I approached one cabinet that caught my eye. Inside it, several blue-and aqua-colored piec-es of glassware sparkled elegantly, the lighting in the room passing through the glass of the curio cabinet and ricocheting playfully back from the glass of the objects.

"They're lovely," I said offhand.

"They are two thousand years old," Alyssa replied. "We are now in the part of the museum dedicated to artifacts retrieved from Pompeii, Herculaneum, and Stabiae. All of the objects in this room were preserved, untouched, beneath several feet of volcanic lava, ash, and mud following the eruption of Mount Vesuvius in 79 CE. That eruption, and the stunning preservation of those cities that accompanied it, gave us the most complete picture of the ancient world we have ever been able to observe."

I peered more closely at the fragile glass items. "How did they survive the eruption without being crushed?"

"Because a four-hundred-degree-Celcius pyroclastic flow of hot gas enveloped the area with such intense heat that the water vaporized out of organic objects, and ash fell steadily for hours, reaching a depth of more than ten feet. Objects were essentially carbonized before the ash fell, and then the ash encapsulated everything, forming a seal which remained for seventeen hundred years."

"Whoa," I said, trying to imagine a heat so intense that it could instantly desiccate an entire city.

We passed through a series of spaces and corridors into another small room containing glass exhibition cases. In the center of one was an instrument that resembled an old, battered loom. Long, knotted strands of a charcoal-colored substance hung suspended from it. I read the English version of the description and then leaned forward, gaping in disbelief. The suspended cluster looked more like curing meat hanging in a slaughterhouse than what it actually was.

"That jumbled mess is made of *paper*?" I asked Alyssa.

"It's papyrus," she said. "This room is dedicated to the *Villa dei Papiri*—Villa of the Papyri. The villa is named for its large library containing approximately two thousand papyrus scrolls. These scrolls were among the objects buried in the eruption of Mount Vesuvius. They were rediscovered during the excavation of Herculaneum that began in the 1700s. They are still legible to this day.

"What you are looking at is the tool developed in 1756 to unroll them, and that 'jumbled mess' is one of the actual scrolls from Herculaneum. It took four years to unwind the very first scroll. We are still in the process of unwinding some of them—an extremely laborious procedure, even with today's technology."

I tore my eyes away from the slaughterhouse meat and scanned the room. On its walls were flattened papyri—torn, faded, and smudged in places but, indeed, legible. I walked over to examine one of them more closely. It was written in Greek.

"This is the focus of my research today," Alyssa said. "As I mentioned on the phone, I am the director of an effort called the Piso Project. The project was named after a man called Lucius Calpurnius Piso Caesoninus. He was the owner of the Villa dei Papiri. He was also the father-in-law of Julius Caesar.

"The Piso Project seeks to unravel, translate, and archive a specific subset of the scrolls unearthed from the library. We believe these scrolls may contain information that can disprove a vast range of common dogma regarding ancient Rome, Greece, and Egypt.

"It was during this work several weeks ago that I translated the section of one of the scrolls that compelled me to phone your husband. At first, I was not sure what I had found. To be honest, I'm still not certain.

"I consulted Jeff to ascertain whether or not the phenomenon described in my translation was even possible from a chemistry perspective. Jeff suggested that it probably was but that to identify the isotope with any degree of confidence would be like finding a needle in a haystack. And, as you know, we have been working intensely toward that goal ever since. With Jeff away on—did you say a family emergency?—I was hoping you could take his place in these efforts."

"Of course," I said, with absolutely no idea what I was agreeing to.

"BULGING TUMORS ON HIS BREAST" MEANS THE EXISTENCE OF SWELLINGS ON HIS BREAST, LARGE, SPREADING AND HARD; TOUCHING THEM IS LIKE TOUCHING A BALL OF WRAPPINGS; THE COMPARISON IS TO A GREEN HEMAT FRUIT, WHICH IS HARD AND COOL UNDER THY HAND, LIKE TOUCHING THOSE SWELLINGS WHICH ARE ON HIS BREAST.

THERE IS NO TREATMENT.

*-THE EDWIN SMITH SURGICAL PAPYRUS*, 1600 BCE

PAPER OF WHATEVER GRADE IS FABRICATED ON A BOARD MOISTENED WITH WATER FROM THE NILE: THE MUDDY LIQUID SERVES AS THE BONDING FORCE. FIRST THERE IS SPREAD FLAT ON THE BOARD A LAYER CONSISTING OF STRIPS OF PAPYRUS RUNNING VERTICALLY... AFTER THAT A CROSS LAYER COMPLETES THE CONSTRUCTION. THEN IT IS PRESSED IN PRESSES, AND THE SHEETS THUS FORMED ARE DRIED IN THE SUN AND JOINED ONE TO ANOTHER.

*-NATURAL HISTORY*
PLINY THE ELDER (23–79 CE)

# Chapter Four

Alyssa Iacovani led me away from the exhibition rooms and into a hallway of private offices. We stepped into one of them, and she closed the door behind us.

Alyssa walked over and sat down in the desk chair while I looked around the cluttered space. Bookshelves lining the walls were double stacked with a collection ranging from various history texts to archeological case studies to basic biology, chemistry, and physics books.

The books were interspersed with a number of small statues and trinkets that I imagined might have come from the museum's gift shop. A large wall calendar resembled a book of papyrus scrolls. Various dates were scrawled with appointments in scarcely legible Italian.

On the desk near a badly scuffed computer lay several disheveled piles of notepads, binders, and manuscripts. Beside them, a small cardboard shipping box lay open, with packing peanuts strewn about it, its precious treasure already pillaged from within.

Also on the desk stood two framed photos. One was a portrait of a dark-skinned middle-aged man with a crooked-toothed but attractive smile and a full head of salt-and-pepper hair. His rounded black eyes shone brightly, but beneath them were heavy bags.

Beside the man's photo was an image of two black-haired youths in their mid-to-late teens. The boy stood casually behind the seated girl, her thick tresses pouring like oil over one shoulder to her slender waist. Both children shared the same dark complexion and rounded black eyes of the man in the photo beside them. I wondered if the teenagers were twins.

I examined the photos on the desk for a moment and then glanced into the golden face and cat-like green eyes of Alyssa Iacovani. Her eyes, too, fell to the photographs for an instant before returning to meet mine.

"Would you like to see the document?" she asked.

Alyssa switched on the desktop computer and sat back in her chair for a moment while the aging machine hummed to life. She clicked with the mouse, and across the room a printer began to whirr.

She stood to snatch up a single page and then handed it to me. "This is the English translation of that section of the scroll I was telling you about. This is what I showed Jeff. The original is much, much longer.

"Each of these texts spans many papyrus scrolls; the ancients were wordy, to say the least. Furthermore, many of the scrolls are horribly fragmented. As researchers, we are tasked with piecing together the full-scale works. This aspect of antiquities research is quite literally the assembly of a large jigsaw puzzle..."

As I read and re-read the document, I barely heard her.

**I HAVE IN MY CHARGE THE CARE OF TEN, ALL STRICKEN WITH THE PLAGUE OF THE CRABS.**

**AGARISTE AND I CREATED TWO EXTRA BEDS FROM THE**

**FEATHERS OF PIGEON TO ACCOMMODATE THE SIX MEN. THE GODS GRANTED THE COMFORT OF MORE SPACIOUS SURROUNDINGS TO THE FOUR POOR WOMEN IN THE ADJACENT ROOM, BUT THEY WAIL WITHOUT STOPPING NONETHELESS.**

**ALL TEN OF MY CHARGES HAVE FAILED THE SCALPEL AND THE FIRE DRILL. THEIR TUMORS CONTINUE TO GROW. THE CRABS CONTINUE TO DEVOUR THEM.**

"Excuse me," I said. "Wasn't it Hippocrates who coined the word 'cancer,' meaning something about crabs?"

Alyssa looked impressed. "Yes, it was!" she said. "Cancer, carcinoma, carcinogen... all of these words descend from *karkinos*, the ancient Greek for 'crab.' Hippocrates' hypothesis of cancer, that it was caused by an excess of 'black bile,' remained fairly unchanged from about 450 BCE all the way until the Renaissance."

"And did the word *tumors*, as used here, have the same meaning in the ancient world that it has today?"

"Essentially," Alyssa said. "Of course the ancients' descriptions reflect a lack of technology—so any deformity of the skin or other imperfection that resembles a tumor will have been written as such. But true tumors have been documented in ancient papyri for thousands of years. The first known case study is a papyrus scroll from ancient Egypt, known today as the *Edwin Smith Surgical Papyrus* after the man who found it. The scroll dates to 1600 BCE but is believed to be a copy of much older texts. It describes breast cancer—in men, oddly enough. The ancients could even distinguish between malignant and benign, based predominantly on the same gross differences in tumor composition that are still utilized for preliminary assessment today."

"Vascularization, asymmetry, et cetera?" I asked, and Alyssa nodded.

"And recurrence," she added.

I glanced again at the last three sentences of text.

**ALL TEN OF MY CHARGES HAVE FAILED THE SCALPEL AND THE FIRE DRILL. THEIR TUMORS CONTINUE TO GROW. THE CRABS CONTINUE TO DEVOUR THEM.**

"What is the *fire drill*?" I asked.

"That was essentially a cauterizer. They basically treat-ed the tumors by burning them off. Each of these patients had endured it, as well as the procedure that today we would call 'surgical resection' or 'de-bulking.' Yet the tumors re-curred. These points are strongly indicative of an aggressive malignancy."

"I agree," I said.

Alyssa printed another document and handed it to me. "The handwriting, ink, and text indicate to me that this piece and the one you just read are two parts of the same docu-ment. We do not know yet what comes between that piece and this one. It is possible that the missing fragment has yet to be unrolled or has not been unearthed from the Villa dei Papiri. Unfortunately, it is also possible that the piece is lost forever."

I read the document translation once, and then again. As I processed the information, my initial enthusiasm gave way to absolute, debilitating despair. Before me was the text from an ancient papyrus that had somehow lured my husband to Italy behind my back. It might also have been what led to his demise.

And it was nonsense.

I blinked back frustrated tears as I stared at the page in my hand, still warm from the printer. Then I closed my eyes and sighed.

"This is categorically impossible," I said.

"That's what Jeff thought, at first. In fact, it's also what I thought. But following several weeks of intensive research, your husband and I are both convinced that it *is* possible."

She looked into my eyes. "You *know* new chemical elements can be created," she said. "Jeff won a Nobel Prize for exactly that. You and he have now co-founded a successful company based on the creation of new elements and the medicinal value of their isotopes. You already have four of them in clinical trials. Why do you think I picked him to consult about this?"

"But... the creation of new elements requires modern technology!" I argued. "There is no way the ancient Greeks, or Egyptians, or whomever else you study, could have done this!"

"You are assuming that modern technology is the only way," Alyssa said. "But nature produces phenomena that no scientist in the world has ever managed to harness. Thanks to this document, I think that Jeff and I may be able to learn how to harness one of them. One that, if we are right, may revolutionize the field of medicine."

WHEN THE SKY OPENED AND THE GODS CAST DOWN THEIR ANGER UPON OUR ENEMIES, THE WINE SOURED AND THE NARDOS BY THE BEDSIDES TURNED FROM GREEN TO RED.

"THE NARDOS HAVE QUICKENED!" SAID ONE OF THE WOMEN, AND SHE REACHED FORTH A FRAIL HAND TO TOUCH ONE BUT THEN HASTILY WITHDREW AS IF STUNG BY AN INSECT. "IT BIT ME!" SHE SAID, WITH THE CRAZY EYES OF THE SICKNESS.

WHAT PART OF HUMANITY MAKES US NEED TO SEE, TO KNOW FOR OURSELVES, EVEN THOUGH THE GODS SO FREQUENTLY PUNISH THOSE WHOSE VANITY DRIVES THEM TO EXPLORE THE FORBIDDEN? IT IS THE GREATEST MYSTERY I HAVE KNOWN. BUT AS THE FIRST WITHDREW, THREE OTHER THIN ARMS REACHED FORWARD AT ONCE, THE OTHER WOMEN ALSO SEEKING WHAT THEIR BEDMATE HAD EXPERIENCED. ALL THREE RETRACTED WITH HASTE.

I, TOO, NEEDED TO KNOW. WHEN I TOUCHED ONE OF THE NARDOS, A GENTLE WARMTH RAN FROM MY FINGERTIPS TO MY HEART, LIKE A QUIET FLAME IN THE BLOOD OF MY ARM. I FEARED THE SICKNESS THAT WOULD SOON FOLLOW! AND THEN, THE SENSATION WAS GONE.

"AGARISTE!" I SHOUTED. "THE NARDOS ARE AFLAME!" BUT BY THE TIME SHE ENTERED THE ROOM AND REACHED OUT TO TOUCH ONE, THE EFFECT WAS GONE.

THE NEXT MORNING, THE FOUR WOMEN REPORTED AN UNUSUALLY PEACEFUL SLEEP, AND THEIR TUMORS APPEARED SMALLER TO MY EYE. AFTER FOUR MORE DAYS, THEY WERE GONE, YET THE CRABS CONTINUED TO OVERTAKE THE MEN. THE SICKNESS I HAD EXPECTED NEVER CAME.

WHY DID THE GODS SPARE THE WOMEN THROUGH MAGIC PLANTS? IS IT BECAUSE WOMEN DO NOT MAKE WAR, AS MEN DO? IT IS NOT FOR US TO KNOW, BUT, IN THOSE FOUR, IT WAS AS IF THE CRABS NEVER EXISTED.

"What is a *nardo*?" I asked, my voice trembling slightly.

"A medicinal plant," Alyssa said. "I have come across the term in other ancient texts. It was apparently used to treat a number of ailments in those days. Unfortunately, today there are multiple possibilities for what a nardo could actually be, and I'm not sure which of today's plants corresponds with the one in this document—*if*, of course, the plant in the document even still exists today.

"Furthermore, none of the possibilities that I have investigated so far are poisonous or stinging, and certainly none of them bite, as all five of these women seemed to agree upon, including the caretaker—who I assume was perfectly healthy to begin with. And if an ancient nardo was poisonous, electrified, or otherwise capable of attacking humans, I can't imagine it would be selected to adorn patients' bedsides in a hospital. So we can probably assume that the phenomenon observed by our author was very rare."

"Then what happened?" I shouted. "Magic? The gods?"

"Exactly," Alyssa said. "Magic. The gods. Except that today we attribute these phenomena to the laws of nature. And as you are well aware, they frequently turn out to be explicable by science."

*She is right*, I began to admit to myself. *Nature precedes science, and science precedes medicine...*

Penicillin is a mold. The medical uses for leeches and maggots, once thought archaic, were revived in the twentieth century after the organisms' legitimate therapeutic properties were brought to light. A drug once marketed worldwide for morning sickness induced devastating birth defects in thousands of babies—but was later revived as an effective cure for leprosy, and is currently standard of care for multiple myeloma.

"You are talking about a cure for cancer," I said. "Not just a treatment—a cure. These women were cured."

"Yes," said Alyssa. "They were. That's exactly what I'm talking about. What we are talking about."

*She and my husband.*

I turned away for a moment, pretending to examine a small sculpture in the corner of the office. It was a figure of a woman in a sheath dress, a crown upon her head displaying two large horns. Between them was an orb.

Then I turned once again to face the beautiful woman Jeff had been collaborating with instead of me. And I wondered if I was looking into the face of his killer.

"Cancer drug discovery and new chemical elements are pretty far outside of your field, aren't they?" I asked.

"They are entirely outside of my field," she said. "That is why I consulted your husband."

*It is the day after we spoke for the first time. The lecture hall is packed for a presentation by the handsome Nobel laureate chemist Jeffrey Wilson. I am sitting front row center, as he had been during my own talk. Jeff mounts the podium and winks in my direction.*

*"Good morning," he says. "In 1984, Barry Marshall demonstrated that stomach ulcers are caused by the bacterium* H. pylori. *He did this by drinking a vial of it. Vile indeed."*

*A chorus of chuckles sweeps through the room, along with a few groans of disgust.*

*"Today," Jeff continues, "my lab has developed an antidote to* H. pylori *infection. As I had no desire to drink a beaker of bacteria, we chose to use chemistry instead."*

*An image projects on the screen above him. He focuses a laser pointer upon it.*

*"As you know, many chemical elements on the periodic table can exist as several variants, or isotopes. My lab has developed a brand new class of therapeutics using isotopes of the so-called superheavy elements.*

*"These are named as such because they are formed by a combination of two smaller elements—which makes them, well, super heavy. We have learned how to force the collision of natural elements to create these from scratch. The trick is in creating those with medicinal properties, and the even bigger trick is in harnessing the best isotope before it decays.*

*"Superheavy isotopes are unstable. They are generated very rapidly, and they decay almost instantly into inert ingredients. But it is also this very transience that lends enormous therapeutic potential to the superheavy isotopes as a class. It is this transience that permits us to target a specific biological or pathological niche without any off-target activity.*

*"An example is the drug we have developed against H. pylori. When an ulcer patient swallows our pill, the drug is converted by stomach acid into a new superheavy isotope, which specifically targets the bacteria and then disperses into its inert ingredients. The result is a highly powerful therapeutic with virtually negligible side effects..."*

I blinked to make my eyes refocus upon the ancient text. My hands were trembling as I read and re-read its message.

**... THE WINE SOURED AND THE NARDOS BY THE BEDSIDES TURNED FROM GREEN TO RED.**

**... "THE NARDOS HAVE QUICKENED!"**

**... WHEN I TOUCHED ONE OF THE NARDOS, A GENTLE WARMTH RAN FROM MY FINGERTIPS TO MY HEART... AND THEN, THE SENSATION WAS GONE.**

**... IN THOSE FOUR, IT WAS AS IF THE CRABS NEVER EXISTED.**

I looked up at Alyssa Iacovani. "Do you realize the consequences for the person who brings this discovery to light?" I asked. "Whoever scientifically proves whatever happened in these nardos will never need to work again. He or she will have cured the plague of our time."

Alyssa's intelligent eyes shone with the electricity of pure ambition, a vulgar neon green against the blood red backdrop of my mind. "Yes," she said, smiling. "You are correct about all of those things. So do you want to be a part of it? Your husband certainly does."

[F]OR SOME OF THE EGYPTIANS THE CROCODILES ARE SACRED ANIMALS... AND EACH OF THESE TWO PEOPLES KEEPS ONE CROCODILE SELECTED FROM THE WHOLE NUMBER, WHICH HAS BEEN TRAINED TO TAMENESS, AND THEY PUT HANGING ORNAMENTS OF MOLTEN STONE AND OF GOLD INTO THE EARS OF THESE AND ANKLETS ROUND THE FRONT FEET, AND THEY GIVE THEM FOOD APPOINTED AND VICTIMS OF SACRIFICES AND TREAT THEM AS WELL AS POSSIBLE WHILE THEY LIVE, AND AFTER THEY ARE DEAD THEY BURY THEM IN SACRED TOMBS, EMBALMING THEM.

-*THE HISTORIES*
HERODOTUS (CA. 484–425 BCE)

[T]HE ROMANS PITIED, NOT SO MUCH HER, AS ANTONY HIMSELF, AND MORE PARTICULARLY THOSE WHO HAD SEEN CLEOPATRA, WHOM THEY COULD REPORT TO HAVE NO WAY THE ADVANTAGE OF OCTAVIA EITHER IN YOUTH OR BEAUTY.

-*LIVES OF THE NOBLE GRECIANS AND ROMANS*
PLUTARCH (CA. 46–120 CE)

## CHAPTER FIVE

A new slide appears on the projector screen, and Jeffrey Wilson aims a laser pointer at the grotesque image. From my seat at front row center of the auditorium, I hear the collective gasp of the audience behind me.

*I do not gasp; it is an image I have seen a thousand times.*

*On the slide is a full-frontal photograph of a small naked boy, his eyes covered to protect his identity. The boy's body is covered with coal-colored sores, sores that appear somewhat like black mold. The sores are the unique, distinctive signature of the bacterium* B. anthracis, *the trademark that gives rise to the name anthrax—derived from the Greek word for coal.*

*"This little boy exemplifies the desperate need for better medicines to combat modern diseases," Jeff is saying, "and current efforts in my lab are aimed at expanding the potential of superheavy isotope technology to address this need. As an example, we are developing a treatment for weaponized inhalational anthrax, which will combine our superheavy isotope technology with the high levels of oxygen present in the lung..."*

Alyssa stood and retrieved a large set of keys and a purse from her desk. "Let's take a walk," she said. She then led me from the private offices, and we began strolling through the museum like tourists.

"I know that you and Jeff are a team," she said. "He raves about you. He says you each act as the other's sounding board, voice of reason, and muse."

*Except for this time*, I thought.

"So I would really love your input on this," Alyssa said.

I could smell her perfume. I had not noticed it earlier, but now she walked so closely next to me that our shoulders were nearly touching. The scent was subtle and delicate, but the weight of her presence and her scent in my personal space made me feel sick again. I was glad to be walking through the museum rather than confined to her office.

Her voice was nearly a whisper. "There is something I have been seeking since I entered graduate school," Alyssa said. "As I mentioned, my dissertation project was conducted at the Fayoum Oasis outside of Cairo. I went to the Fayoum in hopes of recovering an important fragment of the historical record that has been lost for centuries."

"Ambitious project for a student," I said softly.

"Indeed. When I selected my project and began to flesh it out, I knew I was embarking upon something risky. What I could never have predicted was the magnitude of what I would eventually find.

"I had developed an hypothesis that a large critical piece of history had either inexplicably disappeared or, more likely, been deliberately hidden just before the birth of Christ. You asked me earlier what sparked the shift in thinking during that era from superstition to true science. The truth is, we don't know. Nobody knows. That is what I went to the Fayoum to find out.

"I decided to go into field work at the oasis after poking around in a microfiche database at my university library. I stumbled upon an article in a turn-of-the-century American newspaper. The story was about an accidental find in the Fayoum.

"In the year 1900, an expedition was led by the Hearst Foundation and the University of California, Berkeley, into the Fayoum to excavate an archeological site. What they found was an ancient crocodile nursery and a cemetery full of mummified crocodiles.

"The workers were furious. They were being paid to excavate human mummies, not animals. To them, this mishap was just a job they would lose money on. So one of the workmen took a machete and began hacking into one of the mummified crocodiles out of anger. Guess what was inside it."

"I give up." I shrugged.

"A hidden collection of papyrus scrolls, dating to 49 BCE."

"Interesting."

"Indeed. Evidently this site was used by the Egyptian rulers to raise crocodiles to adulthood and then use their mummified carcasses to archive documents indefinitely. Of course, the opportunity to explore it was a dream come true for me. Like browsing through a library of six-foot-long organic vaults containing buried treasure from Atlantis. And since my hypothesis dated to the same era, the Greco-Roman period, I thought that this burial ground might contain the information I was looking for. I went to the Fayoum to complete the excavation of the cemetery and to translate the texts inside the crocodile mummies."

"Did you find what you were looking for?" I asked.

"Unfortunately, no. I had to change my entire doctoral hypothesis. But after I graduated, I came to Naples to resume my search. It was here that I finally found two examples of the documents I had been searching for. Five weeks ago. The documents you hold in your hand. I believe there are dozens, maybe hundreds of additional medical texts from the same era yet waiting to be discovered."

I glanced down at the texts I was still holding in my hands: the first, a case study of ten cancer patients; the second, a vague description of the healing of four of them. "What made you so sure that this type of medical writing would exist at all?"

"Everything we know about the era," she said.

"We know a great deal about the author of these documents in particular. This was a public figure—a reigning queen, in fact. She was an exquisitely well-educated woman. She spoke and wrote fluently in nine languages. She had a well-documented, very sophisticated flair for the sciences. She loved her secrets, and she manipulated public record to suit her interests. She had both the means and the motive to store secret documents in the Herculaneum Villa dei Papiri because the library's owner was Julius Caesar's father-in-law. And Caesar was her lover.

"But then, because her life was cut short, she ran out of time to reveal her work on her own terms. This is why her legacy, her *true* legacy, has been lost to us. And why we have never found a single document of hers. Until now.

"The nardo document is the first writing in existence in the hand of Queen Cleopatra the Seventh. I believe it reveals the true source of her power over the most influential men of her era."

*After his lecture, Jeff steps down from the podium. The audience begins exiting the lecture hall, buzzing with conversation about the rapid advances the Nobel laureate has recently made*

in superheavy isotope technology. *Several eager audience members approach Jeff to shake his hand and express their interest in his work.*

"Impressive," *I hear a man say as he walks past me.* "Wilson can't possibly be very old."

"He's forty," *another voice responds.*

*An elderly woman approaches Jeff and lays a hand on his shoulder.* "You should start a biotech company, son," *she says.*

*Jeff smiles politely and shakes her hand.* "Thank you, Dr. Bower." *A number of heads turn to witness the dialog between Jeffrey Wilson and Sara Bower, who has just cured HIV.*

*But Jeff's smoky blue eyes are on me. He steps away from Sara Bower and approaches me.*

"So what did you think, Doctor?" *he asks.*

"Brilliant," *I say, and I cannot control my grin.* "Except for the colossal fuck-up."

"Excuse me?" *Jeff exclaims, drawing back in surprise. His face is bright red, but he is smiling.* "What colossal fuck-up?"

"I know you're a chemist and all," *I say,* "but I have to assume you at least have a couple of biologists on the payroll. They should know better than what you just said.

"Tell me something," *I say with a cocked head.* "How are those anthrax studies coming along?"

*Jeff frowns.* "We'll get there."

"I know a thing or two about anthrax," *I say.*

"Um, yeah, I realize that."

"How are you targeting a specific biological and pathological niche when no specific biological and pathological niche has been defined?" *I ask.*

*Jeff pulls me aside and lowers his voice.* "You're right! The cells are killing me. Or rather, I can't kill them!"

*I laugh. It is the most confusing paradox in anthrax research.*

*Despite the devastating effects of anthrax in the body, there are really very few human cell types that can be killed by anthrax. Until only somewhat recently, the only cells known to be susceptible to infection were a few types of immune cells that in no way could produce the symptoms of anthrax when infected.*

*The biological terrorist attacks of 2001 and beyond triggered a massive increase in funding for anthrax research. This increase in focus led to the demonstration that additional cell types can respond to anthrax infection, but research in these cell types is still incomplete. The total picture is still a mystery.*

*Except to me.*

*"You just bluffed to an audience of five thousand scientists," I say, grinning. "Ballsy."*

*"I didn't bluff!" Jeff says. He is still red in the face, but laughing. "I said we're working on it, and we are. We'll get there! Just wait!"*

*I shake my head. "So your lab is going to single-handedly solve this puzzle that the Department of Defense has been struggling to solve since 2001?"*

*"YES!"*

*"You're one of those guys who won't ever ask for directions, aren't you?"*

*"What do you mean by that?"*

*"Just that you're the type of person who won't accept anyone's help."*

*"How do you know that? You don't know me!"*

*"Oh, I think I do. It's like looking in a mirror. But what if I told you I already know the answer? What if I said that I have proven the complete mechanism of action for anthrax in an entire panel of new cell types?"*

*"I'd think it's a huge bummer that the woman I was just thinking of inviting out to dinner turned out to be a total crackpot."*

*This time, he is the one with the smug grin on his face.*

*"Oh, really? So then, you're convinced that you can solve it, but it's absolutely impossible that I could have?"*

*"Pretty much," he says, but he jumps back as if I might hit him.*

*"OK," I say. "I'll make you a deal. Take this crackpot to dinner, and I'll bring some of my recent data with me—the stuff I am not yet discussing in public. But first, what are the stakes? What do I get if I'm right?"*

*"Dessert?" he offers, and I refrain from asking what delectable treats are on the menu.*

Alyssa Iacovani's intelligent green eyes were unblinking as she waited for my response to her revelation.

"So you're telling me," I finally said, "that *Cleopatra* was the person who wrote this? That she was the person who discovered this... medical phenomenon? That she was some kind of doctor? That's ridiculous!"

"Is it?" Alyssa smiled, and she motioned with her arm to direct me toward an exhibit room. As she pushed the door open and we stepped inside, she gestured broadly around the room.

"Allow me to introduce you to the queen," she said.

The room's display was entitled *The Ptolemaic Dynasty*. It began with a mosaic. The faded, heavily damaged piece depicted an ancient battle, centered around a lone soldier on a horse.

Painted below the mosaic was a brightly colored full-scale reproduction of the same image. The accompanying description identified the soldier as Alexander the Great, founder of the city of Alexandria, Egypt.

A beautifully illustrated timeline gracing all four walls told of the legacy that followed. Key events were annotated in Italian and English alongside painted images of the players involved.

I walked along the walls and allowed my eyes to absorb the dynasty as it flowed from Alexander the Great through Ptolemy I and eventually to Ptolemy XII.

After Ptolemy XII, there was Cleopatra.

A slender figure in a black sheath dress, she wore upon her head a crown of horns with an orb between them. Centered on her forehead above dark, seductive eyes was the small poised head of a snake, its body wrapped horizontally around her head, partially hidden by her lustrous black hair. An additional snake graced each wrist, these of gold.

The thick eyeliner extending far beyond the corners of her eyes accentuated their warm almond shape. The queen's lips were full and the deepest red, and one hand brought a single purple grape toward them. The other hand was wrapped loosely around the bunch.

"This room," Alyssa said from behind me, "I did *not* put together."

I turned to look at her.

Alyssa glanced at the image of Cleopatra and rolled her eyes. Then she began to motion with her hands across the images on the walls. "The timeline is accurate, at least.

"Cleopatra was the last Egyptian ruler from the Ptolemaic dynasty, but she was of Greek descent. The empire was created by Alexander the Great, who bestowed the kingdom upon a fellow Macedonian, and one of his most trusted generals, who became the first Ptolemy king. Cleopatra's father was Ptolemy the Twelfth.

"There are two images missing from this wall—those of

Cleopatra's two brothers. They did not live long enough to rule the kingdom for any significant length of time.

"When her father died, he left the dynasty to Cleopatra *and* to her brother Ptolemy the Thirteenth, with instructions that they marry and rule jointly. They did this for a brief time.

"But Cleopatra was not satisfied with the arrangement, so she raised an army against her brother and husband. This effort initially failed; Ptolemy overthrew Cleopatra's army and exiled her from Egypt.

"During this exile is when she took up with Julius Caesar. The year was 48 BCE. Caesar arranged a false reconciliation of the estranged couple so that he and Cleopatra could murder her brother. One year later, after Cleopatra married her even younger brother—Ptolemy the Fourteenth—and became the Egyptian queen once again, she gave birth to Caesar's son. Shortly thereafter, Ptolemy the Fourteenth died of a mysterious illness—probably poisoning by Cleopatra. Thus, she managed to secure the Egyptian monarchy exclusively for herself twice in one year.

"In short, this was a highly ambitious woman."

Alyssa paused to lead me from the timeline display and into an adjacent room. This one showcased several collections of ancient coins.

"After Caesar's assassination, Cleopatra was summoned by Mark Antony, a friend and comrade of Caesar's, who believed that Cleopatra might have now played a role in Caesar's murder. After meeting with her, Antony abruptly pardoned her, placed her back into power in Egypt, and impregnated her with twins. He later married her. As I said, this was a highly ambitious woman. She also clearly had an effect on men that has never quite been paralleled."

Alyssa led me across the room as she spoke, reaching into

her pocket to withdraw the hefty keychain from her office. "I'm sure you are familiar with the rest of the tragedy, which culminates in the suicides of Cleopatra and Mark Antony, the end of both the Ptolemaic dynasty and the Roman republic, and the rise of Octavian—who became Augustus, the first Roman emperor. I'm sure you have also heard the idealized, romanticized version of this story, in which Cleopatra is a woman of such beauty and charm that she effortlessly manipulates these powerful men as if they were schoolboys..."

We arrived at a display case in the corner of the room, and Alyssa unlocked it. She raised the glass lid and withdrew a small coin. Placing the coin into my free hand, the hand not holding the document translations, she said, "Katrina, I give you the seductress, Cleopatra."

My jaw dropped.

On the coin in my hand was an image of a face in profile. The figure might have been a female, evidenced primarily by the hair. The most prominent facial feature was one of the longest, most hooked noses I had ever seen. The mouth hung partially agape, and the lower jaw dangled downward as if the figure were disgusted. The expression on the androgynous face was something akin to stupor.

"This coin was minted by Cleopatra during her reign," Alyssa said. "It is the image she wanted to portray for posterity, and it is probably the most accurate likeness of her ever generated."

"*That's* Cleopatra?" I blurted out. "She's *hideous*! I was expecting Catherine Zeta Jones, and you've given me the bastard child of Sandra Bernhard and Howard Stern!"

"Peculiar, isn't it? I guess that's what two hundred fifty years of inbreeding will do for you."

"But... surely the standards for beauty were different in

her time?"

"Yes, they were," she acknowledged. "But ugly seems to have endured through the ages. Even her contemporaries agreed that Cleopatra was not attractive. There were some— Octavian, for example—who never understood what Julius Caesar and Mark Antony saw in her at all.

"So you tell me: What is more likely? That in one of the most misogynistic societies the world has ever known, the beauty and charm of *this* woman could seduce that era's two most powerful men, leading to the collapse of two empires? Or should we, at last, at least consider her mind?"

*I am carrying a briefcase full of documents when I arrive at the eighteenth-century Tuileries Quarter restaurant Jeff has selected. He is waiting for me at the reception desk in a navy blue sport coat that sets off the blue-gray of his eyes. A neatly pressed pair of tan slacks complements both the jacket and the sandy brown of Jeff's thick hair.*

*"Beautiful place," I remark.*

*We are led through the restaurant, the delicate scents of French cuisine wafting through the air, to a window booth over- looking the Seine. Beyond the river stands the Eiffel Tower.*

*A bottle of Bordeaux arrives.*

*"When was the last time you were in Paris?" Jeff asks me.*

*I cast my mind back. "I guess it's been a few years." I take a sip of my wine before adding, "Also for a conference. You?"*

*"Same. And how long have you lived in San Diego?"*

*"Quite a while. I went to grad school there and sort of fell into a job after that. I've been there ever since."*

*"So that means about... ten years?"*

*I smirk as I realize he is flattering me while also setting me up to reveal my age. "Try fifteen," I say. I have just learned this morning in the lecture hall that Nobel laureate Jeffrey Wilson is only forty—just three years older than I am.*

*Jeff takes a sip of his wine. For a moment, he looks deep in thought. Then he says, "I'm quite familiar with your work on anthrax. You developed a treatment for a particularly virulent form of it. Made a killing when you sold it to the Department of Homeland Security…"*

"It is well established that Cleopatra's power stemmed from both her wealth and her knowledge. But I think the latter has been grossly underestimated."

I blinked and returned my gaze to Alyssa, the walls of the coin room once again surrounding me.

"The image of her as a sexy, wanton seductress is nothing but Hollywood propaganda," she said. "Even Plutarch described Cleopatra as nothing special to look at, but bewitching for her intelligence, her wit, and her almost magical knowledge of languages.

"In fact, she was the *only* member of the Ptolemaic dynasty to speak and write both Greek and Egyptian. This is quite significant. Greek was the language of educated Egypt, including the Ptolemaic rulers who, of course, *were* Greek. Egyptian was the language of their subjects. The fact that the kings did not speak the language of their subjects *at all* strongly underscores the harsh class structure that existed in Ptolemaic Egypt. Cleopatra—uniquely—could communicate directly with her subjects.

"Yet, for two millennia after her death, we could not find a single document written by her. Not one. The only definitive writing in her own hand was a one line signature of approval—'let it be so'—scrawled in Greek on one official document. I believe that signature matches the handwriting of the nardo document.

"We have extensive records of her power and of the dynasty under Cleopatra and her predecessors, and of course we have abundant information regarding her relationships with Julius Caesar and Mark Antony and the ends of the eras in both Egypt and Rome. But there is one thing we still don't have, and that's what I have been looking for."

"Evidence that she was a doctor," I said.

To my surprise, Alyssa shook her head adamantly. "Wrong. *Hard proof* that she was a doctor is what we're lacking. We have a frustratingly ample collection of evidence, not the least of which is her choice of patron goddesses. You see, Cleopatra adopted the persona of the 'New Isis,' thus formally and publicly associating herself with…"

"The ancient Egyptian goddess of medicine," I said under my breath.

*Jeff and I forego the third day's sessions of the conference in Paris. With both of our presentations behind us, as well as a promising first dinner date, we decide instead to tour the Louvre together.*

*It is raining, a steady, gentle rain, and a cold breeze is billowing through Paris. I am wearing a long, thick wool skirt over leggings and boots. A heavy coat, a hat, and warm gloves complete my cold-weather ensemble.*

*When I arrive, Jeff is already waiting for me at the glass pyramid that marks the entrance to the museum. He, too, is in a thick coat that falls to his calves. He flashes a grin, and I flush at the memory of the way he smiled at me the first time I saw him. And I wonder if I will ever be able to look at this man without imagining him in the nude.*

*We are walking through the Louvre's Egyptian rooms when we meet the goddess Isis. We descend a staircase toward the sarcophagus of the Egyptian pharaoh Ramesses III, and there she is.*

*The pharaoh's three-thousand-year-old sarcophagus is the central feature of the small room. The staircase is centered between the flanking walls, leading tourists entering the room directly to the foot of the sarcophagus.*

*Carved in exquisite detail into the wood at the feet of the deceased pharaoh is a single commanding figure. Her delicate arms reach out to both sides as if to embrace the mourners approaching the tomb she protects. Feathering down from her arms is a majestic span of wings, straight along the tops in parallel with her arms, then tapering down below her waist.*

*The symmetry of Isis aligns with that of the sarcophagus. Her body is as vertical as a staff, and the wingspan projecting outward calls to mind a symbol I have seen thousands of times over the course of my career. Isis is represented as a caduceus, the ancient symbol of medicine that has endured to this day.*

*"Would you look at that," Jeff remarks.*

*"Incredible," I say.*

"The nardo document was originally written in Egyptian."

Returning to the present, I realized that I was still holding the coin. The androgynous image of Queen Cleopatra seemed to laugh at me.

"You must understand," Alyssa continued, "that very few people of the educated class even *spoke* Egyptian. But Cleopatra did. I believe this document is just one of a vast collection of her writings that were rumored to exist but are now lost. I think she deliberately hid them—"

"Why would she do that?" I interrupted with irritation. "If Cleopatra was as ambitious as you say, and she stumbled upon a treatment for a deadly disease, wouldn't it dramatically *increase* her power to *expose* it? Why would she write a document like the medical text you uncovered only to hide it?"

Alyssa shook her head. "I don't know," she admitted. "That's a big piece of the puzzle that doesn't fit, but I'm trying to understand it. But I can tell you with absolute certainty that, throughout her life, Cleopatra was in the habit of hiding things." She frowned and shook her head again, and I wondered how many times she had mentally dissected that same stubborn puzzle piece.

"I am sure you can understand why this find is so important to me," she said. "If I have found what I think I have found, it will change history. Perhaps it will change medicine as well."

I handed the coin to Alyssa, and she returned it to the case, locking the case before we stepped away.

"But the history and the medicine are by necessity intermingled in this project," she said. "If I can demonstrate unequivocally that Cleopatra wrote this document, then I will have proven that much of what people believe about her is wrong. Moreover, I might be able to pinpoint when and where she was at the moment the event she described took place. If I can do that, Jeff believes he has a real shot at recreating the chemical reaction that produced the isotope in the nardos. And if he—or both of you—can do that, it will prove the authenticity of the document.

"I cannot solve this alone, nor can you. Chemistry, biology, and drug discovery are not my areas, and Egyptology is not yours. So the three of us need to cooperate—"

"I understand," I said. "I know what you are saying. If we are not collaborative, then we are competitive—"

As the words fell from my lips, the obvious question crashed upon me. I whirled to face Alyssa. "Who else knows about this document?" I demanded, stabbing accusingly at the pages in my hand with my forefinger.

Alyssa's response was the last I would have expected. Her eyes welled up with tears.

Alyssa looked down at the floor for a moment and blinked a few times. Then, as quickly as it had come, the emotion was gone, and she was professional once again.

"To be honest," she said, "nobody should know about this except for Jeff, you, and me. The Piso Project is very broad, and the excavations of Herculaneum and Pompeii are even broader. While there are many people working under me, and an enormous number of people in the field, this particular document is one I have kept exclusively to myself since I first personally unrolled it and began translating the Egyptian. Prior to that moment, the document was mute for two thousand years.

"When I initiated the Piso Project—how do I put this?— strange things began happening to me every once in a while. I found the door to my house unlocked when I was sure I had locked it. I found some research notes misplaced, and I'm sure I did not move them.

"But after I found the nardo document, these occurrences intensified and became more frequent. And some of them—like when my brakes went out along the Amalfi coastline—have been more than just strange. They have endangered my life.

"Except for Jeff, you are the first person I have told about this document. To be honest, I was worried about including even you. But Jeff spoke so highly of you that I felt I knew you. And frankly, I'm desperate. So I let you in."

She took a deep breath. "I feel like I'm losing my mind. I immerse myself daily in a world ruled by the supernatural. And I'm beginning to believe in it myself because I'm starting to think this project is cursed. As an educated, logical woman, it makes me crazy to hear myself say that out loud."

Another deep breath. "Realistically, *someone* must know what I have stumbled onto. Someone must have obtained access to my research, or to Jeff's. Someone must be seeking the same answers we are. I must find those answers first, and I must find them quickly. Because if I can expose them, I will have neutralized whoever is trying to beat me to the punch. And I think that's my only option because it's too late to just walk away."

I found it interesting that her pronoun of choice had somehow changed from "we" to "I."

"Why don't you just go to the police?" I asked, even as the image of my dead husband's body threatened to surface, and with it the exact same question from the lips of Larry Shuman.

Alyssa scoffed. "I did," she said bitterly. "They told me to come back if I had anything concrete to report. I guess if at some point I am actually attacked, and survive to report it, then they might listen. They might. The Naples police department is less than helpful..."

Her voice trailed off as a phone inside my purse began to ring.

"Excuse me," I said, and I stepped away from Alyssa. When I saw the caller ID on the screen of my iPhone, a wave of nausea came over me. I glanced at a large wall clock in the museum's exhibit room. It was almost noon in Naples, which meant that in San Diego...

My stomach lurched again. The call coming to me from San Diego at 3:00 a.m. Pacific Time was from Larry Shuman, the mortician with whom I had entrusted my husband's body two days earlier.

~~~

"Are you OK?"

I glanced up. Before me, Alyssa Iacovani's face was a picture of concern. I realized that I had begun to sway on my feet. With the hand not holding my cell phone, I grabbed the display case in front of me and leaned against it.

The phone chimed, indicating that the phone call had gone to voicemail, and that the voicemail was now recorded.

"Yeah," I said weakly. "It's just that I didn't get much sleep on the plane, and I'm also very hungry."

"Would you like to go to lunch?" she asked, glancing at her watch. "Naples has fabulous seafood down in the Santa Lucia district. I'm hungry as well, and it is about lunchtime."

I shook my head. "Thanks, but I haven't even checked into a hotel yet; I came straight here from the airport. My bags are downstairs. I think I should get settled."

"Of course," she said. "You must be exhausted. Why don't you get some rest tonight. We can catch up tomorrow. How long are you in town for?"

"I don't know," I said truthfully, my mind reeling. I had not told anyone I was leaving. My colleagues, my employees, my family, my friends—and Jeff's—would all begin to wonder about our disappearance very soon. With no answers, they would inquire. And if they inquired, there would be a police investigation. And if there was a police investigation, I would be finished.

I said a distracted goodbye to Alyssa and turned to leave the museum. When I was sure I was clear of her, I retrieved the message from Larry Shuman.

"Dr. Stone"—his urgent voice came through—"I must speak with you immediately. You have *not* been honest with me..."

THE SEED OF THE BLACK POPPY... IS A PAIN-EASER, A SLEEP-CAUSER, AND A DIGESTER, HELPING COUGHS AND ABDOMINAL CAVITY AFFLICTIONS. TAKEN AS A DRINK TOO OFTEN IT HURTS (MAKING MEN LETHARGIC) AND IT KILLS.

*-DE MATERIA MEDICA*
DIOSCORIDES (CA. 40—90 CE)

## CHAPTER SIX

The background noises of the museum seemed to instantly grow louder, and more discordant. I stepped into a stairwell to replay the voicemail from the beginning. I was certain I must have misunderstood it the first time.

A gregarious group of teenagers burst in after me, each voice shouting over the other in Italian. I blocked my free ear with a finger, straining to hear the impossible words pouring from my phone.

"... toxicology panel... abnormally high levels of opiates in the system... only survivable following repeated exposure and increasing desensitization..."

The teenagers exited the stairwell on the floor beneath me, and their chatter was cut off by the slamming of the heavy door. In the silence, I learned that my ears were not deceiving me.

"Your husband"—the mortician's voice was clearer now—"died from the two gunshot wounds that passed through several vital organs. However, Dr. Stone, at the time of his death, he also had levels of morphine in his system that should have been lethal. Yet, he showed no signs of morphine toxicity as a contributing factor to his death.

"Obviously, this finding concerned me—to the point that I have worked late into the night to confirm it. The data demonstrate unequivocally that your husband had built up a physical tolerance for the drug over some period of time, and you did not disclose this to me.

"Dr. Stone, I don't know who you think you are dealing with, but drug-related crime is simply not something I am willing to involve myself in. I am completing my post-mortem work-up and reporting my findings in their entirety..."

*It is impossible, and, yet, here I am.*

Nausea overwhelmed me again, and I sat down on the dusty concrete stairs. I leaned over and dry heaved, once, hard. I tilted my head back against the wall and closed my eyes.

*Jeff was a drug addict.*

It all made sense. The secrecy. The total change in both behavior and thinking. The decision not to trust me with whatever he was running from. The decision to run toward a stranger, a beautiful woman. The paranoia. The obsession. It all made sense.

*But it makes no sense.*

*There is no way.*

Stinging tears welled to the surface, and I blinked them back violently.

*There will be no two weeks. Shuman is completing his post-mortem work-up and then turning me in.*

*Jeff was a drug addict.*

*There is no way this is happening.*

In an instant, her disguise fell away, and I saw a different version of Alyssa Iacovani. She was a thinly veiled undertaker, and her museum was a mausoleum, a shrine, a tribute to death. I felt its walls encase me like a burial chamber.

*Take a breath, Katrina,* I told myself, but I could not. The air had grown thick and stale. I could taste the decay of the mummies lying two floors below me.

*You're losing it.*

I fought to appear normal as I moved toward the exit, but I could feel myself hyperventilating, my consciousness quickly fading. In a fog, I found the museum's coat check desk. I reclaimed my belongings and stumbled outside, seeking open air like a drowning woman kicking for the water's surface.

There was a horn and a screeching of brakes. I felt the rush of wind upon my face as a metal blur obscured my vision. I leapt back and turned my head just as a speeding car rocketed away, its driver apparently oblivious. I wondered if I had accidentally stepped into the street, but a quick look down confirmed that I was still standing on the sidewalk. And then I was almost run over again.

This time, an entire family on a moped sped by within inches of my face. A man jerked the handlebars left and right as if boxing. Behind him sat a girl of three or four, not bothering to clutch his waist. A woman straddling the rear of the bike squeezed the girl into place while curling a bag of groceries in one arm and an infant in the other like two footballs.

They scooted deftly over the sidewalk to avoid a slow-moving car, not seeming to mind that they had almost collided with a pedestrian instead. The little girl smiled at me as they passed, perfectly comfortable in her element and apparently unaware that this mode of travel could be dangerous or considered the least bit odd by anyone.

After they were gone, I retreated into the shadows of the museum, away from the edge of the sidewalk, and watched the traffic zipping past me. I breathed deeply and, after a few moments, found that I could think again.

I stepped back to the sidewalk's edge and hailed a taxi.

After loading my bags into the trunk, the driver climbed aboard and looked at me expectantly in his rearview mirror. I suddenly realized I had no idea where I wanted to go. "Uh, hello. Do you speak English?" I asked.

The driver held his thumb and forefinger about an inch apart. *"Un po,"* he said, which I took to mean "a little."

"I need a hotel."

"Hotel? *Quale?"*

*Shit. This isn't going to work.*

My stomach growled violently and my head swam. I thought back to my conversation with Alyssa. "Santa Lucia?" I finally said, hoping I had gotten the name of the seafood district correct.

"Ah, Santa Lucia!" We lurched forward. In contrast to the relaxing limo ride that had induced sleep earlier that morning, this one induced severe carsickness, exacerbated by an empty stomach.

*... abnormally high levels of opiates in the system...*

From within my purse, my phone chimed again, and I started. It had to be a text message this time because the phone did not ring. But instead of looking down to dig into my purse and find out, I had no choice but to watch the road. I hated that motion sickness could render me so incapacitated at such moments.

The taxi raced down a main street, weaving in and out of traffic that had no apparent legal regulation. There were very few road signs, and the traffic signals seemed only to flash yellow. I could not identify a correct side of the road or a speed limit. The sidewalk was open terrain for motor vehicles as well as for pedestrians. I quickly realized that renting a car was not going to be an option.

The streets doubled as supermarket aisles. Like islands in the center of a fast-moving river stood rows of vendors' tents peddling food, jewelry, handbags, and countless other goods, while the heavy automobile traffic swirled around them. Hurried pedestrians zigzagged back and forth across the traffic like ants, jumping from sidewalk to vendor's tent and then biblically parting on cue to accommodate a racing Smart car. Or a bus. Or a moped containing four passengers.

A siren screaming in the background seemed to follow us for the entire drive through the city center. I wondered if it was one siren or an overlapping of the sounds of several.

I began to doubt I would make it to my destination without vomiting, and I leaned forward to ask the driver to pull over. But then I saw the waterfront and knew that we must be close to our destination.

In sharp contrast to the city center, the waterfront district was relatively serene. The vendors' tents had vanished, along with the vast majority of the motor and foot traffic. We zoomed along a well-paved street with clearly marked lanes and, shockingly, a well-defined sidewalk populated exclusively by pedestrians.

"*Questa regione é Santa Lucia,*" the driver said, motioning with both arms, to the detriment of his steering. I neither knew nor cared what he had said, but I could have cried with relief when he screeched to a halt in front of a large nice-looking hotel. "*L'Hotel Santa Lucia!*" my driver announced, and I realized that I had inadvertently requested it.

By this point, exiting the taxi was my only priority. I did not wait for him to open my door. I collected my bags and sent the driver on his way. I stood on the sidewalk for a moment, gulping at the fresh air to quell the motion sickness. Then

I finally began rummaging through my purse to retrieve the message that had come in while I was in the taxi.

When I saw the text message, my nausea quickly returned. It was not from Larry Shuman as I had expected. It was from my daughter. It read: Where r u?

And it was sent to Jeff's phone, not mine.

Once inside my hotel room, I found my phone once again.

I called my daughter, but she did not answer. I hung up without leaving a message. Then I looked at the time signature on the phone's screen and mentally back-calculated. It was now 4:17 a.m. in California.

I walked past the bed and into the bathroom, where I splashed some water on my face. Then I strode across the room and opened the curtains. Brilliant light poured in through a pair of narrow French doors.

I opened the doors and stepped out onto a small balcony. Before me was a large geometrically shaped castle. Surrounding it lay a surprisingly organized aquatic parking lot lined with hundreds of small private boats. Dozens more of its occupants were out for the day, sailing casually through the crystalline crescent-shaped Bay of Naples. Beyond the bay loomed Mount Vesuvius like a massive grim reaper, a fallen angel choosing the moment to rain down its black death from above.

"The castle beneath your balcony is *Castel dell'Ovo*," the concierge informed me in heavily accented, but clear English. "Just to its left is the small Santa Lucia seafood district. You will need to cross the long bridge toward the castle and then follow the road that turns left off of the bridge just before the bridge enters the castle through the gates."

I thanked the woman and stepped out of the hotel. After a quick walk along the frontage street, I turned onto the bridge she had referred to. Even from across the span of water, I could see the bridge leading directly through the front gates and into the castle. Tall, thick pillars flanked the bridge, and docked boats littered the water lapping its sides.

I had almost arrived at the arched entrance of the castle when the side street leading to the left off of the bridge came into view. I followed this street into a quiet neighborhood containing one restaurant after another. Potted plants and umbrellas decorated patios adjacent to charming old buildings. Beyond them lay the castle to one side, water to the other. I selected a quaint bistro with green and white checkered tablecloths and a view of the bridge. To my surprise, the restaurant was relatively empty, and I was seated immediately at a partially shaded table by the water.

As I waited for my food, I was approached by a guitarist and an accordion player, one heavy, the other thin. I breathed another deep sigh as the duo began serenading me with a beautiful romantic song. A sad, numb, exhausted relaxation enveloped me, and I turned to look out over the serene bay.

*I turn to look out over the Seine, finding it necessary to avoid his eyes before I speak.*

*"I have a daughter."*

*It is our third and final evening together in Paris, and Jeff and I are once again enjoying a romantic dinner. Through the window beside us, a breathtaking display of lights accents the river and Notre Dame Cathedral beneath a black sky. A pianist is playing and singing softly in French.*

*Jeff sets down his fork and finishes the last sip of his wine. Then he folds his hands on the table and looks at me attentively. The pianist, too, appears to finish, and she begins gathering her belongings from beside the piano bench.*

"Alexis is eighteen now," *I continue.* "She is a freshman at Berkeley in environmental sciences and has a boyfriend I'm not too crazy about. But he's nice enough, so I guess I should consider that an improvement over some of the others."

*I smile, but I am embarrassed. My daughter's taste in men seems to follow closely with my own. Until now, I realize, as I gaze across the table at the monumentally successful, charming, and handsome man who has become a promising love interest over the past three days.*

*Jeff chuckles softly.*

"When I was still working exclusively on anthrax," *I say,* "Lexi was living with me half of the time. In her earlier teens, she was a bit of an unholy nightmare. At a time when I couldn't trust my daughter at all, I also had Homeland Security tracking my every move.*

"You are correct that I developed a treatment for a virulent strain of anthrax, but you also know it was only effective on that strain. So the threat of anthrax remained, and I became the United States' poster child for anthrax research. Between my daughter's unpredictable behavior and my well-publicized work, I was worried something would come to a head.*

"Then opportunity began guiding my career toward cancer research, so I embraced it. I thought it would be a safer career path..."*

My food arrived, and I tore my eyes away from the Bay of Naples. I glanced around and noticed that the serenading guitarist and accordion player were now singing at another table.

The food was like a drug, and I had to force myself to eat slowly. I dove into the plate of poached salmon with lobster cream sauce on a bed of pasta, and the effects of thirty-six hours of adrenaline began to wane. My stomach gradually settled, and my mind began to clear. At last, I paused for a break from the food.

A large clock on an exterior wall of the restaurant now read 2:33 p.m. It was just after 5:30 a.m. in California. I tried calling Alexis again, this time from Jeff's phone. There was no answer.

"*Prego, signora.*" My waiter laid the bill before me and bowed politely.

I dropped Jeff's cell phone back into my purse and was rummaging for my wallet when the phone began to ring. I glanced at the caller ID. The incoming call was not from Alexis as I had expected. It was from John—Jeff's best friend and personal physician.

I recalled the last time I had spoken to John, when he had called our home after Jeff had missed the Seattle conference. I could feel myself scowling all over again as I answered the phone. "Hi, John."

"Oh, hey, Katrina! How are *you* doing, my lady?"

"I'm doing great!" I lied. "How are you? I'm assuming surf's up or you wouldn't be calling so early…"

John laughed heartily. "Oops, I'm sorry! Yes, I forgot again. Hope I didn't wake you. Anyway, I'm doing great, except I can't seem to get hold of your husband! Did he tell you to answer his phone and get rid of me?" He cracked up at his own joke.

I laughed as well, hoping to sound realistic.

"We were supposed to go golfing this weekend," John continued. "Jeff totally ditched me! Is he still having problems from the stomach flu he had earlier?"

I reflected briefly upon a bout of illness Jeff had endured two weeks prior. Now, I wondered if my husband's "stomach flu" might have been, in truth, morphine withdrawal.

"Nah, nothing like that," I said. "But he *is* currently off surfing. We're in the Bahamas, actually. I guess he must have forgotten to tell you we were going, but, yeah, we'll be here for the next two weeks. We needed a break."

John's joking demeanor changed. "Oh yeah?" he asked with some concern. "In that case, I hope you're getting some rest. It's no wonder, with the way the two of you work, that you'd burn yourselves out once in a while. Well, tell him that Mai Tais and sunscreen are doctor's orders, OK? And hey—have him call me when he has a chance, would you, dear?"

"Will do, John. You take care."

"You, too, my lady."

I hung up the phone and then stared at its screen for a moment, wondering if John knew something I did not about my husband. If so, doctor-patient confidentiality would prevent him from sharing it.

Speaking to John reminded me once again that I had told no one I was leaving San Diego. John's was not the last concerned phone call I would receive following the sudden disappearance of both Jeff and me. So I began preempting the calls.

"Oh, that's *wonderful!*" The perpetually cheerful tone of Jeff's mother was a welcome respite. She glowed across the miles as if travel was a rare treat for us.

"Well, Kat, you two have a *fabulous* time in the Bahamas! Give my son my love. And bring back tons of pictures, OK? I want to see *all* of them!"

"I will, Mom," I promised, choking on tears. "See you soon."

My own mother has Alzheimer's. Her live-in nurse assured me that all was under control and that she would call me if necessary but that it would not be necessary. I found myself marveling that my mother was so much easier to handle than Jeff's. If only we could all forget the past.

Our respective laboratories and offices were also easy to deal with. I diverted both with brief e-mails sent from our iPhones, offering no explanation as to our whereabouts other than "out of the office."

Then I stared for a moment at the speed dial functions programmed into my phone. I had called all of them except for two.

The first number, of course, would reach the other phone in my purse. I avoided the temptation to dial it just to hear his voice.

I also avoided the phone number of my older sister. Because calling Kathy would mean having to tell the truth.

The cacophonous chatter of my small collection of loved ones was reverberating maddeningly through my head. I clawed at my hair and scalp for a moment as if to physically contain the uproar.

*What happened to him?*

As I struggled to connect the disparate pieces of information I had before me, a notion struck. I reached into my purse and withdrew Jeff's phone once again. I clicked into his Internet browser.

It was all right there.

Jeff had our bank accounts bookmarked. The more I rummaged through them, the more I understood of my husband's final actions. In recent weeks, he had sold stocks collected since he was eighteen years old. He had withdrawn enormous sums of money from our long-term investments as well as our liquid accounts. He had obliterated our retirement funds. Jeff had not wiped out our finances entirely, but he had plundered them for millions of dollars.

*Who is Alyssa Iacovani? And what has she done to him?*

*Please, God, please, let me find the truth about my husband, and let me find a truth that preserves all that I cherish of him.*

SEE NAPLES AND DIE

-ANONYMOUS

## Chapter Seven

A soft breeze gently rocked the boats in the Bay of Naples, and the golden rays of sun converging upon their decks began to dance. The image was all too familiar. And then something dawned as if for the first time.

*He is gone. Really. Forever.*

Having just stood up from the small bistro table, I sat down again, heavily. I buried my face in my hands and began to cry. Once I began, I sobbed unabashedly. I could not see. I could not breathe. And I could not stop crying.

When my sobs finally faded to sniffles, I could barely remember where I was. My head was throbbing, and I could feel the puffiness of my face. In a daze, I looked around. The check had been in front of me. I was sure of it. But now the bill was gone, and I did not remember paying it.

I wiped my face on my napkin. There was a tall glass of water in front of me that I also did not remember. I closed my eyes and took a long deep drink. When I opened them again, there was a young man sitting across from me.

"Are you feeling better now, *signora*?" he asked in a thick Italian accent.

"Ah, yes—um, thank you."

"Do you need some help? I could call you a taxi?"

I guessed him to be about my daughter's age. A baseball

cap perched backward on his forehead revealed a kind face lacking the eventual roadmap of experience. His sleeveless shirt exposed arms that looked much less naïve; both were completely covered to the wrists in tattoos.

"Thank you again," I said. "But, no, I'm fine now. Thank you so much, really."

"Why are you alone?" he asked.

"Uh, what?"

"Why are you alone?" he repeated matter-of-factly. "You're a very beautiful woman, sitting and crying in a Naples café by yourself. I don't get it. Have you just been dumped or something? Because, if so, I think it was—how do you say?—his lost!"

"Are you serious?"

He laughed. "*Normale!* Of course I'm serious!"

"For one thing," I said indignantly, "my last shower was days ago, in San Diego. For another, I'm old enough to be your mother. And for a third, if I were your mother, I would kick your ass to kingdom come for sitting down uninvited and hitting on a stranger old enough to be your mother! Excuse me!"

I stood to leave and reached for my purse, and the boy's eyes fell upon my large diamond engagement ring and wedding band.

"I'm sorry," he said, the cockiness gone. "I did not mean to offend you. I was not trying to be rude. You seemed lonely and very sad, and I was hoping I could make you smile. I see you are married." He gestured toward my rings. "I think you are married to that American on TV, Donald Trump. Please, sit down. I will wait with you until your husband returns."

I paused, still standing, and I felt myself smirk. "Thanks. But I really do have to go."

He reached across the table. At first I thought he was

reaching for my purse, and I started. But his hand fell gently onto my arm. "Listen, *signora*, I don't mean to scare you. But Naples is not a good city for a foreigner, especially a woman foreigner, to be alone. Naples has crime. Naples has *camorra*."

"What is *camorra*?"

"Like in the movies, the criminals."

"Mafia?"

"Yes. So, please. When you are out, stay with your husband."

"I'm on my way to meet him now, so don't worry."

"Can I walk with you? I'd feel better. I'm sure he won't mind. I don't think you are old enough to be my mother, but if you say so..." He smiled.

*Charming. Lexi would drool.*

"And how do I know that you are not the Godfather himself?" I asked, and he cracked up.

"If I was *camorra*," he said, "I could afford a car. I would not offer to walk with you. I would offer you a ride."

I thanked the young man profusely for his concern and assured him with some degree of condescension that I would not be requiring any help.

I was so, so wrong.

I gathered my belongings and wiped my eyes one more time with my napkin before heading away from the restaurant. As I approached the bridge leading off the island, I looked behind me. The boy was ten feet away. I scowled.

"I'm not following you, *signora*," he said. "There is only one bridge."

He had a point. But that bridge led almost directly to my hotel, and I could not return to it as long as he was still behind me. So instead of going to rest in my room, I decided to drop in on Alyssa Iacovani again, when she was no longer expecting me.

Well aware that my stomach was now very full, I quickly decided that another cab ride like the one I had taken earlier was not on the agenda. I turned around to face the anonymous boy once again. "Excuse me," I said. "Can you tell me where there is a bus stop and how to get a ticket?"

"*Prego*," he said and led me into a convenience store.

A moment later, armed with my bus ticket, I approached the stop and stood next to a dozen or so locals. And so did he. I glared at him.

"If you don't want me to stand here," he said, "I can wait for you to leave and then catch the next bus."

"Thanks," I said, laughing a little. "I don't suppose that is necessary."

"Do you know what bus number you need?"

"Um..." I began, and he shook his head in a silent scolding.

"I'm going to the Naples Archeological Museum," I said and then quickly added, "My husband is meeting me there."

He explained to me that I needed to take the Number Two bus, which would follow a continuous loop through downtown Naples, stopping at the railway station and at several of the major tourist attractions.

"Now, please, do not be afraid," he said. "I am taking the same bus. But I will get off before you. I live in the Spanish Quarter. You'll be able to wave 'bye bye!' " He waved cheerfully at an imaginary target.

I smiled wearily, feeling a bit stupid. And, admittedly, a bit grateful.

I had not ridden a bus in years. There must have been a

hundred people crammed onto the one that pulled up to our stop. By the time I entered and found a place to stand that was near the driver, my new friend was nowhere in sight. I took care to hold my purse in front of me with my arm over the zipper and the strap laced more than once around my hand. I also had a death grip on the leather.

The bus lurched from one stop to another, and I listened intently for the driver to announce the stop for the Naples Archeological Museum. Two Metro policemen boarded and began shoving their way between the wall-to-wall passengers. The police approached each passenger in turn, and each passenger extracted a ticket for the policemen to see.

"*Billete*," one said when they reached me. I produced my ticket.

The two policemen looked at each other. Motioning between my ticket and my face, they began a heated discussion in Italian. Finally, the dialog ceased, and one of them turned back to me. "*Settanta-cinque euro*," he said.

"Huh?" I asked and shrugged my shoulders.

The policemen turned back to one other, and they began yelling back and forth again, shaking their heads. Finally, one took out a small notepad and wrote on it. "75€" his script read.

"Does anyone here speak English?" I asked, straining to turn my head and peer through the crowd. Dozens of pairs of eyes dropped to the floor of the bus. Others continued to stare straight ahead as if I had not spoken at all.

We proceeded through two or three additional stops, with both policemen yelling feverishly at me in Italian, before the bus screeched to a halt and one of the transit cops grabbed me by the top of the head. He roughly turned my head toward the window, which he pointed through with a long stabbing finger. "*Bancomat!*" he said emphatically.

The policeman was pointing toward a cash machine. Finally, I understood that they were telling me I owed them money. I had been through the procedure dozens of times during college weekend jaunts from San Diego across the border to Tijuana. These officers expected seventy-five euros from me in exchange for leaving me alone.

I thought for a moment. Then I flashed a sweet smile at both policemen and stepped casually off the bus.

The bustle of downtown Naples was around me in full force as the automatic doors of the bus snapped shut with their characteristic metallic sigh. The honking of horns and overlapping voices of hurried pedestrians blended together in a murky haze of sound.

Out of the corner of my eye, I saw the two policemen exchange a look of triumph as I stepped toward the cash machine. I reached into my purse and withdrew my wallet, from which I pulled my debit card. I withdrew eighty euros from my checking account and handed the cash to one of the policemen. I returned my wallet to my purse.

"Thank you, Officer, uh... Carmello Rossi," I said, peering at the name badge on his uniform. "You may keep the change." I smiled again at his partner and made a quick mental note of his name badge as well—Franco Dalfani.

The officers exchanged a few words in Italian as Rossi motioned toward the banknotes in his hand.

"May I go now?"

My eyes had just fallen upon Dalfani when he leapt toward me and snatched my purse from my shoulder. I had no time to react, as Rossi grabbed me by the shirt and began shoving me into the street.

I cowered at the onslaught of cars, brakes screeching and tires squealing as drivers swerved to avoid us. The policemen appeared unconcerned as they marched into the traffic with determination, dragging me roughly alongside them. I dug the heels of my shoes into the pavement, fighting against the inevitable pull toward a destination unknown. But the effort was pointless. Against Rossi, I had no chance.

We reached the opposite side of the street, and before me was a tall building. I looked up at its façade. It was then that I knew I had made a terrible mistake.

My experiences in Baja California had taught me that a cash bribe was invariably the fastest route to getting rid of police of questionable ethics. I had expected that the Naples police would simply pocket the eighty euros and walk away. Instead, Officers Rossi and Dalfani were shoving me into the Naples Police Station.

Which meant that whatever they wanted from me was legitimate.

Dalfani was holding my purse above shoulder level, like a severed head displayed on a spike as an example for other would-be traitors. Rossi's grip on my shirt did not relax until a bone-splitting metal crack on each of my wrists left me handcuffed to a chair in the lobby.

*What do they want? What do they know? How can they know? Oh, God...*

There were so many things they could know, so many possible reasons for them to have brought me here. My crimes were snowballing.

*How did I not see this coming?*

*I need a lawyer.*

A cloud of cigarette smoke swirled around me like gray confusion, and I felt like gagging from the staleness of the air. I blinked, in a feeble gesture to protect my eyes from the smoke, my hands bound uselessly behind me.

Now, there were not two but dozens of policemen shouting at me, and at each other. They descended upon me like a lynch mob, cigarettes waving like torches between their stained fingers. They motioned toward me and toward my purse, each of them grabbing for it in turn as Officer Rossi began rifling through its contents. I watched as he extracted both of the iPhones within and began clicking through their data.

A skeletally thin man was roughly brought toward me and handcuffed to the chair next to mine. Through his worn, filthy clothing, I could see the man's shoulder bones jutting angrily forth. He looked up at me with eyes as dead as night, and I could see in his fixed pupils that he was strung out.

*A buzzer sounds, and the door before me swings open. I step forward.*

*I enter the prison's visiting area and approach a long bank of small booths. I sit at one of them. Then I wait.*

*A moment later, Lawrence Naden enters the room. He shuffles slowly toward me, and the bones of his legs are visible through his paper-thin pants. He sits on the other side of the barrier. He lifts the receiver of the telephone beside him and raises it toward one hollow cheek.*

*As if it is a mirror between us and not a panel of clear glass, I reach for the telephone on my side of the barrier and raise it to my own ear.*

*"Who the fuck are you?" he asks me, a sneer projecting forth, accentuating his crack-rotted teeth.*

*"I'm Katrina Stone."*

The clamor of policemen and civilians echoed through the small smoke-filled Naples police station. I scanned the crowd for a kind face. "Does anyone here speak English?" I kept asking, and I felt as though I might start crying again. And then, as I continued searching through the horde, I did cry. But they were tears of relief as I saw, through the unruly swirl of people, a familiar backward baseball cap.

The young man with the tattooed arms pushed his way aggressively through the crowd as he yelled rapidly in Italian. When he was close enough, he stepped boldly up to Officer Carmello Rossi, pointing a finger no more than two inches from his face. This was a strong, confident, and concerned *man*—a dramatically different person from the happy-go-lucky child who had teased me in a café and then helped me buy a bus ticket.

The formerly authoritative policemen were now almost shriveling. They stood quietly, listening to the onslaught from my unlikely hero. His rant carried on for a few moments to an increasingly sheepish audience.

He stepped toward the officer currently in possession of my iPhones and snatched them viciously from him. He gathered the rest of my belongings and returned them to my purse, offering a brief look of apology in my direction as he did. He pointed at Rossi and then at me. And then, to my sheer amazement, Officer Rossi leaned down and unlocked my handcuffs. I began to rub my bruised wrists and peered questioningly up at him. Without a word, Rossi turned and walked away.

Then the tattooed young man with the backward hat took me silently by the hand, and we walked, unimpeded, out of the police station.

For the second time in less than an hour, I found myself wiping tears from my eyes while the enigmatic stranger waited politely nearby. When I was finished, he spoke. His voice was gentle, but firm. "On the bus there are machines," he said. "They are impossible to see when the bus is full, and half of the time they don't work. But if you don't use them"—he made a stamping motion—"to mark your ticket, it is a crime here. Tourists usually have to pay money. If they don't pay, they go to the police station. Then they do pay. That is why this always happens to people on the bus near the police station."

"But I paid them," I said.

He shook his head. "*Signora*, you were going to jail whether you paid them or not. I heard them talking. The bus ticket was an easy excuse, but... it wasn't really why you were arrested. Now I think"—he paused and took a deep breath—"I think you should tell me the truth about your husband."

My knees buckled, and the world went gray. Through tunnel vision, I could see a strong pair of thick, tattooed forearms flash toward me, and then a pair of large gentle hands was supporting me by my elbows. He guided me to a concrete wall running along the sidewalk.

Trembling, I sat and looked up at him. "What do they want with my husband?"

"I don't know," he said. "But whatever it is, it is in Herculaneum. That cop is going there now."

As yet we have only entered into one room, the floor of which is formed of mosaic work, not unelegant... I was buried in this spot more than twelve days, to carry off the volumes found there... Those which I have opened, are philosophical tracts the subjects of which are known to me; but I am not at liberty to be more explicit.

-Director of the Museum Herculanese
Camillo Paderni (1720–1770)

# CHAPTER EIGHT

The *Circumvesuviana* train lumbered away from the central train station of Naples before picking up a steady, rocking speed. I gazed out the window and watched the city recede. Then I turned to stare unabashedly into the unlined face of my new companion. "Why are you helping me?" I asked gravely.

"Only a monster would allow you to do this alone," he responded. "I wish you would tell me why you need to do it at all."

I ignored his request. "I'm serious," I insisted. "It's one thing to get a crying woman in a café a glass of water. It's quite another to blow off your entire afternoon and chaperone her through Roman ruins."

The train chugged farther and farther from the city.

The boy shrugged. "I felt very sorry for you, *signora*. You looked... lost. And also, I did not want to go to class today, and I was—how do you say?—playing hooker?"

I giggled, despite myself. "Hookey," I said, and he blushed.

"Listen, I really appreciate what you did for me at the police station. And I appreciate your sharing what you overheard there. I guess you could say I am going to Herculaneum to hear the rest of the story." I held out my hand. "I'm Katrina."

"Dante. Dante Giordano."

Dante instructed me that we needed to disembark at the train stop designated for the Herculaneum excavations—*Ercolano scavi*—rather than the stop for the modern province of Ercolano, now sitting atop the ancient ruins. He explained that getting off at the wrong stop was a common mistake among tourists.

I took a deep breath before stepping off of the train.

To my relief, a small gathering of tourists was still entering the Herculaneum ruins, despite the late afternoon hour. I could hear the enthusiastic chatter of more people inside.

I walked to the booth and purchased two tickets. I did not see Officer Carmello Rossi.

"I don't see him," Dante said, echoing my thoughts. "What do you want to do, just walk through the whole site? The Herculaneum ruins are quite large."

"I don't know," I said with a sigh. "I guess I hadn't really thought it through..."

I forced my mind back to my earlier conversation with Alyssa Iacovani, and then I knew where I needed to look. I returned to the ticket booth. "Do you have a map of the ruins?" I asked the attendant.

Still standing at the window, I unfolded the large map I was given and looked through its features. There were two large bath complexes, a forum bath and a suburban bath, and several other marked spaces I assumed to be private residences and temples. In bold, seemingly of utmost importance, were the House of the Mosaic Atrium, the large Palestra, and the Shrine of the Augustales. I did not see what I was looking for.

"Excuse me." I turned once again to the attendant. "Where is the Villa dei Papiri?"

"Oh, it's slightly outside of the main area—right about here." She circled a blank area of the map outside of the annotated region.

"Why isn't it on the map?" I asked.

"Because you can't go in."

I gaped at her. "Why not?"

"It's closed off. It's actually still almost completely buried."

"How did they get the papyrus scrolls out?" I asked.

"They didn't," she said. "The scrolls that have been unearthed are probably just a small fraction of what's there. Most of the collection is still buried in the villa."

I glanced at the young man beside me and then wordlessly sprang into a dead run.

My heart was pounding as I approached the area circled on the map, the area off the tourist trail. Behind me, I could hear the labored breathing of a young man who clearly was not the runner I was. He plodded toward me and then stopped to rest his hands on his knees, wheezing.

Before me was a section of a high stone wall, clearly a remnant of an ancient building. Scattered around it were several large piles of stone, some as tall as I was, which I took to be excavated rubble from within the villa. Surrounding the area was a low chain-link fence bearing a single fading metal sign. The sign bore the name of an Italian construction company.

Thick dust covered the sign and the piles of stone adjacent to the wall. I glanced at Dante and then looked around the area. There was no sign of Rossi. Indeed, there was no sign that anyone had been there for years.

I swung myself over the chain-link fence. A cloud of dust billowed up from beneath my shoes when I landed on the ground near the ancient wall, the only visible trace of the Villa dei Papiri. For a moment, I stood immobile and only listened. Except for the still-ragged sound of Dante's breathing, there was only silence. I timidly stepped toward the wall.

No vegetation was present in the heavy dirt, and the area looked completely uninhabitable. In the dust beside a shoulder-high mound of construction rubble was an abandoned pair of work gloves, also covered with dirt and nearly camouflaged.

I stepped around the pile of rubble. Behind it, invisible to any passerby from the opposite side of the chain-link fence, was a large rectangle of rotting wood that lay flush with the earth like a trapdoor leading into the ground. Crossing it were two four-by-four beams, a crude barrier to block entrance to what lay beneath.

The beams caught my attention immediately. They were relatively new and did not bear the layer of dust that coated every other object around me.

Dante slipped up next to me and whispered, "Someone used something to cover their tracks in the dirt after putting those there." His unexpected voice in the utter silence made me jump.

"I know." I nodded, as my heartbeat settled back to normal. "Here, help me." Dante and I bent forward in unison to push the four-by-fours aside to access the trapdoor and whatever lay beneath it, but before we could move them the silence of the abandoned area was broken once again.

"You should have stayed away, Dr. Stone."

"*Naples has crime. Naples has* camorra."
 "*What is* camorra?"
 "*Like in the movies, the criminals.*"

*"Mafia?"*

I looked up into the face of Carmello Rossi. In his hand was a pistol. As he stepped toward us, he raised his arm and trained the gun on me.

I froze, crouched near the trapdoor. Beside me, Dante looked up into my eyes.

"What do you want with me?" I asked Rossi.

"I only wanted you to stop searching," he said. "But since you will not, then I must deal with you another way. Stand, please, with your hands over your head." He pulled back the hammer of the pistol.

I slowly stood, raising my hands above my head. As I did, I saw a flash of ink and flesh below me, and then a shot rang out as a force like a train crashed into me, knocking me to the ground. My head hit the dirt, and a cloud of dust flew into my eyes, nose, and mouth. I began hacking and coughing.

I heard a sickening thud, and in my blurred peripheral vision I saw Rossi fall backward, clutching his chest. A rock approximately eight inches in diameter was rolling away from him.

*"Hurry!"* Dante shouted and yanked me roughly to my feet with both hands. Still sputtering, I lunged behind the nearest pile of stone just as another shot sent splintered fragments of rock toward me.

Using the piles of stone and rubble as cover, Dante and I raced to hurl ourselves over the chain-link fence. Then without stopping or looking behind us, we sprinted back toward the annotated area of the map of Herculaneum.

The gunshots had ceased by the time we re-entered the populated area of the ruins, but Dante and I kept running. We barely made it onto the train before it left the Herculaneum station. As the doors closed and the train began pulling away from the station, I peered through a window to see Carmello Rossi still trotting after us, now looking casual, his pistol tucked out of sight. As the train rolled away from him, his pace slowed to a walk.

The train picked up speed as it left the ruins of Herculaneum behind. I sat down heavily and gulped in air. My throat was still scratchy from the dust I had inhaled, and my head was throbbing. I reached a hand up to rub it and then looked up at the young man who had just thrown me violently to the ground and pelted a police officer with a boulder in order to save my life.

"I'm sorry," Dante said, touching the top of his head to signify the wound on my own. His face was strained.

For a moment, we sat in silence as I struggled to think. His eyes never left me.

"I want to help you," he finally said. "But I can't unless you tell me whatever it is you are not telling me."

I still paused before answering, but then I said, "OK. The villa we were just at contains a two-thousand-year-old collection of documents. One of them describes an ancient plant called a nardo. My husband and... others... have apparently been looking for that plant. Rossi obviously wanted my husband—wants both of us—to stop looking. I suspect he wants to find it first."

"Katrina," Dante said, "I have lived in Naples all my life. Take my advice. Stop looking."

The train continued its steady chug, and I stared out the window at the passing Campania countryside.

*Rossi killed him.*

I looked up at Dante once again. His eyes were concerned.

"I can help with the Italian if you want to buy a plane ticket to return home to the United States," he said. "And I'm begging you to do that."

What he said barely registered.

"Dante," I said thoughtfully, "let me ask you something. You mentioned *camorra*, the Naples Mafia. They are drug runners, right?"

"Eh, of course. Drugs, and other things."

"Is it possible that Rossi is one of them? Could a Naples police officer be mixed up in that kind of thing?"

"It is possible that a Naples police officer can be mixed up in *camorra*. Yes. It is also possible that a *camorra* boss could impersonate a police officer. Our law enforcement—what would an American say?—sucks."

"So if I go to the police to report Rossi—"

"Don't. Just don't. Katrina, go home."

"I can't go home." Tears sprang to my eyes, and I blinked them back. "Can't you see that I can't just go home? Rossi took something from me. Something dear to me that I will never get back. I need answers. I need justice. Or I might as well have let him shoot me back there."

Dante looked pensive for a moment, and I thought I saw a tear in his eye as well. He looked down at the floor of the train. "He killed your husband." It was not a question.

I nodded miserably, my eyes fixed upon my lap.

"If you keep looking, he will kill you, too."

"If I don't," I replied, "then I'm already dead."

The train shuddered to a halt, and I glanced out the window. "Are we in Naples?" I asked.

Dante's eyes widened. Then he grabbed my hand and pulled me to my feet. "Come on!" he said and led me off the train.

I looked around. "This isn't Naples…" I began, and a moment of panic took me as I wondered why he had led me off the train at the wrong stop.

"I know," Dante explained. "We jumped onto the train so quickly that we took the wrong one. We took the one coming *from* Naples, through Herculaneum, through Pompeii. It goes the wrong way."

As he said it, I realized he was right. We had boarded the train at the same platform where we had arrived from Naples.

"We are now in Pompeii," Dante said.

"Aw, fuck." I began looking around for the platform for the return train.

"No, no… this could be good," he said.

"What do you mean?"

Dante looked up at the sky and then at his wristwatch. Then he turned and looked into my eyes. "Are you sure you want to keep looking? Are you completely sure?"

I gave him a dirty look.

"That's what I thought. Then this is where you should be. Pompeii is bigger than Herculaneum. It is more popular. There is more to see. There are more guides. More of the information is written in English. You can learn whatever you need to learn about the Villa dei Papiri, the history, the plant. Maybe you can figure out what Rossi is after. And maybe I can help."

"How so?"

"I know a lot about the ancient Romans."

"You do?"

"Yes. I study their religion. I'm a pagan theologist."

I glanced at his youthful, heavily tattooed flesh and backward baseball cap, now slightly askew from our dash through the ruins of Herculaneum. "No, you're not," I scoffed.

"Oh no?" His eyes were suddenly challenging. "Look again."

I did, and I could not believe my eyes. "Incredible," I said. "I can't believe I didn't notice before."

Many years ago, I took a backpacking trip through Eastern Europe with a girlfriend. In the Bucovina region of Romania is a series of monasteries. Each monastery is completely covered, exterior and interior, top to bottom, in intricate frescoes depicting Biblical scenes. Each wall tells a story in the universal language of pictures.

Standing at the entrance to the ruins of Pompeii, I realized I was looking at the pagan equivalent, and Dante Giordano's flesh was the canvas. My eyes took in the mythical stories running down his arms. Every square inch was covered. No, not covered. Layered. The images blended into one another so flawlessly as to create a global appearance of pattern, but it took more than a passing glance to notice the purpose. And there was movement within the images. *His tattoo artist is a genius*, I thought. I wondered with some degree of embarrassment how many more stories were hidden beneath his clothes.

Only some of the figures were familiar to me. I recognized Mercury, with his winged sandals and helmet, floating up the young man's forearm. Poseidon was perched on his shoulder, surrounded by an intricate network of sea creatures and flowing water. A chubby, naked little boy fluttering around a wrist with wings and a bow could only have been Cupid. Many of the others were a mystery.

"What..." I began, not really knowing what to ask.

"It started as a way to cheat my way through mythology classes," Dante stated with a proud smile.

I laughed. "Didn't any of your professors catch on?"

"*You* didn't," he observed.

"Pagan theology is hardly a subject I spend much time thinking about," I said, "and, no offense, I wasn't really looking."

"Actually," he said, "one of my professors *did* catch on. He called me into his office to kick me out of his class."

"And?"

"And I left five hours later, after a giant theological debate, with an honor's thesis project. I guess he decided he liked me."

"So you kept inking yourself and he still let you pass the class?"

"Yep." He beamed. "And graduate with honors. He is now my Ph.D. advisor."

I smiled at the notion, but then my purse chirped, indicating a new voicemail. The call must have come in while we were on the train. I withdrew my cell phone. No message. I checked Jeff's cell phone.

With one hand, I paid for tickets to the Pompeii ruins for Dante and myself. With the other, I held Jeff's cell phone to my ear and listened to the message. It was from my daughter.

"Jeff, it's Lexi," Alexis said. "I need to talk to you, badly. I've been trying to call. I texted you a couple of times, too. Just... call me back... as soon as you can. Please..."

*It is the last day of Alexis' freshman year. Jeff and I are still technically living apart, but we spend every evening together.*

106

*Jeff's SUV rolls slowly onto the campus of U.C. Berkeley. From behind the steering wheel, he peers at street signs directing him toward Alexis' dorm. His eyes track a sign on the right hand side of the car before straying to meet mine. He winks.*

*I am both excited and nervous. I cannot wait for my new boyfriend and my daughter to finally meet in person.*

*We round a corner near Alexis' dorm, and there she is. Lexi is standing on the curb with a group of her classmates. Between two fingers, she holds a lit cigarette. She glances up toward our car and smiles at seeing me in the passenger seat. Nonchalantly, she hands the cigarette to one of the girls standing beside her. Then she runs toward the car.*

*As Jeff pulls the SUV to the curb, Alexis lays her upper body across its hood in front of my seat as if embracing the car in advance of embracing the occupants inside. I roll down the window, and she hugs me fiercely through it.*

*"You've grown again," I say as I return her hug. "And when did you start smoking?"*

*She ignores me.*

*Jeff and I step out of the car, and my daughter sizes him up.*

*"So..." she says, feigning suspicion. "THIS is the guy who has turned my mother from a logical, hard-assed scientist into a blushing, giggling teenager!" As if to prove her correct, I feel myself blush and cannot control a slight giggle. Jeff, too, smiles and reddens slightly.*

*"Seriously!" Alexis continues, laughing at her own wit. "You have no idea what a feat this is! Nobel Prize? Piece of cake. Softening up Doctor Katrina Stone? Virtually impossible. Nice job!"*

*She approaches Jeff and hugs him like an old friend.*

"Are you OK?"

I turned to see a concerned Dante Giordano by my side, his eyes upon the cell phone still held to my ear. The message from Alexis had long since finished playing.

"He was shot in our home," I said, more to myself than to Dante. "He was shot in our home and had lethal levels of morphine in his system. But the morphine was not a contributing factor to his death, which means he had built up a tolerance to it. Which also means he was on drugs. Now my daughter is frantically trying to get hold of him. I wonder if Lexi is somehow involved in whatever connected Jeff with Carmello Rossi."

"Which would mean that she, too, is in danger," Dante said.

"Yes."

"The morphine—that's why you were asking about the *camorra* running drugs."

"Yes."

"But it doesn't make sense. Your husband would not have to come to Italy for drugs."

"I know," I said, and we stepped into the ruins of Pompeii.

A tour guide was leading a group and reciting a monologue in Italian. We attached ourselves to his group and followed him.

"He says that we are at the thermal baths," Dante translated. "Romans would go through a few rooms: a cold bath, a warm bath, and a hot bath. The Pompeii baths were heated by slaves. Water would flow in from the aqueducts. Then the slaves put wood into a big heater under the floor to heat the water, and pipes carried the hot water to the baths for the Romans up on top."

I nodded and silently passed beyond the bath complex. Dante remained quietly by my side as I began following the streets of Pompeii and my own thoughts.

It was a stark mental image—obscenely wealthy, hedonistic bathers sprawled lazily in the bright, luxurious baths, socializing and fornicating. Directly beneath them, the slaves—blackened from toiling in a smoky, soot-filled chamber to generate the appropriate water temperature for their masters. The "haves" above, and the "have nots" below. Heaven and Hell.

I am now one of the "haves," after spending most of my life as a "have not." The Heaven I shared with Jeff seemed like a reward for surviving Hell for so many years.

I married my first husband, Tom, while still an undergraduate. Alexis was born six months later. Motherhood and financial struggles delayed my undergraduate degree, but I finally finished college and entered a Ph.D. program at twenty-four, all the while working in addition to attending classes—I had run through a large assortment of odd jobs before settling on bartending for the exceptionally high graduate-student wage of ten dollars an hour plus tips.

When Tom and I divorced, I got virtually nothing from him, and I still had three years of a five-year Ph.D. program in front of me. Mercifully, my Ph.D. program offered waived tuition and a small stipend, which I continued to supplement by bartending. It was a decent income, but with a young child to support it was not sufficient to make ends meet.

My daughter was my reason for living but also my heaviest financial burden. I reduced Alexis and myself to such modesties as living in a garage for a full year and eating nothing but spaghetti for days at a time in order to meet the high costs of child care and living in San Diego. Financially similar is the story of nearly every Ph.D.-level scientist I've known. But very few of them were also single parents during their training, as I was.

Relentlessly, stubbornly, obsessively, I fought through the impossible double shifts and scraped by from paycheck to paycheck for an agonizing three more years. I graduated first in my class.

My hard work paid off. In my first few years as an independent researcher, I developed a treatment for a virulent form of anthrax, and the federal government paid me handsomely for it. Alexis and I were finally able to live comfortably. Then I met Jeff, who had always been wealthy, and who had become even more so through his own dedication and brilliance.

I now live in a different world than the one I was born into. I have left behind the smoky slave chamber below for the bath complex above. It is no wonder my daughter would so cling to Jeff, the first man she ever met whose life was untainted by the blackness of the soot.

My thoughts were interrupted by the whiteness of a human corpse. I halted and then timidly stepped forward to examine the pale body before me.

It was encased in glass, a man. Every inch of his body was displayed in painfully granular detail. He was lying on his back, tilted slightly to one side. Both of his arms were held up, forearms parallel to his body, as if he were shielding his face from an attacker.

His face was frozen in an expression of sheer terror—an expression I had seen far too recently. I looked away as quickly as possible, blinking back tears once again.

"It's plaster," Dante said from beside me. "This is one of the things many people come to Pompeii to see."

"I don't understand." I was still holding back tears.

"When Mount Vesuvius erupted, people in Pompeii were buried alive in ash—you can see that this man tried to block the ash with his arms. Then the ash became very hard around their bodies. When the bodies... eh, decomposed?... it left holes inside the hard ash. When Pompeii was found centuries later, these holes were also found and filled with plaster. So now, this plaster cast shows exactly how this poor man died."

I peered through the glass for a moment, in awe of the detail within the agonized face. I tore my gaze away, only to be confronted by a second glass case containing another example of human horror.

"There are other places here with plaster bodies," Dante said. "Most are people, but I think there is also a dog, and a pig too."

In the single anonymous man's face, I had seen enough. I stepped away from the glass cases and returned to the streets, walking slowly, aimlessly, staring mostly at the ground.

A white, horrified face in a glass case, arms raised upward to protect himself from falling death.

A white, horrified face on the deck of a yacht, arms splayed out sideways to break a deadly fall.

The two images melted into one.

*What am I doing? Did I really think that here, in this ruin, I would find a form of plant life from two thousand years ago? And that this plant would somehow help bring my husband's killer to justice?*

I stepped out of the street, seeking a quiet corner to shrink into. I brought my hands up to my face and wiped from my cheeks and chin the tears that were now falling freely. I rubbed my eyes and looked down at my feet. On the ground beneath my tennis shoes was a large mosaic. Its tiny rocks were arranged to spell a single word:

# HAVE

*Glistening, naked bathers, reclining shamelessly in baths heated to the exact temperatures of their choosing. Glistening, sweating slaves, stoking the fires beneath. The "haves." The "have nots."*

I glanced up and saw that I was standing at the entrance to a villa. I could not distinguish its boundaries—the villa was enormous.

A tour group came up close behind me, its guide speaking Italian-accented English. "This villa is called the 'House of the Faun,'" the guide was saying, "and this mosaic is a... welcome mat!" The tour group laughed. "*Mi scusi*," he said quickly to me, and I stepped aside to let them pass.

The volume of the guide's voice began to wane as he led his group deeper into the villa. "The mosaic," he said, "means 'hail to you' in Latin, and the villa was named after the dancing faun you see here in the atrium. This villa is one of the biggest and most luxurious in Pompeii. While its owner is unknown, the decorations show an Egyptian influence, especially from the Alexandrine era. Its garden, among the largest in Pompeii, featured everything from food plants to opium poppies..."

"*... abnormally high levels of opiates in the system...*"

"*... its garden featured everything from food plants to opium poppies...*"

"*... the nardo document is the first writing in existence in the* *hand of Queen Cleopatra...”*

*“... the decorations show an Egyptian influence...”*

Suddenly, the notion that the ruins of Pompeii could lead to an extraordinary plant, and that this plant could lead to a killer, did not seem so absurd after all.

I spun on my heels and chased the guide and his tour group into the vast House of the Faun.

NOTHING COULD PART US WHILST WE LIVED, BUT DEATH
SEEMS TO THREATEN TO DIVIDE US.

CLEOPATRA TO MARK ANTHONY

-LIVES OF THE NOBLE GRECIANS AND ROMANS
PLUTARCH (CA. 46—120 CE)

# CHAPTER NINE

"**W**hat kind of Egyptian influence?"
I practically shouted the question as I bolted into a large central atrium surrounded by multiple rooms. Within the atrium was the bronze statue of the dancing faun that had given the villa its modern name. A second large atrium lay to my right, and as I approached it I could once again hear the English-speaking tour guide. He was describing the opulent living quarters of the mysterious occupant of the house.

"Excuse me. What kind of Egyptian influence were you referring to?" I asked again. I shoved my way past the small tour group and brazenly withdrew a twenty euro note from my purse, handing it to the tour guide.

"Right this way," he said.

Beyond the main living areas was a massive peristyle garden. The guide led me through it, and his somewhat irritated tour group followed. Trailing behind, a silent, curious Dante.

The garden was relatively nondescript—a very large open green space—but I could easily envision the well-tended foliage that must have existed there in the days of abundant slave labor. Surrounding the garden were tall colonnades.

Beyond the colonnades, something caught my eye. This was the object the guide was leading me toward.

We passed through the garden and into a once-enclosed room. Covering the room's floor was a large mosaic, a heavily damaged image of a battle scene. The central figure was a soldier on a horse.

"This mosaic," the guide said, "is a depiction of Alexander the Great. It is a replica of one of the most priceless works from Pompeii. The original is preserved in the National Archeological Museum in Naples. The scene shows Alexander's victory over the emperor of Persia. When Alexander conquered Egypt, he founded the city we know today as Alexandria, and it became the capital of Egypt. The first Ptolemy king was the first ruler of this city, and many of you probably know that the last Ptolemy ruler of Alexandria was Queen Cleopatra."

I had seen the same image earlier that day. It was the mosaic marking the entrance to the Ptolemaic Dynasty display. The display Alyssa had made a point of showing me. The display that explained the legacy of Queen Cleopatra and her ancestors.

My neck broke out in gooseflesh. *This was not a villa*, I thought. *It was a palace.*

It was one of the largest residences in the wealthy Roman resort of Pompeii. Its décor paid tribute to Queen Cleopatra's heritage. It could only have been owned by the highest of the elite. And its owner has never been revealed.

*It might have belonged to her*, I thought, and the realization guided my gaze toward the vast expanse that was its most prominent feature.

Beyond the mosaic room was yet another peristyle garden.

This one even larger than the first. Easily envisioning my entire home seated within its cavity, I estimated that this garden alone was probably in the range of fifteen thousand square feet. It was almost as large as the rest of the property combined.

"There were opium poppies in this garden?" I asked the tour guide, and he gave me a look of shock.

"*Yes!*" he said. "That's so strange. Someone else asked me that same question just a couple of weeks ago."

My hands were trembling as I rifled through my purse. I finally managed to extract my wallet, from which I withdrew a dog-eared photo. I deliberately avoided looking at the image as I held it out for the tour guide. "Is this the person who asked you?" I whispered hoarsely, my voice on the verge of breaking.

"Yes!" the tour guide said enthusiastically. But then he sucked in his breath as if suddenly realizing he might have said too much.

"And," I pressed, "was he with a blonde lady, about my age?"

This time, the guide just looked down at his feet, a silent acknowledgement. Then he said quietly, "I only remember him because he did something very strange. After asking about the opium poppies, he went over there into the garden and started digging in the dirt."

I could feel him.

I sat in the dirt, grabbing handfuls, letting it slip slowly through my fingers. As he had.

*Jeff was collecting soil samples.*

Suddenly, it was all so obvious, and I was sickened to reflect upon what I had been thinking, what I had been suspecting.

*How could you, Katrina?*

Dante Giordano sat quietly beside me. "Are you OK?" he asked softly.

"Yeah," I lied. "Just resting for a moment."

"Your husband was here a couple of weeks ago. With a blonde lady. And that had something to do with his death.

"Katrina, I know it is not my business, but... please, just try to forget it. Don't seek revenge. It will only eat you alive. I beg you again. Go home."

I smiled sardonically. Of course Dante would say that. Of course he would think that, as I had.

But now, I knew differently.

"I can't," I said. "I can't go home. I can't stop looking. I need to find the plant. I need to finish what my husband started. I owe him that. And I'm not out for revenge, not anymore. Jeff was not having an affair."

*... Jeff became practically obsessed with the document...*

*... nature produces phenomena that no scientist in the world has ever managed to harness...*

*... so do you want to be a part of it? Your husband certainly does...*

Dante looked at me questioningly but did not speak.

"Don't you see?" I asked, and then I was sobbing again. "Jeff came to Naples because of the Herculaneum document, because the document described a cure for cancer. He dug through this garden looking for that cure, knowing that poppies would accompany it. Because opiates are the standard-of-care painkiller for terminally ill cancer patients, as they have been for thousands of years..."

*"Where were you for four days, Jeff?"*

*"Sweetheart, listen, I can't tell you. I am sorry for that, I really am. I have never lied to you before. I have never kept anything from you. I am sorry for lying to you about the conference. I hate myself for that. But I can't tell you now, either. Please, you just have to trust me..."*

My sobs faded to sniffles, and I stared at the ground.

"As the cancer progresses, the opiate dosage increases," I said quietly, more to myself than to Dante.

*... abnormally high levels of opiates in the system... only survivable following repeated exposure and increasing desensitization...*

"Jeff came to Naples to try to save his own life before I could ever find out he was dying."

*I have a lot of patients these days asking about the latest advancements in superheavy-isotope-based therapeutics. Especially the people that... have failed other therapies and don't have many options left...*

I looked up at Dante.

"The opiates were at such a high level in Jeff's system that they should have killed him. Which means that his cancer was already beyond treatment by modern means.

"The nardo was Jeff's last hope. It was the only clinically validated cancer treatment that he had not already tried.

Because it was lost to medicine when the volcano erupted two thousand years ago."

Dante laid a hand on my shoulder.

"No wonder," I muttered under my breath, still sniffling. "No wonder his best friend keeps calling. No wonder he is so concerned about Jeff's condition."

*Is he still having problems from the stomach flu he had earlier?*

"John probably diagnosed the cancer. John is probably trying to call Jeff to update him about recent test results, to check in and find out how he is feeling. And also, just to listen because he knows that Jeff hasn't told me.

"And no wonder Jeff didn't tell me. He knew the losses I have already suffered. He was trying to find the treatment without ever letting me know he was sick in the first place."

I stared at the Pompeii earth and smiled through my tears.

It was just like him.

Dante and I parted at the Naples train station.

"Thank you, Dante," I said. "For everything. Really." I hugged him fiercely. "But I will be fine on my own from here. I have already involved you too much, and it is only a short bus ride to my hotel."

Dante was shaking his head. *They never learn*, his expression said. "May I at least go with you to your hotel? What if Rossi comes back?"

"No, thank you," I said. "If Rossi is still looking for me, it will be easier for him to find us together. Hold on a second..."

I stepped away from him to purchase a sweatshirt and hat from a tourist booth in the train station. I donned the sweatshirt and tucked my hair into its hood before cramming the hat over the top. "See?" I said. "I will be fine. I can see Rossi before he sees me. And I have learned my lesson about stamping bus tickets."

"OK, OK." He gave me a fatherly smile. "But listen to me. Rossi is not the only threat to you in Naples. I meant what I said earlier. It's not very safe here for you alone, especially at night. Don't talk to anyone, not even small children. And, please, I must insist you take my cell phone number. If anyone tries to even talk to you, call me right away."

He said something in Italian to a man standing nearby, and the man pulled a pen from his shirt pocket. Dante scribbled a number on the back of his ticket stub from Pompeii and handed it to me.

"Thanks," I said and tucked the stub into my purse.

He then took out his ticket stub from Herculaneum and wrote the number again. "Now," he said, "put this one in your pocket, in case you have to call me because your purse has been snatched."

I watched the bus pull away with Dante aboard. He waved through the window, watching over me for as long as traffic allowed.

In truth, I needed to take the same bus he had, the one we had taken from the seafood district. But something told me not to share the location of my hotel. Not even with the young man who had just saved my life. He was still a strange man in a foreign city, and I was still unsure of his motive for helping me in the first place.

So now I had to wait for the next bus. The sun was going down, and I suddenly felt very, very vulnerable. I looked around the train station.

A young man in earmuffs was staring at me. *Earmuffs? It's seventy-five degrees outside!* But the look on his face was vacant. I realized that he was not staring *at* me so much as staring absently in my direction. A mustachioed old woman in a bra sat on the floor, rocking back and forth and muttering to herself.

I watched a chatty herd of small children with cloying smiles surround a solitary young woman. While it was clear that they were deliberately portraying themselves as sweet and endearing, they looked far too streetwise for their ages. They reminded me of a flock of vultures. The woman abrasively shooed them away, and I fervently hoped they would not approach me.

Another man, this one in shorts and a T-shirt and with his face partially obscured by a scruffy beard, was definitely looking at me. Unlike the man in earmuffs whose look revealed mental disability, the look of this man revealed interest. *Great,* I thought and looked away.

The bus was far less crowded this time. As I mounted the steps, grateful to be escaping the late-evening creepiness of the station, I immediately saw the bright yellow validation machine located in the aisle a few feet behind the driver. I practically lunged for it with my ticket extended.

I slipped the ticket into the slot, and nothing happened. I retracted it and tried again. Again, nothing happened. I could feel panic closing in as I thrust my ticket repeatedly into the machine, and then I felt a tap on my shoulder. *Oh, God, not again.*

I turned and found myself face-to-face with a portly elderly woman. One hand clutched a fraying vinyl purse; the other held a small bag of groceries. I sighed with relief.

The woman smiled sympathetically, pointed at my ticket, and then extended her hand. I gave her the ticket. She, in turn, gave it to the driver, who pulled a pen from his dashboard and scribbled on it. The woman returned the ticket to me.

*Ah,* I thought. *Manual validation. OK.*

"*Grazie,*" I said to both the woman and the driver.

Still, I should have known that the transit police would get on the bus as we neared the Naples police station. I should have stepped off the bus beforehand and walked the distance of a few stops before re-boarding. I should have done anything, *anything*, besides wait for them to approach me. But by the time I realized that, it was too late.

When I saw the two familiar uniforms on the bus, I turned to look out the window. I pulled the hood of my new sweatshirt a bit closer around my face and the hat over my ears as tightly as possible. Then I pulled my purse in front of me and covered it with my arms as best I could, praying that Rossi—if he was, indeed, one of the cops now aboard the bus—would not see or notice the very handbag he had been rifling through earlier in the day.

I could hear the dialog between the two policemen and the various passengers as the officers worked their way toward me. My heart was pounding. The ticket in my hand was now soaking in sweat, and I took care not to crumple it beyond legibility.

I kept my head down when the officers reached me, simply holding out the ticket for them to see. But I peered out from beneath my hat to read the name badges on the two uniforms. One was a name I did not recognize. The other was Dalfani.

"I validated my ticket, *asshole,*" I muttered.

Dalfani stood next to me for what felt like far too long. Then he said simply, *"Prego,"* and walked away. I wondered if, like Rossi, he had been able to speak English all along.

A few moments later, I recognized the large stone arch leading into the Santa Lucia district, and I knew that we were near my hotel. I stepped off the bus and looked around to gather my bearings. My hotel was almost immediately across the street. I was so exhausted that the thought of room service followed by a good night's sleep in a plush bed was almost painful.

I turned and watched as the bus drove away. I could see Dalfani through its window. He was watching me as well.

It was now completely dark.

I had begun walking toward the light of the hotel when a sudden, intense feeling came over me that I was being followed. Casually, trying to look like I was seeking a street address, I allowed myself to turn around and look behind me.

I recognized him immediately. The man behind me was not Dalfani as I had been expecting. It was not Rossi either. It was the man from the train station—the one in shorts and a T-shirt who had been looking at me with an interest I had taken for romantic. Our eyes now met; his were emotionless.

I quickly looked away.

For the second time that day, I was afraid to return to my hotel. As I deliberately avoided looking toward its façade, I turned instead to face the Bay of Naples. The bridge to *Castel dell' Ovo* came into my field of view. Remembering the lively seafood district just across the water, I kept walking.

Like a ticking clock behind me, I could hear steady footsteps.

*How many people were on the bus? Maybe thirty?*

I walked past the Hotel Santa Lucia.

*How many got off the bus at my stop? Three?* I could not remember. Perhaps I did not even notice, distracted by my second encounter with the Naples police.

Now, I could only see two people. One man was some distance away from me, walking in the other direction. The other was still behind me, keeping pace with my own movement.

*Katrina, stay calm. Your mind is playing tricks on you. This man may be merely another passenger now headed toward his own hotel.*

But I had consciously observed him looking at me.

*He doesn't strike me as a tourist. Are there homes near here?*

I approached the bridge, resisting the urge to break into a run. *Running will only make you look scared, Katrina. It will make you look like a victim. That is what attackers want. Easy prey. Don't give it to him. Be confident.*

I turned onto the bridge.

A teenaged couple was crossing the bridge in front of me, holding hands. I could hear the footsteps of the strange man behind me. Nobody else was in sight.

The street that led off into the seafood district was much darker than I had thought it would be. The only sound I could hear was the rhythmic lapping of the waves against the sides of the bridge, and their ebb and flow washed away my confidence that the restaurants would still be open.

The teenaged couple entered the castle through its arched opening. Instead of turning left and entering the seafood district, I followed them.

The man behind me followed as well.

The castle was wide open; there was no ticket booth of any kind. It appeared that one could just meander through at leisure. A stone walkway wound upward toward the top of the castle. Over the high wall bordering the walkway was a drop to the street of the seafood district below. The couple strolled up the path and I followed.

The walkway passed by a series of dungeons, and the couple faded slyly toward one of them. Wordlessly, the young man pushed his mate roughly against the bars of the gate barricading the dungeon and began kissing her with abandon. As he advanced from the girl's mouth downward and began hungrily kissing her neck, she tipped her head back and caught my eye. His hand was snaking its way into her shirt. Her glance told me to get lost.

I ducked beneath an archway and began briskly climbing a staircase through a dimly lit passageway.

When I heard the footsteps behind me advance to keep pace with my own, I began to understand that I was *not* just being paranoid. This man had been following me from the start and was now deliberately staying only steps behind me.

I reached the top of the staircase and stepped under another archway. To my horror, I suddenly emerged onto a large terrace. It was open almost three hundred sixty degrees around and offered panoramic views of the Bay of Naples. Short, squat cannons pointed out in all directions through low openings in the waist-high stone wall. Beside them were small piles of cannonballs at the ready.

I ran toward a cannon and reached down for one of the cannonballs, but it was far too heavy for me to throw with any accuracy. I let it fall back onto the pile.

The only other object on the terrace was a spindly statue depicting a centaur-like creature. It stood a few feet from the stone wall, positioned as if the centaur was looking out over the water. The statue was clearly too thin to hide behind.

As I hurriedly scanned the expansive space, I realized all too clearly the purpose of it. This had been a formidable fortress. Both its location and its structure were perfect for the function. There was no way to sneak up on the inhabitants of this castle.

I quickly realized the irony of my situation. On the terrace of a two-thousand-year-old fortress designed to offer failsafe protection from invaders, I was suddenly completely exposed and simultaneously trapped. A wrong turn had traded the narrow, cryptic passageways of the castle for a sacrificial altar, and I was the lamb. Except for one skinny statue, there was nothing to hide behind and nowhere to go except back through the archway. And the man from the train station was coming through it.

I ran behind the statue. It provided abysmally thin protection, and the backward cocked head of the centaur suddenly seemed mocking.

The man emerged from the archway, and suddenly the darkness surrounding me was not nearly complete enough. I could see into his eyes. They still bore that same cold, emotionless expression.

"*Katrina!*" he said.

As if reeling from a physical blow, I scrambled backward until I felt the stone wall slam into my lower back. "*What do you want?*" I practically screamed.

"*I have a message from Jeff!*"

But his hand was reaching into his pocket, so I gripped the wall with both hands and jumped.

The water was dark but surprisingly warm.

My only thought was to swim as far from the castle as possible before emerging, and suddenly I was very grateful for my daily habit of running four miles a day through deep sand and then up a steep cliff. I was able to hold my breath for a long time and swam at the lowest depth possible through the dark, murky water for as long as I could.

Still, the weight of my clothes and the purse yet dangling from my arm slowed me considerably. When I could no longer continue, I surfaced and took in deep breaths of the cool night air.

I looked back at the castle behind me and gasped at its height. I was lucky that a boulder instead of open water had not broken my fall. But the desperate jump had served its purpose. Looking up at the castle in the distance, I was confident that my form in the dark water would be nearly impossible to detect from the terrace.

I turned and looked toward the shore. Nearby was a short dock. I remembered it. The dock jutted off from one side of the castle bridge, near the boats of the marina. There had been sunbathers on it earlier in the day when I had crossed the bridge on my quest for seafood. Now, the dock was abandoned. But it was not far from the shore that paralleled the street my hotel was on.

I took a few more deep breaths and continued swimming. When I reached the shore, I looked around before exiting the water, acutely aware that a fully clothed woman with a purse emerging from the bay would scarcely go unnoticed. I saw nobody.

Leaving a trail of seawater behind me, I walked toward my hotel. *You just have to get through the lobby*, I thought to myself. Without slowing my pace, I wrung out my clothes to the best of my ability. I squeezed as much water as possible out of my hair and then tied the thick locks into a knot crudely resembling a bun at the nape of my neck.

After a thorough survey of the area, I finally paused just long enough to dump my purse upside down onto the sidewalk. A small river and all of my belongings poured out of it. As quickly as possible, I wrung out the ruined leather itself and then began picking up objects one at a time, shaking them off, and dropping them back into my purse. At least I was no longer dripping excessively.

The concierge at the front desk gave me a strange look but did not say anything except to wish me a good evening. I returned the greeting politely, as if there was nothing unusual about my condition, and then hurried upstairs to my room.

Campania can get worse because you could cut into a Camorra group, but another ten could emerge from it.

-Galasso Clan Boss
Pasquale Galasso (1955–)

# CHAPTER TEN

*I* *walk down the rows of hospital beds, taking in the hopelessness of the nameless victims. An IV drips into one arm of each. A teenaged voice pleads with me. I look toward her.*

*The girl is my daughter. Alexis is fifteen.*

I awoke feeling almost hung over, as if I had been drugged. After a few moments reviving, I realized how well I had slept. My body was stiff and sore, but, nonetheless, I felt refreshed, calm, and aware.

I finally roused myself from bed and stepped into the bathroom to inventory my belongings. On the floor were my soggy blue jeans and T-shirt, along with my underwear and the one pair of tennis shoes I had brought to Naples. I picked up one damp shoe off the floor and poured a small river of sand into the wastebasket before giving up and adding all of my salty, sandy clothing to the wastebasket.

Sitting in the sink's bowl was my leather purse, still saturated with water from accompanying me into the sea. I reached inside the purse and began withdrawing its soaked contents, sorting through them to distinguish the salvageable items from the hopelessly ruined. The cursory survey made me realize with some relief and a great deal of apathy that *almost* everything in my purse could be replaced.

The absolutely essential items—money, driver's license, credit cards, and passport—were all rinsed in the sink and laid out on towels to dry. The non-essential items that could not be salvaged followed my clothes into the wastebasket.

I flipped through my passport; the pages were intact. I realized that the stamps might not be legible, and I briefly wondered if I would have a problem returning to the United States. I was also all too aware that I might never have the opportunity to find out.

I had no idea what to do with the two waterlogged iPhones that were now my only connection to the world outside of Naples. My cell phone was frozen on the home screen, with no response from any of the icons. I tried to power it off, to no avail. Jeff's phone was also frozen but indicated a new text message, which, of course, I could not retrieve.

I set both phones on the bathroom counter and looked into the mirror. For a long, long moment, I simply stared into my own eyes, asking myself what to do next.

My stomach growled and brought me back to the present. I walked into the bedroom to order room service. Then I drew back the curtains, opened the French doors, and stepped out onto the balcony.

It was another brilliant, sunny day in Naples. Dozens of small boats whirred around the bay like children at a playground. But above them, Mount Vesuvius was like a lurking predator.

I approached the balcony railing and rested my forearms upon its cool metal.

*Jeff and I are now engaged to be married.*

*I am at my desk in my office at San Diego State University, where I lead a large research laboratory. A text message pops up on my phone:* White?

*I frown at the message and then glance up at the clock on my desk. I have lost track of time, again. I rub my weary eyes and look back at my phone.*

*I text back:* What are you talking about?

*Jeff's response:* Maybe pink

*Then, in a second bubble:* With flowers

*My phone rings.*

*"Did you mix the wrong chemicals and kill some brain cells?" I ask.*

*"Yep!" Jeff says. "But that was years ago, in college. And don't tell my mom."*

*I laugh, and the tension from my day begins to dissolve.*

*"Hey, Kat, are you still working? Can you get away?"*

*I glance down at the document in front of me. "Sure. What do you have in mind?"*

*Thirty minutes later, Jeff's car zips into an upscale neighborhood along the coast, just as the sky is fading to shades of red. He turns toward a private cul-de-sac and keys in the access code to open the gate.*

*"Oh, look," I observe. "The house next door must have found a buyer."*

*Jeff glances casually at the real estate sign in the front yard, now tagged "PENDING." "Oh, yeah," he says casually. "I met them. Nice people." He is smiling.*

*Jeff pulls into our driveway. This is the home we have just closed escrow on, and I still cannot believe I get to live here.*

*Jeff opens the elegant front door, and we slide past the various construction items strewn before us, heading straight for the staircase. When we reach the master bedroom, Jeff quickly loops an arm around my waist to stop me. "Careful," he says and points down at my feet. I step around a messy pile of painting supplies on a canvas sheet near the doorway. We walk through the room and out onto the terrace.*

*"Wow," I say, and the breeze from the ocean breathes away the last traces of stress from my work day.*

*I run my hand along the terrace railing. "This turned out beautifully!"*

*"Yeah. They did a great job. I love the design you picked out." Jeff reaches forward with both hands and grabs a section of the brand new ornate iron railing. He gives it a vigorous shake. The metal does not budge.*

*"Hold on a minute," he says and disappears into the bedroom while I lean against the railing and stare, amazed, out at the view that is now mine to enjoy every day. I lazily trace a finger down the black metal design, still warm from the day's sun.*

I leaned upon the metal railing of my hotel room balcony, watching the boats drifting randomly through the Bay of Naples. And I sighed.

The key piece of data I needed at that moment, the one seemingly trivial thing I was most desperate for, I had lost. I needed my daughter's phone number. I needed it more than anything. But I did not know it from memory. I only knew where it was located in my "favorites" on my iPhone. And now, that was useless.

But I did have one number—one single number—that I might be able to use.

I stepped back into the bathroom and shuffled through the damp papers on the bathroom countertop. I found a ticket stub.

Dante Giordano's cell phone number was severely smeared, and I could not distinguish whether one of the numbers was a one or a seven. Another number might have been a four or a nine.

I reached into the bathroom wastebasket and withdrew my blue jeans, now stiffening from the seawater. In one of the pockets, I found the other ticket stub. On it I could see that the numbers in question were a seven and a four.

Together, the two papers in my hand provided the only phone number I had left for anyone in the world.

There was a knock on the door, and a man's voice announced that room service had arrived.

The concierge directed me to Galleria Umberto I, explaining with admirable tact that it was the city's largest shopping mall. It was also less than a mile from the Hotel Santa Lucia and contained Naples' largest Apple store. I thanked the woman sheepishly and dropped the street map she had provided into my damp, and somewhat smelly, purse.

The Galleria was the most beautiful shopping mall I had ever seen. I stepped inside to find an expansive open space topped with an ornately painted dome—architecture I would have found more appropriate in a cathedral than a commercial building. Extending back from the entrance was a long corridor flanked with marble façades that appeared to be at least three stories high. The ceiling was an arched crystalline network of clear glass, exposing the blue Mediterranean sky.

I collected the replacement items I needed, including a new

leather purse, and happily tossed the ruined purse into a garbage can.

The man behind the counter at the Apple store laughed
heartily when he saw the two iPhones I laid on the counter,
but he did not speak a word of English. After a frustrating few
moments, a passerby stopped and offered to translate. The
message I finally got through my interpreter was that Apple
could not guarantee salvation of the phones, but if I bought
two new ones a technician could transfer the data in an hour.
Apparently the SIM cards would survive anything.

I wondered if this was merely a ploy to sell me two new
phones, but I really did not care. I was happy to pay the money
to regain my contact information, so I handed over my phones.

An hour later, the Apple technician handed me two brand new
iPhones. I stood before him as I clicked into one of them. I
recognized the screen saver and breathed a sigh of relief. The
image was of me, heavily bundled, at the top of a ski slope.
Jeff had taken it on a recent trip to Aspen. This was Jeff's new
phone. His data had been retrieved.

I clicked into the other phone. Its screen was blank, exhib-
iting standard iPhone features. I showed it to the technician
and looked at him questioningly. He launched into a rapid and
seemingly defensive rant in Italian.

I began asking around the Apple store for anyone who
spoke English, but, instead of helping me, patrons began to
conveniently disperse. I was reminded of my previous day's
experience on the bus. After a few frustrated moments, I knew
what I needed to do. I withdrew the two damp ticket stubs
from my new purse and dialed Dante Giordano's number.

Fifteen minutes later, he walked into the Apple store. I took in the tattooed flesh, the muscular body, the ever-present backward baseball cap. And the friendly, almost naïve smile. He was carrying a battered backpack, the type of backpack typically carried by a student. I briefly wondered what was inside it.

The young technician in a polo shirt had a brief exchange with Dante before being replaced by a middle-aged man in a suit. I assumed this was the manager. He smiled at me with what I feared might be a look of apology. Then he began speaking to Dante.

Dante listened for a moment and then interjected an increasingly agitated tirade, one that left the manager red-faced instead of smiling, and cowering instead of friendly.

"What? What's going on?" I kept saying, but Dante ignored me until he had finished with the manager.

Then Dante turned to me and spoke more calmly. "They lost the information from one of your phones."

I felt the blood drain from my face. I leaned onto the counter, afraid I might faint.

"How—," I began, but Dante cut me off.

"I don't know, and this donkey won't tell me. He said there was a problem moving the information from the wet phone into a new one. It sounded like bullshit to me."

"Is there anything they can do to retrieve it?" I asked weakly.

"No," he said and placed a soothing hand on my arm. "I'm sorry, Katrina."

I felt sick. I slowly stepped away from the counter and from Dante, walking aimlessly. "It's not your fault," I said softly, unsure if he had heard me. I took a few deep breaths. I could hear him yelling at the man behind the counter again.

I wandered out of the store, and Dante caught up to me.

"They said they will pay for both phones."

"You have no idea how much the data on those phones is worth," I said quietly.

I gazed at the two new phones in my hand. I clicked into the one with the blank screen. It contained only standard features. I consulted its contacts section as if my daughter's phone number would miraculously be there. The section was empty. But I knew her number would be in Jeff's phone; she had texted him just the day before. I clicked past the image of me on an Aspen ski slope and into the contacts screen.

Alexis was nowhere in Jeff's contacts. I clicked into his record of recent calls. There was no evidence of recent communications with my daughter, despite the fact that, in addition to her text to Jeff, I myself had called her the previous day from Jeff's phone.

I returned to the home screen. It once again indicated a new text message. I remembered having seen it earlier that morning on the frozen face of the phone I had carried into the sea. I clicked into the new message, sent from an international number I did not recognize. When I read it, my stomach lurched.

The stranger who had chased me into *Castel dell'Ovo* was telling the truth. My dead husband had sent me a message.

ANTONY WAS SO CAPTIVATED BY [CLEOPATRA], THAT, WHILE FULVIA HIS WIFE MAINTAINED HIS QUARRELS IN ROME AGAINST CAESAR BY ACTUAL FORCE OF ARMS... HE COULD YET SUFFER HIMSELF TO BE CARRIED AWAY BY HER TO ALEXANDRIA, THERE TO KEEP HOLIDAY, LIKE A BOY, IN PLAY AND DIVERSION, SQUANDERING AND FOOLING AWAY IN ENJOYMENTS THAT MOST COSTLY... OF ALL VALUABLES, TIME.

*-LIVES OF THE NOBLE GRECIANS AND ROMANS*
PLUTARCH (CA. 46–120 CE)

# Chapter Eleven

On the screen of Jeff's brand new iPhone was a text message less than a day old. It could only have been composed by Jeff himself, and it could only have been intended for me.

"I need a restroom," I said under my breath.

"Down this hall, on the left," Dante quickly directed me, his face a mixture of horror and concern.

I briskly walked and then ran toward the destination he had pointed at, dropping both new phones into my purse with trembling hands while I did.

I bolted into a stall and surrendered up my breakfast. As I fell to my knees before the toilet, I instinctively brought my hand up to pull my long hair back from my forehead. The effort was a split second too late, and the hand sliced through an already emerging stream of vomit, which I then plastered into my hair.

In the stall beside me, a small child screamed and then began to sob. "*Ssshh*," her mother whispered. "*Andiamo!*" The restroom door was flung open, and the wailing gradually receded as the mother dragged her terrified child away.

As I clutched the sides of the toilet while what felt like my whole life spewed angrily forth, I wondered for the first time, *What's wrong with me?*

When there was nothing left, I sat back and took a breath. *I was sick on the plane*, I remembered. I had thought that it was motion sickness, something I have always been prone to in cars and boats, but not typically on airplanes. *But I also felt sick in the museum*, I remembered. I had attributed it to claustrophobia at the time, and that was something I have *never* been prone to.

I stood up and staggered to the sink. I plopped my shopping bags onto the counter and retrieved a new travel toothbrush and a hairbrush from one of them. I brushed my teeth and then washed my hair in the sink with copious amounts of liquid soap from the dispenser. I rinsed out as much of the soap as I could before brushing out my hair. After a few minutes, I was satisfied with my hygiene, but my hair was still wet, and my face was blotchy and red. I reapplied my makeup using the new supplies, which I then dropped into my purse.

My nerves were slowly calming, but I still felt sick, even with nothing left in my body to cause it.

*Unless...*

I stared again at the text message.

*"Hold on a minute," Jeff says. He steps away from the brand new iron railing and into the construction-rubble-littered bedroom of our future home. I am left alone momentarily, watching the remaining rays of sun dance upon the Pacific Ocean.*

*Jeff returns with two empty five-gallon plastic buckets and inverts them for us to sit on. He then disappears again and comes back with a bottle of wine, a corkscrew, and two wine glasses.*

*I laugh out loud. "What a nice surprise!" I say, and he beams with pride. After I sit down, he grabs the bucket I am sitting on and slides me closer to him.*

*Jeff uncorks the wine and pours a glass for each of us. "To sunsets," he says simply, and we toast.*

*We sit in comfortable silence for a few moments, sipping our wine and watching the changing colors in the sky.*

*"Have you seen your mother this week?" Jeff asks casually, and I frown, my pleasant mood suddenly darkening.*

*"No," I say and take a larger-than-usual gulp of wine. "I'll see her this weekend if it kills me—even though I still really don't have the time. I feel terrible, and every day this week I have tried, but I just haven't been able to drive all the way out to the home—at least, not during visiting hours. I'm so frustrated. My schedule doesn't work with their visiting hours.*

*"My mom barely remembers me anymore," I elaborate. "And talking on the phone is utterly useless. But she is still happy to see me, even if she isn't sure who I am half the time. It's frustrating that I'm not able to see her more often."*

*Jeff rubs my shoulder. "Hang in there," he says. "Your house is sold, my house is sold, and the work on this place will be done before you know it. Once we move in, we can bring her to a closer place. Everything will be easier."*

*"You're right. Having her closer will make the situation so much better." I give him a soft kiss, and we sink back into a comfortable silence, breaking it only once, to refill our glasses.*

*As the sun is just dropping below the horizon, Jeff speaks again. "So... which is it? White? Or pink with flowers?"*

*I have completely forgotten about his bizarre text messages from earlier in the afternoon. I turn and stare at him. "What is wrong with you? What are you talking about?"*

*"For the bedding," he says. His eyes are dancing. "It was the nurse's idea—sort of a fresh start."*

*I continue to look at him like he is crazy, and then I open my mouth to ask again what he means.*

*"Shh," he whispers, placing a finger gently over my mouth. "Just enjoy the sunset."*

*I turn in silence back to the ocean view but find myself distracted. White or pink? My mother's favorite colors. And, like me, she loves flowers. What nurse?*

*The sun drops below the horizon, and Jeff takes the empty wine glass from my hand. He sets it down on the terrace with his own. "Come with me," he says and leads me back into the bedroom.*

*On the wall to our right is a large bay window, presently covered with an ugly beige contractor's sheet. I had not noticed the opaque fabric earlier, but now I realize that it obstructs the view to the house next door, the one with the "PENDING" sign in the front yard.*

*My mind begins to race, and I feel a chill run down my spine. White or pink. For the bedding. The nurse's idea. Once we move in, we can bring her to a closer place. PENDING. I glance at Jeff and he chuckles. I glance back toward the covered window.*

*"You didn't!" I say, racing to the window. I tear down the contractor's sheet and stare blankly in disbelief. Jeff casually steps up behind me and wraps his arms around my waist, gently locking his fingers around my stomach.*

*Across a lovely strip of our backyard garden, I can see over our fence into the side yard beyond it. A middle-aged woman in hospital scrubs is relaxing in a cozy sitting area that graces the yard. She is reading a magazine.*

*Sitting next to the woman is my elderly mother.*

*The woman looks up at us and then takes my mom's hand and points up to our window, waving my mother's hand for her as someone would do with a small child. My mom smiles with recognition and says something to her companion, and Jeff waves back. He then mimics the motion of my mother's new nurse by taking my hand and moving it to wave.*

*"Hi, Mom," he says quietly into my ear.*

*"I don't believe it," I say, still stunned. "You bought the house next door. And you put my mom up in it with a private nurse."*

*"I know they were big decisions for me to make by myself, but I wanted it all to be a surprise. The nurse came highly recommended by John and several of his colleagues. I hope you don't mind."*

*"Mind?" There are tears welling up in my eyes. "This is the most considerate and generous thing anyone has ever done for me."*

*As it turns out, it is also the first instance of* The Game *in our relationship.*

It was like hearing a voice from beyond the grave. Except that Jeff was not in a grave and the message was not a voice. It was a simple strip of text in a white bubble on a handheld device.

The text read: `Trust nobody. Her 2.`

I thought I was being so careful. I was not. Already, I had been too trusting. I had invited a stranger to Herculaneum and then to Pompeii. Dante Giordano saw what I was investigating. I told him Jeff had cancer. I told him details.

I vowed not to make the same mistake a second time.

So I climbed out the bathroom window.

*"White," "Maybe pink," and "With flowers."*

*These words eventually lead me to discover my husband's grand gesture of purchasing the house next door, allowing my mother to live in perfect comfort with a nurse and allowing me finally to see her every day.*

*The confusing texts, sent to me completely out of context, initiate The Game for the first time.*

*I quickly learn that when Jeff talks to me like he has lost his mind, the apparent nonsense he is speaking is actually a punch line. It is up to me to deduce the story that led to it.*

*As our relationship grows, The Game becomes our favorite intellectual pastime. It becomes increasingly elaborate over the next four years as we each concoct new ways to one-up the other.*

*The Game is like a private variation of Jeopardy, with carefully selected answers given to provoke a question, and it is like a treasure hunt in reverse. The first clue provides the very end of the mystery. The goal is to drive the puzzle back to the beginning. At the beginning, there will be a surprise.*

I knew Jeff's habits as well as I knew my own. Jeff would never have written anything as grammatically incorrect as "Trust nobody. Her too." Jeff would freely type "LOL," "ROFL," "WTF," or any of the acronyms that digital-age text conversation dictated. But had he meant what this particular text message implied, he would have abbreviated his thought "Trust nobody. Her either."

This discrepancy in semantics was precisely how I knew the message was from him. He was referring to something else entirely.

HER2 is the name of a protein associated with breast cancer. In recent months, Jeff and I had started up a program to develop a drug against HER2. We trusted nobody with it.

Targeting HER2 is a double-edged sword. While current

therapies against the protein show promise and can powerfully combat breast cancer in many patients, the drugs also carry FDA-mandated warnings for toxicity.

In addition to its role in cancer, the HER2 protein is essential to the normal function of heart cells, and treatment of cancer patients with HER2-targeted therapies can lead to severe cardiac toxicity. Thus, in choosing to take a HER2-targeted drug, a breast cancer patient must decide whether to risk a potentially fatal heart malfunction in order to combat the cancer. Without treatment, however, the cancer patient is likely to die.

When Jeff and I began the program, the risks and potential benefits of targeting the HER2 protein were well established. Our idea was not. We hoped to engineer a new superheavy isotope that would act only in the breast cancer niche, thus targeting the cancer cells while leaving the cardiac cells untouched. We knew the risks we were taking in advancing our program, which was radically different from others already underway and thus completely without precedent.

So we kept our fledgling project under wraps, not even involving our colleagues or employees. The HER2 work was a private effort, solely between Jeff and me.

The reference to HER2 was clear proof to me that the text message had indeed come from Jeff himself and that it was intended for me. It was a brilliant way for him to send a private message to me while also providing the messenger with a red herring.

Trust nobody. Her 2.
Trust nobody.

Dante Giordano waited for nearly twenty minutes before finally stopping a woman coming out of the restroom. He spoke to her, and she shook her head. When she walked away, he stepped inside the women's restroom himself.

I watched from a shop across the mall. On my head was a new hat, over my eyes a pair of sunglasses, and wrapped around my shoulders a new shawl—all hastily purchased following my covert re-entry into the mall.

When Dante came back out of the restroom, he did not appear to notice me. I waited a moment and then followed him.

He stared mostly at the ground, shaking his head mildly as he exited the main doors of the crystalline mall. I followed him for what seemed like nearly a mile.

When Dante finally left the streets behind, it was to ascend a stone staircase into an old building. I watched him go through the heavy iron doors, and I waited for them to close before approaching. I looked up at the building. I was at the University of Naples.

He had been telling the truth. He was a student.

I tore my eyes away from the façade of the university building and reviewed the text message once again.

Trust nobody. Her 2.

*Why didn't you send me a message I could use? Why didn't you write me a letter?*

The questions answered themselves. Because Jeff knew that the cancer was not the only threat to his life. Because he could not hide a message in a place where he was sure I would be the one to find it. And because nobody could be trusted to deliver it to me.

But he did trust somebody to deliver it to me.

The man at *Castel dell'Ovo* was absolutely unfamiliar to me. I was certain I had never met him. Yet, he followed me. He called me by name as I stumbled backward on the castle terrace. He told me he had a message from Jeff. He was reaching for something as I threw myself into the water. I had assumed it was a gun.

It now occurred to me that it might have been a cell phone.

I withdrew Jeff's iPhone from my purse and clicked into the mysterious text message again. I replied: Who are you?

The response came through almost immediately: Is he dead?

A chill crawled over me. I had no idea how to respond. As it turned out, I did not have to. While I paused to gather my wits and compose a response, a second message came through: Katrina meet me at Stazione Circumvesuviana now.

Fifteen minutes later, I entered the train station where I had first noticed the man looking at me. I saw him immediately. He was easy to spot because he was wearing the same touristy shorts and T-shirt that he had been wearing the previous evening.

"Who are you?" I demanded again as I approached him. "Why did you ask me if he was dead?"

The man's bearded face revealed neither malice nor sympathy. In fact, the total lack of emotion was unnerving.

In broad daylight and at close range, I could see how lined his face was. He was probably close to my age, but life had not been kind to him.

When he spoke, his voice was heavily accented, but all too clear. "Because when he dies, I get a lot of money."

The mysterious bearded Italian turned and charged briskly out of the train station without speaking again. With no choice, I followed, almost running to keep up.

The crowd from the train station thinned as he led me down a small side street and into an alley. The crowd thinned even more, and I wondered where he was taking me. Rickety balconies strewn with laundry overhung the alley. The air was stale from the piles of garbage outside of the meager homes. The occasional stray dog looked up with mild interest as we passed, but there were no longer any other humans in sight.

We reached the end of the alley and turned left, only to follow another narrow alley. *This man could be leading me anywhere*, I thought. The warning from the text message echoed once again through my mind, but then, to my relief, I began to hear the sounds of people. As we came upon a group of parked cars, the welcomed sounds of civilization intensified. Finally, we came to a cross street wide enough to support moving traffic, and the chaos of Naples resumed in full.

The street opened up into a large piazza. The tall bell tower of a church rose above the other buildings in the square. This was where he was leading me.

"*Santa Maria del Carmine*," the man announced abrasively as I followed him into the church. We passed through its dilapidated walls and out into a monastic central cloister, and my initial confusion began to fade as I came to realize why he was showing me this place.

The central cloister was serving as a makeshift homeless shelter. Several ragged men and women occupied sleeping bags lined up along its walls. Stolen carts from the Galleria Umberto I were filled with sparse, miscellaneous belongings ranging from blankets to board games held together with frayed bungee cords. When we entered the area, I felt like an intruder, like I had just barged into a stranger's apartment without knocking. But my mysterious companion seemed, literally, at home.

"I live here," he said with his heavy accent, confirming what I had just begun to suspect. "I sleep over there." He pointed to an empty mattress topped with a crumpled blanket.

Aghast, I looked at him again. This was the man with whom Jeff had entrusted a final message for his wife?

The man's shorts and T-shirt were faded, but not noticeably dirty. Regardless, they were clearly secondhand. While this man was not a tourist, he may have been wearing a tourist's former attire—clothing that had been discarded by a traveler who decided it was not worth carrying on the remainder of his trip. Or perhaps it was donated by a local. I realized now why he was wearing them again, why he had not changed his clothes since the previous day.

The man's thick beard was not groomed. It appeared disheveled in a somewhat natural way, but not obviously unkempt. I could now see that his hands were dirty, but not so much as to call attention to himself. Only the lines around his eyes and across his forehead gave away the hard years behind him. So when he asked me again if Jeff was dead, the quiet optimism that shone in his eyes seemed out of place.

"How do you know my husband?" I asked.

"I don't. I just met him a few weeks ago."

"How?"

"He just showed up here. He came in and asked if anyone spoke English. Only a few of us did. He talked to each of us separately for a few minutes. I guess I got the job."

"What job? Why you?"

"I didn't ask why," he said. "I guess because I spoke good English and I'm not crazy like some of the others. I could talk to him. I could understand what he wanted, and I was capable of doing it."

"What did he want you to do?"

"He gave me a hundred euros to get my attention. Then he gave me your picture. He told me to watch for you at the *Circumvesuviana* train station. He told me, if I ever saw you, to give you a message. He gave me a cell phone and texted the message to it, to make sure I got it exactly right and also so I could contact him if I needed to. He told me that if you came to Naples and if I told you everything you needed to know, there would be fifty thousand more euros in his will for me."

"And you agreed to this? Why did you believe him?" I asked.

"It's not like I have very many things to do. I'm usually at the train station anyway. Besides, if there is one skill I have, it is reading people. I was sure he was telling the truth."

"But my husband was very young. Why would he leave money for you in his will instead of paying you in a timely manner for a job done?"

"Again"—and this time there *was* a hint of malice in his eyes—"I can read people. Your husband was rich. He was American. He walked into a church in Naples and begged a homeless man to help him. I agreed because he was desperate. He never told me how desperate, but I could see that I would not be waiting very long for the money. Your husband knew he was going to die."

"Is that the entire message?" I asked.

"That's it," he said. "I had no idea you had received the message until you texted me today from your husband's phone. Texting it back to him was an accident. But I was to show you the exact text message and then tell you how I met him and about our financial arrangement."

"Why didn't you just tell me the message? Why didn't you approach me at the train station when I first saw you looking at me? You scared the shit out of me when you followed me into the castle."

"Your husband was specific that you had to see it typed and that nobody else could know about it, so I had to speak to you absolutely alone. No privacy, no money. He made it clear that specification would be in the will.

"But by the time I got you alone," he said, "you were running from me. When we got to the terrace of the castle, away from those two kids you were following, I was planning to show you the message as he instructed. I had no idea you would jump over the wall.

"I have done everything your husband asked me to do. Now all I care about is my fifty thousand euros. Your husband said that everything would be taken care of, and I believed him. But if I were you, I would confirm that his will is in order according to our deal. If it is not, you should get out of Naples and not come back because Naples will no longer be safe for you if your husband did not live up to his word."

I felt my eyes flash at the matter-of-fact threat, and I could see from his stern expression that he meant it.

This time, I did not take the bus. Instead, I began walking. I followed the bus route I had now memorized, the one leading from *Stazione Circumvesuviana* toward my hotel. I knew it would be a long walk, but I needed to think.

Jeff solicited a complete stranger's help. He solicited a complete stranger who could not possibly be involved in whatever Jeff was running from. He solicited a stranger in Italy. He gave that man a message for me. He told him to watch the train station, the one from which trains leave for Pompeii. He knew that, if I came to Italy, I would follow him there.

Smart.

He knew that, if I came to Italy, I would be facing the same danger he was. And he knew that he would not be able to help me himself.

He solicited a stranger to help me.

Because he knew that if I came to Italy he would already be dead.

I snapped out of my thoughts and glanced up to get my bearings. Before me was an AT&T store. On a whim, I stepped inside and asked if there was any way to retrieve lost data from an iPhone.

The attendant laughed. "Of course there is!" he said in perfect English.

"What do you mean?"

"Madam," he said, his eyes twinkling with amusement, "every time you receive a phone bill, your recent activities are on it! All we need to do is pull your last bill, and you will see all of the numbers you have recently called or sent messages to and all of the numbers that have called you or sent you messages. This should provide a great deal of information. If you want more, we can go back into previous months. I can also provide you with unbilled activities, which will, of course, be the most recent."

It was so obvious that I felt stupid.

On one hand, I was relieved. But I was also mortified. Why hadn't the Apple store reminded me of this?

I could only come up with two possible reasons. They did not want me to have my own information. Or they wanted it for themselves.

It was clearly someone working from within that store that had deleted Alexis' contact information from Jeff's phone.

The AT&T attendant asked me to step behind the counter and enter a string of security information into the computer in order to access my account. Moments later, we had retrieved and printed my last two months' phone records.

I thanked the man and left the store. I scanned the documents as I walked. With phone numbers and cities before me, it was easy to place them with names.

The majority of calls, of course, were to or from Jeff. There were a few other San Diego numbers as well, which I quickly noted as my lab, a couple of colleagues, and my mother's nurse. And there were two phone numbers with San Francisco area codes. My daughter and my sister.

I skimmed through the numbers to the end where the unbilled, most recent activities were listed. The information was completely current, a real-time transaction record of everything up to the moment I had pulled it up on the computer in the AT&T store.

I recognized the phone call I had received the previous day when I was in the Naples Archeological Museum. That was the one from the mortician. I recognized the outgoing calls I had made from the seafood café where I had first met Dante.

Then I saw the calls that had come in over the twelve-hour time frame while my phone was down, and I gasped. My sister had called me five times.

*There is a phone call, and my marriage ends. Then there is a gunshot, and my life ends.*

*I am an invalid. It is Kathy who feeds me. It is Kathy who cleans up after me. It is Kathy who cares for my daughter.*

*And it is Kathy who forces me back to life.*

It was the middle of the night in San Francisco, but my sister was not one to sleep through a ringing phone. It rang for a fourth time nonetheless, and I knew the call would now go to voicemail.

"Kathy, where are you?" I asked aloud.

"Kathy—," I began when voicemail picked up, and then I heard the tone of call waiting. I clicked into the call. "What's wrong?" I blurted out. "What's wrong? You don't call me five times without leaving a single message unless there is something you don't want to say on an answering machine."

"Hold on," Kathy whispered, and for a few moments I could hear nothing but soft, rushed footsteps and my sister's quiet breathing into the phone.

"Sorry," she continued a moment later. Her voice was still a whisper. "I had to get outside so she wouldn't hear me."

"Who?"

"Lexi." Her voice was now stronger, and the word was piercing. "I'm camped out at her apartment until she tells me what's going on, but she won't tell me. You need to get up here and see your daughter, Trina. Now."

"What about her?" A chill ran up my spine.

"I got this weird call from her earlier. She was sort of rambling. Something about needing to talk to Jeff. I didn't understand it, and I thought she sounded nuts. When I started asking questions, she hung up on me. So I came to her apartment to check on her.

"She looks like *shit*, Katrina. I don't know when you last saw her, but I barely recognized her. She's thin. She's drawn. Her eyes, they look crazy. She's not herself. I think she's on drugs. I told her that I'm not leaving her apartment until she tells me what is going on with her. But she won't tell me."

*Oh, God, no! NO!*

`Trust nobody. Her 2.`

*NO! Not her too!*

"Wake her up and put her on the phone," I said. "Tell her it's Jeff."

*I am twenty-six, and Alexis is seven.*

*A phone rings. I jerk up from studying for my Ph.D. qualifying exams and quickly dance around the toys in the living room to answer the phone before it can ring a second time. The call is from Tom. He is cheating on me, and I have just caught him red-handed. I slam the phone down.*

*I bite my lip to contain the rising tears. I cannot let them come. Not yet.*

*I walk down the hall to my daughter's room. Slowly, carefully, I open her bedroom door. I expect her to be sleeping.*

*Alexis is on the floor, playing with her ponies. She looks up at me and smiles, and I remember promising at least an hour ago that I would join her. With a guilty pang, I send Alexis to brush her teeth, and I promise to tuck her in when she is finished.*

*I walk out of her room and step across the hall to the other door. I hold my breath and hope that the door will not squeak and wake the sleeping child inside.*

*My son.*

*Christopher is asleep. He makes a soft cooing sound when I open the door, but then he is quiet again. I watch him for a moment. He is five years old.*

*Christopher's blonde curls spring wildly from around his angelic face, his chubby little fist resting against a flawless rosy cheek. The blanket has pulled down in his sleep, and his pudgy belly peeks out from beneath a soft flannel pajama top. I tiptoe to him and pull up the cover.*

*I blink back tears.*

*Christopher and his sister will now grow up in a broken home. They will divide their time between two parents who can no longer live together. They will learn, at five and seven years of age, that parents can stop loving each other.*

*Christopher's innocence breaks my heart.*

*I quietly slip into the bathroom and splash cool water on my face to calm my nerves. I fulfill my promise to tuck Lexi in for the night. I make up an answer to her question about where her daddy is. And then finally, finally, I am able to run down the hall into my own bedroom, lock the door, and break down into the quietest sobs I can manage.*

*And then I hear a gunshot. And the shattering of glass.*

*And there is Christopher lying on the floor of the living room in a pool of blood.*

*I scream.*

*And there is Alexis.*

The Naples traffic was dizzying around me as I heard Alexis pick up the phone in San Francisco.

"*Jeff!*" she shouted. Her voice was sheer desperation.

"Alexis, are you sick?" I asked, and I could hear the same desperation in my own voice.

Alexis began to cry. A wailing, anguished cry. When she finally tried to speak, she could barely get the words out. But I already understood everything. Perfectly.

*Cancer cluster.*

"Oh, God, Mom, what's wrong with me?" She sobbed and gasped for breath. "I can't... I can't stand it! The pain... it's worse... every day... and the morphine... it's not working anymore... I need more... and John... John won't let me have any more. He says I'm taking too much... he... he says he has never... never seen anything like this... but all of a sudden... it's popping up all over the place. He has dozens... maybe even hundreds of patients. He can't find anything... anything we have in common... and we... we all just keep getting worse. It keeps spreading. It's all through me already..."

I heard her words, but one single phrase was what resonated through my mind.

*Cancer cluster.*

The phrase makes us think of radiation, power lines, something toxic in the local water, some common thread among those who have the same disease.

But Jeff and Alexis don't even live in the same part of the state.

"Alexis, listen to me," I said forcefully. "Just calm down. Relax. I'll fix it. Pack a bag and go stay with Aunt Kathy. She will take care of you. Just hold on, and trust me! I'll fix it! I swear to God, Alexis! I will find what you need! *I will not lose you too...*"

There are two kinds of nardus. The one is called Indian, the other Syrian. Not that it is found in Syria, but because one part of the mountain where it grows turns towards Syria and the other towards India... Applied they stop discharges of the womb and the whites... A decoction (taken as a drink with cold water) helps nausea and stomach rosiones, those troubled with wind, sickness of the liver or head, and painful kidneys... They are mixed with antidotes.

There is also another kind of nardus called Sampharitic from the name of the place—very little, yet great-eared, with a white stalk sometimes growing in the middle, very much like the smell of a goat in scent. This ought utterly to be refused.

-*De Materia Medica*
Dioscorides (ca. 40—90 CE)

# Chapter Twelve

*M*y son is gone. My husband is gone. My daughter is slipping away.

~

There are currently one hundred thirty elements on the periodic table. Of these, thirty-two are man-made. Jeff and I have patented twelve of them.

As I hung up the phone, the desperate wailing of my daughter still resonating in my ears, I was ready to crawl through Hell for the thirteenth.

I called Alyssa Iacovani and asked for her help in picking up where she and Jeff had left off. Twenty minutes later, I climbed into her car.

"Tell me what we are looking for," she said.

"I doubt you remember the acronym CHNOPS from your freshman chemistry class," I began explaining. "It stands for carbon, hydrogen, nitrogen, oxygen, phosphorus, sulfur. These six chemical elements are by far the most abundant elements in the world. The CHNOPS elements constitute an estimated ninety-nine percent of matter. The remaining one hundred twenty-four elements on the periodic table make up less than one percent of life. We are looking for a place that contains these rare chemical elements."

"So, we are looking for less than one percent of the matter existing in the world?" Alyssa asked.

"It's worse than that. We are not even looking for an element that actually exists. Instead, we need to find the appropriate building blocks, and then we need to identify a rare reaction between them that can generate an isotope so transient that it will be difficult to detect, even briefly, and even more difficult to prove the existence of."

Alyssa shook her head. "That sounds impossible."

"It almost is," I replied.

She plunged into the chaotic traffic of downtown Naples, and her driving reminded me of the previous day's cab ride. "I see you've been living here long enough to have attended the Naples School of Kamikaze Driving, and graduate with honors." Alyssa only grinned fiendishly and waved a middle finger at another driver she had just cut off.

After a brief stop for supplies, we hurtled out of the city and began winding our way southward down the coast.

"I know a lot of places that may fit your criteria of rare elements," Alyssa said. "Have you read Dante's *Inferno*?"

"Uh, yeah. Why?"

"Dante Alighieri was from Florence, but it is rumored that he got the idea for his *Inferno* from an area very near here. Today this area is called the Phlegraean Fields.

"Within the Phlegraean Fields there is a whole series of large, shallow volcanic craters shooting geysers of steam, hot springs that are now underwater, smoking caverns, and a huge sulfurous cavity called Solfatara, meaning sulfur—the ancients, of course, called this element brimstone. There's also Lake Avernus, which was thought for centuries to be the entrance to Hades.

"The geothermal activity in this region, together with our natural landscape, is unlike any in the world. And, of course, the source of it all is Mount Vesuvius."

"Then let's start there," I said, and she nodded. "But first, I need to know more about the plant. What is a nardo? Where does it come from?"

"Nardo might be spikenard," she said, "which is native only to the Himalayas. It was a very rare luxury in ancient Rome and Egypt. The upper classes valued spikenard for the perfume oils extracted from it."

"Then why would they have had it at the bedside in a hospital room?"

"Only if they believed in its medicinal value."

I nodded agreement.

"Alternatively," Alyssa offered, "the text from Herculaneum might have been describing lavender, which was termed 'naardus' by the ancient Greeks and is, of course, quite abundant throughout Italy."

"Great," I said. "There must be a million varieties of lavender in this world. So we are looking either for a magic plant that only grows on the highest mountain range in the world or for a quite ordinary one that could have adorned hospital rooms simply for its sheer abundance and nice smell. That narrows it down."

"Exactly," Alyssa said. "But I think the historical record has narrowed it down for us. I believe it is spikenard—*vaffanculo!*" Alyssa shouted as we rounded a curve.

Alyssa slammed on her brakes and jerked the steering wheel, and we narrowly missed crashing into a massive pile-up of halted vehicles. Her small car jumped onto a narrow shoulder. We screeched to a halt, and a cloud of dust engulfed us.

I gulped. "Oh, my God. Are you OK?"

Alyssa coughed and nodded.

I peered across the landscape of cars haphazardly strewn before us, and then I saw the accident. An overturned car was still smoking. Neither police nor medical help had yet arrived. I glanced around, and, as if on cue, a siren began wailing behind us.

After the fire truck passed by, the restless motorists began to coordinate with each other, and traffic slowly resumed. Alyssa shifted her car into gear, and we fell into funereal single file behind a small sedan.

We reached the accident just as a uniformed police officer was laying a sheet over a human body. A small river of blood flowed from beneath the sheet and down a gentle slope in the road. Lying parallel to the body were two others, also covered. One of them looked very small.

I glanced over at Alyssa and was surprised to see her sobbing uncontrollably.

Alyssa pulled her car out of the slow single line of traffic and onto the shoulder once again. There she parked and leaned her forehead against the steering wheel, crying.

I placed an awkward hand on her shoulder. "Do you want me to drive?" I felt stupid as soon as the words escaped my lips, but I could think of nothing else to say.

She only shook her head and continued crying.

A few moments later, her sobs abated, and she leaned past me to reach into the glove compartment. She withdrew a pile of napkins and began blowing her nose and wiping her eyes. She consulted the rearview mirror for a moment and brushed a wisp of hair from her cheek. Then she sat quietly, sniffling for a moment. She stared straight ahead, her hands on the steering wheel.

"My family was killed in a car crash," she said. "It was only a few weeks ago. When I arrived at the scene, it looked something like that."

I opened my mouth to say another stupid thing, but this time I caught myself.

"You're wondering how I am functioning," she said. "The answer is that I have no choice. It was just after the incident I told you about when my brakes went out along the Amalfi coast. I narrowly avoided crashing. The same thing happened to my husband. His brakes went out, but he couldn't avoid the crash. That's when I realized that neither occurrence was an accident. But the police wouldn't listen to what they considered the crazy conspiracy theory of a grieving wife and mother. They ruled the crash that took my family an unfortunate accident."

Alyssa took a shaky breath and exhaled noisily. She turned and looked at me, and her green eyes were exhausted. Only then did I notice the bags beneath them.

"The only thing that kept me going was Jeff. He returned my call at just the right time. If I believed in such things, I would have thought he was sent to me, an angel. He convinced me that the nardo holds the key to saving a lot of lives."

Alyssa gave me a determined look, and I suddenly felt that I knew her. She was as driven as I was.

"Help me find this goddamn plant," she said.

A few moments later, we were breezing along the Campania coastline again as if nothing had happened.

"Why do you think it is spikenard?" I asked.

"Because several species of spikenard are described as

nardo in an ancient text," she said. "The book is *De Materia Medica*. The author, Dioscorides. This man was a traveling physician with Nero's army, and even today *De Materia Medica* is still considered one of the most complete reference books for organic medicine in history. It is the closest thing we have to a contemporary eyewitness account of the plant species we are looking for.

"Furthermore," she went on, "this text was never 'rediscovered.' It never *left* circulation from the time it was written in the first century CE. It was the first written account of medical botany and the extant authority on herbal medicine all the way through the sixteenth century. For almost two millennia, it was the *Physician's Desk Reference*, utilized consistently by the best doctors in the world. So if this text says nardo is spikenard, I'm inclined to go along with it."

We turned off of the highway and wound our way up a short hill. Moments later, we pulled into a large parking lot at the base of Mount Vesuvius. A few buses and vans were also in the lot, and tourists were wandering around, photographing the volcano.

"I hope you're in shape," Alyssa said, examining the mountain from below.

"I'll race you," I challenged.

She was right. The climb was steep. But I estimated it would take no more than about fifteen minutes to reach the top. I charged forward, breathing steadily. Alyssa kept pace with me, and we quickly overtook a family who had paused for a small child to rest. I could hear Alyssa's breathing become somewhat labored as we climbed. She was in good shape, but not a runner like I was.

"Much of Dioscorides' knowledge came from his own travels during campaigns with Nero's army—but much of it did not.

His text mentions plants from all regions of the world, many of which Nero's campaigns never brought him to. Dioscorides describes many, many species that there is no way he saw first-hand."

Alyssa glanced behind her to confirm that the nearest tourists were out of earshot. "Experts agree that these species were discovered on the campaigns of Alexander the Great. Dioscorides must have learned of them from Alexander's records. So isn't it interesting that Cleopatra destroyed these records long before Dioscorides was ever born."

We reached the top of the volcano, and I stood for a moment to stare into the mouth of the killer. The crater looked so quiet, so innocent, but it is still an active volcano.

I imagined the destruction that Mount Vesuvius had unleashed in 79 CE. And I realized that it would happen again. I looked toward Naples and the bay. The boats. The castles. The shops, the restaurants, and the homes. At any moment, it could all be gone.

"What are you talking about?" I asked Alyssa, returning my attention to our conversation.

"The great library of Alexandria," she said. "It was the largest database in the ancient world. Ptolemy I inaugurated the library with the texts of Alexander the Great. And every subsequent ruler in the Ptolemaic dynasty continued to add to it.

"By law, visitors to Alexandria were forced to lend any works that the library did not already contain to be copied; the originals were not always returned. They sought to accrue copies of *every* text written in Greek, Aramaic, and Egyptian. Interpreters were employed to translate the documents that were not written in Greek.

"Two hundred fifty years later, Cleopatra inherited this library. By then, it was legendary, containing approximately seven hundred thousand papyrus scrolls. But neither the library nor the adjacent museum was open to the public. They were used for research purposes by museum members, mostly members of the royal family and their entourage."

"So the Ptolemies created the knowledge capital of the *world* and hoarded it amongst themselves?" I asked.

"Exactly. The Ptolemies were not just curators of knowledge. They were pirates. But because they kept the books to themselves, an illegal book trade grew up around the Alexandria library. It was through this underground network that many texts from the ancient world—real and fabricated—were made available to the general public over the centuries. The lack of any regulation in the trade has dramatically complicated the identification of genuine versus bogus texts.

"Within the Alexandria library were the greatest achievements in literary scholarship and applied sciences, including the first documentation of what is now established scientific method. There were many works of Herophilos and Erasistratos—third century BCE doctors—revealing fundamental discoveries concerning anatomy, which they made through dissection of corpses and criminals.

"Cleopatra herself was rumored to have written dozens of books on a variety of subjects, ranging from weights and measures to cosmetics to magic. Yet, none of her writings can be found today, with the exception of the Herculaneum document I myself discovered. And the majority of texts that existed in the Alexandria library during Cleopatra's reign, including the descriptions of plants discovered on the campaigns of Alexander the Great, were lost on her watch."

I reached down and grabbed a handful of earth and then

allowed it to slip through my fingers. A brisk breeze carried it, and it billowed to one side before falling to the ground once again.

"How could the 'highly ambitious' Cleopatra let that happen?" I asked.

"I think she arranged it," Alyssa said. "The library was burned down by her lover, Julius Caesar."

I pulled a ziplock bag from a shopping bag and opened it. I grabbed another handful of soil from beneath my feet, dropped it into the ziplock bag, and sealed it. I then withdrew a permanent marker from the shopping bag and labeled the sample.

"May I ask a silly question?" Alyssa asked.

"Sure."

"Instead of gathering small samples, wouldn't it be better to collect large quantities of dirt and attempt to grow the plant? Wouldn't that be the best way to find out what compounds are generated?"

"Of course," I said, "once we find the plant. But right now we aren't even sure what it is. And in the meantime, I can start with a basic analysis of the composition of the soil. I can do this with very little material."

What I did not tell Alyssa was that I had no intention of growing any plants. She was right that cultivating plants under the appropriate conditions was the most logical path forward. But it was not an option. There was no time. My uneasy alliance with a skeptical mortician was over. And my daughter could not wait.

My alternative was to independently analyze the elements within the soil, the water, the air, and the plants—if I could get my hands on the right ones. It was a dirtier approach, but a much quicker one, and there was a chance that, if I was very lucky, it would yield the isotope.

I already knew what to do with the isotope if I found it. I would examine its interaction with the HER2 protein on human cells. And, if I was very, very lucky, that interaction would block the cancer shared by my husband and my daughter.

~~~

**WHEN I TOUCHED ONE OF THE NARDOS, A GENTLE WARMTH RAN FROM MY FINGERTIPS TO MY HEART, LIKE A QUIET FLAME IN THE BLOOD OF MY ARM.**

I moved quickly. The work was mindless, and, as I carried it out, I reflected upon what I knew of the isotope and the nardo.

"I think the isotope might have some effect on the heart," I said, bending down to scoop a blackened patch of soil from the center of a more brightly colored area. "But Cleopatra didn't leave us as many clues to it as I would have liked. Why would she burn her own library down?"

I sealed the ziplock bag containing the sample and scrawled a descriptive label onto the plastic. Then I stepped a few yards further into the crater. Alyssa followed.

"I'm not sure," she said. "But it certainly seems to have been deliberate. It happened when Cleopatra joined forces with Caesar to battle her brother Ptolemy the Thirteenth to the death.

"The *hypothesis* is that the fire was a strategic military maneuver, meant to frustrate a traitor's attempt to communicate by sea, and that the library burning down was just an accident. But the *fact* is that Caesar set fire to his *own* ships, and the fire spread rapidly to the docks and the Alexandria library. The seven hundred thousand papyrus scrolls within were decimated."

Deeper within the volcano's crater, the soil was rockier, lacking the fine sandy texture of the well-trodden dirt on the tourist paths. I collected a few more samples.

Alyssa continued. "We know the importance of the library to Cleopatra by the fact that Antony's wedding gift to her fifteen years later was two hundred thousand new scrolls to re-populate it. Yet at the time, she didn't seem bothered by the fact that her lover had destroyed two hundred fifty years of accrued knowledge and information. Indeed, she followed Caesar to Rome twice in the next four years with their son, Caesarion, who had been born within a year of Caesar and Cleopatra's first meeting.

"And remember, all this time Caesar was married to another woman. His wife was Calpurnia, the daughter of Lucius Calpurnius Piso Caesoninus, who was the owner of the Villa dei Papiri in Herculaneum. And that, of course, is where the nardo document was unearthed.

"I believe Cleopatra and Caesar staged the fire that consumed the Alexandria library. They had obviously already removed important works from this library and hidden them elsewhere, including the nardo document."

I motioned for Alyssa to follow me, and we began walking toward the other side of the crater.

"So..." I said. "Cleopatra witnesses an extraordinary medical phenomenon in the nardo—"

"And she writes about it in Egyptian," Alyssa added, "to conceal it from her peers who don't speak the language."

"And then she moves the document from her own personal library in Alexandria into the Herculaneum villa of Caesar's father-in-law, just before Caesar burns the Alexandria library down," I said and bent down to collect another sample.

"Yes," Alyssa said. "In fact, I now know of three locations containing hidden documents from Cleopatra's reign. Two, of course, are the Villa dei Papiri in Herculaneum and the crocodile cemetery in Fayoum, Egypt. There was also a daughter library located elsewhere in Alexandria. Remains of that library still exist. Who knows how many hiding spots may have existed worldwide?

"I am sure that by the time of Dioscorides at least one of these sites had been found. Dioscorides was Roman. He would have had full access to the Egyptian archives after the Ptolemaic dynasty fell to Rome.

"It is clear that Dioscorides was a student of Egyptian medicine. His text, *De Materia Medica*, is full of ancient Egyptian remedies. He wrote of nardos and of some of their medical uses. But he wrote nothing about their potential to treat cancer, which means he did not know of the phenomenon described in the document you read."

I ran through the sequence of events in my mind once again. When I spoke at last, I spoke with conviction. "Of course he didn't. He couldn't. The document was trapped beneath the ash in the Villa dei Papiri throughout his lifetime."

A DEEP CAVE THERE WAS, YAWNING WIDE AND VAST, OF JAGGED ROCK, AND SHELTERED BY DARK LAKE AND WOODLAND GLOOM, OVER WHICH NO FLYING CREATURES COULD SAFELY WING THEIR WAY; SUCH A VAPOUR FROM THOSE BLACK JAWS WAS WAFTED TO THE VAULTED SKY WHENCE THE GREEKS SPOKE OF AVERNUS, THE BIRDLESS PLACE.

*-THE AENEID*
VIRGIL (70—19 BCE)

# CHAPTER THIRTEEN

An hour later, the Solfatara crater gaped and belched at me like a suppurating wound. "I agree with Dante Alighieri," I said. "This place is the gateway to Hell."

The stench of sulfur invading my nostrils was overwhelming, and that was just the beginning of the vileness of the place. Thick black boiling mud burped globs of putrescence. As I watched, a steam geyser spewed to a height of nearly three feet from a yellowed mouth. When the wind shifted, the geyser turned toward me, and the onslaught of sulfurous vapor was multiplied.

"*Shit*," I said under my breath when I remembered what I had come there to do.

Alyssa looked amused. "I dig up mummies," she said. "This is all you."

Rickety waist-high fencing separated Alyssa and me from the volcano, and I could not believe that the word "dormant" was used to describe it. I wandered for a few moments through the area that was open to tourists. As I did, I reached down and touched the earth with a flat hand, feeling around to gain several reference points. Some spots were considerably warmer than others. And then I understood why Alyssa had included a collection of small microwave- and oven-safe containers when we stopped for supplies. Ziplock bags would melt.

"I'm glad there are no other tourists here," I said. "I have no desire to watch someone's three-year-old follow me into an abyss of boiling quicksand from which I'm not guaranteed to emerge." I took a deep breath and jumped over one of the fences. The closer I came to the thermal mud lake, the more I could feel its heat radiating up my legs beneath the cuffs of my jeans. When my one-day-old sneakers began to sink, and then stick slightly, and then produce audible sucking noises as they came out, I decided I had gone far enough.

"This is why I don't do field research," I muttered under my breath, and I quickly dunked one of the small heat-resistant containers into the mud. The container did not melt, but I could feel the intense heat through it. *Earth's vomit*, I thought and popped a lid onto the container.

"Does it feel like Satan is reaching up to pull you into Hell?" Alyssa shouted from the safety of the other side of the fence.

"This *is* Hell," I fired back.

The momentary cessation of movement had sunk my feet even deeper into the mud, and I really did wonder for a moment if I would be stuck there permanently, like a mafia informer in cement shoes. After a brief struggle, I yanked myself away from the hungry, angry, sucking mud and returned to the safer side of the fence.

I repeated the procedure at the *bocca grande*, or "large mouth"—the largest of Solfatara's steam geysers. Although the geyser shot only a couple of feet high, it projected steam at scalding temperatures. The day was windy, and I was approaching a boiling geyser with a plastic container and the sleeve of a sweatshirt as the only protection for my arm.

"You look like someone offering a sardine to Jaws!" Alyssa shouted, and she was giggling.

Fortunately, the earth around the *bocca grande* was solid.

During a momentary stillness in the breeze, I rushed in and hastily gathered a sample of the steaming emission. Without bothering to cap the container, I leaped away as quickly as possible, hoping fervently that the wind would not shift.

"OK," I said to Alyssa, finally breathing easily again. "I guess that does it. I need a shower."

Alyssa smiled. "Don't you want some water from the River Styx?" she asked.

"The name *Lago d'Averno* is Greek," Alyssa said. "It means 'lake of no birds.' It was once believed that birds flying over the sulfurous water would drop out of the sky, dead from the fumes. Of course, we have now confirmed the presence of fowl, but the lake is... well, foul."

Nonetheless, I found the lake infinitely more pleasant than Solfatara. I was happy to discover that it was easily accessible and even populated by a handful of brave swimmers. It was also surrounded by lush greenery, and I ordered myself to cross-reference the plant life—clearly adapted to grow in highly concentrated sulfur—with anything that could be referred to as nardo. I did not see any lavender. I certainly did not see any spikenard.

After I gathered some water from the lake, Alyssa led me back toward the parking area and then beyond it for a couple hundred yards. "This is where the *real* entrance to the underworld is supposed to be," she said. "It's called Sybil's Grotto."

A man stood at the entrance, and Alyssa negotiated with him for a few moments in Italian before he led us into an underground passage. As the guide led Alyssa forward, I allowed myself to fall behind. I scraped a small pile of dirt from the floor and a bit from the walls of the tunnel.

We stepped back out into the daylight, blinking against the glare, and Alyssa thanked the man before we walked away.

"There are several ruins around here," Alyssa said, gesturing with her arms as we walked. "There's an old Roman temple, an arch, and the ancient city of Cumae. Of course, the spots we have already been to are probably more important for your research. If we need to gather soil from every Roman ruin in the area, we're in trouble."

Nodding agreement with her, I asked, "What now?"

Alyssa chuckled. "Do you dive?"

"Are you serious?"

"I am. Just a couple miles away are the ruins of Baiae. It was a summer resort for the Romans, and a villa still standing there was the summer home of Julius Caesar. Fairly extensive ruins remain, including a bath complex and a more modern castle. But the majority of the site is underwater. You can see it via glass bottom boat tour, or you can take a diving tour."

I thought for a moment and then said, "Yes, I dive, but I don't think it's worth it. It's one thing to gather the native soil of an area by collecting samples. It's another to hope that the composition has remained unchanged after two millennia of being submerged in seawater."

"But they haven't been underwater for two millennia," Alyssa said. "The bradyseisms—uplift and subsidence events—that submerged much of the city only happened in the mid-1500s. Many of the ruins were discovered from aerial photographs of the region taken during World War II. So Baiae, now an underwater park, has only relatively recently become available for exploration and is still very much preserved.

"And that's not the only reason for you to gather samples there. The bath complex was originally built on a natural mineral spring of highly reputed medicinal value. These baths were where doctors in Caesar and Cleopatra's time sent patients for treatment. I wouldn't be surprised if Cleopatra herself had frequented them for medicine. And the sources are still active, still producing the same medicinal output. But it is all under water."

So I dove into a secret world beneath the sea, a world unassumingly frozen in time and space.

The tour for advanced scuba divers began with a brief refresher course on diving, followed by a description of the sites we were about to swim to. By the time my English-speaking guide finished his monologue, I could not wait to get into the water. But the tour began on the ground.

The ruins of *Le Terme di Baia*, the "Thermal Baths of Baiae," remain above sea level. Had I been passing through the largest and most important medicinal bath complex of the ancient world on virtually any other day of my life, I would have been fascinated. Instead, I was looking at my watch, and then out at the water, and then at the rapidly lowering sun, anxious to start diving while there was still sufficient daylight. But once we boarded the small boat that would take us to the dive, the wait was only minutes.

Conversation necessarily ceased when we dropped into the water, instead becoming a compilation of improvised hand gestures. "Sign language is genetically programmed into Italians," Alyssa had quipped. "But you might need an interpreter."

Our guide led us first to the nymphaeum. He had told us that the amazingly intact collection of statues was a tribute to the lineage of Mark Antony with Octavia, his first wife. The one Cleopatra supplanted.

Alyssa had filled in other details more pertinent to our

search during the boat ride. Octavia was also the sister of Octavian, the rival who ultimately defeated Antony and Cleopatra, leading to their suicides. Antony's daughter with Octavia was Antonia Minor. Antonia's great-grandson was Emperor Nero, the emperor under whom Dioscorides would document the botanical discoveries of Alexander the Great in *De Materia Medica.*

I swam in a circle around the life-sized statue of Antonia, marveling both at its preservation and at the fact that I was observing it accompanied by a school of fish. Contrasted with the blue water surrounding her, Antonia's white marble figure shone, illuminated by the few rogue sunbeams that penetrated through the natural filter of the water.

Tiny rivulets of bubbles flowed upward from the earth like the artificial aeration mechanism in a modern aquarium. I pulled a ziplock bag from the sleeve of my wetsuit and inverted it over one of the sources. I held it there until it filled with air and then zipped it shut.

Antonia was surrounded by several other equally well-preserved statues, and the other four people on my tour, including Alyssa and the guide, swirled curiously around each of them for a few moments.

After we left the nymphaeum behind, we passed over a series of large marble slabs and several amazing mosaics embedded in the sea floor. These had been walkways and patios. Our guide called attention to the structures by passing a hand over each, clearing away the silt that had settled onto the black, white, and multi-colored marble pieces.

Then he brought us to the summer villa of the man whose main residence was the Villa dei Papiri. The summer residence of Lucius Calpurnius Piso Caesoninus was decadently expansive. Our guide motioned for the four of us to follow him to a thinly covered expanse of lead pipe. He brushed a hand over it, and the silt feathered away, revealing the inscription in Latin letters:

# L.PISONIS

Near it was an enormous courtyard. A series of arcades and passages led us through several private rooms and, eventually, to the private thermal mineral baths belonging to Lucius Piso. As I had near the statue of Antonia Minor, I collected several samples of the gases bubbling up from the sea floor.

We spent a great deal of time exploring the expansive Portus Julius, which covered more than ten hectares and featured mile-long canals and tunnels connecting Lake Avernus, Lake Lucrine, and the city of Cumae. It was this site that had first been detected in the intelligence photographs of World War II.

But I was most interested in the "Smoky Reef," so called because of the fumaroles, columns of gaseous bubbles escaping from the sea bed.

It was there that I began to lose consciousness.

Several massive pillars constituted an entrance that rose almost to the water's surface. I swam between them and into an aquatic ecosystem unlike any I had ever seen.

Despite its depths, the reef was filled with life more commonly seen nearer the surface. The pillars were coated with algae. A network of fish and other shallow-water sea creatures wove around them. I watched a school of fish and came slowly to the realization that the organisms within the Smoky Reef lacked natural competition. They benefited from an increase in physical space, fewer predators, and more abundant food. They bore a biological advantage.

*But why are they here at all?*

I could feel why. The area was unnaturally warm. The deeper within its depths I swam, the more its heat enveloped me, like the warmth of a coral reef. But instead of the sun above, the Smoky Reef's heat source was constant volcanic activity from below.

I swam deeper.

The giant pillars and the life forms housed within them indeed shared a smoky appearance. I allowed my eyes to trace the grayish lines of sulfur deposits streaking the surfaces of the pillars, and I was able to detect the active fumaroles that bubbled gently around them. I collected several more samples.

My work completed to my satisfaction, I turned to return to the boat. It was then that I first noticed how lightheaded I had become.

I stopped swimming for a moment and looked around in an effort to regain my bearings. I realized I had no idea where the boat was. I began swimming aimlessly, but my limbs felt heavy. I was suddenly so, so tired. I just wanted to sleep. More than anything. I *needed* to sleep.

I changed directions, and suddenly there before me was Alyssa. In slow motion, she grabbed my arm and looked into my face. Behind her scuba mask, her green eyes flashed. She disappeared behind me, and then a thin arm slithered around my waist from the direction she had gone.

No longer caring, I allowed myself to drift into unconsciousness.

~~~

*I still have three years of graduate school left, and the bullet comes crashing through the living room window.*

*And then Christopher, my baby, my five-year-old little boy, is bleeding to death in my arms.*

I awoke lying on my side, vomiting. My joints were burning. Each involuntary heave of my stomach sent another jolt of fire through them.

"Welcome back, *signora*," a man said. His accent was Italian. An Italian accent sounded familiar, but I could not remember where I had recently heard one.

The waves of convulsions in my stomach finally subsided, and I rolled over onto my back. Slowly, a vertical staff wound with symmetrical snakes came into focus. The man's uniform bore a caduceus, the eternal symbol of medicine, and behind the man was a dilapidated ambulance.

The medic looked up from examining me, his gaze directed over my head, and said something in Italian. An angry female voice answered. From the depths of a cave, I remembered that voice. It was Alyssa Iacovani's. I turned my head and looked toward her.

Alyssa's eyes fell upon me as a large rubber bowl descended over my nose and mouth. "It's one hundred percent oxygen," she said. "You lost consciousness, and I had to rush you to the surface. Now you have the bends and will need decompression. I'm sorry, Katrina."

I nodded.

Slowly, carefully, I sat up. The pain in my joints was almost unbearable.

"Be careful," Alyssa said.

I reached up and pulled the oxygen mask away from my mouth so that I could speak. "The tank..." I said weakly, and I forced myself to turn and scan the area for my scuba apparatus.

"I'm sorry, ma'am," another voice said, this one in perfect English. "You can rest assured we will conduct a thorough investigation into what might have caused your gear to malfunction. This is the first incident of this kind that our diving company has ever experienced. The safety of our customers is paramount."

I realized then that there was another man standing over me in addition to the medic. The second man's smile was unnaturally wide, and he was sweating profusely. His eyes reminded me of the eyes of a reptile.

"No!" Alyssa said sharply. "You will listen to me! This is a prominent American doctor with connections to Homeland Security. She almost died in your company's care. You will give me the fucking tank. Right now."

I was rolled onto a stretcher, lifted into the ambulance, and then carried into a hospital and placed in a pressure chamber. There I remained for almost five hours as the nitrogen content in my bloodstream slowly normalized. When I emerged, I felt almost normal.

"We need to keep you overnight for observation, *signora*," a man said as I began gathering my belongings.

"You almost have," Alyssa said. "Step aside."

He stepped toward her as if to prevent us from leaving, but the blaze in her green eyes made him stop. He stepped backward.

Alyssa led me to her car. Once we were alone inside it, I finally asked the question that had been running through my mind. "What are the odds that this was an accident?"

"Under normal circumstances," Alyssa said, "I would say huge. Safety regulations aren't the same in Italy as they are in the United States. These things happen. Tour buses fall off cliffs all the time. Trains derail. But lately, I don't assume anything is an accident."

"My thoughts exactly," I said. "Thank you for saving me. And for making sure we got the tank. It will only take a few minutes in a laboratory for me to understand what I was actually breathing down there."

But first, I needed the laboratory.

I turned to survey the back seat of the car. It was all but overflowing with biological samples, and the trunk was full as well. Each of the unique chemical environments that I had sampled in just one afternoon would exponentially expand my work load.

"Alyssa, I can begin the analysis of these samples immediately if I can have access to a lab, but I need at least a skeleton staff to operate it. I need a basic molecular biology facility and a basic organic chemistry facility. And I need help, especially on the chemistry side, from people who know what they are doing and won't ask too many questions. Can you get me these things?"

"You already have them," she said.

FOR THE POOR PEOPLE FROM THE STREETS NEAR THE DI SANGRO CHAPEL, THE NEAPOLITAN INCARNATION OF DR. FAUSTUS MADE A PACT WITH THE DEVIL, AND ALMOST BECAME A DEVIL HIMSELF, TO MASTER THE MOST SECRET MYSTERIES OF NATURE.

*-STORIE E LEGGENDE NAPOLETANE*

BENEDETTO CROCE (1866–1952)

# CHAPTER FOURTEEN

It was nearly two in the morning when we finally returned to Naples. The trunk of Alyssa's car was loaded with plastic bags and containers holding more than one hundred biological samples, their labels providing an itinerary of every location we had visited. I had gathered dry dirt, boiling mud, steam that had now condensed into liquid, seawater, and sulfuric deposits from cave walls. I had even collected air, in the form of millions of tiny gaseous bubbles emerging from the sea floor.

Spiraling around me now were the millions of tasks ahead of me. Each sample mandated a new data set, each data set a new analysis. And now I had reason to analyze the contents of a scuba tank as well.

Still, I was eager to begin the analyses of the samples and also curious about the labs themselves. "Where did these labs come from?" I asked.

"The labs are mine, sort of," Alyssa said. "I began setting them up when I first found the nardo document. With all the strange things that kept happening to me, I wanted to keep the document away from the rest of the Piso Project team at the archeological museum. So I pulled some strings and secured a separate location for a research facility. It's in the basement beneath another museum, the *Cappella Sansevero*.

I have known the curator there for years; he is a good friend.

"I have been very interested in the Sansevero since I began working on the Piso Project. I'm even more interested in it now that I've found the nardo document."

"Why?" I asked.

"Because the chapel is a shrine to our isotope."

We pulled into a narrow, crooked alleyway in the heart of Naples, and Alyssa parked the car. "Just leave the samples here for now," she said. "We can grab some big trash bags from inside to carry them in."

We exited the car and began walking through the alley.

"The Villa dei Papiri was first rediscovered in the 1700s, after nearly two thousand years beneath the ash," Alyssa said. "The king of Naples at that time was Charles of Bourbon. Raimondo di Sangro, the Prince of Sansevero and patron of this chapel, was a good friend of his. Charles enlisted di Sangro to attempt the unrolling and deciphering of the papyrus scrolls."

"And?"

"Di Sangro tried using mercury to soften the charred papyrus."

"What was the result?" I asked.

"The scrolls dissolved."

"Damn."

"I'll say."

We approached a nondescript brown building. A molded archway surrounded a heavy wooden door. Alyssa produced a key, and we entered the building. Inside was an information and ticketing desk for the museum, but at that late hour it was vacant. A tall A-frame sign announced the entrance to the Sansevero chapel.

"Raimondo di Sangro was one of the first people to become truly obsessed with the documents buried within the Villa dei Papiri. And I believe he was searching for the same thing we are searching for. He was clearly onto something resembling our isotope. But I'm not sure if he found it."

"How close did he come?"

"Much closer than we are."

Alyssa pushed open a second heavy wooden door, and we entered di Sangro's chapel.

The moment I saw what was inside, I sucked in my breath and stopped short. I could make no sound. I could only stare. I have no idea how long I stood there.

My mind was not my own as I stepped forward.

Beneath the altar was a single prominent display—whispering, seducing, drawing me toward it. I approached it with no free will to do otherwise.

A display case of clear glass enclosed a body. Inside the glass was Jesus Christ.

He was lying on his back, his face tilted to one side, his eyes closed. Beneath him was a thick, fluffy, padded bed, and his upper body was propped upon two soft pillows. His entire body, from head to toe, was covered with a thin, transparent veil. Its gentle folds were spun from a silken cloth so delicate that Christ's every feature, every muscle, every detail of face and body could be clearly discerned beneath it.

But it was not cloth. It was marble. The soft shroud, the warm and comforting bed, the perfect body, and the peaceful face—the entire masterpiece had been freed from within a single slab of marble.

The expression on Christ's face was one of serenity. He

appeared to be sleeping rather than dead, and the sense of peace he projected contrasted sharply with the broken shackles and crown of thorns lying near his feet. These objects of torture from his mortal life lay next to the body but outside of the veil, as if rejected from the warm cocoon protecting the Savior.

Christ's body was thin but not emaciated as I had seen in so many depictions of this moment. His shoulders and biceps were muscular, the forearms and hands extending from them long and lean. His right arm lay gently alongside his body; the left was resting casually and comfortably upon his hip. The details of each finger could be observed from beneath the soft folds of the marble veil, and they spoke not of the pain of the cross but of the many miracles born from them. The rising arch of his chest sloped down into a flat abdomen, and I was almost certain that I could see him breathing beneath the veil.

"You share your husband's curiosity," Alyssa said softly from beside me. "Jeff had the same reaction."

"I have never seen anything so amazing," I whispered.

"It's entitled *The Veiled Christ*. It was created by Giuseppe Sanmartino at the behest of Raimondo di Sangro. It is sometimes also referred to as *The Dead Christ*."

"This Christ is not dead," I said. "He is the personification of vitality."

"You're absolutely right. He is awaiting the moment of resurrection."

I cast my eyes again upon the liquid veil and the perfect body beneath it. "How did Sanmartino do it?" I asked. "This could not possibly have been sculpted with a chisel."

"For over two hundred fifty years, the veil was believed to have been created by Raimondo di Sangro himself using some secret alchemy. But modern analyses have confirmed that it was in fact done with a chisel. Legend also held that di Sangro gouged out the eyes of Giuseppe Sanmartino, after Sanmartino completed this work, so that he would never again be able to create something so beautiful. Of course, the fact that Sanmartino sculpted many other pieces later in life disproves this myth pretty definitively. None of his subsequent works compare to *this* one, but certainly they were not carved by a blind man."

I laughed softly. "Then why would people have thought that of di Sangro?" I asked.

"Such was the reputation of the Prince of Sansevero."

Alyssa began walking as she continued. "Raimondo di Sangro was the Grand Master of the Neapolitan Freemasons. He did not build this chapel, but in the last years of his life he completely remodeled it into a tribute to his beliefs.

"Unlike many of his contemporaries and other art patrons through the ages, di Sangro maintained full control over the artwork in this chapel. Rather than giving a rough idea of what he was looking for and then leaving it to the artist's imagination, he gave very specific instructions as to how he wanted his own thoughts expressed in each piece. Many of the things in this room were literally done by di Sangro's own hand. The rest of the pieces are his visions.

"This whole section is filled with statues of the virtues. Among them are *Modesty, Divine Love, Self-control, Liberality, Religious Zeal,* and *Education.* When we have more time, I can explain all of them to you if you like. But this one is important."

She directed my attention to a statue almost as impressive as *The Veiled Christ.* But rather than a thin, transparent veil, the central figure in this one was enveloped within a binding net. And unlike the Christ, at peace beneath his veil, this figure was struggling to escape. He was assisted by a small spirit bearing a flame on his forehead. At the feet of the two figures were a globe and an open Bible. I marveled at the intricacy of the netting that ensnared the man, and I was stunned—once again—that such a feat could be attained in marble with a chisel.

"There was a triad including this piece and *The Veiled Christ*," Alyssa continued. "They were the masterpieces, devoted to artistic excellence."

She pointed to the bas relief on the pedestal. "The Bible is open to the story of Jesus restoring sight to the blind. But this piece is entitled *Disillusion*. It refers to the very Masonic idea of light from the darkness, an obvious metaphor for knowledge.

"Di Sangro was a follower of Enlightenment principles, but like so many of his era he was stifled by the Church over the course of his lifetime. One of the more well-studied essays he wrote, his *Lettera Apologetica*, communicated some of the more radical Enlightenment notions, including free thought and hostility toward Church interference. Of course, the Church was mortified. They banned it."

"But wouldn't di Sangro have actually been a member of the Church?" I asked.

"Publicly, yes, of course. But he was also believed to be a Rosicrucian."

I squinted. "Which means what, exactly?"

"Rosicrucianism is a... I hate to even use the word *religion*... it's a philosophy. The order was founded by a circle of doctors. Like the Freemasons and so many other secret societies of the time, their purpose was, to put it in far overly simplistic terms, to *learn*—without the interference of the Church.

"There is a Rosicrucian maxim: to know, to will, to dare,

and to keep silent. Di Sangro seems to have lived by it. He studied the arts, philosophy, military tactics, printing presses, pyrotechnics, physics, pharmaceuticals, mechanics, you name it. His scientific work was at the cutting edge of several fields, including the budding transition from alchemy to modern chemistry. Indeed, he was one of the preeminent scientists to make that transition.

"Di Sangro created this chapel to showcase his accomplishments. But his work was secret, and his laboratories were secret. And just before he died, he burned all of his research. So there are many things to this day that we know he did, but nobody has any idea *how* he did them."

"Sounds like Cleopatra burning her own library down after hiding her most critical documents in other locations," I observed.

"He *was* like Cleopatra in almost every way," Alyssa agreed. "He had an appetite for the sciences and spoke and wrote fluently in multiple languages. He was completely secretive about his work, and very deliberate in choosing which messages to share publicly. But he left tributes in plain sight so the very *enlightened* could see them. And that is why I think we can find the isotope through him."

I stepped away from *Disillusioned* and began surveying more of the chapel. In my compulsion to reach the sculpture of Christ, I had scarcely noticed the chapel's details upon first entering. Now, they were critical.

"What parts of this chapel are works of di Sangro's own hand?" I asked.

Alyssa took my arm and led me back toward the entrance before pointing to the amazing frescoed ceiling.

"Look at the colors," she said. "Di Sangro didn't paint the ceiling, but he invented the paints. Nobody understands how they have remained so well preserved for so long. Baroque period frescoes never look this good unless they have been actively restored. Except for this one. It's timeless."

We then stepped into a small alcove along the side of the chapel, and I realized I was looking at di Sangro's tomb.

"Look at the inscription," Alyssa prompted.

"What?"

"It was written by Raimondo di Sangro himself," she teased.

"So?" I asked. Aside from the fact that it seemed a bit self-promoting, heralding di Sangro as "gifted," "extraordinary," and "famous," I had no idea what she was getting at.

"The inscription on this tomb was produced chemically. To this day, nobody knows how. He must have used some form of acid, or something similar, but it's not documented. What is clear is that it was *not* chiseled."

Alyssa then pointed to the floor beneath the tomb, and I noticed for the first time how anachronistic it was in this setting. The contrasting light and dark shapes reminded me of an M.C. Escher pattern, something totally out of place among the baroque style that was prevalent throughout the chapel.

"Are those... *swastikas*?"

"Alternating with concentric squares," Alyssa said. "The swastika in ancient tradition symbolized cosmic movement. The concentric squares refer to the tetragon of the elements—earth, fire, wind, and water.

"This pattern, which in di Sangro's time covered the *entire* floor, represents the difficulty of the path that one must follow to gain knowledge."

Alyssa led me toward a staircase, and we began to descend. "Raimondo di Sangro was brilliant," she said, "and, apart from

196

the Church, his contemporaries acknowledged this, but many of them feared him. He was ahead of his time and, on top of that, absolutely secretive about his actions. Not a good combination for building trust or dispelling myths. He gained a reputation fairly comparable to Victor Frankenstein."

We entered a small basement beneath the chapel, and I understood why.

Two display cases in a small round underground chamber each held a human corpse. Both bodies stood erect. One was a man. The other a pregnant woman.

Their entire circulatory systems were wrapped, immobile, around their skeletons, having emerged from hearts forever frozen to their open chests. The skeletons stood intact, and the intricate networks of tiny veins and arteries crossing their faces reminded me of the netting I had just seen carved from marble and covering the *Disillusion* figure.

"*Oh, my God,*" I said, venturing closer. "Are they real?"

"The skeletons are definitely real," Alyssa said. "The fetus in the woman's womb *was* most definitely real, until it was stolen a number of years ago."

"*Stolen?*" I asked, feeling a sudden wave of nausea.

I redirected my gaze again to the webbing of veins over the male corpse's face, and I wondered how it could have been achieved in the eighteenth century.

About a decade ago, a traveling scientific exhibit passed through San Diego. The exhibit was called *Bodies*. It featured anatomical models similar to those one would observe in a high school science class, except that they were real. One could wander through the various sections of the exhibit and observe, *in situ*, the entire circulatory system, the respiratory system, the reproductive systems of both males and females—even neurons.

The bodies of the exhibit were preserved using a technology called plastination, a brand new preservation technique that had been invented at the turn of the twenty-first century for the specific purpose of preserving the bodies. As I stood in the basement beneath Raimondo di Sangro's chapel, I realized the *Bodies* exhibit had precedent more than two centuries prior.

"How did he do this?" I asked incredulously.

"Legend held that these were two of di Sangro's servants who had angered him. The belief was that he preserved the circulatory systems by injecting the victims with mercury while they were still alive."

"Is that part true?" I asked.

"He certainly did have an affinity for science, as you have seen. And he also had an affinity for using mercury, as I mentioned about the scrolls. But how he made these, nobody knows. Chemical analyses have yielded evidence of all sorts of organic substances associated with the capillaries and veins, including beeswax. So it appears that these models are, um, partly real. The rest is a mystery.

"Di Sangro's palace was adjacent to where this chapel was built. He had a laboratory in the basement of the palace. His contemporaries documented strange noises and strange flashes of light coming from the laboratory at all hours of the night. It's really no wonder they were afraid of him. And he moved secretly between his lab and the outside world through an underground tunnel connecting the laboratory under the palace to this chapel basement.

"Officially, the tunnel no longer exists."

"And unofficially?" I asked.

"Where do you think we're going?" Alyssa said and pushed aside the display case containing the pregnant female.

I had begun to feel like I was in a dream, but reality quickly returned when we emerged from a short tunnel and into a modern laboratory. I felt a deep breath force its way into my constricted airway, and I suddenly relaxed in the familiar environment.

"Wow," I said. The equipment was brand new. There were no damaged linoleum floor tiles or discolored countertops—the ghosts of chemical spills—or piles of dust bunnies behind computers. At 2:15 a.m., the lab was unoccupied. Rarely had I seen a lab so new entirely devoid of activity. Had it not been for the characteristic hum of a functional laboratory, the objects before me might have been theater props.

"This is the laboratory I have set up dedicated solely to work on the nardo document," Alyssa said. "Before I contacted Jeff, I wasn't sure what needed to be done or who was going to run the project. I knew roughly what types of studies we'd want to do but had no idea how to do those studies myself. However, I knew I'd get *someone* to lead the effort if not Jeff.

"The equipment is brand new and is just now almost in place. Jeff only began hiring scientists over the last couple of weeks. A few people have been qualifying machines and developing protocols."

I ran my eyes once again over the gleaming machinery. *Of course*, I thought, as the realization struck me, but I asked anyway. "Where did all the money for this come from?"

Alyssa looked surprised. "Well, most of it came from *you!*"

A basic biological laboratory costs millions of dollars in set-up expenses alone. The six-figure salaries of Ph.D.-level staff and the exorbitant costs of consumables can easily reach millions per year.

I now understood where our money had gone.

Together, Jeff and I were incredibly wealthy. But to build and maintain a research facility without the help of additional investors would quickly drain our collective life savings.

Jeff had gambled it all on the Vesuvius isotope.

"Gosh, where are those trash bags?" I asked, the events of the day finally taking their toll.

"You read my mind," Alyssa said. "I can give you a proper tour tomorrow, but right now I'm hitting a wall. I need a bath and a good night's sleep."

"That makes two of us," I said, bending one arm to assess any residual pain from the bends.

We each grabbed a handful of large black trash bags and re-entered the tunnel. We walked through it in silence, the dim lighting along the walls guiding our way, each of us deep in thought and too tired to speak. We stepped into the underground chamber containing di Sangro's mysterious corpses, and Alyssa pushed the female back into position before we ascended into the chapel.

As we walked back through the chapel, something caught my eye that made me forget my exhaustion. I could not believe I had not noticed it the first time through this area. Among the statues of the virtues, and not far from the netted *Disillusion* I had observed earlier, stood another veiled sculpture, a counterpart equally as impressive as *The Veiled Christ.*

In sharp contrast to the Christian Savior, this statue depicted a woman very much alive and standing erect. Her posture was both self-confident and defiant. She leaned against an enormous plaque, which was broken across the corner where her arm rested. The thin veil enveloping her form did nothing to conceal her body; her breasts were thrust forward, her shoulders back, and her face was cocked to one side. The woman's eyes were half closed. Over her hips was casually slung a garland of roses.

Alyssa must have noticed me staring. "The inscription on the plaque refers to a Gospel story. Christ appears to Mary Magdalene dressed as a gardener."

"This statue is Mary Magdalene?"

"The statue is called *Modesty.*" It was a non-answer. "It's the third in di Sangro's triad of artistic excellence."

"She hardly looks modest," I said.

"Exactly. Just as *The Dead Christ* hardly looks dead. This statue is an allegory of wisdom. It represents a veiled Isis. This chapel was erected on the site of an ancient Temple of Isis. Di Sangro had this statue placed in the exact location where a statue of Isis once stood. This one is making the statement attributed to the veiled Isis for centuries."

"What statement?"

"Nature loves to hide."

She paused to allow me to fully absorb the meaning of the sentence and then continued. "Like I said before, di Sangro was very selective about what messages he left behind for posterity. One of his most public pursuits was a quest for an 'eternal flame.' Near the end of his life, he claimed to have actually invented one, but of course he never published the details of the science so nobody can verify today whether or not the flame was real. The claim might have been a chemical reference exclusively—a chemical element or mixture that could burn without ever dying. But I don't think so.

"This statue, the veiled Isis, is exactly where it belongs. But the statue of *The Veiled Christ* is misplaced. It was intended to go in the underground chamber. Di Sangro detailed in his plans for this chapel that *The Veiled Christ*—the Christ not really dead, but merely resting—would go in the center of the underground chamber. Beside it would be di Sangro's eternal flame.

"The metaphor is obvious. Di Sangro was seeking immortality. He was seeking a substance that could restore life to the dying, a substance capable of doing exactly what our nardo document describes.

"What if di Sangro found the first evidence of his 'eternal flame' in the Villa dei Papiri? Or what if he found it at another one of the secret locations in which we know Cleopatra hid documents? That might have been his reason for exploring the villa, once it was rediscovered, with such a passion in the first place. It might have been his reason for following Cleopatra's example of burning his own research notes. It might have been his reason for erecting a tribute to her patron goddess, on the site of a former Temple of Isis. What is clear is that his quest for immortality led di Sangro to those papyrus scrolls.

"Now, consider the nardo document. Put it in the context of the 1750s when the Villa dei Papiri was being excavated. Had di Sangro discovered a similar text, there is no doubt he would have pursued it in secret.

"An extensive network of Herculaneum document hunters grew up out of the discovery of the scrolls in the villa. I am talking about some of the most powerful leaders in the world. Certainly, they sought treasure—the statues, bronzes, coins, jewels. All of those things were pillaged rampantly when Pompeii and Herculaneum were discovered—you saw a large collection of the recovered pieces in the archeological museum. But they also sought the science that had been introduced to the world by the Ptolemy leaders in Alexandria.

"And remember, any science considered too radical in di Sangro's time was thought to be magic or witchcraft or the work of the devil. One had to hide not only from the Church but also from anyone *else* who was pursuing the same goals. A competitor could either usurp the work or simply turn the rival in to the Church authorities.

"Katrina, I think this rivalry is still active today. I am trying to sort out the details of exactly who knew about di Sangro's work and who else has known about the papyrus scrolls in general over the centuries. It's a daunting task. But I can tell you this, the more I look into it, and the more I learn who has been involved with this discovery since the 1750s, the more I feel that... I'm not losing my mind. Someone really is trying to kill me."

I looked over at the woman who had just that afternoon saved my life, and I decided that I owed it to her to return the favor. "I know who it is," I said.

SINCE, THEREFORE, IT CANNOT BE DOUBTED THAT THIS IS A TRUE LIGHT, SIMILAR TO OUR CANDLES OR LAMPS, AND HAS BURNED THREE MONTHS AND SOME DAYS WITHOUT ANY REDUCTION IN THE MATERIAL USED FOR FUEL, IT CAN RIGHTLY BE CALLED PERPETUAL, MUCH MORE SO THAN THOSE IMAGINARY LIGHTS WHICH CAN SOMETIMES BE FOUND IN THE ANCIENT TOMBS AND ANY OTHER LIGHT WHICH DOES NOT HAVE THE SAME PROPERTIES AS MINE, I.E. ALL THE QUALITIES OF OTHER NATURAL FLAMES, DOES NOT DESERVE TO BE CALLED ETERNAL.

-LETTERS OF RAIMONDO DI SANGRO (1710—1771)

# CHAPTER FIFTEEN

*J*eff is lying on his back. He is naked. He is dead. A pool of red ripples outward from his body, spreading quickly over the deck of my yacht. From my vantage point on the terrace of our bedroom, I scream.

*I turn and run. I tear through the bedroom, down the hallway, and onto the staircase. I descend the stairs two at a time, but it is dark, and the farther I run the more disoriented I become. When I reach the lower floor, I fumble in the dark until I find a light switch. When I flip it on, a brilliant light fills my vision. I shield my eyes.*

*But then my eyes adjust, and I realize that the light is not blinding after all but soft and comforting. And I am not in my house but in a beautiful underground chamber.*

*And Jeff is not dead. He is sleeping.*

*Jeff lies in the center of the space, illuminated gracefully by a single eternally burning flame. It is not a red pool of blood surrounding him but a soft veil, spun from a delicate silk of the purest white I have ever seen.*

*I approach him. He awakens and smiles at me. His smoky blue eyes shine gently up at me through the translucent veil. Slowly, he slides the veil down over his body. Its thin, iridescent folds puddle at his feet.*

*"Morning, love," he says and sits up.*

*I begin to sob uncontrollably, and a look of confusion darkens Jeff's countenance.*

*"What is it, Kat?" he asks with concern.*

*I can barely speak. "I thought... I thought you were... you were dead!"*

*Jeff wraps a comforting arm around me. I bury my face in his chest and throw my arms around his shoulders. I can feel the bullet hole in the center of his back. But I also feel him breathing.*

*"Come with me." Jeff takes my hand and leads me out of the chamber.*

*When we emerge, we are in the depths of a beautiful private garden. Slowly, lazily, we stroll through, silently enjoying the fragrances and the beauty of the lush foliage around us.*

*"Open-toed shoes are OK," Jeff says, and across his face spreads an enormous mischievous grin.*

*I stare up at him for a moment, questioning.* Huh? Open-toed shoes? Did I hear that right? *Then I feel a similar grin crossing my own countenance. "That's good," I say. "I'm so glad to hear that because I have lots of cute ones that are very comfortable this time of year." I pause to think before asking, "What do I wear them with?"*

*Game on.*

*We walk.*

*Jeff is no longer naked, but he still bears the bullet hole through the center of his chest that somehow does not kill him.*

*I ponder his latest puzzle. It is about open-toed shoes. But in the end, it will have very little, if anything, to do with shoes. And I already know everything I need to solve it.*

*"Hmm," Jeff says. "What to wear them with? Nothing too*

*revealing. Nothing flashy. Nothing tight. You don't want to call attention to yourself. It's a different culture."*

*Jeff leads me to a climbing vine and wraps one of its tendrils around a finger, staring at the winding plant with fascination. "Isn't she amazing?" he asks.*

*"Who?"*

*His response is a single word. "Nature."*

*I frown. "Sometimes she's a bitch."*

*Jeff chuckles. "Yes," he says. "She loves to hide. But you can find her."*

*"How?" I plead, with tears once again springing to my eyes. "I don't understand any of these things! Chemistry is not my area! Egyptology even less so!"*

*"You're wrong," he says. "You are exactly in your element. The answers are right in front of you. Just open your eyes and see them."*

*We come to a gentle river flowing lazily through the vast garden. There is no bridge across it. Jeff releases my hand and smiles at me, and then he winks and dives into the water.*

*I want so badly to dive in after him, but something holds me back. Instead, I watch in silence as my husband swims across the flowing river. When he reaches the far bank and emerges, he is naked again, his wet skin glistening in the brilliant sunlight. He looks back across the water and blows me a kiss. Then he turns and disappears into the lush greenery along the river bank.*

*I turn around. Before me stands my house, and I suddenly realize that the garden I am standing in is the one in my own backyard.*

My hotel room's alarm clock blared. I struggled not to hear it, to stay asleep, because to wake would be to lose him again. But waking was inevitable, as it always is at such beautiful moments, and I finally conceded.

I awoke with tears in my eyes. It had been so nice to be with Jeff again. It was now so painful, so cold, so harsh to be alone in reality once more.

For a few moments, I lay staring at the hotel room ceiling, reflecting on the dream. It had felt so real. But it was nonsense. How could The Game exist in a dream? How could Jeff taunt me with a secret in a dream?

I shook off my confusion, sad beyond description that it was only a dream, and that he was still gone.

Beside me, I heard my purse vibrate. I reached toward the nightstand and rummaged through my purse until I found one of the iPhones. It was Jeff's.

There was a new text message from John. It read simply: Jeff. Call me.

I felt a sudden chill, and I pulled the hotel bedding more tightly over my body, all too aware that it was not the least bit cold in the room.

*John knows that Jeff is sick,* I thought. *He knows because he diagnosed Jeff. And he diagnosed Alexis. That's the reason for his concern. Now that I have spoken to Alexis, he probably knows that I know. About both of them. But he doesn't seem to know anything further about what Jeff has been doing in Italy.*

*Why not?*

I deleted his text and pulled the bedding even more closely around my body, but I was still shivering. Because he was the link. John. Jeff's best friend. John was the only connection.

The sudden, unambiguous revelation was paralyzing. John

was the only common denominator between my husband and my daughter—two people with dramatically different lives, living in different cities, and with no genetic relationship. They shared nothing except for the same, very rare form of cancer. And the same personal physician.

As I forced myself to emerge from the warm cocoon of a Naples hotel room bed, I was terrified that my husband had been murdered on the orders of his best friend.

Our attorney sounded both surprised and perturbed to be receiving a business call, on his home phone, at 10:30 p.m.

He sounded even more perturbed when I asked if my husband had made any recent changes to his will, and when I made it clear I needed to know the answer to that question immediately. My voice was steady, but my hands were shaking, as I could only hope attorney-client privilege would compel his silence should Jeff's murder be discovered before I could finish what I needed to do.

That was three days ago.

I was surprised to discover in myself that morning a sense of calm. It had come to me quietly in the form of a wonderful, terrible, haunting, poetic, and bittersweet dream.

I was still thinking of the dream as I sat on a Naples public bus once again, absentmindedly nibbling a pastry and sipping hot coffee. I marveled at the mysterious core of the human psyche that produces dreams like a belching volcanic crater buried deep in the mind, the Freudian Phlegraean Fields.

My mother used to tell me that all dreams have meaning. Despite my innate sense of logic, I believed her. Now, I knew that the Jeff in my dream was not really Jeff. He was the subliminal materialization of my own subconscious, manifest in the familiar form of my most trusted loved one. The objective part of my mind had finally found a way to speak, and I had heard it.

I *was* exactly in my element.

I had spent a lifetime accruing an encyclopedic knowledge of biology and had rigorously educated myself in the fields of cancer research and drug discovery. I had the insatiable inquisitiveness of a lifelong researcher and the critical eye of a highly trained scientist. I was following the trail of the man I loved more than anything and whom I knew better than anyone else in the world. My memory was as sharp as a razor. And I would stop at nothing. If I could not solve this puzzle, it could not be solved.

The more my self-doubt dissolved, the more clearly I understood what I needed to do. Alyssa would be expecting my call, but she would have to wait. Despite Jeff's warning to me in his text message, he himself actually *had* trusted someone. He had trusted just a single soul. And with that one act, he had instantly created a long list of those whom he had deliberately *not* trusted.

Everyone we knew was on it.

Her too.

A few minutes later, I stood before the one man Jeff had trusted.

I asked him his name, but I already knew it. His name was Aldo de Luca. I had learned it that morning from my attorney.

My next question was more complicated than the first. I asked him why he was homeless.

Aldo de Luca glared at me. "That's an easy question for you to ask, standing there instead of sitting because you don't want my sleeping quarters to dirty your expensive jeans."

Suddenly, I realized how out of place I must look in the makeshift homeless shelter of the central cloister of *Santa Maria del Carmine*. I sat down next to de Luca on the ragged mattress on the floor. "I apologize. What I meant was that you are obviously an intelligent, capable man. What happened in your life to make you end up here?"

He took my hand and examined it, turning it over to look at both the back and the palm. "Your husband was born into his charmed life," he said matter-of-factly. "Not you. You have known hardship. So you should already know the answer to your question."

I looked into his tired eyes, stunned at his sense of perception. He was right. I needed only to reflect upon my own history to understand how many variables can affect the course of one's life. Was Aldo de Luca born into this situation? Was he thrown into it? Did he make some huge, devastating mistake and bring it on himself? It was probably a combination of all three, and it didn't matter anyway. Whether sitting on a floor in a homeless shelter or behind a desk in a corner office, he was still the same person. And he was the closest thing to a friend that I had.

"I need your help," I said.

"I'm listening."

"I double-checked on the fifty thousand," I said. "It's in Jeff's will."

"Of course it is, or you would not be here."

"I will make it a hundred thousand, payable immediately. But first I need you to help me do something."

"What do you need me to do?"

THE DIRECTION OF THE WORK WAS GIVEN TO A SPANISH ENGINEER NAMED ROCH JOACHIM ALCUBIERRE. TO BORROW THE ITALIAN PROVERB, THIS MAN KNOWS AS MUCH OF ANTIQUITIES AS THE MOON KNOWS OF CRABS. HIS INCAPACITY CAUSED THE LOSS OF MANY ANTIQUITIES.

-OPEN LETTER ON THE DISCOVERIES OF HERCULANEUM
JOHANN JOACHIM WINCKELMANN (1717–1768)

# CHAPTER SIXTEEN

When the lost city of Herculaneum was rediscovered in the early 1700s, one of the first artifacts located and retrieved was a statue of Cleopatra. It was excavated along with a trio of female statues, each woman draped in a flowing silken tunic carved of the purest white marble. All four of these statues have since been lost once again.

It was Alyssa who told me of their existence. After leaving Aldo de Luca, I called her and accepted her offer of a full tour of the lab beneath Raimondo di Sangro's chapel. As we once again walked single file through the cramped underground tunnel toward the lab, I began asking questions.

Every scientist understands that inconsistent data is not the exception but the rule. Rarely does an entire package of evidence come fitting neatly together with no anomalies. If it does, one should be very skeptical. There is always at least one piece in the otherwise flawless jigsaw puzzle that stubbornly refuses to fit with the others. And it is usually this piece that ultimately leads to the *true* conclusion, formerly masked by the overshadowing, seemingly cohesive majority of the pieces—which turn out to have presented a distracting fallacy all along.

I asked Alyssa about the piece of the puzzle that didn't fit.

"Why was the Villa dei Papiri never fully excavated?"

She smiled. "Excellent question. One I have been seeking the answer to since I first came to Naples. There is absolutely no shred of doubt that this villa is one of the most important archeological resources in human history. Other areas of Herculaneum *have* been excavated. The fact that this villa has been relatively neglected over the centuries while digging has continued at these other sites is a truly glaring omission in the archeological record. It's like unearthing the fossil of an extraterrestrial humanoid and then just walking away from it."

We reached the end of the tunnel, and Alyssa opened the door leading into the laboratory. This time, the space was bustling with activity.

I immediately felt at home. The constant, loud whirring of assorted machinery was a comforting sound. It was accompanied by a crackling radio blasting a Lethal Factor tune at full volume.

> *I've got something so, so bad*
> *Something in me I never wanted to know I had*
> *And it's changing all I know*
> *Raging inside, every day I can feel it grow*

*This is my lab*, I realized.

We had entered the facility into the biological sciences space, as evidenced by the familiar objects before me. Three parallel rows of lab benches spanned the room. Their shelves were stocked with bottles of clear and colored liquids, only a few of which were properly labeled with the appropriate universal hazard stickers. The remaining solutions were identified by strips of colored tape labeled with the scrawled handwriting of a rushed scientist. Lining the outer perimeter of the large main room were metal cabinets. I knew without looking inside that they would contain glassware, chemicals, assorted reagents, and specialized laboratory supplies. Four people, all of whom I guessed to be under thirty, were at work.

"Hi, Jackie," Alyssa said to one of them as we passed. The girl waved without looking up from her experiment.

"This is the main bio lab," Alyssa said. "Over here we have a cold room, a warm room, and a radioactive room"—she pointed to the doors of each in turn and then to a fourth door—"and this door leads to a separate space for tissue culture. You need to walk through it to get into the chemistry and analytical labs."

We stepped through the fourth door, passed between the tissue culture hoods, and entered the chemistry lab, crammed with fume hoods and additional benches. Lethal Factor became markedly louder.

*Try, can you keep it locked inside?*
*Deep within the secret place it hides*
*Block it away from you, trapped within*
*But this can devour you through my skin*

Neatly sorted on one of the benches were the biological samples Alyssa and I had collected the previous day. A pimple-faced young man was feeding test tubes into a machine. He glanced up and offered a distracted greeting as we stepped past him.

Lying on the bench next to the collection of samples was my scuba tank. Alyssa picked it up and led me away with a subtle nod toward the young man.

Once we were alone, she leaned toward me. "The tank held both the normal scuba air mixture and carbon monoxide. The carbon monoxide percentage was low—it would have taken quite a while for the gas to get to you. But the more you breathed, the more it overwhelmed your body. There is no doubt that was what caused you to faint."

"Interesting," I said. I took the tank from Alyssa and examined it. "They don't make this model of tank in the U.S. anymore."

She shrugged. "They probably don't make it here either. This particular one is clearly past its prime."

"See the connection here"—I pointed to a fitting—"these can take in a certain amount of air from the environment. The presence of carbon monoxide inside the tank could mean that someone tried to kill me. Or, it could just mean that someone stupidly set the tank down next to an idling VW bus before I used it. We will never know. But it doesn't matter. Even if this was an attempt on my life, it certainly wasn't the first. We need to move on."

"I know," she said.

"Have you procured a source of nardo?"

"No, I didn't make it out to the Himalayas yet this morning," Alyssa scoffed. "And, anyway, we're still not sure what a nardo is. But it's time to find out. Now that we have collected these samples, positively identifying the nardo plant has become the rate-limiting step in this entire endeavor."

"Then bring me up to speed," I said. "What can we learn, and what have you learned already, from Raimondo di Sangro and the others who have searched for the nardo before us? Tell me what you know, and I will tell you about the man I believe is trying to kill us both."

Alyssa opened a door and led me past a series of private

offices. A nameplate on the door of the corner office read "Jeffrey Wilson, Ph.D."

We entered a break room with a small kitchen, and Alyssa headed straight to an espresso machine on the counter. She quickly prepared two large cappuccinos, and we sat across from each other at a small table, upon which sat an assortment of pastries. Alyssa motioned for me to help myself.

I walked Alyssa through my two encounters with the Naples transit policeman named Carmello Rossi. She appeared totally unsurprised.

She then began telling her story, the story of the rediscovery of the Villa dei Papiri in the 1700s. It began with a statue of Cleopatra, and three others eerily resembling the veiled Isis standing above us in Raimondo di Sangro's chapel.

Like so many of the world's most amazing discoveries, the lost city of Herculaneum was rediscovered by accident. The year was 1709, and Naples and the surrounding regions were under Austrian rule.

While digging a well, a feat accomplished in 1709 by leading oxen in a circle to drive a drill into the ground, a farmer began unearthing pieces of marble. The farmer began selling the marble fragments, and one of his first customers was Emanuel d'Elboeuf, the French prince commanding the Austrian cavalry.

Eager to complete his summer residence, the task that had brought him to shop for marble in the first place, d'Elboeuf confiscated the poor farmer's well on behalf of the Austrian government. D'Elboeuf began digging in earnest, and the three female statues were unearthed. They were quickly followed by the statue of Cleopatra. The statues were claimed as property of the Austrian government and placed in the king's garden in Vienna.

D'Elboeuf and his workers pillaged the building that had been drilled into until it was stripped clean. When the booty was gone, they filled in the holes. With no interests whatsoever in art, no such field as archeology existing at the time, and no apparent concept of historical preservation, no real records of the find were made.

The story might have stopped right there had it not been for a succession of women as ambitious as Cleopatra herself.

Twenty-five years after d'Elboeuf abandoned the site, two factors converged to revive the excavations at Herculaneum. The first was the ascension of a new king of Naples, or rather, the *true* monarch—his mother.

In 1734, Austria ceded Naples to Spain, and Naples fell under the rule of the Spanish royal dynasty controlling the Kingdom of the Two Sicilies, although neither king nor queen was either Spanish or Sicilian.

King Philip V was the grandson of Louis XIV of France and was raised at the court of Versailles with aspirations to the French crown. Instead, he was granted the lesser Spanish crown. Philip's wife Queen Elisabetta was an Italian princess descended from the Medici dukes of Florence and the Farnese dukes of Lombardy. Throughout his reign, Philip suffered from severe depression that left him categorically incapacitated most of the time. So the kingdom was managed by his queen.

Queen Elisabetta installed her firstborn son,

eighteen-year-old Charles, upon the throne of Naples. Four years later, Charles married. King Philip had sought a French bride for his firstborn in a feeble effort to cling to the French throne. Elisabetta's wishes prevailed, however, and Charles married a Prussian, Princess Maria Amalia, who coincidentally had grown up in the very Austrian palace containing the first statues excavated from Herculaneum—the three veiled females and the statue of Cleopatra.

While Charles nominally ruled his kingdom, it was his mother, the Italian-born Queen Elisabetta, who became determined to convert the run-down, poverty- and disease-infested cesspool that was Naples into "the Florence of the South." And this she did, funding her ambitious endeavors by taxing the Catholic Church on its lands. As the Church was the largest landholder in Campania, tax revenues tripled.

Elisabetta used the newly acquired funds to build three new palaces, a royal opera house, a prison, hospices, a cemetery, and a number of factories. The palaces were intended as museums as well as royal residences; therefore, she set the course to transfer a vast number of pieces from her family's priceless Farnese collection to Naples.

At the same time, in hopes of finding further additions for her collection, Elisabetta ordered that the Herculaneum excavations be resumed. Under the official direction of Charles, and the unofficial direction of Charles' mother, the vast ruins of Herculaneum and the recently rediscovered Pompeii were systematically plundered.

These efforts were led by a Spanish artillery engineer named Captain Rocque Joaquin de Alcubierre, whose sole mission was to find everything of monetary value and pluck it from the earth. As Alcubierre exhausted one source of buried treasure, he would delve unthinkingly into the next, backfilling each prior section with dirt from the new one.

It was under Alcubierre that the Villa dei Papiri and its library of scrolls were discovered.

Raimondo di Sangro, Prince of Sansevero and friend of King Charles, became the first to attempt opening the papyrus scrolls. In an effort to soften the charred, brittle papyri, he immersed them in mercury. This dissolved the scrolls, and many of them were lost. Of course, di Sangro chose the most well-preserved of the scrolls for his experiments, thus leaving behind those that were even harder to decipher.

King Charles himself was fascinated with the scrolls. In addition to allowing di Sangro to work with them, Charles sent to Rome for assistance with them as well. Vatican calligrapher Padre Piaggio was the first to manipulate some of the scrolls *without* destroying them. Piaggio's infinite patience and sense of innovation produced a device that could at last unwind the scrolls, at a rate of one half inch per day. It was this device that I had seen in the Naples Archeological Museum on my first day in Italy.

Slowly and painstakingly, Padre Piaggio succeeded in being the first to unroll one of the papyrus documents recovered from the Villa dei Papiri. This single act took four years.

Piaggio continued unrolling additional scrolls and set to diligently copying their text. The Vatican calligrapher produced remarkably faithful reproductions of the text despite the condition of the scrolls and also despite the fact that he neither spoke nor read modern Greek, let alone ancient Greek.

Translation of the content was equally difficult. The papyrus was in such terrible condition and so many pieces had been lost that much of the author information and content were either missing or misunderstood. Indeed, several scrolls were literally translated backward in their entirety, and only many, many years later were the mistakes even recognized as such.

Meanwhile, the second factor involved in bringing Herculaneum to light was the expanding influence of the Enlightenment itself during the eighteenth century. This philosophical movement prompted a great interest in the study of antiquities.

A Grand Tour of Europe was considered an essential element of an upper-class education, and the aristocratic travelers known to Italians as *milordi*—"my lords"—came from far and wide throughout Europe. Rome was a quintessential stopping point, and soon Naples became one as well. As rumors of the ancient treasures began making their way across Europe, increasing numbers of Grand Tourists became determined to see the ruins for themselves, as well as to purchase the many replicas of Herculaneum booty that were suddenly all the rage.

Artists who could faithfully reproduce these coveted artifacts found abundant work in Naples. One such artist was Camillo Paderni, who was fascinated by the flawlessly frozen cross-sections of ancient Roman life. As he toured the excavation sites, Paderni produced image upon image of a world formerly unbeknownst to the public.

Paderni was also appalled that these cross-sections were being so brutally destroyed and began writing letters of complaint about Captain Alcubierre's methods. When antiquarian and well-respected writer Johann Joachim Winckelmann chimed in with his scathing critique that Alcubierre knew "as much of antiquities as the moon knows of crabs," Alcubierre was sent to a different post.

Alcubierre was replaced by Karl Weber, a Swiss architect and engineer, who produced the first true maps of the Villa dei Papiri and its surroundings as well as the many tunnels still present throughout the area today. Approximately eleven hundred additional scrolls were found and removed from the villa during Weber's supervision of the project.

Then the inevitable fate of monarchy politics intervened and set in motion another end to the Herculaneum excavations. King Charles' father, Philip V of Spain, had died in 1754. By 1759, Charles could no longer shirk his responsibility to the kingdom, and he reluctantly left Naples for Spain. Governing in Naples in his stead was a temporary stand-in until Charles' spoiled eight-year-old son Ferdinand could come of age.

Without the king's support, money for the project was diverted elsewhere. Excavations at Herculaneum were forcibly halted in favor of ongoing efforts at Pompeii, which lay considerably closer to the surface, making it easier and cheaper to explore. The death of Charles' mother, Elisabetta, the woman who had first initiated the work, sealed the fate of Herculaneum. The secrets still contained within the Villa dei Papiri would once again be forced to wait.

Charles' son Ferdinand came of age in 1767 and became the arrogant, ignorant boy-king of Naples—an event that would no doubt have represented the final nail in the coffin of Herculaneum and the villa if not for one unlikely variable.

Her name was Maria Carolina, and she would become Ferdinand's queen despite her loudly voiced opinion on the matter: "You might as well cast me into the sea." She was also the elder sister of the girl who would become known to history as Marie Antoinette, and whose notorious fate would only intensify Maria Carolina's hatred of all things French.

Maria Carolina became a close friend of Padre Piaggio, sitting with him for hours as he painstakingly unrolled a scroll. She safeguarded the papyrus scrolls from the Villa dei Papiri throughout the extensive fallout in Naples resulting from the French Revolution, and she successfully kept them from the hands of the pillaging Napoleon Bonaparte—for a while.

At the exact moment Alyssa mentioned Napoleon's name, I felt my chair shift beneath me, as if the disembodied head of Marie Antoinette had spoken.

At first, I thought I was experiencing a sudden attack of vertigo, a residual effect of the bends. I took a deep breath, my eyes scanning the small space of the subterranean kitchen. Then, an audible rumbling began beneath me, and a cupboard over the break room's small countertop swung open. The contents of the cupboard slid out, hitting the countertop and the floor beneath and shattering.

Alyssa stopped talking and looked curiously around her. "Get under the doorway," she said authoritatively.

"I'm from California," I reminded her, already moving into the most earthquake-safe area of the kitchen. For perhaps forty seconds, Alyssa and I huddled together under the thick doorframe leading out of the break room and into the lab. The rumblings continued, and we could hear the sounds of additional items crashing to the floor.

"Is this lab earthquake-compliant?" I asked, already casting my mind back to the tour she had just given me to try and recall what I had seen. I remembered that there were acid cabinets underneath the fume hoods. I was reasonably sure that there were also cabinets for flammables and other combustibles. But I had not paid enough attention to notice if the lab's occupants had been using them.

All too frequently, scientists, in their haste, fail to store chemicals properly. They take a bottle of acid from an acid cabinet, and, when finished using it, they just stash it on the shelf over their bench. That is fine, until there is an earthquake and they are standing beneath that shelf. It is a very real concern in California, and evidently in Naples as well, I observed.

We heard a scream, and I had my answer.

Alyssa and I raced into the chemistry lab, where we found a young girl struggling to operate the laboratory shower. While labs are universally equipped with such devices, and they are operated with a simple, clearly marked, user-friendly lever, most scientists have never had the misfortune of occasion to use one, and the girl before us was panicking.

I ran to her and pulled the lever. A heavy spray of fresh water instantly doused the young lady from head to toe.

"*Strip*," I ordered sternly, and she looked at me with wide eyes. "You heard me! *NOW!*"

With shaking hands, the girl quickly removed her top but then had trouble with her jeans, which were wet and glued stubbornly to her legs. After a few moments of struggling, she managed to get out of them.

As she stood under the water in bra and panties, I quickly scanned the girl's body for signs of rash or other trauma to her skin. I saw nothing. "What did you spill?"

"Concentrated acrylamide."

Her answer explained the lack of visible symptoms. She

would show none today, perhaps not ever. The effects of acrylamide poisoning, if there are any, can take years to manifest. It is a powerful neurotoxin, and exposure to it can induce Parkinson's-like symptoms. I hoped this young girl would never experience them, but the only way of knowing would be to keep in contact with her for the rest of her life. And there was nothing either she or I could do about it anyway.

"Stay under the shower for fifteen minutes," I told her. "I'm getting you a lab coat to wear home. Leave your clothes here. They will need to go for analysis to record the exposure to your body."

Alyssa showed me to a storeroom where I collected a towel and a clean lab coat. When we returned, the girl was still under the shower, and shivering. This time, I was sure her shaking was from the cold water. She looked much calmer now, and understandably embarrassed.

"Who are you?" she asked me.

"I'm Katrina Stone," I said and watched her for signs of recognition. There were none.

"I'm Jeff Wilson's wife," I added, and then she smiled and enthusiastically offered a waterlogged hand.

"Oh!" she said. "I'm so sorry! *You're* Katrina! I thought you would have Dr. Wilson's last name!"

"It's common for a female scientist not to take her husband's name," I found myself explaining for the millionth time since my wedding. "When you have already established a publication record under your maiden name, you lose that record by changing your name. People conduct Internet searches by last name to find the work of a scientist. They don't know when someone gets married."

*And why don't you already know this?* I wondered.

"Oh, gosh," she said, blushing. "I didn't know that. I'm just an intern. I make solutions like the acrylamide I was working with when the earthquake hit."

No longer surprised at the girl's naïveté, I sent her on her way home, all the while assuming she would be sprinting to change her career path away from any form of science. Then Alyssa and I conducted a brief check of the lab.

We saw the spilled acrylamide bottle near the fume hood, and I donned two pairs of chemical-resistant gloves to clean up the mess while Alyssa stood by. Unlike our adventures at the Phlaegrean Fields the day before, I was comfortable in this situation. Several other items had fallen, and a few broken bottles were present, but clear labeling indicated that nothing else that had spilled was chemically dangerous. We cleaned up the remnants and then decided to step above ground and get some air.

We entered the tunnel between the lab and the Sansevero chapel, and for a moment neither of us spoke. Then Alyssa brought something to the front of my mind that had been huddling near the back since the moment I myself had been huddling in the doorway.

"That earthquake is why we are in so much danger," she said. "This whole area is highly unstable geologically, just like Southern California."

I could feel a chill creep up the back of my neck. "Which means," I said, "that at any time the ruins of Herculaneum and the Villa dei Papiri could be buried again."

"Exactly," she said. "And they might not survive another major geological event like they did the volcanic eruption in 79 CE. They could be completely destroyed. Everyone knows this. It is why the people who want those papyrus scrolls, like the man who shot at you and might have poisoned your scuba tank, are not waiting. They have no patience. They can't afford it. They are desperate. They know that this entire region is a ticking time bomb."

As we emerged from the underground tunnel and into the Chapel of Sansevero, I felt what I thought was an aftershock. I stopped moving. "Did you feel that?" I asked Alyssa. Her look was blank. I felt it again. "That, right there," I said.

Alyssa shrugged her shoulders. "I didn't feel anything," she said, and I realized that what I had felt was the vibrating of my own purse. I reached into it and retrieved the vibrating iPhone, and it dawned on me that there was probably no reception in the underground lab.

It was my phone, signaling a voicemail. The time signature indicated that the message was several hours old. But it had not come through until now.

I gaped at the message and at the time signature, and I knew that my time had already run out.

That was three days ago.

THERE IS NOTHING I WOULD RATHER KNOW THAN THE CAUSES OF THE RIVER WHICH LIE HIDDEN THROUGH SO MANY AGES AND ITS UNKNOWN SOURCE.

-JULIUS CAESAR (100—44 BCE)

HAIL TO THEE, O NILE! WHO MANIFESTS THYSELF OVER THIS LAND, AND COMES TO GIVE LIFE TO EGYPT!

-*HYMN TO THE NILE*, CA. 2100 BCE

# CHAPTER SEVENTEEN

The message was from Larry Shuman. His post-mortem findings had just cemented his conviction that I had killed my husband.

"Dr. Stone"—the message came through—"the cancer in your husband's body is the likes of which I have never seen in twenty-seven years in this business. I am sure you were aware of his condition.

"The suspicious nature of his disease, combined with the suspicious circumstances of his death, led me to run additional tests beyond the normal toxicology panels.

"What I have found is a molecular substance being metabolized through the liver. This is clearly a man-made substance. It functioned as a powerful carcinogen when I tested it on human cells.

"Dr. Stone, I am certain that as a professional drug discovery biologist you understand the implications. This substance is what caused the aggressive cancer throughout your husband's body. Your husband was given this cancer deliberately.

"All of these findings will be in the detailed report I am preparing for the San Diego Police Department. Dr. Stone, if you are innocent of this crime, then may the authorities find you so. But I am willing to wager exactly one million dollars that you are not.

"May God forgive you."

*He made it. Rossi made the cancer. He gave it to my husband. He gave it to my daughter. And the easiest way he could have done that would have been through John. Our family physician.*

Even as I began to wonder if they could have also somehow inoculated me, I knew I was going to be sick again. With my cell phone still to my ear, I hastily excused myself from Alyssa Iacovani. I dashed out of the Sansevero chapel and around the corner into the alley behind it, where I vomited my two morning cups of coffee.

I rinsed out my mouth using a spigot in the alley. Against my better judgment, I withdrew an empty water bottle from my purse and refilled it from the spigot.

I was rounding the corner to return to Alyssa when she stepped out of the chapel. Her face was clouded with worry.

"I'm sorry," I said. "I have a problem at home I need to deal with." And as soon as I could, I caught the first bus that would take me away from her.

*Of course Shuman suspects me.*

When my husband died, I inherited the multibillion-dollar drug discovery company that Jeff and I co-owned. I had both the motive and the knowledge to poison Jeff with a compound that would induce a fatal form of cancer. From those two facts, one is easily led to the conclusion that if my husband—an equally if not more competent scientist—discovered this, I would also have reason to shoot him dead.

From the terrace of our bedroom.

With my own gun.

And then hide his body.

Only then did I realize that there were actually *two* links between Jeff and my daughter. The first, of course, was John.

The other was me.

The bus rocked, and I thought about the cancer.

I thought about Alexis.

*Alexis is fifteen, and she has now advanced from the generally peaceful PETA organization to the more radical Animal Liberation Front. This organization is known for sabotaging animal research facilities and for freeing the animals inside, with the best of intentions. It is through the Animal Liberation Front that Alexis is finally able to target her worst enemy—her mother. It is with them that she goes after my biosafety level 3 facility, an infectious disease laboratory currently housing a cohort of anthrax-infected monkeys.*

As I sat on the rocking bus, I realized that the police would not need to dig very deep to discover a motive for me to harm Alexis, as well as Jeff.

If I could not find the isotope before the police found me, my daughter would lose the opportunity to clear my name.

And I would lose her.

I shook my head in disbelief and swallowed. My throat hurt.

I pulled the water bottle from my purse and tried to take a sip, but the water was appallingly bad. I spat it back into the bottle as discreetly as I could. I looked with disgust at the bottle itself, as if its contents had somehow knowingly offended me, and then sighed and cast my eyes forward. They fell upon two young women on the bus.

For some reason, I found myself staring. The women were seated together, near the driver. I was a few rows behind, on the opposite side of the aisle, and I only had a clear view of one of them. I guessed them to be about Lexi's age, but that was where the similarity between these young women and my daughter ended.

They seemed so out of place in Naples. Both were dressed in traditional Muslim garments. Their faces showed, but that was all. Black scarves covered their hair and shoulders, blending indistinguishably into the formless robes that flowed all the way to their feet. The woman seated nearest the aisle, the one most fully within my line of sight, had her arms folded demurely in front of her. I could not even see her hands; they were enveloped in her robe. I wondered if that was customary.

The women huddled discreetly, confined within their own private black hole, like two drops of oil adhering together within a pool of water. They spoke almost in whispers, their eyes directed downward. They looked and smiled comfortably at one another, but neither so much as glanced at anyone else. I found myself fascinated by the stark contrast between these young women and my daughter.

The bus stopped, and the women stood to exit. I continued watching as the one nearest the aisle gathered her floor-length robe to step forward. Her black-gloved hand poked out from beneath her sleeve like a turtle's head. For just a moment, the robe shifted to give her the freedom of movement she needed. For that brief moment, the woman's sandaled foot was exposed to the ankle.

*Open-toed shoes are OK.* Jeff's smile and his voice flashed back again from my dream.

The woman looked up and saw me staring at her. She glared. I glanced down. My eyes fell again onto the water bottle in my hand, and I suddenly understood the puzzle in the dream.

*"The Pompeii baths were heated by slaves."*

Dante's voice echoed toward me as if taunting.

*"Water would flow in from the aqueducts. Then the slaves put wood into a big heater under the floor to heat the water, and pipes carried the hot water to the baths for the Romans up on top."*

The aqueducts. Of course. Water was life. The Romans, above all others, had harnessed it. The Romans had brought the aqueducts to Pompeii. The aqueducts supplied running water to the entire city.

The infrastructural capabilities of the Romans were ahead of their time. The capacity to divert flows of water at will was one of the main advantages of their culture. The Romans could populate any area they chose. Their cities did not have to be built on a river.

And water would not only have been an advantage for city life. Aqueducts enabled agriculture at a distance from any fresh water source. The diversity of plant life available to the Romans would have been far more extensive than that of any culture that relied on immediate proximity to a river. This would have given the Romans access to the largest medicine cabinet in the ancient world.

In Pompeii I had seen, but failed to really notice, the aqueducts. As I had strolled through a lush garden in a dream, my subconscious mind disguised as my husband had been teasing me. He had teased me with the answer that had been right in front of me since my excursion to Pompeii.

It had taken the Muslim dress of two women on a Naples bus clashing so noticeably with their sandaled feet—

*Open-toed shoes are OK.*

—to bring me the answer to the riddle.

If the aqueducts were introduced to grow a particular plant, say in the enormous garden of the House of the Faun in Pompeii, then that particular plant was clearly not native to the region. It must have been transplanted there.

By whom? And from where?

*What to wear them with? Nothing too revealing. Nothing flashy. Nothing tight. You don't want to call attention to yourself. It's a different culture.*

The answer was in the one woman who held every key. The woman who had literally positioned herself in bed with the Romans and thus had acquired access to the world's leading agricultural technologies. The woman who was the only member of her dynasty to speak Egyptian—the native language of the slaves who tended her gardens.

She needed the Roman aqueducts to grow nardo because it did not grow naturally in Italy.

*The plant is Egyptian, and Egypt is where I will find it.*

I yanked the cord to signal that I wanted to get off the bus. Then I leapt from my seat and ran toward the rear exit.

A hurricane was raging through my mind.

*Shuman still needs to write his report. How long will that take? When did he start? Was he already finished before he called me? Why did he call me? Why did he forewarn me? Why would he give me an opportunity to contradict him before he turned me in?*

*Was he giving me the chance to flee or hoping I would be caught trying? Maybe his report is already turned in and the authorities are already on my trail. Maybe Shuman set me up, to make me appear even guiltier.*

I stood at the rear doors, waiting for the bus to reach its next stop. As it finally began to slow, I glanced out the windows on both sides, scanning for police. Instead, I saw a familiar face. I was immediately relieved because I knew that he could help me, as he had so many times before.

Dante Giordano was walking briskly down the street, weaving between pedestrians. He was carrying the same battered backpack I had seen him with before, and he was smiling.

"*Mi scusi,*" I said softly to a man standing next to me on the bus, and he stepped aside so that I could reach for the window. I leaned forward to tap on it and get Dante's attention. But just before I did, Dante reached an arm up to wave at someone else on the packed sidewalk.

I lowered my hand and scanned the faces of the bustling pedestrians on the sidewalk, those who were walking toward Dante. Several yards in front of him, another arm went up in the air. I gasped and clasped my hand over my mouth.

The man approaching Dante with the friendliest of gestures was Carmello Rossi.

The bus stopped, and the doors opened. Mindless of my own safety, I stepped off. As the bus pulled away, I was drawn into the street, staring. I was only distantly aware of the scores of cars swerving and honking to avoid me.

The gap between Dante Giordano and Carmello Rossi closed. I watched in disbelief as they embraced and kissed one another, once on each cheek. Then Rossi slapped Dante affectionately on the back, and they began walking, together, in the direction from which Rossi had just come.

Traffic swirled around me like a tornado.

*He set me up.*

*The whole scene on the bus. The whole scene at the police station. The whole scene at Herculaneum. Dante was soliciting my trust. And I gave it to him. I led him to Herculaneum. I led him to the poppies. I might even have led him to the nardo.*

To follow them would be to bring Jeff's killers to justice and clear my own name. But to leave them was the only chance I had of saving Alexis.

I watched them walking a moment longer. Then I turned and walked away without looking back.

"There's been a change of plan," I said. "We can't wait until tonight."

"Let me check my schedule." Aldo de Luca looked dramatically around the homeless shelter before returning his gaze to me. "What do you need me to do?"

His eyes were as cold as ever.

An hour later, I returned to the underground lab accompanied by a handsome professional in a shirt and tie. A handful of devoted scientists remained at their work, apparently uninterrupted by the earthquake—an event that now seemed to me like days rather than hours earlier.

"Is Dr. Iacovani still here?" I asked the first person I saw.

"No," the boy said. "She left a while ago." His English was perfect, but his accent was German. "I think she went back to her museum."

*Good*, I thought. *This might work.*

"Excuse me!" I said loudly, to command the attention of the scientists. In unison, they looked up from their work and stared curiously. A few drifted in from an adjacent room.

"For those I did not meet this morning," I continued, "I'm Dr. Wilson's wife. This is Inspector de Luca of the Naples Fire Department. As I understand it, he needs to conduct an inspection as some kind of post-earthquake measure?" I looked at de Luca, faking timidity. "Is this right?"

He shrugged and looked at me with irritation.

"We must check labs!" he said in a thick Neapolitan accent and then emphasized this with something unintelligible in Italian. After a moment, he returned to English to say, "*Go, go!*" He waved his hands as if to shoo the occupants from the lab like flies.

"I'm sorry for the disruption," I said, "but the Inspector needs to do this with no interference. You all have the remainder of the afternoon off. Please wrap up your efforts to the best of your abilities in the next fifteen minutes. I promise that you will have plenty of leeway from Dr. Wilson for lost work."

Two employees grinned at each other and promptly strolled out without a word. The other three exchanged frustrated looks of disbelief. One looked at his watch, rolled his eyes angrily, and threw a rack full of test tubes into the garbage. One began frantically clicking buttons on one of the beautiful new state-of-the-art lab computers. The third continued her pipetting, but at a much expedited pace.

We stepped into the adjacent lab spaces, dismissing the occupants of each. "Thank you for your cooperation," I said to them all and led de Luca into Jeff's office.

"OK, let's get started," I said.

I pulled a file from Jeff's file cabinet and showed de Luca how to scan its contents using the copier/scanner near Jeff's desk. Then I showed him how to send the scanned documents to my e-mail address. I quickly sifted through the file cabinet and generated a pile of work for him, basing the prioritization upon my own rushed assessment of the file names.

I pulled five new memory sticks from my purse, sat down at the desk, and opened Jeff's computer. It only took a moment for me to locate the secret e-mail account I knew would be there. It came up automatically when I opened his web browser. While he clearly needed ready access to the account, he also took the precaution of keeping it out of the computer systems he frequently used in San Diego. It took two tries to get the password. It was not HER2 as I had expected. The password was Katrina.

My heart was thumping as I scanned through the messages in the inbox of an e-mail account deliberately not loaded onto Jeff's iPhone. There were many, many messages from aiacovani@gmail.com. Curiosity overcame me, and I clicked on one of the recent ones. It was all business.

I memorized his username and then continued with the task I had come there to do. I clicked quickly and efficiently through Jeff's desktop and hard drive and began copying every file I could find.

Two hours later, both Aldo de Luca and I had made considerable progress, but many files and documents remained to be copied. Nonetheless, it was now 4:00 p.m., and I needed to move on.

"OK," I said. "That's it."

"That's all?" he asked, shocked that fifty thousand euros had been so easy to earn.

"That's all," I reiterated. "Just, please, look around the lab and make sure we are alone before we leave."

He did as instructed and then returned to assure me the

coast was clear. I tucked the memory sticks back into my purse, and we cautiously exited the office.

As we passed back through the facility, I found a few notebooks and flipped through their contents. For a moment, I considered taking them. But I knew that they were still needed by the scientists.

I poked around through the lab for a few more minutes before leaving. Because I knew that I would not be returning again.

As we passed through the underground tunnel toward the chapel above us, I chose my words carefully. "I know you can read people. Eerily well. So I will ask you honestly: Do you trust me?"

"Depends," de Luca answered. "What do you want me to trust you with?"

"The one hundred thousand euros I owe you."

"Go on," he said.

"I want to know if you believe I am good for it." He did not respond, so I explained further, "I want to know if you will believe me when I say that I simply can't give it to you immediately. I need all of my liquid assets for myself right now. But I promise that within a matter of days, if I'm still alive, I will set up an account for you and wire the money there."

"And if you're not alive?"

I had been expecting the question, but I still had no answer. We emerged from the tunnel and paused to allow our eyes to adjust to the light in the underground chamber of *Cappella Sansevero*. De Luca gazed for a moment at the anatomical model of the pregnant female, apparently deep in thought. Then he looked into my eyes briefly before he continued walking.

We both remained silent as we passed up the staircase into the chapel, beyond *The Dead Christ*, and through the front doors into the street. I was speechless, and he was evidently waiting for an answer to his question. When he changed the subject, I knew my silence had answered the question for him. He knew I had no idea how to pay him in the event of my untimely death. He also knew this was a strong possibility.

"Where are you going?" he asked, and I knew lying to him would be a mistake.

"Egypt."

"Why?"

"Because I have just become a fugitive. I need to get out of Italy."

De Luca stared without speaking, waiting for the rest of the story.

"And because... because that's where I'm going to find something I need to save my daughter's life."

We stood at a crosswalk in the street next to the chapel. De Luca looked me up and down for a moment in silence. When he finally spoke, I realized that I truly had no idea how to read people. I would never have predicted his response at that moment.

"*Buona fortuna*," he said, and he turned and walked away.

I watched Aldo de Luca go, and as the distance between us grew my stare in his direction became increasingly absent. I wondered if I was making the right move.

As if to answer, the familiar tri-tone of a new text message rang through from my purse. I reached inside and extracted Jeff's iPhone. On it was a text message from John.

Please hurry. The first patient just died.

And so I have come to Egypt.

I suppose that, subconsciously, I had known all along that my quest would bring me here. Two Muslim women on a Naples bus juxtaposed incongruously with a nasty bottle of Naples tap water had been the force that channeled me, like the flow through a Roman aqueduct. But in retrospect, I had actually learned two days earlier that Egypt, not Italy, was where I would find the nardo.

This answer was presented to me in Pompeii, and in Naples. It had come to me in so many ways that I could not believe I had missed it.

*How did I miss it?*

*As I stood in the garden at the House of the Faun, how did I not see it?*

Now, it was so obvious.

The last time Katrina Stone was seen, she was entering the Arab Republic of Egypt through Cairo International Airport. After that, there was just another woman in a niqab.

FOR HER ACTUAL BEAUTY, IT IS SAID, WAS NOT IN ITSELF SO REMARKABLE THAT NONE COULD BE COMPARED WITH HER... BUT THE CONTACT OF HER PRESENCE, IF YOU LIVED WITH HER, WAS IRRESISTIBLE... SOMETHING BEWITCHING. IT WAS A PLEASURE MERELY TO HEAR THE SOUND OF HER VOICE, WITH WHICH, LIKE AN INSTRUMENT OF MANY STRINGS, SHE COULD PASS FROM ONE LANGUAGE TO ANOTHER; SO THAT THERE WERE FEW OF THE BARBARIAN NATIONS THAT SHE ANSWERED BY AN INTERPRETER; TO MOST OF THEM SHE SPOKE HERSELF.

-*LIVES OF THE NOBLE GRECIANS AND ROMANS*
PLUTARCH (CA. 46–120 CE)

IF ONE TRIES TO NAVIGATE UNKNOWN WATERS, ONE RUNS THE RISK OF SHIPWRECK.

-ANCIENT EGYPTIAN PROVERB

# CHAPTER EIGHTEEN

Passing through security in Naples was the most terrifying moment of my life. And when I arrived in Egypt, I held my breath at passport control and jumped when I heard the loud strike of the entrance stamp. I approached the customs kiosk wondering if I was charging head-on into a Middle Eastern prison.

At a cash machine in the Cairo airport terminal, I drained my bank accounts, taking a moment to study the large wad of Egyptian pounds before dispersing it into various locations in my pockets and bags. I buried my passport, my credit cards, and every other form of personal identification in my possession within the depths of my luggage. Then I shut off both iPhones, with their GPS tracking features, and buried them in my luggage as well. With that, I erased my own existence.

Following the example first set two millennia ago by Cleopatra, I began creating a new identity. Where Katrina Stone had been, a new, anonymous woman began to emerge.

I inquired at an information booth for transportation to Alexandria. The lady at the booth advised me kindly and in good English that it was too late in the night to travel to Alexandria. In the morning, I could fly or take a bus from the airport or a train from the Ramses station downtown. I asked if there were hotels near the airport.

"Of course," she said. "The Cairo Traveler's Inn is just next to the airport. Would you like me to help you reserve a room?

"No, thank you," I said and smiled politely as I collected my luggage and stepped away. Because I knew that to assist me she would need my passport.

I gathered a few tourist pamphlets and maps of Cairo and stepped outside. The automatic doors had not yet closed behind me when I was assaulted by stifling heat and at least a dozen cab drivers. I struggled to think through the avalanche of broken English pelting me.

"Where you going?"

"Where you from?"

"Which hotel?"

"English?"

"American?"

"Cairo Traveler's Inn," I said, and the taxi drivers universally lost interest. They were looking for a fare into downtown.

Only one driver stayed with me. "Fifty pound," he said, and I was sure it was a considerable rip-off.

"I will give you one hundred," I told him. "But you have to wait outside for me. Do you understand?"

"*Mesh mushkela!*" the driver said enthusiastically, and then, "No problem!" But I was not convinced.

*Oh... my... God...*

Whatever chaos I had experienced in Naples traffic paled in comparison to Cairo. It was now the middle of the night, yet my taxi pulled out into traffic that was unlike any rush hour I had ever seen.

The street was about two lanes wide, but four to five cars traveled abreast at any given time. They traveled bumper-to-bumper at top speed, screeching, honking, and weaving around each other like bleating goats in a panicked herd. My taxi swerved between two cars that were not occupying any lanes I could identify, and we passed into an intersection at which eight different streets converged.

My stomach lurched. *Oh, no, not again,* I thought, as the inevitable motion sickness hit me. But then, we arrived.

After a five minute language struggle, I had to place my bags back into his cab to make the taxi driver understand that I wished for him to wait for me. With that hurdle behind me at last, I stepped inside the hotel.

"Hello," I said at the reception desk, as sweetly as I could. "I am looking for a room." I extracted a handful of cash from my pocket.

"Passport, please," the attendant said and held out his hand.

"I'm sorry," I said. "I have lost my passport traveling. I was planning to go to the embassy tomorrow."

"Driver license," he said.

I grimaced apologetically. "I'm afraid I lost all of my identification." I began rifling through the money and then extending it toward him with no attempt at subtlety.

"I am sorry, madam," he said without a glance at the cash. "We have no rooms."

It took several tries and significant downgrading of standards before I found a hotel with rooms available for a woman with money but no identification. It was in a dark alley in downtown Cairo. The staff spoke virtually no English. As I looked around the lobby, and then my room, I wondered if perhaps I should have slept at the airport.

That night, I became my dead husband.

I dropped my suitcases off in my filthy hotel room and stepped out. Now reluctant to turn on my phones for fear of being tracked, I found an Internet café just a few doors down from my hotel.

I first went into my own e-mail account and handled the pressing business from my lab in San Diego, replying to a selection of correspondence from colleagues and employees. Then I logged off and entered Jeff's e-mail account, from which I did the same.

There were two new e-mails from John. Both asked why Jeff had not been responding to his text messages and phone calls. The second message ended with: I have test results. Call me.

I stared at the message for a few moments, and it occurred to me that my suspicions of John were off base. At the very least, he had not killed my husband—John had no idea Jeff was dead.

*Unless the texts and e-mails are a cover*, my forever skeptical mind prodded me.

I clicked the "reply" button and stared at the blinking cursor for a few moments longer. Then I typed: What can you tell me about the dead patient? Autopsy? I sent the e-mail.

I finally went into Jeff's other e-mail account—the secret one he had created without my knowledge. I located the names and contact info of a number of scientists employed by Jeff to operate a new chemical biology facility in Naples. I began scanning through the correspondence between Jeff and a chemist who appeared to have the highest position.

His name was Romano Moretti. It seemed familiar. Although not a chemist myself, I was reasonably certain that Moretti was somewhat famous among his peers. I clicked into PubMed—the international database for peer-reviewed scientific publications—and searched for him. An extensive publication record appeared. I skimmed through a few of Moretti's most recent papers and saw that the majority were in the world's top chemistry journals. This was the man Jeff had hired to run the chemistry lab in Naples in his absence. Jeff had selected the best.

I e-mailed Moretti from Jeff's account. I instructed him to begin processing the mounds of samples that had appeared in the lab the previous day, although I had seen for myself that the work had already been initiated.

I paused as a thought struck me, *Was the whole day I spent collecting those samples a wild goose chase?*

I was sure I would find the nardo in Egypt, if at all. But the environment in which the isotope was produced—the soil, the air, the elements—could have been Italian. Or they could have been Egyptian. Or even Nepalese, had the nardo originated in the Himalayas. I shrugged, sighed wearily, and pressed the "send" key for the e-mail.

Just before leaving the café, I ran two Google searches. One for my own name. The other for Jeff's. No evidence of anything amiss popped up. Despite his promise to the contrary, Shuman had still not turned me in.

I stood up from the computer and paid the dark-skinned attendant. Then I stepped out again into the Cairo night.

CAESARION'S... EVERY FEATURE RESEMBLED THAT OF HIS FATHER, THE GREAT CAESAR

*-CLEOPATRA*

GEORG EBERS (1837–1898)

# CHAPTER NINETEEN

Aniqab has three layers, affording the woman wearing it three options for revealing—or concealing—her face. When all three layers are flipped backward over her skull, the woman's face is completely exposed. The first layer, when pulled down, covers her face but not her eyes. Each subsequent layer affords an additional screen. If all three layers are down, the woman's eyes are shielded completely, but she can still see out. In theory.

I quickly found that, in practice, trying to see through all three layers was like looking through a porthole smeared with black mud. A small porthole. But it was my only choice.

I learned how to wear the niqab the day before yesterday.

I awoke in a seedy downtown hotel room with something tickling my arm. Lazily, I opened my eyes and struggled to adjust them to the light filtering in through a dingy window. Finally, my vision came into focus just inches from an enormous cockroach. I shrieked and quickly sat up, simultaneously flinging my arm. The roach flew across the room and hit a wall before falling to the floor and scampering out beneath the hotel room door. I shuddered.

I shook the last remnants of sleep from my mind and

climbed out of the lumpy bed. I flipped a light switch. The light flickered and then came on with a loud hum. Several other roaches scurried out of the room or into darker corners. *I've got to get out of this shithole*, I thought.

I stared down at the two large, wheeled suitcases I had not bothered opening after returning from the Internet café the previous evening. Navigating Cairo with both of them would be impossible, so I consolidated the two bags into one and left a mountain of expensive clothing for the hotel maids. Fifteen minutes later, wheeling one bag behind me, I stepped out of the room and onto the streets of Cairo.

I didn't know any better.

Nearly every passing man who was without an accompanying woman either whistled or shouted something at me on the street. They turned a full one hundred eighty degrees to follow my movement as I passed by in my jeans and T-shirt, my long auburn hair flowing freely behind me. They leaned out of car windows. They honked at me, even more than they honked at each other.

The most common question was "Where you from?" Or simply "American? Australian? English?"

One man, from the driver's seat of a passing taxi, wondered, "Are you Egyptian?" And then declared, "I hope you are Egyptian!"

I imagined some form of international law enforcement posing questions to random passersby on the street. Everyone, but everyone, would have noticed the woman they would be describing.

I stopped walking and looked around. Every person on the street was Egyptian. There were men in khaki slacks and long-sleeved, button-down shirts. The women wore anything from niqab to jeans. Some covered their faces. Others only wrapped their hair in brightly colored scarves. Still others walked with thick dark hair flowing freely. I did not see a single light-haired person. And there were no short sleeves.

I reached up and ran a hand through my long red hair before tying it into a knot behind my head.

*I'm probably the only Western woman in all of Cairo walking around by myself right now. And these people, casually going about their business, will form a human trail that leads straight to me.*

*I need to be invisible.*

So at the first opportunity, I purchased the niqab—veil—the accompanying Arab robe called a galabia, a hijab—headscarf—and a pair of gloves. The entire ensemble was pure black.

I was grateful that the woman who sold it to me spoke no English. I had no idea how I would explain such a purchase if asked. She simply wrote a price on a piece of paper, using the numerals I know as arabic. I handed her the money and walked out, my purchase still in the bag.

*Now what?*

I hailed a taxi.

The only thing I knew logistically about Cleopatra's life was that her ancestors founded the city of Alexandria. Alexandria had been her home. It was the best lead I had.

I could don my new outfit in the Cairo train station restroom—the Ramses station, according to the information desk at the airport—and thus leave town anonymously.

"Where you go?" The cab driver looked at me expectantly.

"I need to go to Ramses Station."

"Oh, Ramses!" the cab driver said enthusiastically.

I climbed into the taxi.

A nauseating twenty minutes later, the taxi pulled into a large square. Traffic converged in three dimensions, with cars coming down from overpasses and up from tunnels to intersect with multiple traffic lanes, but I did not see anything that resembled a train station, or train tracks for that matter.

"No," I said. "Ramses!"

"*Na-am!*" he insisted, nodding. "Ramses!" He pointed to a large hotel. The Ramses Hilton.

I paid the cab driver and pulled my suitcase from his trunk. Then I stepped inside the hotel and asked how to get to the trains. The Ramses Hilton concierge looked somewhat bewildered and amused as he explained that I was nowhere near the Ramses train station. He offered to hail another taxi for me.

"No!" I said immediately and asked where I could find a Metro.

The concierge pointed across an intersection of ten streets that included an overpass. Still nauseous from the cab ride, I looked wearily across the stormy ocean of cars toward the Metro sign. I looked down at my suitcase and the shopping bag in my hand and sighed.

Feeling shackled to my baggage, I stepped toward the streets. My eyes were drawn to a woman in niqab. With one black-gloved hand, she held a large basket steady on top of her head. Her other arm was looped first through a medium-sized handbag and then through the arm of a small child. Her galabia dragged the ground, and I wondered how well she could actually see through the veil. I would soon find out for myself: not very well.

The woman stepped out into an intersection that was an undulating sea of cars. Yet, the woman and her child appeared protected by some kind of supernatural force field as they walked slowly and nonchalantly between the cars and somehow miraculously reached the other side of the intersection unscathed.

I stepped out into the traffic with my eyes closed.

Somehow, I made it across.

I approached the Metro station the Hilton concierge had indicated. But then I stopped short, fervently scanning my surroundings. I realized that the area I stood in was familiar.

In early 2011, the period that would later be termed the "Arab Spring," this very spot had been the focus of every international headline. I was in *Midan Tahrir*—Cairo's "Freedom Square"—the gathering place for the thousands upon thousands of Egyptian protestors who would set the stage for the revolutions throughout the Middle East.

At one end of the square was a large red building. I knew from the events of the Arab Spring that within it was the information I needed.

I smiled and stepped confidently toward the Museum of Egyptian Antiquities.

I checked my clunky suitcase at the ticketing building outside of the museum but kept my purse and the shopping bag containing my new clothing. Just inside the museum's entrance was a small gift shop. I purchased a guidebook for the museum and two travel guides for Egypt. I dropped the travel guides into the shopping bag and began flipping through the museum guide as I approached the security line.

The museum was not air-conditioned, and it was packed.

It was sweltering inside. Sweaty tourists in shorts and tank tops fanned themselves with brochures while Arabs in long robes flowed like black water around them, apparently unaffected by the heat, many casting disapproving glances at the skimpy Western clothing.

I approached the metal detector. Observing the people passing through it before me, I noticed that they almost invariably set off its alarm. Yet, the security officers waived them through anyway.

When I stepped through the detector, it remained silent. I was unsurprised, with nothing on my person except clothing, books, and my wedding rings. The guard waved me through, and I walked into the museum, searching my guidebook for directions to the Greco-Roman exhibits.

As I turned a corner, something made me glance back at the security guard. He was speaking to another guard. He pointed in my direction. Suddenly cautious, I increased my pace slightly, hoping the change in demeanor would go unnoticed. In my peripheral vision, I could see the guard. He was approaching me. I closed the guidebook and dropped it into my shopping bag.

My eyes began darting around me. There was very little signage either on the exhibits or indicating directions for the museum. The guard was proceeding more quickly in my direction. I thought I saw another behind him, following in his footsteps.

I turned another corner and almost smashed into a large group. Behind me, men were yelling in Arabic. A sea of shiny, straight black hair spread out before me, and I could hear a museum guide chattering in Japanese. Panic began to consume me as I realized just how easily I would be spotted in this crowd.

Desperately, I scanned the room, looking over the heads of the Japanese tour group. I breathed a sigh of relief when I spotted a sign reading "W.C."

I rudely shoved past a few of the Japanese tourists and dashed into the restroom. There were only three stalls and two sinks, but at least twenty women were stuffed into the tiny space. The musk of far too many bodies was heavy, and the restroom itself was filthy. Two women who appeared to be custodial staff sat, immobile, on chairs next to a basket for tips.

Standing nervously in line for a stall, I kept my eyes trained on the entrance to the crowded restroom. The guards did not come bursting in after me. I turned to watch as a young woman adjusted her hijab in front of the mirror. My eyes took in the details of how it was pinned, neatly and decoratively around her skull. I had never before noticed the intricate layering of such a garment. It appeared to be somewhat of an art form.

*Shit*, I thought. I had not even known to purchase pins for my own hijab. And I had no clue how to affix it.

I approached the woman. "Do you have any more of those?" I asked, pointing to her head. She looked confused, and I pointed again, nearly touching her head, while she looked into the mirror to see the location of my finger. I pulled a fifty pound note from my pocket. Understanding dawned, and the woman reached into her purse. She pulled out a small case full of tiny straight pins and exchanged it for my money.

I returned to my former place in line. While I waited, I looked around at some of the other women in the restroom. I noticed several different styles of wearing the Muslim clothing and felt a bit relieved. If there was freedom in the way the pieces were worn, I could probably pass.

A moment later, I was inside a claustrophobic restroom stall and sweating profusely. It was easily well over a hundred degrees Fahrenheit in a space smaller than an airplane restroom. I pulled the long black galabia out of its bag and over my head, careful to avoid a pool of unidentifiable liquid on the floor. The flowing folds of the garment enveloped my purse, still affixed to one shoulder, and the shopping bag I had slung over the other.

I wrapped the hijab onto my head and pinned it the best I could, struggling to envision the way the woman before the mirror had been wearing hers. Then I added the niqab, all three layers down. Finally, I donned the black gloves. I felt like fainting. I had never been so miserably hot in my entire life.

I emerged from the stall, struggling to adjust to a new standard of vision through the screens over my eyes. I did my best to observe the other women in the restroom. None of them seemed to notice me, or to have registered my transformation. The woman who had sold me her hijab pins was already gone.

I further adjusted my clothing with the benefit of the mirror, until I convinced myself that what I wore could pass for an acceptable form of the Muslim woman's fabric origami. Then I stared at my reflection for a long moment. The bags hanging beneath both of my arms were unrecognizable as such, but they made me appear much chubbier than I actually am. I scrutinized the woman before me in the mirror as objectively as possible. I could find no trace of Katrina Stone.

Three security guards were standing outside of the women's restroom as I emerged within a cluster of niqabis.

"*Marhaban*," one of the guards said and nodded courteously.

"*Ahlan wa sahlan*," answered one of the women without looking up. The other women were silent.

The guard said something else to the women in Arabic. His

tone and inflection suggested a question. The woman who had initially spoken offered a one word answer, shaking her head gently, and then passed by.

Behind and alongside her emerged a steady stream of women. Some were completely covered. Others wore hijab, but their faces were showing. Still others were completely exposed.

None of them had long auburn hair and blue eyes.

The combination of adrenaline and merciless heat was manifesting as a flu-like alternation between fever and chills. My knees were weak, and I hoped I was not visibly swaying in my step as I passed within mere feet of the three guards waiting for me by the restroom door. I concentrated on holding my breathing steady.

I knew without question that Larry Shuman had turned me in and I was now being hunted. My last known location, the location recorded by my passport and visa at entry, was Cairo. The tunnel vision induced by the niqab seemed to narrow even more as I walked briskly yet casually—I hoped—out of the museum.

A light breeze struck me. It felt like heaven. I habitually reached for my iPhone to check the weather. Then I remembered that both my phone and Jeff's were now in a suitcase that had been sacrificed indefinitely to the Museum of Egyptian Antiquities. I had no earthly possessions except the clothes on my back, the contents of my purse, a few guidebooks, and a dwindling supply of cash.

On the street, I flipped up the top two layers of the niqab in order to pass through several lanes of traffic. That was when I began hearing the word *zuro*.

The first instance was from a street vendor.

I ducked down an alley and found myself in a small open market selling everything from questionable-looking fish to questionable-looking handbags. At a small stand selling jewelry, I pointed without speaking at a watch that had the correct time and was ticking. The vendor rattled emphatically in Arabic as he pulled down the watch for me to examine. I donned it over a black glove and handed him a few Egyptian pounds. He was still half shouting at me when I walked away, and I wasn't sure if he would follow me and demand more money. But he didn't.

The only word within his rant that I caught, the only word he said more than once, was *zuro*.

I looked around for a quiet corner devoid of other people. There appeared to be no such thing on the streets of Cairo. *I'm going to be spending a lot of time in restrooms*, I thought and entered a McDonalds.

Safely inside a stall, the one place I could think of that afforded privacy, I lifted up my galabia and withdrew a guidebook from the shopping bag. In it I found a subway map. *God bless*, I thought, upon discovering that the Metro connected easily with Ramses Station, which, of course, was nowhere near the Ramses Hilton.

On the way out of the McDonalds, I heard the mysterious word *zuro* again from a man at one of the tables. On the street, I was sure I heard it again from a passerby mumbling to his friend. And when I bought a subway ticket, I was positive the ticket vendor was referring to me when he said it. So on the subway, I asked.

I was pleased to find Metro cars designated strictly for women, and I wearily sat beside a kind woman who had moved over to offer me room. She explained to me the meaning of the word *zuro*.

"Do you speak English?" I asked.

At first the woman looked surprised, and she surveyed me up and down in my black Muslim ensemble as if she had just been spoken to by a passing bird. I realized with dismay that this would be the reaction of anyone with whom I tried to communicate in American English. "Little," she said, her accent heavy.

"What is *zuro*?" I asked. "What does that mean in Arabic?"

"Eh, how to say?" she said, half to herself, and then she said something in Arabic to the woman beside her.

"It is color," the other woman offered, her accent heavy as well. "Blue. Like your eyes." And she pointed through the open slit of my niqab.

So the other two niqab layers came down, their screens like two layers of heavily tinted glass. But even with total physical invisibility, I felt exposed. I was now an Egyptian Muslim with no understanding of the religion, culture, or traditions I should have been taught from birth. And to maintain anonymity, I could not speak. In any language.

The Cairo train station was in shambles. The entire station was under construction—yet business as usual appeared to be taking place.

Stumbling like a drunk, I tripped over construction rubble, the two bags on my shoulders banging awkwardly at my sides like the prodding heels of a rider on a horse. I searched for a ticket window through the veil. *Do women actually get used to these?* I wondered, fighting the urge to pull back the niqab.

"Alexandria," I said in a muted voice at the ticket window. The ticket seller gave me a strange look and rambled in Arabic for a moment, but I was relieved to see a ticket emerge through the window. I passed him some money. He handed some of it back.

"Alexandria?" I asked of an elderly woman who was clearly not law enforcement. She looked at my ticket and pointed me vaguely to the left, also rambling in Arabic.

"Alexandria?" At the first fork in a road paved with construction rubble, I was waived onto a platform.

"Alexandria?" A woman standing on the platform nodded. I hoped she was right.

Nobody looked at my ticket until the train had been under way for nearly an hour. During that hour, I hoped fervently that I was really headed to Alexandria. Over the course of the two-hour train ride, I read. I devoured the introductory history and the Alexandria-specific portions of my new Egypt guidebooks. And I came to realize I had just made a terrible mistake.

There is virtually nothing left of Cleopatra's Alexandria.

The library itself is gone—I had already known as much. But what I hadn't known was that Cleopatra's palace, her gardens, her army's fleets—*everything* associated with her reign—had long since gone, literally, into the sea.

It was all under water. And unlike the earthly samples I had obtained from beneath the sea in Naples, this time I had no hope of retrieving what I needed. There was no way I would find any trace of a living plant underwater that had been surviving above ground in her day. I had reached a dead end.

I buried my face in my hands and cried.

I had just failed my daughter.

*It is our third night together in Paris.*

*"I have a daughter," I say. I tell Jeff the story of how my daughter's teenaged fanaticism had been a driving force in my decision to stop working exclusively on anthrax, how it had led me increasingly to cancer research.*

*"I thought that cancer would be a safer career path," I explain, and then Jeff asks me the question I have been dreading since I first spoke to him two days ago.*

*"Is Alexis an only child?"*

*I take a deep breath. "She is now," I say. "I had a son. I lost him eleven years ago. He was murdered."*

*I reach across the table and squeeze his hand briefly, and then I stand and excuse myself to the restroom, having learned that this is the best way to allow my news to sink in. And to give my new love interest the way out that he needs.*

When I return to the table, *I think,* he will have received an emergency phone call in my absence and he will need to regretfully cut the evening short.

*At least I will have gotten it over with quickly.*

*I remain in the restroom much longer than necessary, perfecting my makeup and my hair, giving my date time to absorb the death of my son. Then I return to the table.*

*Jeff immediately takes my hand. "Listen, Katrina," he says, squeezing gently. His hand is warm and strong. "I'm really, really sorry to hear about your son."*

*"It was a long time ago," I offer, glancing down at my lap.*

*"I know," he says. "But it's a part of you now."*

*I nod.*

*"To be honest," he says, "I am a bit embarrassed that I*

*didn't know how to respond. As for myself, I have never been married."*

*I wonder, How can that be?*

*"I have no children," he continues, "although..."*—*he pauses for a moment*—*"I would have liked to, I think. And I can't imagine how it must feel to lose one."*

*"To be honest," I say, "it is unbearable. My daughter saved my life. Without her, I don't know how I would have survived."*

The train arrived in Alexandria, and I was numb as I gathered my belongings. Suddenly, the world was gray. I walked with no direction, and, some time later, I arrived at a rocky beach. Before me stretched the Mediterranean Sea. I stared across the water.

A crescent-shaped strip of land was jutting out to my left, forming a small bay. At the crescent's very tip protruded Fort Qaitbay. I remembered the large castle from the guidebook I had been reading on the train. Fort Qaitbay stood at the site of the lost Alexandria Lighthouse—the creation of the Ptolemy kings and one of the seven wonders of the ancient world.

*What a shame. Everything falls to time.*

The Fort Qaitbay castle reminded me of *Castel dell' Ovo* in Naples, also perched at the very tip of a jutting piece of land, also surrounded on all sides by water, as if it, too, could easily topple into the sea at any moment. I remembered having jumped from *Castel dell' Ovo* into the Bay of Naples, terrified of the man who turned out to be an unlikely ally. Aldo de Luca. The man carrying a message for me from my dead husband. `Trust nobody. Her 2.`

I was standing on the Corniche next to a large open green space. I had read about this area on the train. I was in *Midan*

*Saad Zagloul,* the site at which Cleopatra's Needles—two enormous obelisks—once stood. Of course, they too were now gone.

Cleopatra had erected the obelisks as part of her Caesarium, a tribute planned for the deification of Julius Caesar, and of her son with him, Caesarion. The Caesarium was to be built in this very square. But she died before its completion. The Caesarium was finished by Octavian after he became Emperor Augustus.

As I recalled this, something clicked. I glanced out again at Fort Qaitbay, and then I turned to look behind me at the square. Beyond it were modern buildings, buildings that had been erected where the ancient library of Alexandria once stood. The lighthouse would have been visible from the library, and vice versa.

The lighthouse. The library. The Caesarium. All three lost to time.

But in my mind, the three ancient monuments appeared before me in all their grandeur, and I felt a chill through the warm Mediterranean air. Because I suddenly knew what I needed to do.

"I'm sorry, Jeff," I said aloud.

I stepped across the square and into a pharmacy, where I purchased a bottle of sleeping pills.

# PART III: IMMORTAL

Fool! Don't you see now that I could have poisoned you a hundred times had I been able to live without you?

-Cleopatra (69—30 BCE)

There is another building, too, that is highly celebrated; the tower that was built by a king of Egypt, on the island of Pharos, at the entrance to the harbour of Alexandria. The cost of its erection was eight hundred talents, they say... The object of it is, by the light of its fires at night, to give warning to ships, of the neighbouring shoals, and to point out to them the entrance of the harbour.

-Natural History
Pliny the Elder (23—79 CE)

# CHAPTER TWENTY

Trust nobody. Her 2.

Trust nobody. Her 2.

*The lighthouse. The library. The Caesarium. The Caesarium. The library. The lighthouse.*

*The world's largest, most renowned library. The world's largest, most renowned lighthouse. Within line of sight of each other. Both built by Cleopatra's ancestors.*

*The Caesarium. A shrine to her son.*

"I'm sorry, Jeff," I said again through the fog as I nodded off to sleep.

⌒⌒

*There is an underground chamber. Within it burns an eternal flame. Above it burns a tribute to light—to light, coming from darkness.*

*There is Enlightenment.*

*There is a gentle rolling, like the rocking of a ship floating out to sea.*

⌒⌒

*There is a gentle rolling, like the rocking of a ship floating out to sea.*

*I awaken.*

*A light is shining down upon me. I reach forward.*

I awoke.

I reached forward. I parted a curtain and watched the swaths of green rolling past me. Beyond them were mounds of desert sand.

"Luxor," I heard a voice call, and I retrieved my galabia from the rack above the bed. I was rocking back and forth as I dressed, my legs unsteady from the constant motion of the overnight train, my head cloudy from the sleeping pill.

The early morning light was pouring in through my open curtain.

The train slowed to a halt, and I stepped off.

Rarely in my life had I felt an innate biological need like the one I had for food that morning. As I sat salivating in a Luxor café, with the glorious scents of Egyptian cooking surrounding me, I realized just how little I had eaten the previous day.

The overnight train from Alexandria had served a miserable excuse for dinner. I had only taken a few bites while poring over my guidebook before reading a section of the book specifically about Egyptian food. The book warned, with a bit of ironic humor, that Western visitors to Egypt are almost certain to be sick from the food at least once during their stay. It then specified that food on overnight trains between Upper and Lower Egypt should be avoided at all costs. So I had put down my fork, feeling a bit nauseous, and instead popped a sleeping pill.

The food surrounding me now could have come from a different universe than that on the train. Tantalizing piles of eggs, meats, beans, cheeses, breads, and fresh fruits graced the tables near me, and at first, through force of habit, I tried not to stare at other patrons' plates while waiting for my own gluttonous order. But then I realized it did not matter. They could not see me watching them. My face was completely covered.

Through the distraction of my rumbling stomach, I observed the tables around me, and I noticed something. In this café, unlike on the street, there were very few women in niqab. Apart from myself, there were only two: one was accompanied by a man, and the other by a man and two children.

I suddenly understood why I had been seated in a back corner of the restaurant. We all were.

Women with exposed faces, whether alone or in groups, were seated at the central, more public tables in the dining hall. The other niqabi and I were given the best seclusion that the restaurant's dining room could afford us—the corner tables. Grateful that they could not see my gaze, I glanced back and forth between the other two women as it suddenly occurred to me that I had no idea how to eat in the outfit. Or if custom even allowed it.

When a waiter brought food to the table of the couple, I was happy to see two plates. The man moved his chair slightly closer to the woman's left side, shielding her as best he could from the open dining hall. Her right side was close to the wall, and she mostly faced into the corner. When she flipped the niqab upward on the right side only, the side of her face nearest the other patrons was shielded by the veil's other half and by the man. And so she began to eat.

The ritual vaguely reminded me of my own experiences, more than two decades ago, breast-feeding my infant daughter in public.

*What a cruel, bizarre path my life has taken since then.*

Over the front door, a TV was mounted to the wall. Footage of bombed-out buildings and angry, fist-shaking protestors was accompanied by an anchorwoman in hijab and a line of squiggly Arabic script marching backward across the screen, to be read from right to left. I stared absently up toward it through my veil as I chewed my food, deep in thought.

Cleopatra's ancestors built the largest library the world had ever seen. They demanded that all ships docking at Alexandria surrender any books on board. Not treasures. Not gold. Neither incense nor myrrh. Books. And they used them to populate that library, which they kept to themselves.

Near the library, they built a lighthouse, one so magnificent it would become known as one of the seven wonders of the ancient world. With the light it emitted, the Ptolemies drew the ships to Alexandria like spiders casting a web across the sea. And then they pirated every single book—every single piece of intelligence—from the victims they ensnared with their lighthouse.

*I'm sorry, Jeff,* I thought again. Because I had every intention of following the example of the Ptolemies. And to do so, I needed to deny my late husband's final wish. I needed to trust somebody.

It was yesterday that I learned how to eat in niqab.

After the meal, feeling remarkably refreshed, I took a deep breath and laid down my fork. I briefly considered the possibility that I had never enjoyed eating a meal so much in my life. Then I headed, once again, to the private sanctuary of a restroom stall and consulted the contents of my purse.

My euphoria was short-lived.

My hands began to shake as I withdrew a pair of ticket stubs, stiff from having been soaked with seawater. As I mentally reconciled the two parts of the phone number once again, I was reminded of the last time I had seen Dante Giordano. He had been kissing the cheeks of the man who had tried to kill me. I took a deep breath, held it, and closed my eyes. The shaking of my hands subsided.

There was a small phone booth near the restroom. I stepped inside and dialed.

"*Buon giorno*," a familiar voice said a moment later.

"How would you feel about a free trip to Egypt?" I asked in my most playful tone.

"Are you kidding?" He laughed. "Where's the plane?"

"There's a catch," I said. "I need you to bring someone with you. I've lost her number, but you can track her down in the Egyptian section of the Naples Archeological Museum. Her name is Alyssa Iacovani. And, Dante, please tell her I need her to bring the original document and its translation. She will know what I'm talking about."

"Wait a minute," Dante said. "I get to tour Egypt with *two* women? What did you say the catch is?"

Even across the miles, his laugh was infectious, and I almost believed in his innocence.

*Be careful, Alyssa*, I thought as I stepped out of the phone booth.

I slowly passed between the tables of the restaurant, cautious not to bump into anything or anyone.

As I approached the exit, I felt my smile fade into a frown. How badly I had misjudged Alyssa. I had come to Italy on a pre-conceived notion that she was, or was somehow connected to, Jeff's murderer. And that she and my husband had possibly been lovers. How mistaken I was.

She had lost her husband, too. She had lost her entire family.

I could have believed Alyssa guilty of murder if there had been an illicit affair between her and Jeff. She could have been motivated by passion gone awry, by jealousy of me, or by scorn if he had changed his mind and dumped her. But there was no such motive. I had read private e-mails between them. Their relationship had been strictly professional. She had solicited his help as a scientist, and as a scientist he had offered it.

Why, then, would she kill him before the mystery she had solicited that help for was solved? There was no reason. She wouldn't. It didn't make sense.

I had nearly made an enemy of an ally, one Jeff had trusted. His message to me—"Trust nobody. Her 2"—clearly could not have been a reference to Alyssa.

I wondered again what my husband had meant by his message.

*Was he referring to Alexis? Was he warning me that the cancer ransacking his body had infected her, too?*

And then suddenly, there he was before me.

I halted in my tracks. For a moment, I stood motionless in the middle of the restaurant's dining hall. Then I felt myself start to sway on my feet. With trembling hands, I clutched the nearest table, which mercifully was empty. I sat down quickly and hard on the chair beside it. And I continued to stare.

On the TV over the door was a full-view, still image of Jeff. I watched in disbelief as the image changed to a newscast.

*What is he saying?* I wondered desperately as the news anchor rambled in Arabic, the image of my husband now confined to a small corner of the screen.

The screen changed again, and this time it was my picture on the TV. I did not need a translator to understand what the image meant. Jeff's body had been found, and now I was wanted.

I glanced around the restaurant.

*They can't see you. They can't see you. They can't see you.*

I mentally repeated the words over and over, struggling to remain calm and, more importantly, to stay in control of my breathing. I tried to envision myself at this moment from an outsider's perspective, sitting in this café in my black niqab, black hijab, black galabia, with bags at my sides that made me look chubby. Nobody would ever guess that I was the woman on the TV. I had to believe that.

I glanced around the café again and saw a few patrons looking up at the TV nonchalantly, but none appeared to pay much attention. I felt myself calming.

*It's OK. It doesn't mean anything. Except what you already knew. You knew Shuman would turn you in. Now he has.*

Then the image on the screen changed again, and my breath caught in my throat.

My stomach protested in a sickening gurgle, and the ominous paragraph from my guidebook about Egyptian food and Western stomachs came back to me. Trying not to imagine the act of vomiting while dressed in niqab, I closed my eyes and swallowed hard. The moment passed.

I looked back up at the TV. The image now on the screen was one quite familiar to me. It was a laboratory. But this particular laboratory had been ransacked. A few reagent bottles appeared to have crashed to the floor, but, in general, the wet lab spaces themselves were intact.

The break-in had focused on the offices. Computer cables lay like severed limbs across barren desks where the machines and monitors had been. File cabinets were gutted, their drawers yanked out, their contents strewn about wildly.

I instantly recognized the office that the camera had focused in on. It was Jeff's. It was not the office space in Naples, which I had personally invaded with the help of Aldo de Luca. The burglarized office now on the screen was Jeff's office in our building in San Diego.

The news camera panned through the office space, and I recognized one of the file cabinets. One of its drawers was open and tilting downward, just inches from teetering off its tracks and out of the cabinet. Where its collection of files had been, there was now just a large empty space.

It was the drawer that had contained Jeff's files for our secret HER2 project.

From the heights of these pyramids, forty centuries look down on us.

-Napoleon Bonaparte (1769–1821)

# CHAPTER TWENTY-ONE

WHY DID THE GODS SPARE THE WOMEN THROUGH MAGIC PLANTS? IS IT BECAUSE WOMEN DO NOT MAKE WAR, AS MEN DO? IT IS NOT FOR US TO KNOW, BUT IN THOSE FOUR, IT WAS AS IF THE CRABS NEVER EXISTED.

I tore my veiled eyes away from the television screen and glanced quickly around the café one last time. Its patrons appeared engaged in their own conversations, their own meals, their own lives. Nobody seemed to notice that the woman sitting near them was the American murder suspect being talked about on the TV. I stood and walked as nonchalantly as possible out of the restaurant.

I strolled down the Corniche along the Nile, with the final three sentences of the nardo document mocking me.

HER2 is a breast cancer gene. While its presence has been confirmed in tissue other than breast tissue, and its relevance in other types of cancer has been explored, the effectiveness of HER2-targeted medications was demonstrated in a subset of breast cancers, the subset with the highest quantities of HER2.

The patients that had benefited from the nardo's effect were all women. I had assumed this to be merely an experimental artifact—an error—because the women and men were housed in separate rooms of the hospital, and only the plants near the bedsides of the women had been observed by the document's author. One woman had noticed a change in the plant and then reached forward to touch it. The other three and their caregiver had quickly followed.

*Damn it!*

I had no way of knowing what had—or had not—taken place in the other room, the room housing the men. Were there nardo plants at their bedsides? Or were those in the women's room only there as a feminine gesture? Assuming the men *did* have a nardo plant next to each bed, did the same phenomenon strike those plants as well? Did the men simply fail to observe it? Did they lack the interest of the women—the need to reach out and touch the plants during that transient moment? Or was the phenomenon ineffective on their diseases? One thing was certain—the men had not been spared. The document clearly stated as much.

~~~

Trust nobody. Her 2.

The text message was a warning, on so many levels. The HER2 gene itself, to a frustrated scientist, epitomizes the double-edged sword. HER2 treatments are toxic. They can lead to cardiac malfunction. The oncologist must perform the precarious balancing act of freeing his delicate patient from the cancer while not murdering her with a heart attack.

*Could I be on the wrong track with HER2? Could Jeff be warning me not about the gene itself but about duplicity? Could the latter half of the text simply be underscoring the former? Reminding me that someone I'm inclined to trust might be exactly that—a double-edged sword? A wolf in sheep's clothing?*

*John.*

I found another Internet café. This time, my story ranked Number One among trends on the web.

I clicked into one of the news videos.

"A world-famous biotechnology company in San Diego, California, has been robbed, and its husband-and-wife owners are both missing. Security was breached at Collisogen Research, and the theft of large quantities of research data has been reported. The co-founders of Collisogen are prominent scientists Jeffrey Wilson and Katrina Stone. Wilson and Stone, who serve as the company's chemistry and biology department heads respectively, have both disappeared..."

I clicked out of the newscast and then scrolled through several more stories. My racing heartbeat began to slow, and my breathing became steadier. There was no evidence that Jeff's body had been turned in, or that I had been reported by Larry Shuman. But authorities were seeking any information concerning our whereabouts.

An unrelated news story detailed the emergence of a new, aggressive form of pancreatic cancer, to which three patients had now succumbed worldwide.

My face felt hot beneath the niqab.

With trembling hands, I clicked into Jeff's secret e-mail account.

There was a response from Romano Moretti, the Naples chemist Jeff, and now I, had employed under the table, on conditions of secrecy. Moretti asked no questions about the publicized disappearance of his employer or his wife.

Instead, he simply offered the latest lab results. Moretti and his team had spent the previous day completing the processing of the biological samples that Alyssa and I had collected. They had found nothing of interest.

There was no response from John.

*Please hurry. The first patient just died.*

The message had come in two days earlier.

*He has dozens... maybe even hundreds of patients...*

Now, there were two more deaths.

Which meant that additional deaths within the cluster of cancer patients John had been treating were now imminent. And that Lexi may have very little time left as well. Perhaps, so did I.

I felt sick again.

The Luxor sun was already nearly unbearable. Even at five in the morning when my train had arrived, I had stepped out into a hot, sweltering Upper Egypt. Now, at seven thirty, I was certain the temperature was already well over one hundred ten or even one hundred twenty degrees. There was no hint of a breeze.

It was to be my first full day in a black galabia and niqab, and I knew that I could not possibly travel through Luxor and Thebes without a car. In addition to the prohibitive heat already upon me, I had learned from my guidebooks that the sites I needed to visit were spread too far apart to walk, even in the most pleasant of circumstances.

I glanced again at my watch, as if seeing the time again could help me plan my next move. Assuming that Dante had found Alyssa, the two of them would now be traveling to Luxor from Naples and could not arrive before evening. But with my daughter's tortured wails pushing me forward, I could not afford to lose an entire day of research, especially now that I knew what to look for to help her. So instead of a pagan theologist and an Egyptologist to help me, I had an Egyptian tour guide.

I figured I had two choices: hire a taxi or take a tour. Either way, I would be speaking to someone. In English. I decided it might as well be an English-speaking tour guide rather than another taxi driver like the one in Cairo who accidentally drove me to the wrong location. Or worse, one who might do so deliberately.

I took a deep breath and walked into the office of the nearest tour agency and announced through my veil that I needed a tour of Luxor.

The agent at the desk appeared surprised but then complied with my request. "Would you prefer a woman, madam?" he asked kindly.

"Yes, please," I said, and a wave of relief washed over me. It had only then occurred to me that I was about to drive out into the Egyptian desert with a complete stranger.

As it turned out, I felt perfectly safe. My tour guide was a friendly middle-aged woman, and a young British couple was my only other company on the tour. The driver did not speak to us, but the tour guide occasionally spoke to him in Arabic.

The air conditioning felt like heaven, and the van itself was surprisingly new and comfortable. As we rolled gently out into the desert, I found myself lulled into a surprising sense of calm. My ingrained intellectual curiosity, coupled with the research nature of the task at hand, almost made me forget my reasons for being there.

I found myself marveling at the landscape. The greenery along the banks of the Nile was stunning. As we followed a frontage road parallel to the river, I tried to pick out different species of plant life that I knew. Some, like the many giant palms lining the road and the river banks, were the same species popular in Southern California. Other plants were unrecognizable to me.

The river itself coursed through a shallow trough, flowing northward from mountainous Sudan, thus leading to the counter-intuitive designations of *Upper Egypt* in the south and *Lower Egypt* in the north. The green trough containing the river met harshly with steep low cliffs on both sides, above which there was only desert. The Nile was a swath of verdant green cutting through a vast sea of brown.

The desert was unlike any I had ever seen. Having driven on numerous occasions through the California and Arizona deserts, I was familiar with deserts containing cacti, snakes, scorpions, and other heat- and drought-tolerant life forms. In contrast, this desert appeared to support no life at all; there was only sand. Dune upon dune of absolutely uninhabitable sand billowed away forbiddingly from the lush, life-giving Nile. The stark and abrupt contrast between the two landscapes was breathtaking.

Our tour guide broke the ice by asking the three of us if we had seen the pyramids. The British couple, who at first seemed a bit afraid to speak to me directly, nodded. I shook my head and lied. "I'm afraid I haven't been to Cairo yet. I will be heading up there after Luxor."

The young Brits looked as shocked as the woman on the Cairo Metro had when I had asked her the meaning of the word *zuro*. The tour guide, who knew I had requested an English-speaking guide, was prepared. She continued speaking. "The Old Kingdom built pyramids," she said simply. "The ancient Egyptians believed in resurrection. They built pyramids to help their kings find their way to the heavens. They built them in the west because the sun sets in the west. The east was for birth, and the west was for death, like the birth and death of the sun every day.

"But the pyramids kept getting robbed. So by the time the New Kingdom came and the pharaohs moved to Upper Egypt, they finally said, 'No more pyramids. Pyramids get robbed. This makes the gods very angry.'

"So they built the Valley of the Kings. They buried their kings underground instead, where nobody could find them. But they were *sneaky*." The middle-aged woman smiled at the British woman. "This time, they built the tombs under a rock that is shaped like a pyramid. That way, they could still send their kings to the heavens, but they could also fool the robbers."

Our van pulled into the entrance of the Valley of the Kings, and I immediately recognized the rock she had mentioned. The tall pyramid jutted out of the sand as if it had been carved there. But it was a natural formation. Had I not been looking for it, I would not have noticed it. The rock blended right into the desert.

"Your ticket is good for three tombs," my guide said, and she motioned to a man at the entrance, who brought her a packet of postcards. "You can't take pictures inside," she explained, "but you can buy these if you want." She began flipping through them to demonstrate to us what to look for inside the tombs. As she began pointing out the various gods and goddesses on the walls, I cocked my head when she pointed to an image of the goddess Isis.

"Whose tomb is that?" I asked.

I carefully scanned the reliefs within Merneptah's tomb,

dumbfounded.

*These tombs were each built and decorated during the reign of the pharaoh,* I recollected from the tour guide's monologue. *In most cases, that was only a matter of a few years.*

I recalled an international episode that had taken place almost fifteen years prior. A mine had collapsed in Chile, trapping thirty-three miners. It took months to extract them through the rock, and the survival of all thirty-three men was considered nothing short of miraculous. A brand new rock drill was pioneered in the rescue effort, and a variety of space technologies designed by NASA were incorporated in the process—both to keep the miners alive and to subsequently bring them to the surface.

These tombs were built through labor alone, more than a thousand years before the birth of Christ. The effort that must have gone into burrowing into this rock was scarcely fathomable to my modern mind.

And then there was the art work. Every square inch of the tomb was not only painted, it was engraved and then painted. And that was just the surviving art after three thousand years. I tried to imagine how these walls had looked during the time of the pharaohs. I tried to imagine modern technology, modern artists, modern methods creating the reliefs before me. I could not do it.

The image of Isis drew me into the tomb.

I would learn that day that the goddess Isis was everywhere in ancient Egypt. She graced the walls of nearly every temple, every tomb, every shrine. She was easy to recognize because she always looked the same. I desperately wanted to understand *why*—because the patron goddess of Cleopatra, the Egyptian goddess of medicine, never looked anything like I had expected. And this discrepancy was frustrating my search for the medicine that could save my daughter.

She came to me again in the Valley of the Queens. She presided over the tomb of Nefertari. The same Isis, so different than the one I had imagined.

*Alyssa, I wish you were here to explain this*, I thought, and then I remembered what I needed to do before her arrival—and Dante's.

I stepped out of Nefertari's tomb, and my attention turned to my modern surroundings rather than the ancient ones. I was shocked at how quickly and easily I formulated a plan for something I never would have thought I could do.

Luxor was vastly different from Cairo. In Cairo, I had seen tourists only in the Egyptian museum. There were none walking the streets except for me. Luxor, in contrast, was like a theme park. Hordes of tourists poured from buses and filtered through tombs like ants through the tunnels of a child's ant farm.

And, inevitably, with the tourists came the touts. Children and adults alike peddled postcards, small statues, miniature pyramids, T-shirts, and very expensive bottles of water. Men in long galabias and women in headscarves offered maps of the tombs and personal tours. Many of them spoke remarkably good English.

Several pairs of uniformed, armed police stood guard over the tombs but afforded tourists no protection from those seeking to take advantage.

I watched as a pair of dark teenaged boys followed a group of tourists toward a tomb. The taller of the two boys motioned toward a handsome thirty-something man wearing jeans and a polo shirt. The second boy smiled, and I stepped forward to follow from a distance as they approached the man and his young family. As the family stepped into the crowded queue to push forward into a tomb, the tall boy accidentally bumped the man as he passed, offering a shy apology. The shorter boy then stepped away from the crowd with a hand in his pocket. And I knew that the handsome thirty-something man had just lost his wallet.

I had just found my accomplices.

The two young pickpockets had resumed their duties selling sheesha pipes when I approached their makeshift booth. An older man and woman, who might have been their parents, were sitting on boxes in a small recess of shade provided by the tables.

I began examining one of their pipes with feigned interest, and the shorter boy materialized before me. "Four fifty," he said.

"I'm sorry? Four hundred fifty Egyptian pounds?"

The boy shook his head. "American dollar," he said with a smile that was missing a few teeth, and I laughed.

I set the water pipe back down. "You've got to be joking, kid."

"OK, three hundred. Two fifty! Two fifty!"

"Two fifty Egyptian," I said, and the boy looked as if he was considering it. Egyptian pounds were worth one fifth the value of American dollars.

"Let me ask you a question," I said then, and the taller

boy approached to involve himself in our conversation. "How long does it generally take you to make five thousand Egyptian pounds?"

The tall boy frowned. "This is tourist time," he said. "Uh, *sayf...* summer. We make a lot of money in summer."

"Still," I said. "Five thousand. How long?" It was the equivalent of one thousand American dollars. A lot of money by any standards, but possibly more money than these children would possess in their entire lifetimes.

The boys did not answer. I glanced at the older couple still sitting nearby and lowered my voice. "I have five thousand Egyptian pounds for you here," I said, and to prove my sincerity I held out the money for them, letting them touch it, letting them imagine how it would feel in their hands. "But I need you to do something for me. And you will do it because, if you don't, I will put an end to your *real* business." Without warning, I snaked a hand forward and yanked the stolen wallet from the shorter boy's pocket.

A few moments later, the two boys disappeared inside the crowded tomb of Queen Nefertari, easily the most popular tomb in the Valley of the Queens. Within a few moments of that, a commotion arose that led a few tourists, mostly with young children, to rush out of the tomb. But considerably larger numbers forced their way inside.

As if on cue, one of the uniformed policemen stood upright and stepped away from the tall jutting rock he had been leaning against. He motioned toward his partner and then toward the tomb. The partner approached it, turned and waved at his superior, and then stepped inside.

Within minutes, the shorter of the Egyptian teenagers

emerged. He walked nonchalantly over to his sheesha stand, which I had since vacated. I waited for a few moments and then wandered over toward a smaller, less populated tomb. I stared toward the tomb from the outside, and I could feel the boy's presence as he walked up beside me.

"Did you get it?" I asked without looking at him. I opened my gloved hand just enough for him to see the money within.

Wordlessly, the boy took the money and replaced it in my palm with the heavy, cold metal of the uniformed officer's pistol.

Back in the tour van, I asked my guide about the Greco-Roman period. She laughed.

"Everyone comes to Egypt looking for Cleopatra," she said. "They are all disappointed. We know so little about her.

"After the New Kingdom fell in 1070 BCE, there were almost eight centuries of—how do you say?—big mess in Egypt. Other countries invading. No government. Big mess. Alexander the Great and the Ptolemies, Cleopatra's family, they stopped the big mess.

"The Egyptians accepted them. They accepted them because the Ptolemies acted like Egyptians. The Ptolemies made government again. They ruled like pharaohs ruled. And they built temples to Egyptian gods."

This statement seemed to contradict what I had learned from Alyssa. *The Ptolemies built hospitals, not temples. They followed empirical evidence, not superstition.*

Now it appeared that they built both. *Why?*

"Why did they do that? Surely, they didn't worship the Egyptian gods? They were Greek!"

She looked impressed. "You're right!" she said. "They were

Greek! But, they acted like Egyptians. And this is how they ruled the Egyptians. The Ptolemies understood that people want to make *their* gods happy, but not other people's gods. If you appeal to the gods of the people, the people listen to you. To make their own gods happy.

"After Cleopatra, the Romans brought Christianity to Egypt, and the Arabs brought Islam. And all of this brought back big mess. Nobody can agree on which gods to make happy. Big mess is still today.

"Where are you from?" she asked me.

"America," I said, and she looked puzzled.

"You're Muslim?"

I was prepared for the question. "My husband is Egyptian," I said.

"Then you speak Arabic? You asked for English tour."

"No, I'm afraid I don't speak Arabic," I said.

Beneath her pastel-colored hijab, she frowned in confusion. And as her natural curiosity about this unusual tourist in her charge took hold, I began to realize I had made a horrible mistake. Whereas in Cairo I had been totally out of place in jeans and a short-sleeved shirt, and especially with my auburn hair flowing freely, now I was almost out of place in traditional Egyptian dress. In Luxor, there were shorts and tank tops, sundresses, and giant hats to offer pale flesh some protection from the unrelenting sun.

I should have taken off the niqab. I should have purchased a huge touristy hat and a large pair of sunglasses and done my best to conceal my face. I should have done anything but pretend to be Muslim. Because now, I was enmeshed in a line of questioning I had no idea how to free myself from. If I answered incorrectly, she would know I was a fake. And that might lead to my undoing.

"Then how do you read *Qaran?*" she finally asked. "It can only be read properly in Arabic."

How could I have known that the Koran is supposed to be read in Arabic? How could I have known that a language I did not speak would be the one triviality that could blow my cover? Of course, I could not have known, but with every answer to this friendly, curious tour guide's questions, I began to feel more and more as if I were digging my own tomb.

"My husband and I haven't been married very long," I said. "I only recently converted to Islam. I still need to learn Arabic in order to properly learn the Koran." I hoped it was an acceptable answer, but I was now feeling as if I were under a microscope. *Should I have already learned Arabic in order to convert to Islam?* I began sweating, even in the air-conditioned van.

"And your families accepted your marriage?" she asked.

"Yes. I agreed to convert to Islam."

"What were you before?"

"I was raised Catholic, but mostly I was an atheist. I didn't have any religion."

The woman shook her head. "Everyone should have religion. In my country, religion is from your family. It is who you are."

"Yes," I said, hoping to dig my way out. "I look forward to learning my husband's religion."

Then she asked the question I had no answer for. "But why you take Luxor tour without him?"

Of course, at that moment the benefit of hindsight came to me. It was far too late. I realized at that moment that I had seen many, many veiled women in Egypt since my arrival and that not one of them seemed to be out sightseeing alone. I had seen them with husbands and families at the various tourist attractions I had visited. I had seen them with husbands and families in the restaurant that morning. I had seen them with groups of other women. But I had not seen a single woman who was out alone for a seemingly frivolous purpose.

*God, please, let us arrive at the next stop*, I thought. Through the veil, I looked eagerly out the van's window, wondering how far away we still were from wherever we were going next.

I wasn't sure whether my friendly tour guide was still waiting for my answer, or if she had given up and was now mulling over our conversation. Perhaps she had already concluded that the woman before her was lying through her teeth. Perhaps she thought I was hiding from an abusive husband. Perhaps she thought I was hiding from something else.

Or perhaps she thought I was the missing American woman on the news. Perhaps she thought she should say something to someone.

The British man in our small tour group broke the uncomfortable silence. "I read a story a few years back about Cleopatra."

"Do tell!" his wife practically shouted, evidently dying for a change of subject.

"Do you know the legend about Cleopatra and the pearl?" he asked, speaking to his wife but also glancing around the van.

"Of course!" his wife said. "She bet Mark Antony that she could spend some exorbitant amount of money on one dinner. To do so, she dropped a pearl into her drink and then drank it! I always thought that was a myth."

"*Everyone* thought it was a myth," the man said. "Well,

the ancients took it for fact, but in our time we all assumed it was impossible. A few years ago, I read this article. Someone proved it! A researcher at a university actually did the experiment and proved that Cleopatra could have dissolved a pearl in vinegar under the appropriate conditions."

"*No!*" The wife said in disbelief. "How?"

"According to the researcher, it doesn't take anything but vinegar and a pearl. Cleopatra might have softened the pearl first using some other technique we still haven't figured out yet."

The man laughed and threw an arm around his wife but then looked at my veiled face. He addressed me directly for the first time. "I bet you didn't know Queen Cleopatra was a chemist."

Cleopatra was busied in making a collection of all varieties of poisonous drugs, and, in order to see which of them were the least painful in the operation, she had them tried upon prisoners condemned to die.

...

Some relate that an asp was brought in amongst those figs... Others say that it was kept in a vase... But what really took place is known to no one. Since it was also said that she carried poison in a hollow bodkin, about which she wound her hair; yet there was not so much as a spot found... nor was the asp seen within the monument.

-*Lives of the Noble Grecians and Romans*
Plutarch (ca. 46–120 CE)

# CHAPTER TWENTY-TWO

It is amazing how even the most discerning eye can miss something obvious. And it is humbling when that discerning eye is one's own.

I had heard the story of Cleopatra and the pearl many times. And I remembered reading the Discovery News article back in 2010 when her pearl cocktail was scientifically proven possible.

There was another age-old legend having to do with the manner of Cleopatra's death. The legend held that she had committed suicide by enticing a snake—an Egyptian asp—to bite her. But this interpretation has been deemed impossible. It was not only Cleopatra who died a mysterious death that day but two of her female servants as well. Even if the snake could have been enticed to bite all three of them, no asp carries enough venom to kill three full-grown women.

The more accepted interpretation of their deaths is that Cleopatra self-administered some form of poison, also dosing her handmaidens with the same toxic formula. I even vaguely recalled having heard that she had studied various poisons beforehand to select those most effective and least painful.

*I thought Alyssa was crazy*, I remembered, reflecting upon our conversation in the Naples Archeological Museum. *I thought her hypothesis that Cleopatra had been some sort of physician or research scientist was outrageous.* I realized now that Alyssa's notion was not only plausible but, in fact, the most realistic interpretation of everything we have always known about Cleopatra.

As my tour van rolled across the Nile to the East Bank of Luxor, I thought about Raimondo di Sangro, the first man to attempt chemically unwinding the scrolls recovered from the Villa dei Papiri.

Like Cleopatra, di Sangro developed and utilized scientific methods, including specific solvents, that have baffled scientists for centuries. She dissolved a pearl to win a wager. He dissolved the marble of his own tomb to etch his epitaph. Cleopatra's chemical mystery was only solved in 2010. Di Sangro's has yet to be solved.

Di Sangro took his technologies to the grave.

*Did Cleopatra do the same?* I wondered. *Could she have destroyed her own records before her death?* The existence of the nardo document was proof that she had not. Perhaps she only wanted her enemies to believe that she did.

But di Sangro left behind proof of the existence of his methods: the chemically etched tombstone, the "anatomical machines"—human corpses mysteriously embalmed using beeswax and God knows what else.

He left behind a code for the enlightened to follow. My mind's eye saw again the statues in his chapel, the self-written legacy of Raimondo di Sangro. *The Veiled Christ*, a symbol of eternal life. *Disillusion,* the figure emerging from a binding net, a symbol of enlightenment. Light from darkness—a symbol of knowledge—like a grand lighthouse illuminating an even grander library. The veiled statue entitled *Modesty*—a symbol of wisdom. It was a clever representation of a veiled Isis, strategically placed in the exact location formerly occupied by a statue of the goddess herself in a Temple of Isis.

*"Nature loves to hide,"* Modesty's veiled figure had been saying.

*And that is why Alyssa became a follower of di Sangro,* I recalled. Alyssa believed she had traced the nardo document from Cleopatra to him. And she was now trying to trace it forward in time to the present. To herself. To the veiled threats she had been receiving since its discovery. And to the code Cleopatra may also have left in plain sight for the enlightened—the code that would lead to the isotope.

*How far has she gotten?* I wondered.

She had been trying to tell me. When we were interrupted by the earthquake, she had gotten as far as the elder sister of Marie Antoinette, the woman in possession of the papyrus scrolls when Naples was invaded by Napoleon Bonaparte.

I needed to know the rest.

I glanced again at my Cairo watch. It was 1:00 p.m. Alyssa and Dante would not arrive in Luxor for several more hours.

*What did Isis teach you?* I asked Cleopatra, not realizing I was about to embark upon the first lesson.

The first ancient plant life I found was at Karnak Temple.

A relief on the wall at the Karnak Temple Complex depicted a large, diverse botanical garden. The relief dated to the Syrian campaigns of the pharaoh who had built that section of the temple fourteen hundred years before Cleopatra ruled Egypt.

I purchased several disposable cameras from a tout at the temple entrance and began taking photos of as many specimens as I could find. Some of the species looked like ordinary lilies, some like shrubs, and some like palms. Others looked as if they could have been grown in outer space. I had no idea how accurate they were. But it hardly mattered, as I had no idea what a nardo actually looked like.

I was in Luxor Museum when I saw the next plant the ancient Egyptians had deemed important enough to immortalize. I would have completely missed it. The plant was disguised.

This image had also originated in Karnak Temple. The scene was of a person making an offering to the sun. The sun's rays pointed down in straight lines at all angles from the large yellow globe, like those in a child's drawing. But the tips of the rays were hooked, and it was sheer luck that I was standing next to an English-speaking tour guide as he explained why to his group.

"The sunbeams are depicted as a papyrus plant," he was saying. "Papyrus was sacred to the ancient Egyptians and became the symbol of the Old Kingdom and the area we now know as Lower Egypt. Not only was the material used to make paper, a process dating back as far as 4000 BCE, it was also used to make rope, boats, and many other things the Egyptians relied upon to live."

*Papyrus.* I found myself tilting my head in an effort to visualize the sunbeams upright, as the plant would have grown. Then I shrugged. Aside from the interesting fact that the Egyptians have been making paper for six thousand years, I could find no real relevance to my quest in the image of the plant.

*Is it significant that the papyrus is represented as the sun?* I wondered, thinking again for a moment about the metaphor of light from darkness. It was certainly possible. Every piece of knowledge passed down in writing for thousands of years was owed to it.

"Did the Egyptians have an understanding of the distinctive properties of various plants, like the papyrus?" I asked the museum tour guide. "Or did they just take advantage of plants that were abundant?"

"They had a strong understanding," he said. "And they *decided* which ones were abundant. The Egyptian leaders strictly controlled what crops were grown throughout their kingdoms."

*So the most important ones*, I thought, *were probably the most abundant.*

As we exited the museum, my Luxor tour came to an end. I bid an awkward farewell to the nice British couple and to my tour guide. And I hoped that they would keep their mouths shut.

Again, I checked Jeff's e-mail. And again, there was no response from John. It was now early morning in San Diego.

*John abruptly fell out of touch just as our San Diego laboratories were burglarized and Jeff and I were both declared missing*, I realized. *Was he the one who reported us missing?*

*Or was he the one who broke into the lab?*

I wondered what Jeff had hidden within the files of our HER2 project. And I wondered if our physician friend could benefit from it.

Of course, there was also another possibility. There was the possibility that John had found the item that Jeff had been killed for and that he, too, was now dead.

I watched through my niqab from a distance as Dante Giordano stepped out of a taxi in the small Luxor square. He was alone.

He sat down at an outdoor table of the café I had described to him over the phone.

I waited for fifteen minutes.

Dante appeared to grow increasingly agitated. He looked around the square. He looked at his watch. He leaned over and asked a passerby a question. The man shrugged and replied and then walked away.

Finally, I walked over to the café. I sat at a nearby table, but I faced the opposite direction. I unfolded an Arabic newspaper and pretended to read it.

*Right to left, back to front,* I had to remind myself.

When Dante extracted his cell phone, I could overhear his conversation. It was animated and sounded emotionally charged. But it was also in Italian. I could not understand a word.

Eventually, he stood up, took a last look around, and left the café. When I was reasonably confident he would not notice, I left the café as well and followed at a comfortable distance.

Dante looked lost. I was not surprised. He had come to Egypt on a moment's notice for the sole purpose of meeting with me, and I had not shown up. I assumed he was now wondering what to do with himself. I was curious to see what Dante Giordano *would* do with himself when he did not know anyone was watching.

He walked the streets for quite some time, scanning the hordes of tourists out and about in Luxor. He paused to step into a small souvenir shop, and when he stepped back out he was examining a large fold-out map. He found the waterfront and walked along the Nile, still scanning the crowd.

*You won't find me,* I thought.

He entered another shop, and this time a man followed him out. The man gestured toward a street corner, rambling in Arabic. Dante smiled and nodded, thanking the other man in Italian. Then he approached the corner and sat down.

He was sitting at a bus stop. And I knew it was time to move in.

When I knelt down to peer into his face, Dante looked up in shock. Instinctively, I leaned in toward him to whisper, but the effect was the opposite of what I had intended. He gasped audibly and lunged backward as if a large spider had just dropped from the sky to dangle before his eyes.

"Don't react," I said as quietly as I could, and his eyes widened again. Then he seemed to relax. He peered inward as if trying to see the eyes behind my veil. I could feel other eyes upon me as well.

"Katrina?" Dante said softly.

"Let's go," I said and stood up to leave, gathering the folds of my galabia and straining to see through the mud-caked porthole of my niqab.

"Where's Alyssa?" I asked as we walked.

"Katrina…" he said. "She…"

Just like that, I knew.

"She's dead, isn't she?"

"I went to the museum like you said," Dante said quietly. Tears had welled up in his eyes. "I couldn't find her, so I asked around. I found someone who worked with her. They said she had been shot and killed in her apartment."

My chest was constricting and I was struggling to breathe. I sat down on a swath of grass running along the bank of the Nile.

I saw Jeff lying dead and naked on the deck of my yacht. I saw a bloody, smeared handprint on a metal banister and a pistol silencer lying next to his body. Now Alyssa, too, had been killed in her own home. And for what? For a two-thousand-year-old message on papyrus? A message that—according to Alyssa—nobody even knew existed except for him, her, and me?

"*Oh, God,*" I groaned, wondering if I had been her undoing, if I had guided her murderer toward her, if I had offered her up as a sacrifice just as I was now offering myself. And with Alyssa dead, my odds of finding the answers I needed had just become exponentially smaller.

I looked back at Dante but then had to look away.

"Katrina?"

I slowly came back to attention, with no idea how long I had been sitting there lost in thought.

"Yeah?"

"Why are you dressed like that?"

I took a breath. I had to tell him something. But I did not have to tell him everything.

"Because I think someone is after me," I said. "And because the best case scenario is that it's Middle Eastern law enforcement."

I paused and then continued, "That's why I wasn't able to meet you at the café earlier. I thought I was being followed. I was planning to call your cell again, but then I ran into you at that bus stop. Were you planning on leaving Egypt?"

Dante shrugged. "Uh, yeah, I guess so. I didn't know what else to do. I thought you stood me up." He smiled with a sincerity that made me question, just for a moment, if he could really be a killer.

A moment later, I bolted upright.

"Oh, *fuck!*" I said inelegantly.

Dante smiled with relief. "That's my girl."

I leapt up from my position in the grass, nearly falling back down as I tripped on the long galabia. I surveyed the area around us for police, or worse.

I grabbed Dante's arm and jerked on it as if I could physically lift him. "We need to go!"

Following my lead, he stood abruptly and quickly dusted off his jeans.

"Where?" he asked, but he was already following me down the street, jogging for a few paces to catch up with me and then slowing to the same brisk walk I had adopted.

"What's wrong?" he asked.

"I bought this outfit to get out of sight in Egypt. At first, it seemed to work. Then I received a crash course in fundamental Islam, and I learned that I stood out anyway just by being alone. At least, by being alone, touring ruins, and speaking English.

"Now there is a new reason that I stand out—you and I your typical Egyptian couple do not currently make."

Without speaking, Dante removed his backward baseball cap and tossed it into a sidewalk garbage can as we walked. Now, he understood. But he was still probably the only man in Egypt wearing a sleeveless shirt, covered in tattoos, and escorting a woman in niqab.

I HAVE COME TO BE A PROTECTOR UNTO THEE. I WAFT UNTO THEE AIR FOR THY NOSTRILS, AND THE NORTH WIND WHICH COMETH FORTH FROM THE GOD TEM UNTO THY NOSE. I HAVE MADE WHOLE FOR THEE THY WINDPIPE. I MAKE THEE TO LIVE LIKE A GOD. THINE ENEMIES HAVE FALLEN UNDER THY FEET. I HAVE MADE THY WORD TO BE TRUE BEFORE NUT, AND THOU ART MIGHTY BEFORE THE GODS.

*-Egyptian Book of the Dead*
FUNERAL CHAMBER SPEECH OF ISIS

# CHAPTER TWENTY-THREE

The pair that stepped out of the Luxor tourist bazaar might have been a typical American mother and grown son on vacation. Both wore nondescript blue jeans and black sneakers. Both wore long-sleeved, loose T-shirts of neutral colors. And although the relentless Egyptian sun was now finally subsiding for the day, both wore wide-brimmed hats and sunglasses. A passerby would not have paid notice to either of them.

I was now a brunette. A highly capable seamstress at a dilapidated fabric store had questioned her understanding of my English when I asked her to shear off more than a foot of my hair. And then I ducked into a public restroom and dyed the remaining shoulder-length locks while Dante waited patiently outside.

As I slipped into the body of a stranger once again, I also forced myself to slip into the mind of a different woman. A woman who had not befriended a man she now believed was involved in her husband's murder. Because I needed him.

"So what now?" Dante asked when I emerged from the restroom.

"Luxor Temple," I said, pointing to the massive ruin adjacent to the bazaar.

"My original plan was to meet you and Alyssa here and not at the café," I told Dante as we passed through the temple's entrance. "But I have come to learn in no uncertain terms that I stand out in a big way touring ruins by myself in Egypt—no matter what I am wearing..." I trailed off when I noticed that he was not listening.

His neck craned backward, he was gaping upward at the massive colonnade of pillars we were walking through. His expression was sheer awe.

When his gaze returned to me, he was smiling. But then he frowned. "Come here," he ordered abruptly and led me out of the main temple.

We passed back through the colonnade and approached the two formidable rows of sphinxes lining the street that led to the temple. The enormous man-cats bore expressions of duty, of loyalty, of power.

The entire area surrounding the temple was sealed off to prevent unpaid visitors, but a crowd naturally congregated at the temple itself. As we progressed along the avenue of sphinxes and away from the temple entrance, the crowd thinned. Panic began to consume me as he led me farther away from other people.

The pistol, stolen from a Luxor policeman, was in my purse. I had thought that I would not need it until Dante and I were alone. And now we were, and I was unprepared. I tried to appear casual as I slipped a hand into my purse to feel for the weapon.

Dante leaned in toward me, and I shrank back as if from a predator. But he merely asked me a question. "Why are you here? And tell me the truth. I've just traveled for a whole day to a country I know nothing about because you asked me to. I was happy to do it. But if you don't tell me why, then I came here for no reason. Don't you agree?"

I looked up at him, and for a moment I did not answer. This was my last chance to back out. My last chance to make up some other answer, something to send him away rather than drawing him in. But I knew I had already crossed that line. I crossed it the moment I first saw my husband's corpse and decided to conceal his murder.

So I slipped into bed with my enemy, just as Cleopatra had married her two brothers in succession before having each of them murdered. The bait used by the Ptolemies was the lighthouse. With it, they lured their enemies into bringing knowledge to the Ptolemaic library. My bait would be that knowledge.

"OK, Dante," I said. "Remember what I told you back in Pompeii? I told you that I'm looking for an ancient plant called a nardo. It appears that under some very rare circumstance this plant can produce a cure for cancer. It is the reason my husband was killed. It is also the reason I'm now in danger. And I think the plant originated here in Egypt. I also think it was discovered by Queen Cleopatra during her era as the New Isis, reigning queen and goddess of medicine.

"So I called you and Alyssa to help me find it. I called Alyssa because she was an Egyptologist and I am not. I called you because I need a male escort and because I know you are an expert in pagan theology, another area where my knowledge is severely lacking.

"Without Alyssa, this search will be much, much harder. But I know plant biology, and I know how to make medicines. Together, you and I can find the right plant. And hopefully we can also figure out why that cop Rossi was trying to kill us for it."

*And if I have to, I will kill you both before bringing the iso-tope to my daughter.*

We walked slowly back toward the temple and the crowd, my purse heavy with the weight of the pistol.

Dante appeared deep in thought.

"I went to Alexandria," I told him. "I saw the site where the Caesarium once stood."

"Yeah?" Dante asked as if wondering what I was getting at.

"It was Cleopatra who started building the Caesarium, the shrine to her immortalized lover, Julius Caesar, and their son, Caesarion. But then she committed suicide, specifically to escape death or enslavement at the hand of her mortal enemy Octavian. And guess who completed the Caesarium?"

"I give up," Dante said.

"Octavian."

"What the hell?"

"You heard me." I paused for a moment to allow Dante to assimilate this information, and then I continued. "Dante, I can only think of one reason why Octavian would have immortalized Caesarion after effectively killing his mother. He wanted something Cleopatra had, and he failed to obtain it when he failed to capture her. So he wooed her son."

"Didn't he later kill Caesarion, too?"

"Yep."

Another pregnant pause.

"So, if you're on the right track," Dante said, "then maybe he killed Caesarion after discovering that Caesarion didn't have what he was looking for either."

"That's exactly what I'm thinking. Otherwise, it doesn't

make sense for him to deify the kid one day and kill him the next."

"I still don't follow. What does that mean? And why are we in Luxor?"

"Because Cleopatra had three more children."

Dante smiled broadly, and I knew that he now understood.

"Your plan is to find the plant by examining the temple art," he said. "The reliefs, the hieroglyphs, the colonnades." It was not a question.

"Exactly. I have every reason to believe that Cleopatra may have left a code in plain sight, something only the enlightened can understand. I think that, between us, we have enough knowledge of her and her patron goddess to understand it. Cleopatra's past can tell us where the nardo came from. Her future can tell us what became of it. Her ancestors and her children will help us solve this."

"And that's why you need me."

I looked up to search for menace in his eyes but did not find it.

We re-entered the colonnaded temple. As we strolled through its vastness, taking in the thousands of years imprinted upon its walls, I was reminded of the mythical scenes imprinted upon Dante's skin. *What do they mean to him?* I wondered.

I glanced up at the tops of the pillars and noticed something. They had been carved into a shape I had seen earlier in the day. I pointed toward them. "Dante, look at that."

He craned his neck and looked up toward where my finger was pointing.

"It's papyrus," I said. "The entire colonnade was carved to look like rows of papyrus stalks. I found out this morning that papyrus was the symbol of the Old Kingdom. It symbolized Lower Egypt."

I stared up at the papyrus colonnade for a moment longer and then returned my attention to Dante. He was gazing at a relief of a figure. My eyes followed.

It was Isis. She was admiring a plant in a vase. It was not papyrus.

For a moment, I focused in on the plant. It was tall and slender, and its flowers were pointed at the tips. Spiky.

*Spikenard?*

I withdrew from my purse one of the disposable cameras I had purchased earlier in the day and snapped a few photographs. Then I returned my attention to the figure of Isis.

She wore a long sheath dress and a crown from which two large horns protruded upward with a slight inward curve, like those of a bull. Between them rested an orb. In one hand she held a symbol I had seen before but could not recall the meaning of. In her other hand was a staff. The staff touched the ground, but Isis did not appear to be leaning on it. Instead, her arm was extended toward the plant before her as if she were reaching for it with the staff.

I glanced between the plant and the figure of Isis for a moment. Then I asked Dante the question that had been burning in my mind all day. "Why doesn't she have wings?"

Dante jumped as if I had startled him, and blushed slightly. Then he turned to me. "Huh?"

"Why doesn't this Isis have wings?"

He looked at her again as if he hadn't noticed. "Um, I don't know. Isis is sometimes represented with wings and other times not."

Apparently not understanding the weight of my question, he elaborated on something else. "Her crown is the horns of Hathor," he said. "Isis is often associated with the cow goddess Hathor for many things, fertility and motherhood, reincarnation. The sun disk between the horns is also from Hathor. The ankh she holds represents eternal life."

*Of course*, I thought, remembering di Sangro and his eternal flame.

"The papyrus scepter is a symbol of the gods or of power—"

"But what about the wings?" I asked again.

Dante shrugged. "Why?"

I cast my mind back to that day at the Louvre, my second date with Jeff. I closed my eyes, and for a moment I could smell the scent of his cologne and the wooden walls of the Egyptian rooms. I saw the sarcophagus. I saw the winged Isis.

"I saw an image of her," I explained to Dante. "She had wings. Her arms were outstretched like this"—I stretched out my arms to show him—"and, with the wingspan behind her, she looked like a caduceus. A medical staff. Medicine, Dante. I can't help think that *this* is the Isis that we want to find. We need one with a plant. Where is she?"

Dante suddenly paled. "*Vaffanculo*," he said under his breath. "I can't believe it. You're right. I don't know how I missed it, but you're right. Isis was one of the only Egyptian deities with wings. The wings symbolize wind, and the wind symbolizes healing. It's from the original legend of Isis and Osiris.

"The legend is that Isis used her wings to fill Osiris' mouth and nose with air, giving him life. This was after she put all his parts back together, of course."

"Sorry, what?"

"Oh. Isis brought Osiris—her husband—back to life after he was murdered by the god Seth. When Isis and Osiris married, they ruled Egypt. Seth was jealous, so he murdered Osiris and cut him up into fourteen pieces, which he then scattered across Egypt. Isis found every part except for Osiris'... uh..."

He appeared to forget the appropriate word, so he instead gestured toward his own genitals, blushing.

"Penis?" I asked.

"Yes," he said sheepishly. "Isis couldn't find the... *penis*... because it had been eaten by a crab."

**I HAVE IN MY CHARGE THE CARE OF TEN, ALL STRICKEN WITH THE PLAGUE OF THE CRABS.**

**ALL TEN OF MY CHARGES HAVE FAILED THE SCALPEL AND THE FIRE DRILL. THEIR TUMORS CONTINUE TO GROW. THE CRABS CONTINUE TO DEVOUR THEM.**

"Eaten by a crab?"

"Yeah," Dante said. "Eaten by a crab. Isis put the rest of her husband back together anyway and then used her wings to breathe eternal life into him."

"So her wings are associated with her ability to restore life," I said.

"Yes," he said, now with conviction. "You find the winged Isis and you will find what you're looking for. And I know where to find her.

"In Aswan is the largest Temple of Isis built in the ancient world. It was built by Cleopatra's ancestors. And it bears the only image I know of in which a winged Isis presides over some form of plant."

The sky had grown dark, and it became increasingly difficult to make out the reliefs on the temple walls. As I stood staring again at the mysterious plant beheld also by the goddess Isis, I suddenly realized I was straining my tired eyes to see. I blinked, and a tear of exhaustion came to each. I could delay the inevitable no longer.

"Dante, I need you to get me a hotel room."

He looked at me with a raised eyebrow.

"I have no clothing except for what's on my back, an Egyptian galabia, and the rest of the touristy stuff we bought today. I also have no identification, and even if I did I couldn't use it. I spent last night on a train, and the night before that in a hotel so nasty I woke up with a cockroach on my arm. I need a good night's sleep. If you can use your ID to get me into a hotel room, I'll pay you back in cash and with interest."

"No problem!" he said and quietly chuckled for a moment at my summary of the last two days of my life. "And if you don't have tons of money on you, you can pay me back any time. Or, not at all. I don't care. I know you have lots of money—or, at least, you did once—but right now you seem pretty much at the end of your rope. Just... you have a friend. Don't worry. We'll figure it out."

I glanced across the street, away from him.

We checked into adjacent rooms, and, as soon as my door was closed and locked behind me, I dug into the bottom of my purse to retrieve the pistol. It was fully loaded. At first, I placed it on the nightstand and lay down for a few minutes on the bed. Then a door slammed somewhere in the hotel, and I jumped.

I got up from the bed and carried the pistol with me into the bathroom.

Instead of calming me down, a rushed shower only heightened my sense of nervousness. I repeatedly reached out of the shower for the gun, every sound convincing me that Dante was breaking into my room. The Temple of Isis in Aswan was where the answers were. I needed Dante Giordano no further. And I was all too aware that he no longer needed me either.

After dressing once again, I poked my head cautiously out of the door of my room. Dante's door was closed, and a "Do Not Disturb" sign hung from the doorknob. I quietly stepped out and tiptoed down the hall.

I found the concierge in the lobby and requested the use of a computer. There was still no mention of Jeff's death in the news. He and I were still being reported as missing persons, which meant that Larry Shuman had still not turned me in. And, evidently, Romano Moretti was also still keeping his silence.

From Jeff's account, I e-mailed Moretti, a scientist I had never met but upon whom my daughter's life now depended. I asked him to include the papyrus plant in his studies, to determine whether some element contained within it could somehow have produced the Vesuvius isotope.

There was still no response from John. I e-mailed him again. In the subject line of the e-mail, I typed two question marks. The body I left blank.

That was last night.

You see me here, Lucius, in answer to your prayer. I am Nature, the universal Mother, mistress of all the elements, primordial child of Time, sovereign of all things spiritual, queen of the dead, queen also of the immortals, the single manifestation of all gods and goddesses that are. My nod governs the shining heights of Heavens, the wholesome sea breezes, the lamentable silences of the world below. Though I am worshipped in many aspects, known by countless names... some know me as Juno, some as Bellona... the Egyptians who excel in ancient learning... call me by my true name, Queen Isis.

-*THE GOLDEN ASS*

APULEIUS (CA. 123—180 CE)

# CHAPTER TWENTY-FOUR

When I awoke this morning, I went back down to the hotel lobby and accessed the computer, happy to see the "Do Not Disturb" sign still hanging from Dante's door. My latest e-mail to John had been returned as undeliverable, with a message that his inbox was full.

But I—rather, Jeff—had already received a reply from Romano Moretti, who had been able to locate an online vendor of live papyrus. He had placed a rush order.

His group had also completed the chemical analyses of the biological samples Alyssa and I had provided him. Aside from an almost uniformly high concentration of sulfur, to be expected from their proximity to the volcano, the samples had not yielded anything unusual. Moretti was seeking advice regarding additional work on those samples, as he appeared to have arrived at a dead end.

I quickly realized that abandoning Dante for a second time would be futile. We would both be heading to the same place—the Temple of Isis in Aswan. And to leave Dante now would possibly also blow my cover, to admit that I knew the truth about him and Rossi. So instead, I knocked on his door and told him I had made arrangements for our transportation to the temple.

I had signed the two of us up for a van tour from Luxor to Aswan. The tour would take us through Esna Temple, Edfu Temple, and Kom Ombo Temple en route to Aswan. The Temple of Isis at Aswan would be the final attraction.

We learned on the tour that the plant we had seen the night before was a lotus.

The plant we had seen being examined by the goddess Isis at the Luxor Temple was the symbol of *Upper* Egypt. To the ancients, the lotus complemented the papyrus, the symbol of Lower Egypt. And it was everywhere.

I was amazed at the sheer number of times the lotus and the papyrus appeared together. They graced the walls of every ancient monument, their stalks intertwined, their leaves kissing. The lotus and the papyrus. The papyrus and the lotus. But no nardo.

The goddess Isis was everywhere as well. She always looked identical to the image we had seen in Luxor Temple. And she never, ever had wings.

The Temple of Isis at Aswan is located on the island of Philae. The boat taking us to the temple made a semi-circle around the island to reach the entrance, which is located on the far side of the island relative to the Aswan shore. I was able to take in the vast ruins from a distance before the boat docked and the temple was upon me.

I stepped off the boat and looked up at the monument. Though it was quite a distance away from the dock, it seemed to tower just over my head, so large in relation to the island itself that it almost appeared as if the temple could topple right off the land.

As we disembarked from the boat, a gathering of touts converged upon our tour group. Just as I had seen in Luxor, they offered T-shirts, miniature statues, postcards, and other assorted souvenirs. Their Arabic and English chatter swirled hazily around me as I looked up at the temple. When a particularly persistent woman in niqab took my hand and laid a roll of paper into it, I paid no attention.

"This is map of ruin," she said in heavily accented English. "It will help you find what you are looking for."

Absently, I reached into the pocket of my jeans and handed her a small handful of change. "Thank you," I said, without tearing my eyes from the temple.

At the temple's entrance was a large relief showing Ptolemy XII, Cleopatra's father. Beside him stood his family, including the young princess, Cleopatra. According to a guide leading a small group through the temple, Ptolemy XII had been the last ruler to significantly add to the temple. His contributions could be found throughout the temple, but the majority were focused within the inner sanctuary at the far end.

Dante and I headed there at a brisk pace, noting as we went the thousands of years of history and myth sprawled before us. We passed next to a smaller temple, colonnaded as Luxor Temple had been. As at Luxor Temple, the colonnades were carved to resemble papyrus. We passed through a larger such temple. Papyrus colonnades again. We passed by a seemingly infinite number of Isis reliefs. All of them wore sheath dresses. All wore atop their heads a crown of the horns of Hathor with the sun disk in the center. Most carried an ankh or a staff. None had wings.

We passed row upon decorative row of ankhs, aligned with each other in perfect grids. We passed a low relief resembling a picket fence. Slowing for a closer examination, I saw that the image was actually an alternating pattern of papyrus and lotus plants.

We continued forward.

At last we approached the inner sanctuary, and the vast, open, colonnaded spaces were replaced with a series of progressively smaller enclosed rooms. As we passed from one into the other, I noticed that their walls and ceilings became increasingly adorned with birds in flight. Flocks of soaring birds gradually replaced the ankhs and plants I had seen in the outer spaces. Their flight patterns pointed from doorway to doorway as if always leading the way into the next room.

As we followed their path into the depths of the temple, the spaces surrounding us became noticeably darker and much, much cooler. The brilliant Egyptian sunlight, formerly beating down mercilessly, was now filtering in gently through a scattering of small windows. Through them, I could at last feel a gentle breeze wafting across the island from the Nile. It was as if the fluttering wings all around me had brought it.

The birds guided us into the inner sanctuary, their wings outstretched, their heads held arrogantly erect. They began to resemble the symbol.

The caduceus.

Suddenly, I understood the ancient Egyptian legend Dante had described the previous day. In a desert land where temperatures could reach well above a hundred degrees, a soft breeze was life. And it was the winged Isis—one of very few winged deities—who could provide that wind and renew life.

And then, as if to confirm this, there she was.

*It is our second date, and Jeff and I step out of the Egyptian rooms of the Louvre. We have just spent an intimate moment*

*marveling at the winged Isis on the sarcophagus of Ramses III, the oldest image of the modern caduceus that either of us has ever seen.*

*"I had no idea our medical symbol was so old," I say.*

*"A professor of mine once regaled the class with the accepted story of its origin," Jeff says.*

*"Oh yeah, what did he say?"*

*"That the caduceus—a winged staff wound symmetrically by two snakes—had historically been associated with the rod of Asclepius. But that is a different staff, without wings, wound asymmetrically by one snake. Asclepius was the Greek god of medicine, and his rod is also found today. But it is not the same symbol as the caduceus, which is much more commonly used today to depict medicine."*

*"So how did your professor explain the mistake?"*

*"He couldn't. I told him it sounded like bullshit. We debated the point for the rest of the school year." Jeff grins widely. "Now I have proof I was right. The caduceus symbol came from the ancient Egyptian goddess of medicine. Isis. But I have no idea where the snakes came from..."*

In a relief covering the entire wall of the innermost sanctuary stood the only winged Isis I had seen in all of Egypt. Her message was as clear as if she had spoken it out loud.

On the head of Isis were the horns of Hathor. But that was the extent of the resemblance this Isis bore to the thousands of other images I had seen here.

Beneath the horns of Hathor, a serpent circled her head like a crown, its triangular head stretched before Isis as if it wanted to see what she saw. For the first time, the goddess did not wear the constricting sheath dress, the dress that would certainly bind a broad span of wings.

Isis folded her wings protectively around another figure. The figure's face had been obscured over time, but the dress was male.

"Who are you protecting?" I quietly asked the goddess.

"That's Horus," Dante said. "Horus is her son."

In Horus' hand was a staff. The serpent jutting out from the head of Isis pointed toward it. Across from Isis and Horus was another figure, also a male. On his kilt were two serpents, winding up his body, the snakes of the caduceus staff itself.

*Here is your answer, Jeff. The staff, the wings, the snakes. Here is the legend that gave us the timeless symbol of medicine. This is how the wings of the goddess Isis became entwined with the snakes of the caduceus forever.*

Between the kilted figure and the protective wings of Isis around Horus stood a large bouquet comprised of the same repeating elements. The same two plants. The lotus and the papyrus.

"There they are," Dante said breathlessly beside me. "Those are the plants you need. Both of them."

I soaked in the details of the relief, the snakes adorning the two figures, the two plants, the protective wings of the goddess Isis enfolding and protecting her child. And I knew how to save mine.

I stepped toward one of the openings in the wall to feel the breeze upon my face. Inhaling deep breaths of cool air, I glanced through the window at the lush foliage growing along the Nile. They could both be out there. The lotus and the papyrus. The nardo. And if they still grew anywhere in Egypt, I was willing to bet they would still be growing here, at this temple.

I unrolled the map of the ruins handed to me by the veiled tout at the entrance. For a moment, I only stared at the paper, confused. The document in my hands was not a map at all. It was a long section of text written in Egyptian hieroglyphs. I stared at the symbols for a moment before they began to blur from the shaking of my hands.

The paper was thick. It appeared brittle to the eye. But to the touch, it was surprisingly supple. And when I folded a corner between two fingers and then unfolded it, only a barely perceptible crease was left behind.

I vaguely remembered Alyssa telling me at her museum that ancient papyrus was one of the most resilient types of paper ever invented. And that once an ancient scroll is unwound, methods finally exist today for softening it.

This was not a modern, commercial document made to look like ancient papyrus. This was ancient papyrus.

It was the original nardo document.

And Alyssa Iacovani was still alive.

I glanced around. Dante was examining another relief in the inner sanctuary, a grouping of birds. Their wingspans seemed to point toward the winged Isis and her companions. I casually re-rolled the nardo document and stepped outside.

She was standing on the outskirts of the temple, at a serene spot devoid of tourists. Beside her was a steep slope that led down to the Nile.

The tout in the black galabia and niqab was looking out over the water. When I approached, she turned toward me. This time, I noticed her green eyes through the mesh of the niqab's second layer. She glanced at me only briefly, and then her eyes fell to the shoreline of the river.

"It's here," she said. I followed her gaze and saw the plant she was referring to. It was the lotus.

"This is how they kept secrets," she said. "They hid half of the puzzle in a document somewhere, perhaps buried within a mummified crocodile. Or even in a library. The other half is encoded.

"In this case, the document actually *is* the first half of the puzzle. The text was written on the first plant you need. The papyrus.

"The encoded half is the nardo. Spikenard. It is the lotus."

"Why didn't you tell me?" I asked quietly.

"I didn't know myself, until yesterday," she said. "Yesterday, I broke the code.

"The lotus of Upper Egypt translates to 'S N' in ancient Egyptian—the very language that, among the educated classes of Egypt and Rome, only Cleopatra could speak and read. Lotus is S N. Spikenard. Nardo.

"When I learned that the lotus was the plant we sought, I knew that I would find the most authentic source of it here, in Upper Egypt, at the largest Temple of Isis in the world, the one completed by Cleopatra's father.

"But even if I had known all of this before yesterday, I still couldn't have told you, for the same reason Cleopatra could not tell her children. The danger to both of us has grown too great.

"Two days ago, a group of strange men came looking for me at the museum. I wasn't there, but a colleague of mine had a horrible feeling about them. I told the colleague that if anyone returned he should tell them I had been killed. And that is why I am dead." She flipped down the third layer of her niqab.

"Katrina, be careful," she said. "You have to stay hidden."

"Because you think Rossi or his thugs might have followed you here?"

"No," she said, "because the body of a prominent San Diego scientist was turned over to the police a few hours ago."

For seven days, I had been expecting this moment. But now that it was upon me, I could hardly process the information.

*Jeff's body was turned over. Turned over. It is over.*

But it wasn't over.

"Wait," I said.

Alyssa turned back toward me. I could no longer see her green eyes.

"Did they release his name?" My voice was weak and quivering.

"Not yet," Alyssa said, "pending next-of-kin notification. I'm so sorry, Katrina."

I pulled a small cassette tape from the pocket of my jeans. My hands were clammy and trembling as I handed it to her. "This is a voice recording of one of them on his cell phone. I recorded it yesterday. He did not know that I was sitting nearby. I was dressed as you are now.

"The conversation is in Italian. My hope is that it may have evidence that can put them away." I handed the recording to Alyssa, and she slipped it beneath her galabia.

"The man on the tape..." I glanced around the ruins.

Dante was nowhere to be found.

I watched for a moment as Alyssa walked away. Then I looked back toward the water. The nardo swayed gently in the cool breeze.

I slipped cautiously down the treacherous slope toward the Nile and reached for the plant. My hands clasped its foliage and found the stalks and leaves to be strong. Gently, tenderly, I wiggled the nardo loose from its bed in the water.

*There is a crash.*

   *I feel wetness and pain.*

   *I see a thousand memories.*

   *I feel myself slipping beneath the surface...*

*The bite of a crocodile holds more force than that of any other creature on earth—even that of a great white shark. Yet, crocs almost always kill their prey by dragging them into the water and drowning them.*

*This trivia from a TV show from another lifetime flashes through my mind as something crashes into me, and then my head strikes the ground. The sunlight around me dims, and all I can see are teeth. I feel the earth shift beneath me. I feel a cool, somehow comforting wetness, and then darkness falls— as if the lamp has been put out in a closed room...*

*There is an image in my mind. It is an image of my husband, but he is not my husband. He is a handsome stranger, naked on a sunny beach. He looks up at me and smiles, and he tries to shield himself with a towel...*

*There is an image in my mind. It is an image of my husband,*

*but it is not my husband. It is a twisted corpse lying naked on the deck of a yacht, a pool of red expanding rapidly around him. There are two gunshot wounds.*

*There is a gunshot...*

There is a gunshot. It is a noise I know.

There is quiet. There is pain. There is a voice.

"*Katrina,* hold on, sweetie," it says. It is a voice I know.

There is a light. There is softness beneath me, and there is pain. There is movement around me. I open my eyes. I look around. I am in a hospital bed. There are nurses nearby. I scan the room.

I remember the crocodile. I remember the nardo. The spikenard. The lotus.

*Where is it?*

"Where is it?" I try to ask, and one of the nurses turns to me. Her eyes widen. She is surprised to hear me speak. She is surprised I am awake.

"*Al hamda le lah,*" she says calmly and approaches my bed. She places a soothing hand on my forehead. "What did you say, *ya sayeedatii?*" Her accent is heavy.

My tongue is thick, and my mouth is dry. My throat hurts.

"Where is it?" I try again. "Did I lose it?"

"*Laa, ya sayeedatii,*" says the nurse. "You've not lost it."

"Then where is it?" I repeat again.

The nurse looks up as another nurse approaches. They look at each other.

"She's delusional," the other nurse says. Her accent is faint. "*Heeya tatakheyya.*" She steps away. Then I feel a pinch, and the light is gone again.

The light fades back in, and I am awake. I blink. I look around. The hospital room looks familiar. I see a shadow. Someone is approaching. I blink again.

*You can't be here*, I think, and then I am gone again.

I awaken again, and he is still here with me.

"You can't be here," I say, and he smiles.

"Well, *someone* had to come rescue my lady from the crocs," he says cheerfully and leans in to hug me gently.

I begin to weep, and he holds me without saying more.

When I am able to speak, I ask him.

"How are you here?"

"Your HER2 data brought me here," he says, smiling.

"John—," I begin, my voice shaking.

"I know," he says, quietly. "You don't have to say it—I already know."

He leans in and hugs me again, more tightly this time, and I think about Jeff's text message: Trust no one.

*Can I trust John?* I ask myself, and then he answers the question for me.

"I have to tell you something," he says, and his voice is cracking. "It's the hardest thing I've ever had to say."

"Katrina, Jeff would have died from his cancer."

"I know."

"And so will Alexis if we can't finish what he started. And so will thousands of other patients.

"I have never seen anything like this disease. I don't know what to make of it. Neither did Jeff. But the cancer cells are loaded with the HER2 protein, even though this cancer starts in the pancreas and not the breast."

"What else?" I ask, and he looks confused.

"What is the common thread between the patients? I can't think of any just between Jeff and Alexis alone."

"I don't know," John says. "Maybe you can help."

He reaches down into a small briefcase at his feet and hands me a folder. At the top, it reads "CONFIDENTIAL."

I open the folder and run my eyes down a list of patient profiles defined blindly by patient number. There is no common denominator—no race, no locale, no smoking or health history.

I turn the page. The second page is the key that connects patient numbers with names. It is this information that is confidential, known only to the physician coordinating the clinical study.

I recognize the list instantly. I lean over and vomit beside the hospital bed, and then I am gone again.

*I walk. I walk down the rows of hospital beds, taking in the hopelessness of the nameless victims. An IV drips into one arm of each. A teenaged voice pleads with me. I look toward her.*

*The girl is Alexis, and she is fifteen.*

*I continue walking, and I realize that I know their names after all. As I glance at each tortured face in turn, the associated name now sears my memory like a brand. Lisa Adrian.*

*Tracy Hallenback. Aakash Bhat. James Donahee. Alexis Stone. Jeffrey Wilson.*

When I come to again, I am surprised to find John smiling.

"How are you feeling, my lady?" he asks. His voice has reverted to its usual cheer, and just a hint of sadness still shines behind his eyes.

I find his question completely inappropriate, and I am confused. It is not like John to be insensitive. I glare at him.

He steps back.

"Oh!" he says and blushes. "Oh my goodness! I'm so sorry! You don't know?"

"Kat, have you been sick a lot lately?" John asks.

"I... well..." I stammer, and I am crying. "I have been sick every day lately. Do I have it, John? Do I have the same cancer?"

John wags his finger in mock scolding. "Doctor, you should know better," he says, and the smile upon his face is sheer agony.

"No, no, my dear, you don't have cancer. You, my lady, are going to have my best friend's baby." His eyes well up with tears again.

*It is our third date, and Jeff takes my hand across our dinner table.*

*"I have no children," he says, "although..."—he pauses for a moment—"I would have liked to, I think..."*

*"Where is it?" I ask. "Did I lose it?"*

*"Laa, ya sayeedatii," says the nurse. "You've not lost it."*

*"Then where is it?" I repeat again.*

I am crying, and I am laughing. No wonder they thought I was delusional. I had been talking about a plant.

I *am* delusional.

OH ISIS, THOU GREAT ENCHANTRESS, HEAL ME, DELIVER ME FROM ALL EVIL, BAD, TYPHONIC THINGS, FROM DEMONIACAL AND DEADLY DISEASES AND POLLUTIONS OF ALL SORTS THAT RUSH UPON ME, AS THOU DIDST DELIVER AND RELEASE THY SON HORUS!

-*THE EBERS PAPYRUS*, CA. 1500 BCE

# CHAPTER TWENTY-FIVE

John and I step out of the hospital onto a busy street, and the infernal Egyptian heat engulfs us. The air has a familiar sweet, thick scent. Pedestrians rush through converging lanes of traffic, and none of them look like tourists. The men wear long pants and long sleeves. The majority of women are in hijab or niqab.

I am wearing a new pair of jeans and a new long-sleeved T-shirt, clothing brought to the hospital by John to replace articles that had been shredded and soaked in a crocodile attack and then cut from my body by doctors.

"Where are we?" I ask, but I already know.

"Cairo," John says. "I had you airlifted here, to a better hospital."

"I don't have any ID..."

John raises an eyebrow and smiles sardonically. "This is Egypt. I forked over some money to get you patched up, and nobody cared who you were. But they did a nice job. I watched."

I turn and smile gratefully at my husband's best friend.

The crocodile had grabbed me by the upper leg. Its teeth had, fortunately, missed major arteries, and the wounds were mostly superficial. But I still feel like I'm walking in skinny jeans made of fish hooks.

John wraps a supportive arm around me. We begin slowly down the street, when a woman in a black galabia and niqab shoves her way rudely between us and whispers urgently into my ear, "Get out of sight! Right now!"

As if to reinforce her statement, a bullet whizzes within feet of my head and smashes into the stone wall behind me.

Whether by instinct or weakness, I am not sure, but I hit the ground. John falls as well, almost on top of me, shielding my body with his own. Another gunshot rings out, and we crawl behind a large dumpster in the street.

I do not need to guess the identity of the woman who lunges behind it with us. "Can you walk?" she asks.

"I think so," I say, "but I'm not sure how fast or how far."

"This way," she says, and I am relieved to remember that Alyssa Iacovani knows Cairo as well as she knows Naples. She was educated here.

I stand again, grimacing from the pain in my leg. I reach into my purse and withdraw the pistol still in my possession. It is a model similar to my own.

*The gunshots assaulting my ears, even through thick, protective earmuffs, used to startle me. Now, they do not.*

*My five-year-old son is dead.*

*Some of the men at the gun range used to make me uneasy. Now, they do not. I know many of them by name.*

*My son was shot through my living room window by a gangster named Lawrence Naden. It was a stray bullet, the by-product of a drive-by shooting aimed at another gangster. I don't feel safe anymore. In fact, I never did.*

*Without taking my eyes off the target before me, I reach down and feel for the lever that will move it swiftly backward.*

*The target flutters, and the concentric circles on the generic fig-ure's chest become smaller and smaller.*

*Naden is in prison. But this fact provides no comfort.*

*When I am satisfied with the distance, I release the lever and train the pistol on the center circle. I imagine the face of Lawrence Naden as I begin rapidly pulling the trigger.*

The metal is familiar in my hand. I hold onto John's strong shoulder for balance with one arm as I pivot on my good leg and begin shooting.

Ducking as frequently as possible behind whatever cover we can find, the three of us flee down the street. I can see nobody behind us, only transient flashes of clothing and steel as our pursuers also take cover behind various objects. At the corner, we turn and begin making our way down a cross street. Gunshots continue to ring out, and, with each, I cringe and look at Alyssa and John. Nobody is hit.

John is still supporting me like a human crutch.

"Can you run for a moment?" Alyssa asks.

"For a *moment*," I reply.

"You will need to. Because there is no cover in the alley we need to go through."

"OK," I say and take a deep breath of the hot, sweet, cloying smog of Cairo. "Let's go."

We enter the alley Alyssa spoke of. She was right. There is no cover; the alley is not even wide enough for a single car. I let go of John, and the three of us run blindly toward the other end of the alley.

Behind me, I hear hurried footsteps. Then I hear another gunshot and a scream. I turn just in time to see Alyssa fall to the ground.

I halt in my tracks. At last, I am able to make out the shooter. It is not Dante. It is not Rossi. I don't care. I take aim and shoot, and he falls.

Alyssa is lying on the ground. She clutches her shoulder and moans. John looks hastily from her to me, and back again.

"Help her," I say. "I can run."

The alley is short, and we have almost reached a corner where it merges with another street. I can hear commotion beyond, and I realize that Alyssa was leading us directly into a dense, massive crowd.

*Good move*, I think.

I prepare myself for the pain in my leg and then make a last mad dash through the alley. I can hear John following, slowly, with the weight of Alyssa in his arms.

We emerge into pedestrian chaos. Both sides of the narrow, crooked street are crammed with haphazardly erected vendors' tents. The aromas of spices, tobacco, and other goods mingle into a scent as familiar as it is centuries old. Within the never-ending jumble of tents, I see jewelry, hookahs, clothing, foods, and trinkets of every kind. Men in galabias and children in blue jeans reach toward me, motioning for me to come closer, beckoning me into their shops like clowns enticing me into a circus funhouse. A woman in a brightly colored hijab darts into the street to display a rich fabric for my eyes and hands to explore.

The gunshots have ceased.

I turn to Alyssa, who is still in John's arms. Her eyes are half open, and she smiles wearily.

"*Khan al Khalili*," she says. "This market is as old as Cairo itself."

She looks to the woman beside us still holding a fabric for sale, and the two exchange a few hurried words in Arabic. Then the vendor leads us into the back of her shop.

John sits Alyssa down on the stone floor of the fabric shop. A broad, angry red oval marks the area of John's tan shirt where Alyssa's left shoulder had been. The shop owner pulls a curtain around us, and the light of the Cairo sky is gone.

"Ask her for a light," John says, and Alyssa addresses the shopkeeper again. The woman disappears.

"I need to take this off," John says, tugging gently at the front of Alyssa's black galabia. She gives him a look.

"I'm a doctor," John says. Alyssa looks at me.

"He is," I assure her. Alyssa finally concedes to allowing John to remove her galabia, wincing as he pulls it over her wounded shoulder and then her head. Blood is pouring from the bullet hole through the hollow just beneath her collarbone. Her once white bra is now bright red.

John pulls Alyssa's upper body toward him and examines the exit wound in her upper back. Then he rips the galabia into two pieces. He wads them up and holds one piece firmly against each side of the wound.

A moment later, the shopkeeper returns with a flashlight. John uses it to peer into the depths of Alyssa's eyes.

"You're lucky," he says. "All they hit was some muscle. Your biggest concern right now is bleeding, but later it will be the risk of infection."

"*She* is lucky," Alyssa says and cocks her head almost imperceptibly toward me. Her voice is fading, and her eyes are mere slits. She says something in Arabic to the shopkeeper. Then she grimaces as she turns back toward John. "They were aiming for Katrina when the crocodile got her. They shot the croc instead."

"Who?" John asks.

"The people who want the nardo." I look into John's eyes. "They killed Jeff. And they killed Alyssa's entire family." I blink and then wipe a tear from one eye.

Alyssa motions for me to draw closer, and I lean in to hear her barely audible words.

"You can make them kill each other," she says. And then she is gone.

John leans over Alyssa and listens to her chest.

"She will be OK," he says, "if she gets to a hospital quickly." He stood to look at me. "These are the decisions doctors hate having to make. We need to prioritize the many over the one. There is nothing more I can do for her here in this market. And you and I need to go, right now. Because there are thousands of others whose lives also depend on us."

He reaches into a pocket and withdraws a wad of cash, which he hands to the kind shopkeeper guarding over Alyssa. Then he takes my hand, and we quickly slip out the rear entrance of the shop.

In an adjacent shop, we buy new clothing yet again.

I step behind a curtain and emerge in another galabia and niqab. I am surprised to discover that I am, in fact, becoming accustomed to the view through its screens. And without the bulky bags I had previously carried at my side and blue jeans underneath it, the galabia offers a freedom of movement almost akin to nudity. My body is remarkably cool.

John has changed from his blood-soaked tan shirt into a dark long-sleeved, button-down shirt and a pair of black slacks. His salt-and-pepper hair will blend seamlessly into the ancient marketplace of *Khan al Khalili.*

As I look over his new outfit, I realize that John's briefcase remained looped over his shoulder throughout the entire chase that led us here. A dark red stain on the tan shoulder strap is now the only reminder of what we have just been through.

Together, we look like any other Egyptian couple.

"How did you find me?" I ask him.

"I was the one who broke into your lab. I knew something was wrong from your first phone call when you fed me that bullshit line about you and Jeff being in the Bahamas. Then when Jeff wouldn't return my calls or e-mails, I knew I had to do something."

I realize now how ridiculous it had been to lie to him.

"So I raided Jeff's file cabinet, and I found the HER2 project data. Within it was a huge pile of notes about some medical project in Italy seeking a cancer remedy. The contact phone number was for Alyssa Iacovani. I remembered her from UCLA. We had freshman chemistry together."

Freshman chemistry was also the class in which Jeff and John first met. I smiled and blinked back a wistful tear.

"So I called Alyssa," John continues. "I met up with her in Naples and then followed her to Aswan."

"And that's why you weren't responding to my e-mails from Jeff's account," I say. "You were traveling."

"No, I wasn't responding to your e-mails from Jeff's account because I knew they weren't from him."

John smiles, and I smile back for a moment. Then I frown.

"I lost the nardo," I say. "And the document."

John grins, reaches into his briefcase, and retrieves both items. The roots of the nardo are wrapped in damp cloths and protected in a plastic bag. The papyrus document is now dry again.

"I figured out that they were important to you when you didn't let go of either one of them, even with a croc dragging you into the Nile."

The papyrus is remarkably smooth and supple, not like the charcoal-colored meat I saw hanging in a Naples museum more than a week ago. I roll a corner of it between my fingers for a few moments, peering curiously at the hieroglyphs. Then I hand the document to John.

"I need your help," I say. "I seem to have a bit of an immigration problem, and I think I am stuck in Egypt for the moment. So I need you to do something for me.

"In Naples is a chapel called *Cappella Sansevero*. In its basement is a pair of human corpses as well-preserved as Egyptian mummies. And behind one of them, behind the pregnant female, is a corridor leading to a laboratory. Take these items there.

"In the lab you will find a chemist named Romano Moretti and a shitload of commercially purchased papyrus. Tell Moretti that the key to what we are looking for is in the combination of that plant and the one you hold in your hand.

"Tell Moretti to do whatever it takes to find the isotope. And for God's sake, save my daughter's life."

REALLY, I CAN'T SEE WHAT USE ALL THAT SCIENCE IS TO YOU.

-KING "BIG-NOSE" FERDINAND (1751—1825)

# Chapter Twenty-Six

I am an anonymous Egyptian woman once again.

After sending John to Naples, I walk. The streets are getting dark, but I am not afraid. Cairo is pulsating. I am amazed to find a nightlife akin to Las Vegas. Loud music pours from large boats docked at every twist and turn of the Nile. The overlapping cacophonies of techno beats might have come from any night club in the United States, but the lyrics are in Arabic.

Pockets of galabia-clad men sit in the shadows of the docks. I watch them stopping the groups of tourists passing through the streets, offering boat rides and shows with belly dancers. But they leave me alone.

I walk slowly in my black galabia and niqab. I limp heavily, favoring my wounded leg, but the fresh breeze wafting beneath my long gown feels healing. I envision the wings of Isis.

The isotope is out of my hands now. If it exists, and I must believe it does, then it is incumbent upon a chemist I have never met to create it from a collection of building blocks I have provided. A chemist my husband trusted above any other. And if Moretti *is* able to create the isotope, then it is up to John to get it to Alexis in time.

I have picked the right people to finish the job, and there is nothing more I can do. In this regard, I feel helpless.

But now I have another life to consider as well. There is a new life inside of me. There is a reincarnation of Jeff growing there, developing.

*What world will I bring this young life into? Not one where his mother remains at large in Egypt, hiding from the authorities as well as from his father's killer. No. I need to finish this.*

*"You can make them kill each other."*

Those were Alyssa Iacovani's final words to me. But who are they? What do they want?

*"I'm still trying to sort out the details of exactly who knew about... the papyrus scrolls... over the centuries..."*

I realize again that Alyssa had never finished telling me what she had been trying to tell me in Naples. She had been answering my question as to why the Villa dei Papiri was never excavated, when we were interrupted by the earthquake. She had arrived at the rise of Napoleon and the rule of Naples by King Ferdinand and his wife Maria Carolina.

I need to know the rest.

I step into a twenty-four-hour Internet café, and I drop enough money for the entire night.

In 1765, excavations at Herculaneum were halted, and the focus shifted to Pompeii. Two years later, King Charles' son Ferdinand came of age and officially became the king of Naples, a ruler so unpopular among his subjects that they began to refer to him publicly as "King Big-Nose."

Although Ferdinand had no interest in the papyrus scrolls from Herculaneum, his queen, Maria Carolina, was fascinated by them. Maria Carolina befriended Padre Piaggio, the Vatican calligrapher tenaciously working to unroll and translate the papyrus scrolls from the Herculaneum villa. She wholeheartedly supported these efforts despite—or perhaps because of—the complete lack of interest by her husband.

Then a world event utterly personal to Maria Carolina interrupted the priest's work. Louis XVI of France was overthrown and beheaded, and shortly thereafter Louis' queen also fell to the guillotine. Maria Carolina's outrage was two-fold. First, the infamous queen, Marie Antoinette, was her much-loved younger sister. Second, Napoleon was now marching toward Naples.

As Napoleon's army approached, Maria Carolina packed up the scrolls and fled south to Sicily with her husband.

After pillaging what the royal family had left behind in Naples, Napoleon's interest in the ruins of Herculaneum escalated to obsession almost overnight. From Italy, Napoleon headed directly to Egypt, and from there back to France, from where he immediately established a new Institute of Egyptian Studies in Cairo.

Seven years later, Napoleon returned to Naples. This time, the papyrus scrolls were still there for him to seize.

The kingdom of Naples was granted to Napoleon's sister Caroline and her husband. Caroline personally financed excavations at Pompeii and took an interest in the scrolls of Herculaneum. She raised the wages of workmen unrolling the scrolls and funded the hiring of additional apprentices. When Napoleon became emperor, Caroline sent him her prized scroll as a gift. It described in detail the Battle of Actium and the fall of Cleopatra and Mark Antony.

Then Napoleon was defeated, and King "Big-Nose" Ferdinand was back on the throne in Naples for a third time, but without his queen. Maria Carolina had died while in exile.

By 1870, Naples was in shambles following a long succession of Ferdinand's offspring, all of whom were as incompetent as he. The king that finally ended this legacy was Vittorio Emanuele, who brought about the Unification of Italy that has remained to this day. He was the first king of a united Italy in over a thousand years.

Under Emanuele, the church and state divided. The fledgling unified Italian state used every weapon imaginable to defeat the Catholic Church. The secularism of ancient Rome proved to be an invaluable one and sparked a new interest in the ruins of Pompeii. Emanuele and the architects running renewed excavations posed—literally with shovels in hand—for the recently developed medium of film. The perfectly preserved slice of ancient Rome that was Pompeii inspired an Italian nationalism never seen before.

This set the stage perfectly for a young journalist coming to power as Italian premier in 1927. Benito Mussolini exploited the nationalist fervor that was sweeping the nation and developed a cult that tightly associated Roman antiquity with Italian racial superiority. According to Il Duce, the ruins of Pompeii held the archaeology to prove that superiority.

The ancient Eastern good luck symbol that was found repeatedly in the ruins, and that I had noticed in the pattern on the floor of di Sangro's chapel, was picked up by Mussolini's German counterpart. Hitler's hijacking of it as the symbol for his political party tarnished the swastika globally and forever.

By the end of World War II, Pompeii and Herculaneum had been excavated, bombed, and excavated some more. But the Villa dei Papiri remained submerged. By that time, approximately four hundred scrolls had been opened and read. With approximately only one in ten of those scrolls written in Latin as opposed to Greek, despite the fact that most ancient Roman authors wrote in Latin, it was believed that a still-buried Latin library probably existed within the house. If so, it is still there.

Throughout the 1980s, the 1990s, and the first decades of our new millennium, the Villa dei Papiri excavations have been reopened but then halted several times. There have been three obstacles in the way.

The first is the constant flooding and poisonous gases of the ancient ruins, which lie several feet below sea level.

The second is the now-contested location of the Villa dei Papiri. The first map of the villa was generated in the 1700s by Karl Weber. Weber's contemporaries were amazed at its accuracy and detail, and the exact location of each room within the villa was undisputed for two hundred years. Until today.

The most recent effort to excavate the Villa dei Papiri was initiated in the 1990s. Following the reliable maps of Karl Weber, an excavation crew bored into the belvedere, or pavilion, first described by Weber's men in the 1700s. They discovered that Weber had only identified the uppermost story of the building; in fact, there were three levels to the sprawling villa.

Then the modern crew changed their minds. Weber's original map of the villa was declared erroneous. The tunnels proving otherwise were filled back in, and the Villa dei Papiri has been inaccessible ever since.

The third obstacle is the modern town of Ercolano, which now sits directly on top of the ruins of Herculaneum.

The sun is beginning to come up as my Internet search takes me to modern news articles, white papers, and petitions centered around Ercolano. And I am beginning to understand exactly who Carmello Rossi is, and the extent of the blood bath Jeff has involved us both in.

With no identification and little money, I return to the same filthy Cairo hotel in which I slept during my first night in Egypt.

I am taken by surprise when, in broken English, the concierge bubbles forth with enthusiasm at my arrival. He has placed my voice and my accent. I smile beneath my niqab at the realization that the hotel staff probably doubled their annual income with the contents of the suitcase I left behind on my previous visit. And at the realization that they almost certainly think that I have now converted to Islam. The concierge asks me to wait in the lobby while my room is prepared.

The hotel upgrades me for free to their best room, and I am surprised to discover that, while much more basic than the hotel rooms of my former life, this one is reasonably sized and—more importantly—spotless. They have prepared it especially for me.

I deadbolt the door and draw the curtains, and in just minutes I am in bed, well aware that I need to be rested for what I am about to do.

WOMEN ARE NOTHING BUT MACHINES FOR PRODUCING CHILDREN.

DOCTORS WILL HAVE MORE LIVES TO ANSWER FOR IN THE NEXT WORLD THAN EVEN WE GENERALS.

HISTORY IS A SET OF LIES AGREED UPON.

-NAPOLEON BONAPARTE (1769–1821)

# CHAPTER TWENTY-SEVEN

*Somewhere, a phone is ringing.*

*I drift into consciousness. Is it daytime? Is it nighttime? There is light filtering in through the closed curtains of my bedroom. My prison. So it must be daytime. I don't really care.*

*The phone stops ringing. I pull a pillow over my head to shut out the light, and I beg sleep to come to me once again.*

*A door creaks, and a moment later there is a warm, soft hand on the small of my back.*

*"Trina," my sister says. "The police called. They caught him."*

*Lawrence Naden. My son's killer.*

*I am sure Kathy's words should be comforting, but they are not.*

There is light filtering in through the closed curtains. I wake up. Slowly, lazily, I open my eyes. The light seems to be keeping any cockroaches at bay. I glance at the bedside clock. It is mid-afternoon.

The familiar dream is still rolling in a constant loop through my mind. Lawrence Naden was a gangster, an American who ran drugs out of Mexico.

And I understand now why Herculaneum was never fully

excavated.

The modern town of Ercolano sits atop the ancient ruins. Ercolano happens to be Italian crime territory. From within the town, a two-thousand-year-old drug network is run.

Ercolano is the hub of *camorra*, the Neapolitan Mafia. But unlike Sicilian Mafia, which is largely centralized, *camorra* operates as a loosely tied network of families or clans. Because there is no centralization, the individual members of the *camorra* network—much like those of al Qaeda—are much more difficult to flush out and prosecute. The Italian government, Europol, and Interpol have been trying without success for a very long time.

I am pleased to find a modest assortment of toiletries in the bathroom, and I bathe slowly. My bandaged leg juts rudely from the bathtub like an inappropriate erection, and I wince as I gently sponge the skin surrounding the crocodile bite. When I am finished, I step out of the bathtub and don my galabia—the only clothing remaining in my possession—but I leave the niqab sitting on the hotel room bed.

I understand now why the Villa dei Papiri was never fully excavated.

If a major medical find authored by Queen Cleopatra were unearthed from the ruins of the Herculaneum villa, the modern town of Ercolano would be swarmed. The Pompeii and Herculaneum fever of the Enlightenment and beyond would once again explode. The area surrounding the ruins would become a veritable hotbed for archeology, tourism, and international press. And as the legitimate money poured in, the clandestine drug network running out of Ercolano would be destroyed.

So I was not surprised to learn, during my overnight Internet searching, that the landowners of Ercolano—mostly *camorra* bosses—repeatedly block the excavations of Pompeii and Herculaneum. They demand exorbitant sums of money from the Italian government for even a cursory, non-disruptive dig. And they interfere with every effort made to re-enter the Villa dei Papiri.

The tension between *camorra* and the government has been increasing dramatically since 2010. That was when a new, massive eruption of Mount Vesuvius was predicted to occur within the next eight years.

It is now five years overdue.

The situation is becoming desperate. Many of the buildings of Pompeii and Herculaneum, as well as many of the major historical sites of Naples, have begun to crumble. Some of this is attributable to natural wear-and-tear, and some not.

On February 15, 2013, a corruption probe into the most recent excavation of Herculaneum was announced. This had been the dig that revealed the second and third stories of the Villa dei Papiri, just before the maps of Karl Weber were declared erroneous and the excavation halted.

Two weeks later, arson destroyed a prominent Naples museum. *Camorra* was highly suspected. No charges were ever filed.

And so the rift continues between archeologists, the Italian government, and the ubiquitous *camorra*. The *camorra* bosses seem to be winning, and the evidence of this is the fact that one of the richest archeological databases in history remains virtually untapped despite the fact that it may soon be lost forever.

This time, I drape my purse over my shoulder, unconcerned about whether or not its soft camel-colored leather is recognizable. I grab the pistol off the nightstand and eject the magazine. There are only three bullets remaining. I hope that two will be enough.

My shoulder-length brunette hair is flowing freely as I limp slowly out of the hotel.

I ride the subway to the Museum of Egyptian Antiquities. I enter the baggage claim area and find an employee who speaks English. I explain that I lost the claim check for my bag. A description and a wad of cash are sufficient to retrieve it.

I sit in a café long enough to charge my iPhone, and then I find a secluded park. I walk to a bench and sit. When I am sure I am alone, I withdraw my phone, and I begin making calls.

Although I desperately want to, I cannot call Jeff's mother because what I need to say to her must be said in person. And I'm not in a position to do that. Not yet.

So I call my own mother, even though she has no idea who I am anymore. I call her just to hear the familiar voice of someone who I know holds no hidden agenda. I need to hear the voice of someone I can trust.

"Hi, Mom. It's me!" I say enthusiastically.

"Oh, hi, honey," she says in her relaxed, tired, carefree tone. "How are you?"

"I'm great!" I say, always as cheerful as possible when speaking with the woman whose only connection to reality is the voice of another person.

"That's wonderful," she says. "Who is this?"

"It's me, Mom. It's Katrina."

"Are you my sister?"

"No, Mom. I'm your daughter."

"Oh," she says. "Do you live with me?"

"I live next door to you."

"Have you seen my parents? I'm looking for my parents."

"Mom, your parents died a long time ago."

"Oh." Silence for a moment. "Who is this? Are you my sister?"

And the conversation begins again.

My mother's caregiver assures me that all is fine at home, and I hang up the phone.

Then I call Alexis. My sister Kathy answers the phone.

"Alexis is sleeping," she says quietly. "She sleeps a lot these days." Her voice becomes barely more than a whisper when she says, "Trina, I don't know how much longer she's going to hold on."

"Wake her up," I say.

"Hi Mom," Alexis says groggily.

"How are you feeling, sweetie?"

"Like ass," she says, and a distant memory comes back to me. I push it aside.

"Listen to me," I say. "I'm almost there. I swear to you, I am *so close*. You just hold on. It can't be more than another day or two. So hold on. Because I'm going to need you. When this is all over, you will have a new little brother or sister to babysit."

I hear Alexis laughing softly for a moment before she answers.

"Are you serious?" she finally asks. "Aren't you a little old?"

"*I'm forty-two!*" I say indignantly. "And I have wanted Jeff's baby since the day I first saw him naked on the beach."

I call John. When he answers his cell phone, I ask him if he found Moretti.

"Yeah, I found him," John says. "He's here now. I'm in the lab in Naples. We've been working our asses off. But, Kat, we're not having any luck. What did you expect to see? Did the document give any hint about what to do with the two plants?"

"Not really," I say. "It read 'when the sky opened and the gods cast their anger upon our enemies, the wine soured and the nardos by the bedsides turned from green to red.' It also indicated that the effect was quite transient, over in just a matter of moments."

"Well, the gods aren't doing anything now," John says.

"Let me speak to Moretti."

"Sure," John says, and his voice becomes more distant as he holds the phone away from himself to call for the Naples chemist.

"Romano," he says. "Jeff's wife is on the phone. Her name is Katrina Stone. She'd like a word with you about the isotope."

I hear a muffled voice in the background and the shuffle of feet.

*I know that voice*, I think.

Then there is a thud, and the line is disconnected.

A moment later, my phone is ringing. It is a video call.

The camera on John's cell phone is evidently projecting from a desk or table. I can see a horizontal edge at the bottom of my field of vision. Beyond it, John is seated in a low chair.

Blood is trickling down one cheek from a gash in his forehead. Behind him, I can see the Naples laboratory. It is unpopulated.

A pistol is held to John's head. There is blood on the muzzle.

*"Katrina!"* John says urgently. *"Hang up! Hang up the phone! Don't let him see where you are—"*

The muzzle of the gun crashes into John's skull again, and his head drops to his chest for a moment. When he looks back toward the camera, the blood running down the side of his face is flowing steadily. He stops trying to speak.

The chest of a man comes into my field of vision as someone steps in between John's chair and the cell phone propped on the desk. He stoops down casually and stares into the screen.

"Hello, Dr. Stone," Carmello Rossi says casually. "It's nice to see you again."

*"You bastard!"* I shout. *"I'll fucking kill you!"*

"Oh, that would be magic indeed," he says. "And it appears you are incapable of such tricks. Perhaps your New Isis has led you astray."

"You let him go—," I begin.

*"Shut up!"* he shouts. "No, no, no, you will listen to *me!* You will listen to me, or your friend will have the privilege of dying just as valiantly as your husband did. Except, of course, for the fact that, while Dr. Wilson died utterly alone, this man's death will have an audience of one.

"So instead, here is what you'll do. You will hang up the phone now, and you will call my sister's son. I am sure you have his phone number. You will give him your location in Cairo, and, when he has reached you, the two of you will call me back."

*"NO!"* John shouts from behind him. "Don't do it, Katrina!"

Rossi turns, and the muzzle of his pistol smashes across John's head a third time.

"*Shut up!*"

"What he wants is in this lab—," John manages, before the gun crashes down a fourth time, and this time he is out.

"Why did you kill Jeff?" I demand. "My husband was no threat to you!"

"Incorrect again, Doctor Stone. He would have found it. You—I underestimated you. I will soon fix that. But I knew from the start that your husband would find it. He would have brought international attention to my hometown. And that, I could not have.

"My network has survived for two thousand years. Without the interference of you and your husband, that Italian bitch, and this poor gentleman"—he points the pistol at John's head—"it is sure to survive for two thousand more."

"Now call my nephew," he says again and leans into the phone once more so I can see his face. "This should not take so much thinking about. Do you not realize that I still have the power to kill your daughter? Your mother? Your sister? Perhaps I have not yet clarified the extent of my power. Just hang up the phone and call Dante—"

"That won't be necessary," a voice says from behind me.

I try to turn, but there is a flash of ink. Dante's thick, tattooed arm snakes forward and snatches the purse from over my shoulder. And with it, the stolen gun that was my only means of self-defense.

"I warned you about Naples," he says. "It's never a good

idea for a woman alone to carry a purse." He tosses the bag to the ground.

Slowly, I raise my arms and turn around. Dante is aiming a pistol at me. He shakes his head sadly. "I tried to tell you back in Naples. I tried to tell you in Pompeii. I tried to convince you to just go home. Just let it go. Just forget about it. You wouldn't listen.

"We make our own medicines, Katrina. They bring us a lot of money, but they also kill a lot of people. I'm tired of it. The isotope is our chance to finally control the traffic of a legitimate drug."

*You can make them kill each other.*

But I cannot. Not when one is in Naples and the other in Cairo.

"Dante, do you really believe that?" I ask. "Do you really believe that the killing will end if you monopolize the isotope?"

My arms are still raised over my head, but Dante doesn't seem to notice when I slowly lower them.

"My uncle said—"

From my laboratory in Naples, I can hear Rossi laughing.

"Of course it will, *figlio*," he says. "It is the reason I dedicated my life to the study of chemistry. It is the reason I built a legitimate name for myself as a chemist. Do not listen to the woman. She has her own agenda." He chuckles. "And besides, you should realize, my dear nephew, that the isotope is safer in our hands than in those of her pharmaceutical industry."

Dante leans down toward the screen of my video phone and glares at Rossi. As he moves toward the phone, I, too, look into its screen. Rossi's expression is sorrowful as he pleads with Dante.

"You must kill her," he says. "And it will all end."

He steps out of view of the screen, and I can see John

361

again, unconscious and immobile.

Rossi approaches him. "Thank you, Doctors, for your sacrifice," he says.

I squeeze my eyes shut and simultaneously turn away as the shot rings out.

I am sobbing. I am sobbing so hard I can barely breathe. I set the phone down on the bench beside me. I cannot look at the screen.

"It's over, Katrina," Dante says. "It is finally over. For whatever it's worth, I never wanted any of this. I didn't want it for you, and I didn't want it for myself."

He motions with the pistol, directing me to walk. Slowly, I comply, lacing my hands over my head as I limp, resigned, toward a small thicket of trees in the park. Dante follows from behind.

"Turn around," he says. "Look at me."

I turn to face him, but I cannot look into his eyes, the eyes of the boy who just days ago was my only ally.

Dante raises the gun in my direction one more time. Then he turns it around in his hand and offers me the butt.

For a moment I only stare at him, confused.

"Go ahead," he says. "Take it."

Timidly, I reach forward, almost certain he will whirl the pistol around and shoot me at the last moment. But he does not. My fingers wrap around the butt and my forefinger touches the trigger. The pistol is cold and heavy in my hand. But I am not trembling as I aim it at him.

"Don't shoot me," he says, and I wonder why, then, he has

given me the choice.

"Come with me to the Italian embassy," he says. "I will turn myself in to Interpol and confess everything I know about my family.

"My uncle made me believe that the isotope was our way out. But I can see now that he was lying. I could see the greed in his eyes through the video phone. He is never going to stop. Ever. Not for one legitimate drug. Not for a thousand. Not ever.

"I am the family's computer hacker. I've never actually killed anyone. I mean, I've never pulled the trigger. I know that isn't much of an excuse. But maybe if I tell them everything, they will go easy on me. Maybe one day I can even be the pagan theologist I would have been had I not been born into the Rossi crime family.

"But, please, don't shoot me. All that will do is ruin you. And I don't want to be responsible for destroying yet another life. Especially yours."

It is hard to believe that the broken man before me now is the charming student who led me through the ruins of Pompeii. It is hard to believe that the compassionate young man who led me from the Naples police station is the same one who set me up to be brought there, who twice tracked me through the GPS on my phone, and who turned my private data over to the oldest crime family in Naples. And it is hard to believe that this remorseful boy has been involved in so many murders.

*How many have there been in his lifetime?* I wonder.

I pull back the hammer of the gun.

Now my hand is trembling, with rage.

I cannot see Dante Giordano. I can only see Lawrence

Naden. I can only see the man whose gang warfare killed my son, Christopher, sixteen years ago.

I can shoot him between the eyes. Right now. My aim is true. I know it is true because I have rigorously trained myself. I have envisioned this moment for sixteen years.

And when I am finished, after I have finally snuffed out the source of my hatred, I can walk away from this Cairo park, and nobody will ever know, or care, what happened to this drug runner from Naples.

I move toward him. I am practically shoving the gun into his face, and he does not move. I begin to weep sixteen years worth of furious tears. They pour from my blackened heart.

And then I lower the gun and collapse onto the grass in front of Dante.

"*You... are right,*" I sob. "Killing you... won't bring back Jeff. It won't bring back John. It won't bring back... Christopher, either. It will only make me a killer. And I don't want to be a killer again."

Dante looks at me intently, and I realize that we understand each other.

She took one earring off, and dropped the pearl in the vinegar, and when it was wasted away, swallowed it.

-*Natural History*

Pliny the Elder (23–79 CE)

# CHAPTER TWENTY-EIGHT

*hat he wants is in this lab...*
**IS IT BECAUSE WOMEN DO NOT MAKE WAR, AS MEN DO?**
*... We make our own medicines, Katrina...*
**WHEN THE SKY OPENED AND THE GODS CAST THEIR ANGER UPON OUR ENEMIES, THE WINE SOURED AND THE NARDOS BY THE BEDSIDES TURNED FROM GREEN TO RED.**

It is too late. At last, I understand how to generate the isotope, but it is too late. John is dead, and only Rossi remains in my laboratory in Naples.

With Dante, I return to the bench I had been sitting on. My phone is still upon it, and the video call is still connected. I cannot look at the screen.

The image is in my mind nonetheless. I envision John lying on the floor of a laboratory in Naples. His head is blown open.

But Dante picks up my phone. He gasps. "What—? Who are you?"

He turns the phone around to show me the image on its screen, and I have no choice but to see it.

"Oh, my God," I whisper fiercely as the creased, bearded face of Aldo de Luca smiles up at me. It is the first time I have seen him smile.

De Luca steps away from the camera, and behind him John is waking up again.

"What happened to Rossi?" I ask.

"Oh," de Luca says casually. "This piece of shit?" He retrieves John's smartphone from the lab bench and turns the video screen toward the floor. The camera's field of vision falls upon the body of Rossi. He is lying almost peacefully, having fallen onto one arm. There is a single gunshot wound through his back. Aldo de Luca kicks him.

"I... I don't understand..." I trail off.

"Thank you," I say then, and tears are streaming down my face once again.

Aldo de Luca smiles. "You don't promise someone a hundred thousand euros and then expect them to just disappear, do you? You showed me this place. You told me you were in trouble. And..."

His smile widens.

"What?" I ask.

"Do you remember that day when we came to these labs?" he asks. "Do you remember taking me through the tunnels, walking past the corpses in the underground chamber?"

I cast my mind back, but I cannot comprehend where he is leading.

"I looked at that pregnant woman, and I looked at you. And I knew then what you know now."

*He knew I was pregnant before I did. And he was looking out for me all this time.*

"Thank you" is all I can say, again, through my tears.

"I did what anyone would have done for a pregnant lady who has just lost her husband," he says. "And besides, Naples is my city."

I can only stare at the screen of my phone, confused.

"Don't misunderstand me," de Luca says. "I am where I am in life because of my own mistakes. But Naples is not easy on people like me. It is not easy for someone like me to improve his own situation. And that is because of people like this piece of shit." For emphasis, he kicks the body of Rossi one more time. "I guess you can say I have had enough."

When John is awake, I tell him I now know how to generate the isotope.

"I don't get it," he says. "We tried everything. We put the two plants together. We mashed parts of them up. We put parts of them in water. We even set parts of them on fire. Nothing happened."

"Try acetic acid," I say.

"The legend of Cleopatra and the pearl is true," I say. "It was true in her day, it was true when it was documented by Pliny the Elder, and it is true today. Cleopatra dissolved a pearl in vinegar and drank it.

"She obviously kept vinegar around for personal use. Possibly for experimentation. It is, after all, an acid. And it exists in hospitals and laboratories everywhere.

"I don't know if the phenomenon she observed in the nardo was accidental or deliberate. Maybe there was an earthquake—maybe that was the sky opening—and a bottle of acetic acid tipped over onto a bouquet of lotus and papyrus like the bouquets I have seen decorating almost every temple in Egypt. Maybe someone walked by and bumped something. Or maybe she was really experimenting.

"All I know is that, in the nardo document, she describes how to generate the isotope. Soured wine is vinegar. She speaks of it. She speaks of the nardo—the lotus—and she uses the medium of papyrus.

"Try acetic acid," I repeat. "Try dropping a small sample of each plant into acetic acid, just as Cleopatra did with the pearl."

John does as instructed, and nothing happens.

*"God damn it!"*

I throw the iPhone as far from myself as possible and begin pacing through the park. I am vaguely aware that I am waving a semi-automatic pistol randomly.

*What are we missing?*

Nothing.

The obvious answer is upon me, and I bury my face in my hands, the hard metal of the pistol smashing into my cheek.

The isotope was never real. It was a myth all along. And I, a scientist all my life, have just been desperate enough to believe in magic.

"Katrina?"

I hear a voice behind me, and I turn.

"Try using the document." It is Dante.

"Huh?" For a moment, I just stare at him in disbelief, but then my heart jumps. I clasp a hand over my mouth. *What if?*

I run to retrieve my discarded phone from the dirt beneath a tree. A large, jagged crack now runs down its screen, but the video is still running. John sits with one hand on his forehead, staring absently at the floor.

"John!" I say, and he looks up. "There's one more thing we can try. Try ripping a corner from the nardo document itself. Because that document is composed of Cleopatra's papyrus, the papyrus from two thousand years ago. Just like the lotus I pulled from the base of the Aswan Temple of Isis is Cleopatra's nardo. Spikenard. S N. Lotus, in ancient Egyptian."

One more time, John follows my suggestion, and I watch intently. Aldo de Luca watches intently. Dante, now standing beside me, is watching intently. And a flush of red passes momentarily through the nardo.

The battery on my phone is dying as I leave John with last minute instructions. He is to gather patients into the largest groups he can because the ancient papyrus in the nardo document is finite. And the effect of the isotope lasts only minutes.

The patients must be there when it occurs.

John leaves Naples with a logistical nightmare on his hands as he reaches out to the long list of people who need to come into contact with the transient superheavy isotope we have just named Vesuvium.

HE IS EITHER HEEDLESS OR MAD—FOR, INDEED, I HAVE HEARD AND BELIEVED THAT HE HAS BEEN BEWITCHED BY THAT ACCURSED WOMAN.

OCTAVIAN, ON ANTONY AND CLEOPATRA

*-ROMAN HISTORY*
CASSIUS DIO (CA. 150–235 CE)

# CHAPTER TWENTY-NINE

Six months have passed, but the city of Cairo is instantly familiar. I smile at the honking of horns and the faint sweet scent of smog as I step out of the airport into a whirlpool of taxi drivers.

I remember the cumbersome suitcases I was dragging when I was here six months ago. This time, a small overnight bag is slung over my shoulder. It is now January, and the weather is warm but not uncomfortably hot—a welcome change from the cauldron I endured here in July.

My hair is auburn again, and longer. Soon it will once again be down to my waist. I no longer mind the attention directed at me in the Cairo streets.

I negotiate a cab ride into the city and then catch a Metro from *Midan Tahrir*. The women in the car kindly move aside to offer me the seat closest to the doors. I smile and thank them in English, waving a weary hand before I sit down heavily. I know they understand my gratitude if not my words.

Twenty minutes later, the Metro screeches to a halt. I use the metal hand rail to heave myself to a standing position. I step out and begin walking. My limp is almost gone now, but the characteristic waddle of a woman in the end stages of pregnancy is creeping into my gait. I walk more slowly now than I used to. Yet, I am eager as I approach the destination I have traveled from San Diego to Cairo to understand. As the birth of my son approaches, it is time to face the consequences of my actions. And, hopefully, time to close this chapter of my life.

I pay my entrance fee and purchase a small street map. Then I step into the walled, ancient city of Coptic Cairo.

I am early. Slowly, I stroll through the dusty, crooked streets of the birthplace of Egyptian Christianity. Churches and convents line both sides of the streets. I wander into a church and am greeted by an ornate interior of gold and ivory. An old man is at its altar, lighting candles. I leave him alone and return to the street.

I reach into my bag and withdraw the map I purchased at the entrance to the city. I turn and continue down another street. At its end, the ancient city opens into a large pair of cemeteries, separated by a narrow walkway. One cemetery, historically, is Greek Catholic. The other is Greek Orthodox. But within them, I see a diversity I would never have imagined.

Each cemetery contains hundreds, maybe thousands of final resting places ranging from simple headstones to elaborate mausoleums. They are inscribed in Aramaic, Arabic, Hebrew, Greek, Latin, and, occasionally, even English. Some of the monuments are centuries old, and others quite recently erected. Some of them are graced with flowers. Some with photographs.

I brush the fallen leaves off of a stone bench, shaded beneath a tall tree, and sit down to wait.

*It is our second date. We step out of the Louvre, and Jeff takes*

*my hand for the first time. I am terrified.*

*"Are you going to contact the chemistry teacher?" I ask. "The one who told you the bogus story of the caduceus?"*

*"Hell yeah!" he says. "I can't wait to call Dr. Bond and gloat!"*

*I giggle and elbow him in the ribcage. "Why am I not surprised?"*

*"Because we are two of a kind," he banters back and throws his arm around me as if it is the most natural of things.*

*We wander without speaking into the quiet solitude of the Tuileries Gardens behind the Louvre. The rain has now abated to a soft drizzle, and we walk through the garden slowly, hand in hand. At first, neither of us speaks. My eyes, always avoiding his, shift between the ground before my feet and the soft grassy area surrounding us. I feel drunk with the words echoing through my head.*

*We are two of a kind.*

*Never before have I met a man whose intellect aroused me as much as the chemistry between us. Forever skeptical of the old cliché that I would know when I met the right man, I now feel with conviction that I know. And it has only been two days. I struggle to retain my comfort zone of logic, but my heart is pounding.*

*We reach a large circular fountain in the center of the garden, and Jeff voices my inner thoughts exactly. "You seem too good to be true," he says. I stop walking and am grasping for a safe response when he pulls me toward him and kisses me for the first time. And every remaining shred of my instinctive resistance dissolves.*

I hear quiet footsteps, and I awaken from my daydream. She is approaching.

Her gait is light, and I am happy to see that she seems to have made a full recovery since the last time I saw her. She smiles and slowly, cautiously raises her arm to wave. It is then that I realize that her shoulder may have suffered permanent damage from the bullet that passed through it six months ago.

I stand and hug Alyssa Iacovani gently, taking care not to crush either her injured shoulder or my own swollen belly.

"Now I understand," she says as we sit back down on the bench. "I did not know." She smiles and looks down at my stomach.

"Neither did I!" At first, I laugh gently, but then a familiar tear wells into each eye. "I'm so glad he survived," I say softly. "He survived a near drowning, a crocodile attack, and an emotional nightmare unlike any I have ever experienced. And he is still strong. It's almost a miracle."

"He?"

"Yes. The baby is most certainly a boy."

"Jeff Junior?"

"No," I say, and Alyssa looks surprised.

"He is all I have left of his father. But he is a different person. I don't want to try to recreate Jeff. I want our son to be... whoever he is. I can't wait to meet him." My eyes are still brimming with tears, but I am smiling again.

"And that's why you needed to see me," Alyssa says with certainty. "You need to know if he is safe in this world."

"I can't step out onto my terrace without scanning the bedroom behind me for shooters," I say. "I'm not sure if I will ever be able to again."

"Have you considered moving out of the house?"

"I've thought about it. But what good would it do? If Rossi's family has a vendetta, they will find me no matter where I go. And anyway, I can't leave the house. My mother is next door. And there are too many good memories there. Every square inch of the house we bought together reminds me of Jeff. And I want our son to share in those memories. Except for the last one."

The image of my husband's dead body is still as fresh as the day I found it, but, slowly, I am becoming accustomed to that memory as a permanent fixture in my mind. I am grateful that I have years to decide just how to explain his death to our son, but our son will know that his father died a hero.

"As to your concern," Alyssa says. "I don't know if you will ever be safe. But I think you can probably relax. Ever since the healing properties of Vesuvium were made public, the excavations at Herculaneum have gone forth full bore—pardon the pun. The Villa dei Papiri has become to researchers what your California gold territory once was to prospectors. Everyone wants to dig. Everyone wants to know what additional surprises are hiding in those documents."

I frown, deep in thought.

The superheavy isotope proved efficacious. But the transient phenomenon only occurred when using papyrus from Cleopatra's era. Just enough of the precious resource had been made available to us, most of it unearthed from an ancient crocodile cemetery in the Fayoum Oasis. The isotope was only effective on the rare, new, HER2-elevated, pancreatic cluster cancer that John named Wilson's Disease—after my husband. Jeff. John's best friend, and Patient Zero.

I, too, cannot help but wonder—despite all that has happened—if there is still a secret lying buried in Herculaneum or elsewhere, a further explanation of what Queen Cleopatra once observed in a bouquet of nardos at a bedside in an ancient hospital.

"Since the excavations were renewed," Alyssa continues, "the *camorra* families that were operating from within Ercolano have almost entirely been displaced. The majority of their estates have already been bulldozed to the ground to facilitate the excavations. Moreover, your friend Dante has royally fucked the Rossi crime family. His testimony, along with the testimonies of John and the homeless man, and your voice recording, has put away more than a dozen of the *camorra* bosses. And killed one of them, as you know."

The image of a dead Carmello Rossi lying on the floor of a Naples laboratory is a striking parallel with that of Jeff on the deck of our yacht.

"By the way, whatever happened to them?"

"Who?" I ask.

"John and the homeless man."

Suddenly, I am grinning. "Believe it or not, Aldo de Luca—the homeless man—did not accept a lump payment of the money I owed him. He preferred I help him monthly—a sort of trust fund—just until he gets back on his feet. I've put him up in a modest home in Naples, and I'm paying for his counseling, and his education."

Alyssa laughs. "Oh my! Education in what?"

"Child psychology. He wants to help troubled kids, kids like he was once. He wants to see if he can stop some of them from making the same bad choices that he made."

For the millionth time, I envision my daughter at fifteen—arrogant, angry, tortured, spiteful, and brilliant Alexis. I imagine her attempting to lie to Aldo de Luca in a counseling session.

"He will be perfect," I say.

I do not share with Alyssa the bond that has grown over

the last six months between myself and John—the only other person in the world who really understands what I have gone through. It is still far too early to tell where our friendship will lead. But something tells me that Jeff would approve.

"You haven't really made me feel any better," I say. "I mean, I'm glad to have broken up the drug ring, and I'm particularly glad to have discovered Vesuvium in time to save the lives of the Wilson's Disease patients. Not least because my daughter is still alive to meet her new brother.

"But I know how these things go. If you cut off the head of a Naples crime boss, ten new heads spring up in its place. Why wouldn't they continue to come after me? Or you, for that matter?"

To my surprise, Alyssa is now the one grinning. "I knew you wouldn't believe me," she says. "That's why I insisted you meet me here. Let me tell you a little story."

She stands and motions for me to follow her through the cemetery.

"After the death of Cleopatra," Alyssa says, "Egypt was absorbed by Rome. Octavian, the Roman who defeated Cleopatra and Mark Antony, became Emperor Augustus. Augustus became obsessed with Egypt.

"I think that he was looking for something he knew Cleopatra possessed. I think that something was the source of her power. Many believed it was magic. But it wasn't really magic at all, of course. It was science. Chemistry. The creation of poisons and medicines.

"We have ample evidence that Cleopatra was a scientist.

But all this time, for reasons unknown, we have thought she was exploiting some extraordinary political skill—or, even more preposterous, her feminine wiles—to raise herself to a deity as Caesar had been raised. I realize now that we were all mistaken. She did not intend for her peers to elevate her to a god. *They already thought she was a god.*

"Cleopatra dedicated her life to developing the image of herself as the New Isis. The goddess of magic and medicine. And she produced one magic trick after another, to the fascination of her peers. The vinegar and the pearl. The nardos and the cancer patients. Even her own mysterious death.

"I think Octavian was the only one who saw through her charade. I think she fooled everyone—Mark Antony, Julius Caesar, all of them—except for Octavian. I think that at one point he might have even seen the nardo document, or another like it, and learned that her 'magic' was actually explicable and reproducible through natural phenomena. I think he was the only one who realized she was just a woman with extraordinary knowledge, and not a goddess, or even a magician. And I think that is how he was the one who finally had the *courage* to defeat her.

"Katrina, Octavian was the one who brought the aqueducts into Pompeii and initiated the agricultural pursuits there. I think he brought them in to reproduce her nardo phenomenon. I think he knew that if he himself could do what she had done, it would prove there was nothing supernatural about her, and thus he could destroy her.

"But she also took up residence in that very city and usurped the aqueducts he had established there for exactly the same purpose. And that was the initiation of the world's first drug war, the one that continues to this day."

We approach a row of elaborate mausoleums beneath a

cluster of enormous, aging trees. I admire the architecture of the buildings while simultaneously reflecting upon Alyssa's words. I begin reading the names and dates upon the monuments. And I come to understand why she has brought me here.

THE MOON HERSELF GREW DARK, RISING AT SUNSET,

COVERING HER SUFFERING IN THE NIGHT,

BECAUSE SHE SAW HER BEAUTIFUL
NAMESAKE, SELENE,

BREATHLESS, DESCENDING TO HADES,

WITH HER SHE HAD THE BEAUTY
OF HER LIGHT IN COMMON,

AND MINGLED HER OWN DARKNESS WITH HER DEATH.


-EULOGY FOR CLEOPATRA SELENE

# CHAPTER THIRTY

The mausoleum at which we are standing holds a photograph. It is the black-and-white image of a woman—a dark-haired, dark-eyed beauty. I glance into her lovely black eyes for a moment and envision the Cleopatra of Hollywood—the Elizabeth Taylor, the Angelina Jolie. The woman's epitaph is inscribed in Greek; I know the letters from science. The dates of her life and death are listed: 1873–1957. The woman's name is Selena Zenobi. It is a name I recognize.

"What happened to Cleopatra's other children?" I ask Alyssa. "I know that Augustus killed her first-born, Caesarion... what happened to the other three?"

Alyssa smiles. She must know I have caught on to her game.

"I'm sure you won't be surprised," she says, "to hear that the *boys* disappeared from history. Cleopatra had borne twins by Mark Antony, a boy and a girl. The boy was named for the sun—Alexander Helios. The girl, the moon—Cleopatra Selene. Cleopatra's third boy, her second son by Mark Antony, was named Ptolemy Philadelphus, after Cleopatra's own lineage.

"Augustus allowed Cleopatra's three children by Mark Antony to live but brought them to Rome to be raised by his sister, Octavia—the very woman who was Mark Antony's wife prior to Cleopatra. Further details about the upbringing of the three children are murky until the marriage of Cleopatra Selene to King Juba II of Mauretania. The memoirs of Cassius Dio inform us that the two boys were still alive at the time of the marriage. Subsequently, they disappear from the record.

"I'm sure it won't surprise you that, together, Juba II and Cleopatra Selene built a large library and a lighthouse in Mauretania. She bore two children: a son, named Ptolemy, of course; and a daughter, Drusilla. In this generation, it was the daughter who was lost to history. But her name survived.

"The son of Cleopatra Selene was educated in Rome and became part of the court of Antonia Minor—the niece of Augustus and daughter of Mark Antony and Octavia and, thus, Cleopatra Selene's half-sister.

"Ptolemy enjoyed a very long reign as King of Mauretania, as both co-ruler with his father, Juba II, and as his successor. He married Julia Urania of the royal family of Emesa in what is now Syria. They had a daughter—again, Drusilla.

"Drusilla first married Marcus Antonius Felix, the Roman governor of Judea, and then King Sohaemus of Emesa—also known as Gaius Julius Sohaemus of Emesa. Thus, Drusilla became Queen of Emesa and bore a son, Gaius Julius Alexio, who later succeeded to the throne of Emesa.

"It is through Alexio that Zenobia, Syrian Queen of Palmyra, is descended. Zenobia was nicknamed the 'Warrior Queen' for having led a powerful revolt against the Roman Empire. She rode out in front of her army and fought alongside them. She also conquered and ruled Egypt for a period of time.

"Zenobia married a Roman governor, whose name has been lost, and, by him, had multiple offspring. Several were daughters, who later married into Roman noble families. Their one known son was Septimius Odaenathus. And it is from Queen Zenobia through Odaenathus that Cleopatra's lineage descends to Zenobius—the first Christian bishop of Florence.

"We find Zenobius throughout Florentine art—"

"I've seen him," I interrupt. "I have traveled to Florence numerous times and toured the art museums there. Botticelli. Three Miracles of Saint Zenobius. *Saint Zenobius?*" Suddenly, I am shivering.

"Yes," Alyssa says. "As depicted in that piece and others, Zenobius was sainted for miracles of resurrection, the exact skill—the exact magic, if you choose to believe in it—first attributed to that ancient Egyptian goddess, Isis. And it is through the lineage of Cleopatra that he acquired it."

"Descending from Cleopatra is an entire legacy," I say.

"Indeed," Alyssa agrees. "The legacy begins with the birth of Cleopatra Selene—which, by the way, occurred on December 25, exactly forty years before the accepted birth of Jesus Christ. And if you follow Cleopatra's bloodline, you find her miracles throughout.

"Johann Winckelmann selected a very wrong metaphor in 1762 when he said that Alcubierre knew as much of antiquities as the moon knows of crabs. The moon—Cleopatra Selene—was nine or ten years old when her mother was documenting the conditions of ten terminally ill cancer patients on a sheet of papyrus. So the moon might have known a great deal about the plague of the crabs. Cleopatra's knowledge of science and medicine has flowed through her bloodline for two thousand years. And so has some of the 'magic' that accompanied it.

"When we exposed one of Cleopatra's magic tricks to the world, we defeated the *camorra* in battle. They can never reverse what we have done, so I don't think they have any reason to come after us again. But the war continues, as it has all along."

Alyssa reassuringly pats my shoulder. "And that is why you

need not worry, my friend. Today's descendants of Octavian have many others to concern themselves with besides you."

The sun is beginning to fall behind the mausoleum, and I am growing cold in my short-sleeved shirt. I still need to find a hotel for the night, before my return tomorrow to the United States.

"How many are there?" I ask. "How many descendants of Cleopatra?"

"I have no idea."

"Do you think Raimondo di Sangro was one of them?"

"It's possible. He certainly went after those papyrus scrolls with a fire in his belly. He certainly followed the cult of Isis. And he certainly produced science the world had never seen—some of it with acid, much like Cleopatra with the pearl. And, like her, he hid his work for the purpose of forever maintaining his own immortality. His eternal flame. Even if he wasn't Cleopatra's descendent, he was unquestionably her follower."

"Will you try to contact them?" I ask. "Her living descendants?"

"No," Alyssa says. "What would be the point? You don't really think they would tell me anything, do you?"

I imagine a cemetery of mummified crocodiles, each one a vault filled with secret information.

"I suppose not."

We exit the walled city and board the Metro, this time together. Again, the women move aside to offer me a convenient seat, and again I am grateful. Alyssa stands, holding onto the metal railing with her strong arm. She looks as tired as I feel.

For a moment, we ride the rocking train in silence. When I can contain my thoughts no longer, I speak. "Rossi killed your family. Your husband and your son and your daughter."

I remember their images from the photos I had seen in her office the first day I met Alyssa Iacovani. I had thought she was having an affair with my own husband. And possibly that she had killed him.

"Yes," she says, and her gaze drops to the floor.

"Were they twins?"

"Yes," she says again.

"What were their names?" My voice cracks with the question.

"My son was Giuseppe. My daughter was Sofia. Of course, they carried the last name of my husband, Samir Ratib.

"He was Egyptian. I met him here, in Cairo, when I was doing my doctoral research. The twins were sixteen when I initiated the Piso Project. They were seventeen when my husband's brakes failed and all three were killed.

"So I understand your grief," she says, and now she is looking into my eyes. "And I'm so sorry to have caused it."

The morning sickness I had endured for the first two months of my pregnancy is entirely absent now. But at this moment, I feel queasy. I draw a deep breath. "You knew the danger you were involving Jeff in before you ever called him."

"Yes," Alyssa says.

"You knew that he could easily be killed."

"Yes," she says.

Alyssa looks into my eyes again. "I knew Jeff was the most likely person in the world to help me solve the nardo puzzle. I believed that if he didn't, this battle that has gone on for two thousand years might continue for a thousand more. How many husbands have been killed? How many children?" Her voice catches in her throat and she takes a breath.

"You followed Jeff's career for a long time," I say. "That was how you knew he would be the best person to help you. And I am sure you discovered a thing or two about my past as well. And that was why, even in his absence, you could bring yourself to involve me."

Alyssa looks down again. "I knew that, if you were in my shoes, you would have done the same thing."

The train comes to a halt at *Midan Tahrir*. I step off and approach the Ramses Hilton, grateful for the passport and money in my overnight bag.

Alyssa begins to walk in the other direction, but I reach forward and gently touch her arm to delay her a moment.

"He would have died from his cancer if you hadn't called him," I say.

She nods.

"And I also would have lost my daughter, and we would not have saved the thousands of people who contracted Wilson's Disease, all within days of each other."

She nods again. A tear runs down each of her cheeks, and she looks down at the sidewalk.

"So you see," I say. "You have nothing to feel guilty about. Together, we saved thousands of lives. And you did not kill Jeff. As a matter of fact, I did."

Alyssa only stares, and in her eyes is the dawning of understanding. It is the understanding that I have known since, lying in a Cairo hospital bed, I first saw John's list of cancer patients. First, and again. It was the same list that has visited me in my nightmares for eight years. Alyssa places a hand on my arm, and her empty gaze tells me that reassuring words escape her.

I hug her one more time before leaving. As I approach the hotel that will be my home for my last night in Egypt, I rub my swollen belly with both hands. I imagine the young life inside of me. And I wonder what his legacy will be.

*The glaring lights upon the brilliant white beds only accent the appalling conditions of the patients. They are crammed together, side by side and end to end. Thousands of adjacent hospital beds.*

*Beside me, a feeble plea comes forth from a teenaged voice. "Please..."*

*I step forward. I pull a wheeled IV pole toward the bed and hang upon it a clear plastic bag, heavy with liquid. I tap the child's vein and insert a needle as gently as I can.*

*"I'm here, Lexi," I say. "And you will be OK now. All of you will."*

*I gently squeeze the bag, and the solution inside it begins to flow.*

MAGIC IS EFFECTIVE TOGETHER WITH MEDICINE.
MEDICINE IS EFFECTIVE TOGETHER WITH MAGIC.

-*THE EBERS PAPYRUS*, CA. 1500 BCE

# EPILOGUE

Eight years ago, I created a monster. I thought that I was doing the right thing. I made it for my daughter. In a way, I also made it for my son—my first son, Christopher. And, admittedly, I made it for myself.

I created a molecular monster. Of course, I had no way of knowing at the time that eight years later my blockbuster cure for a virulent form of anthrax would induce a new, rare cancer that would come to be known as Wilson's Disease. Or that this cancer would lead to the murder of my husband, a man whom I had not even met when I generated the molecule.

It made me rich. It made me famous. And had I not been rich and famous, I might never have met Jeff. I certainly would not have been speaking about the drug at the International Conference on Emerging Infectious Diseases that day in Paris. And he would not have been sitting front row center for my lecture, his smile interrupting my train of thought.

The drug saved my daughter's life. But eight years later, it almost killed her. Her, too. And more than three thousand others who, thank God, I have now found a way to rescue from the drug's long-term effects.

Of course, I have yet to see the *new* effects that may come still, effects that may be caused by the treatment for Wilson's Disease, the treatment revived after two thousand years to treat a cancer born again in the twenty-first century. Perhaps I have now created another molecular monster. Perhaps I initiated yet another nightmare when I revived the isotope from the ruins of Herculaneum, the isotope that would come to be known as Vesuvium.

What if I *had* known? What if I had known that Jeff, the one true love of my life, would die from it? Would I still have produced the drug that came to be known as the Death Row Complex?

What choice did I have?

**COMING IN 2014**
**THE DEATH ROW COMPLEX**

# Selected References

1. Burstein, Stanley. *The Reign of Cleopatra.* Westport: Greenwood Press, 2004.
2. C. Seutonius Tranquillus. *The Lives of the Twelve Caesars.* ca. 69–122 CE. Trans. Alexander Thomson, M.D. Amazon Digital Services, 2012.
3. Croce, Benedetto. *Storie e Leggende Napoletane.* 1919.
4. Ebers, Georg. *Cleopatra.* 1894. Trans. Mary J. Safford. Teddington: Echo Library, 2007.
5. Harris, Judith. *Pompeii Awakened.* 2007. New York: I.B. Tauris, 2009.
6. Kleiner, Diana E.E. *Cleopatra and Rome.* Cambridge and London: The Belknap Press of Harvard University Press, 2005.
7. Plutarch. *Lives of the Noble Grecians and Romans.* ca. 46–120 CE. Trans. John Dryden, 1819–1861. New York: Random House, 1992.
8. Schiff, Stacy. *Cleopatra, A Life.* New York: Little, Brown and Company, Hachette Book Group, 2010.
9. Sider, David. *The Library of the Villa dei Papiri at Herculaneum.* Los Angeles: Getty Publications, 2005.
10. Tyldesley, Joyce. *Cleopatra: Last Queen of Egypt.* New York: Basic Books, 2008.

# THE DEATH ROW COMPLEX

## KRISTEN ELISE, PH.D.

COMING IN 2014 FROM:

Murder Lab Press

San Diego, CA

# PROLOGUE

By the time they caught up with him, he had forgotten to keep running. Lawrence Naden was incoherent and scarcely recognizable—the sloughed, discarded skin of a human being.

It had been a rainy week in Tijuana. A brown river carried trash along the gutters of the squalid street. Piles of refuse collected in rough areas, generating dams that would eventually break from the weight of the water and garbage behind them.

A burst of static abbreviated the heavily accented warning from the megaphone. *"You've got nowhere to go, Naden!"*

The dark-skinned officer holding the megaphone motioned, and several *federales* carrying M16 rifles filed steadily across the sloping yard, taking care to maintain their footing in the thick mud. Others were already entering the house from the back.

Except for a handful of onlookers, most of them ragged children, the street was abandoned. The regular occupants had fled at the first rumor of approaching law enforcement. This time, however, the *federales* were looking for a single individual. Drugs were only a secondary concern.

As the majority of uniformed men congregated at one rickety house, they shouldered the M16s and began instead withdrawing pistols. A few stepped onto the porches of flanking shacks. They peered suspiciously through the dirty windows or through plastic taped over holes where windows had once been.

The men entering the house were greeted by the familiar rank combination of sweet-smelling rotting food, human waste, and burning chemicals. The front room was abandoned but had recently been occupied, as evidenced by a smoldering spoon on a card table against one wall. Needles and syringes, plastic bags, and glass pipes littered makeshift tables, moldy couches, and the concrete floor.

Silently, the *federales* crept through the house with firearms raised. As those behind him assumed formation along the wall of the narrow hallway, the lead officer kicked a bathroom door, and it flung open as he shrank backward against the doorjamb.

The evasive maneuver barely saved the officer from being shot in the face.

As the bullet cut through the thin drywall behind him and embedded into a rotting wall stud, the officer instinctively leaned in and flicked his index finger three times. The brief staccato of semi-automatic fire rang out, and the ambusher fell gurgling into the bathtub.

Coldly, the officer lowered his pistol to look down at the body. Then he turned to his team.

"*Esto no es lo*," he said and then reinforced in English, "This isn't him."

There were two other doors along the hallway. One was wide open. The lead officer caught the eye of the man nearest it and cocked his head toward the room. The flanking man immediately stepped in, gun drawn. He strode to the closet and opened it and then stepped back out into the hallway and shrugged. The attention of the team turned to the other door. It was closed.

After making eye contact with the rest of the team, the lead officer repeated the practiced kicking of the door then stepping out of the line of anticipated fire. There was none. Cautiously, he followed the barrel of his weapon into the room, noticeably relaxing as he did. The others followed.

A man was sitting cross-legged on the floor across the room with his back against the wall. His disturbingly gaunt body slumped to one side. A trickle of fresh blood flowed down the inner part of his forearm from a newly opened wound. The entire area of flesh was scarred, scabbed, and bruised. As the officers filed into the room, his half-open eyes registered a slight recognition. A needled syringe dropped from his hand and rolled toward the officers in the doorway.

The brief lucidity that had momentarily graced Lawrence Naden's eyes faded as the heroin flooded his bloodstream. His pupils fixed into a lifeless gaze onto a spot on the floor, and then the rush overtook him.

# CHAPTER ONE

The image was lovely in a somewhat odd, geometric way. A bouquet, or maybe, a tree? The flower heads were a jumbled mess. The stems, in contrast, were perfectly arrayed, an intertwined cylinder projecting downward from the flowers piled on top of them. The overzealous, rainbow-coloring of it all was unlike anything existing in nature.

The leaves around Foggy Bottom were turning, and it was getting cold already. Rain was beating against the windows, and White House intern Amanda Dougherty scratched her back with a letter opener while frowning curiously at the image on the greeting card.

The card had probably been white; it was now a slightly charred sepia from the UV irradiation. Despite its ugly signature on the paper, Amanda had been much more comfortable taking this job after Mr. Callahan had explained that decontaminating irradiation was a mandatory process for all White House mail. It was done in a New Jersey facility following processing and sorting at Brentwood, the facility that had made national headlines years earlier when anthrax spores intended for U.S. government officials had infected several people and killed two of its employees along with three others.

Today, by the time the mail reached Amanda, it was safe.

Amanda flipped open the greeting card. "Oh, my word,"

she said quietly. The handwritten text was small and neatly aligned, but Amanda most certainly could not read it. She thought it might be Arabic or Hebrew or Farsi. She could not tell them apart.

After a moment of thought, Amanda got up and walked to Mr. Callahan's office, where she rapped softly on the door. He yelled through the door for her to come in.

"I'm sorry to bother you," Amanda said timidly. "We got a greeting card in a foreign language. I don't know what I'm supposed to do with these."

"What language?"

"I don't know. Something Middle Eastern. It has all those funny double-you looking things with dots over them."

Mr. Callahan motioned for her to enter and took the card from her. He glanced briefly at the image on the front and then flipped it open to look at the text inside.

"It's Arabic, but I don't speak it. I'll give it to an interpreter. Thank you, Ms. Dougherty."

Ten minutes later, Jack Callahan handed the card to an interpreter who had just entered his office.

The interpreter frowned.

"What?" Jack said.

"This card may have a cute bouquet on the front, but the text..." He trailed off, skimming silently down the card, and then read aloud, slowly translating from the Arabic.

*Dear Mr. President,*

*Your nation will soon know at last the full weight of the terror you have inflicted upon our people for years. You will soon reflect upon 11 September of 2001 and consider the date insignificant.*

*A glimpse of the pain we promise has already been put to course. You will shortly learn what it is. You will then have the privilege of living in fear for two months, as our people have lived in fear of the genocide inflicted again and again upon us by the Crusaders.*

*At last, on your Christmas Day of this year, there will begin a nightmare in your country unlike any you have ever seen, unlike any you can even imagine. It will blanket your nation, and no man, woman, or child will be spared. There will be nothing you can do to stop it.*

*We have been imprisoned by the tyranny and oppression of your leaders for too long. The world will now see that you are the prisoners, and Allah will praise the final victory of al Qaeda."*

On the other side of the country, a man and a woman whispered as intimately as possible through a chain-link divider.

Arms extended and fingers intertwined through the barrier, they leaned in almost close enough to kiss. His dark hands enveloped her lighter ones. The woman's figure was concealed within an ankle-length, flowing skirt and a chunky black sweater. Her long black hair hung in thick ropes along the sides of her face, shielding her from everyone but the prisoner.

Their conversation was hurried, urgent.

The guard on duty passed by, slowing ever so slightly in a casual effort to overhear them. For a few seconds, he could hear the man impatiently reassuring his mate.

"It's OK. I've taken care of it. You don't have anything to worry about. So shut up already."

The guard strained to listen, but the woman said nothing. She glanced up, and her face was revealed to the guard for just a moment. She looked afraid. The inmate's expression was one of anger and defiance. To the seasoned guard, it was a familiar combination. He strolled leisurely away to watch over another visiting couple.

The prisoner glanced over his shoulder to watch him go. Turning back to his visitor, he raised one dark eyebrow and gave a subtle nod.

The woman disconnected one hand and tucked it gently and deliberately into a fold of her long skirt. A moment later, the hand returned calmly to the barrier and assumed its former position against her lover's. The guard was still across the room, but, overhead, electric eyes faithfully recorded the scene.

Couples were beginning to kiss goodbye through their dividers, and the room was clearing out. Visiting hours were almost over. She would be ordered to leave soon. They hurried to finish their vital conversation.

"Stay in contact," the prisoner whispered. "I will be calling on you."

His visitor's eyes flared in shock. This was supposed to have been their final meeting. They had agreed.

*"What are you talking about?"* she hissed.

He smiled menacingly, revealing a broken fence of rotten teeth. "Oh, did you think it was going to be that easy for you, bitch? That I'd do all the work and you'd get the glory? I know a good negotiation when I see one. Don't fucking think I'm kidding."

"Never mind then! I'll get someone else!" she said quickly.

"Too late, lover," he said with a grin. "The cat's already out of the bag."

As the prisoner and his visitor were saying their goodbyes, an inmate in a remote wing of the prison was vomiting into his private toilet for the second time that hour. He half-heartedly cursed the prison food. The truth, however, was that he did not think he had food poisoning. He felt like he was coming down with the flu.

The interpreter paused and looked up, his dark eyes a question mark. Jack Callahan seemed relatively unconcerned.

"We get letters like that a lot," Jack said. "They almost always turn out to be a hoax."

"This one might be too," his colleague concurred. "Something about the Arabic is unusual. I was paraphrasing, of course. Most of what is here doesn't translate directly. But... it reads like it was written by someone who might not be a native speaker. Or, maybe they're just very poorly educated. I don't know exactly. Also, the handwriting. It is sort of, ah, overly meticulous. Like someone who doesn't speak or write Arabic is trying to copy something they saw written, not like someone writes in their native language."

Jack made a related point. "It is strange to me that the al Qaeda organization is mentioned but the author gives no other details. Usually, when we get a direct threat from al Qaeda, or they claim responsibility for an attack, there are very specific references, things that had to have come from them in order to lend credibility. For example, they usually include specific names. And since when do they send a greeting card to general White House mail instead of making some kind of grandiose announcement over international airwaves? Those bastards thrive on publicity."

A moment of silence passed as each man considered the

card again.

"So, there's allegedly something about to happen," Jack mused. "And something else on Christmas Day. Can you put the translation into writing for me? I still need to log it into the database, and I'll send the card to the Postal Inspection office. I assume if no shit hits any proverbial fans in the next couple of weeks, then we're probably fine."


Forty hours passed, and death row was redefined. Convicted murderer Nathan Horn struggled for air as he lay dying on his bed. Every feeble breath felt like lightning in his chest.

Much of Horn's present state was ironically akin to the once familiar sickness of heroin withdrawal—a sensation he had not experienced in twenty-two years. His lungs had become increasingly thin over the last hour, and he now continuously felt light-headed and nauseous. There was nothing left to vomit, but he was vaguely suspicious that maybe he had soiled himself again.

Horn had stopped getting up eight hours ago, after he had fainted in the throes of a violent retching spell and hit his head on the concrete floor hard enough for blood to trickle down his agonized face. Too weak to care that his body was shutting down, he could only be grateful that the violent illness he had been engulfed in throughout most of the morning had finally subsided.

The rotten meat smell of the sores was everywhere, even though only some of the inmates had them. Horn was covered with them, and the pain was excruciating. Someone was screaming. Someone else—or maybe it was the same man—was vomiting. Horn had no option but to lay in misery and absorb the sounds and smells of the mortally ill.

Mercifully, his vision was totally gone. He could not see the disgusting mess that had become of the six-by-eight cell where he had spent the last eighteen years of his sentence. He was also unaware that Buzz, the child molester on the other side of the wall, had been dead for three hours, or that Sam—who two years earlier had raped and murdered his sister at the age of nineteen—was now on his hands and knees as he sobbed, mumbling an inarticulate prayer to a God that had never existed to him until that morning.

Drifting in and out of consciousness, Horn's ravaged mind was a collage of people and events from his past. His mother. His parole officer. The sixteen-year-old girl he had shot in the chest in her apartment because it turned out that she didn't have any dope after all. A parade of lawyers. The judge who had asked God for mercy on his soul. Horn had laughed out loud.

The sores were like fire, and their flames were spreading. He could no longer feel the distinct patches of corroded flesh; they were all melting into one surreal torture. Internally, he was being slowly devoured. Externally, he was burning alive. His last semi-lucid thought was a forlorn one. They had all been right. Nathan Horn finally believed in Hell.